INTO THE DARK HEART OF THE MOUNTAINS...

"There are only her tracks and the blood," the M.E., Khan, said. "She could have been shot here, I suppose, but I would expect to see her footprints stagger or her body print in the snow because the bullet impact would a considerable blow." He crept closer, Egorova at his shoulder, documenting as he closed in on the bloodstain.

"She went to her knees there."

It confirmed what Kazakov had thought. "To rest?"

"Could be," Khan said.

Kazakov crouched down in the snow where he was. The drift of snow blocked his view of the trail and could potentially block anyone's view of him. "It was early morning when she was found, which means it's highly likely that she was killed at night. If that was the case, she could have ducked down to hide from someone she expected to come on the trail."

Khan studied the scene. "That fits with what is here."

Kazakov turned and looked up the slope that was gradually being squeezed into a narrow pass between two massive mountains. His gaze followed the faint gray line of the trail used by villagers and the occasional skier and he set out along it, questions parading through his mind.

What was an old woman doing here in the middle of the night? What or who was she running from? Where had she come from?

Ignoring his cold toes and using the palm of his hand to warm his nose, he started up the hill.

THE TSARINA'S MASK

A DETEKTIV KAZAKOV MYSTERY BOOK 3

K.L. ABRAHAMSON

COPYRIGHT

For more information about Twisted Root Publishing, please visit our website at *http://www.twistedrootpublishing.com*.

THE TSARINA'S MASK

A DETEKTIV KAZAKOV MYSTERY BOOK 3

K. L. Abrahamson

1

———————

S omewhere in Holy Mother Russia there lived a tsar who had a beautiful wife and a beautiful daughter who looked much like her mother. When his wife died, the tsar grieved deeply. Then he noticed how his daughter looked so much like his wife and determined to marry her. He came to his daughter and proposed marriage.

The princess was so upset that she went to her mother's grave and poured the story out. From beyond the grave, the mother told her daughter to have a dress made, covered with silver stars. The princess did as her mother bade, but when she wore the dress for her father, he proposed their marriage again.

Again, the princess went to her mother's grave and again poured out her story. Her mother told her to have a dress made with a silver moon on its back and the golden sun on its front. The princess did as bid and again her father told her that he loved her more than ever.

For a third time the princess went back to the graveyard to tell her tale. This time her mother told her to have a dress made of pigskin. The princess obeyed and this time her father was so incensed that he threw her out of the castle.

The princess wandered into the forest and when a young tsarevich and his hunting party came by, the princess hid in the branches of a tree. The tsarevich's hunting dogs leapt at the tree and the tsarevich, being curious, sent his servant into the tree to see what had his dogs so upset.

"What is it?" the tsarevich called to his servant.

"My Lord, there is some kind of beast in the tree—a marvelous wonder, a wonderful marvel."

"What manner of wonder are you?" the tsarevich demanded. "Can you or can you not speak?"

"I am Pig Skin," the disguised princess replied.

"What a marvelous wonder! What a wonderful marvel!" the tsarevich said and brought her down from the tree and into his coach to take back to his palace to show his father and mother. He would keep the marvel there.

Voices outside the hospital room door interrupted Detektiv Alexander Kazakov's reading. He closed the book around his finger and inhaled the urine- and disinfectant-tanged air. The room was filled with shadow and lit only by a single spotlight that illuminated the page of the book of fairy tales he had been reading out loud to the comatose figure on the bed. Young, blond Detektiv Pavel Chelomeyev was still unconscious from a beating he had received two months ago.

The room contained three other beds, though they were thankfully now empty, their bedding pulled crisply across the mattresses, awaiting patients. Chelomeyev's bedding was pulled tight, too. Uncomfortably so for anyone who moved. It crossed the slow rise and fall of Chelomeyev's chest and tucked in around him as if he was a manikin or a child's life-size doll. On the other side of the bed the slow beep, beep, beep of the medical monitor was all that said that Chelomeyev still lived. Though the bandages that had swathed his head had been removed, the young detective was a shadow of his former self, his floppy head of pale hair shaved off and now growing out, the skin of his pale face seemingly pulled tight over bone and shadow. His lashes were dark crescents against the shadowed hollows of his eyes.

"There you are! Is this how you spend all your evenings? But then, don't tell me. I already know." Detektiv Chief Inspektor Valerian Rostoff filled the doorway just as his voice filled the room. An agitated nurse in white uniform stood behind him.

Kazakov stood—whether to greet his boss or to guard Chelomeyev from him, he wasn't certain.

Rostoff turned back to the nurse. "That is all. You can go. We have private matters to discuss." He waved her away and stepped into Chelomeyev's room.

Rostoff was a big man, a bear of a man in the old Russian style. Though he was only in his mid forties like Kazakov, his ruddy face was marred by a bulbus nose, veined like a drinker, and deeply etched frown lines that dragged down his expression. He carried his fur hat, for the weather had changed for the better as the days lengthened in March, but he still wore his greatcoat. In the hospital heat it reeked of warm wool steeped with human sweat. He glanced over Kazakov's shoulder.

"Still unconscious, I see. A shame, really. The boy had promise. I hear his mother is most distraught."

Chelomeyev's father, a big man in the New Moscow Police Department, had done nothing to push the investigation into Chelomeyev's beating. Given what Kazakov had learned about the event, Chelomeyev Senior's inaction had filled Kazakov with concern—concern he had shared with Rostoff.

"Has promise," Kazakov corrected. "He is not dead and the doctors say there is no sign of brain damage. It is simply as if he has decided not to wake up."

"And so you spend your evenings here? Doing what?" Rostoff's gaze slid to the book in Kazakov's hand and yanked it loose. "Fairy tales? You read a detective fairy tales?"

"He studied literature in university and did his thesis on fairy tales. I thought they would bring him comfort," Kazakov said through gritted teeth. He, too, had always loved the old stories. "Now why are *you* here?"

Rostoff sniffed and dropped the book on the bedside table. "There are better things to discuss over a man who cannot hear you." He shook his head again at Chelomeyev.

At least he was alive. That was the only blessing Kazakov could think of and the one he clung to. If he'd only listened to the young detective. If he'd only allowed him to finish his stories, there was every chance Chelomeyev would not be here. Kazakov sighed and looked back at Rostoff.

"What do you want? You wouldn't be here if you didn't want something."

Rostoff went to the door, checked the corridor, and then pulled the door closed.

So something clearly had Rostoff spooked. The fact that he was here at all suggested that something was happening, though why he would come to Kazakov was a mystery. The two men had trained as police officers together, but beyond that they had nothing in common. Rostoff had used his connections and his propensity to be a "fixer" to advance quickly, while Kazakov had become a detective with a nose for corruption and a high conviction rate, and that was where he wished to stay. He had refused to work with partners because few other detectives would put in the long hours that Kazakov would dedicate to his cases. Unfortunately, he made few friends of men like Rostoff, who preferred to smooth over cases involving influential figures.

"Have you been paying attention to the news?" Rostoff asked. He shifted uneasily to the room's lone window that looked out onto the parking lot and the dirty snow melting away in the park that fronted Our Lady Yekaterina Hospital.

"The news?" Kazakov pondered the question. "The election is only a month away." And all the polls said that the people of Fergana were most concerned about their security. Fergana was a small pimple of a country, caught between the superpowers of the Ottoman and Chinese empires. So far, that had worked to Fergana's advantage, because neither superpower dared to encroach on Fergana without rousing the ire of their great foe. But recent attacks in Fergana had raised the specter of domestic terrorism. The most recent had blown up the statue of beloved Tsarina Yekaterina. Her statue had stood in the central square of New Moscow as memorial for her leadership in the horrific diaspora of Russians after Moscow fell and Holy Mother Russia was lost. Their people had wandered through the Siberian wilderness until the kind tribal people of Fergana had taken them in.

In thanks, the Russians had gradually excluded the original people from the new Ferganese culture the Russians had built. Now some people were blaming the tribal people for the attacks and finding a solution had become an election hot potato.

"Is there some problem of Boris Bure's you now wish to solve?" asked Kazakov bitterly. Boris Bure was the current front-runner in the election. He was also the stepfather of a recent sixteen-year-old murder victim and the father of her unborn child, but the evidence of this had been withheld —for now.

Rostoff turned back to him. "The man has power. We both know it. Better to remain on his good side, if a man wants a career."

Kazakov shook his head and felt sick to his stomach. He looked down at Chelomeyev. Was this what the New Moscow Police Department had come to? Chelomeyev had tried to do something more and look where it had got him.

But Rostoff shook his head. "It is not Bure. You may have heard about the murder of an old tribal woman in Biysk. It was on the news this morning."

The room ticked around them and the soft beeping of Chelomeyev's heart monitor ticked off the moments as Kazakov waited for Rostoff to explain himself. Biysk was a ski resort in the mountains enjoyed by Fergana's wealthy. The death of an elderly tribal woman should barely make the news at all.

When Kazakov didn't respond, Rostoff turned back to the window. Apparently, a slush-filled parking lot in the late afternoon's fading light was more interesting than Kazakov or Chelomeyev's room. Or perhaps safer.

"I received a call this afternoon from the Chief Inspector of the Biysk Police Detachment. He has recently experienced a spate of retirements amongst his officers. He has no one with the experience to conduct a murder investigation and is seeking our assistance. You have something of a reputation for your interest in our tribal citizens and you did your part in the investigation into the explosions. I thought perhaps you would appreciate a lighter duty—given your recent injuries, of course."

Kazakov shifted where he stood. His side still ached from where he'd been shot four months ago. It had slowed him down, but he *was* recovering. He'd investigated Chelomeyev's beating last month and had chopped a cord of wood just this past weekend. Of course, now he paid the price in stiffness.

"And what of the investigation into the explosives? Who will pursue the source of the bombing plan? And what of the other missing explosives? They have not been found yet."

"I know. I know." Rostoff waved his questions away, his thick mop of hair shadowing his eyes. "But there are other detectives who can pursue this. You—you are a valuable commodity given how the tribals trust you."

The tribals. Therein lay the issue. He did not treat one Ferganese citizen differently from another. One might be a tall blond Russian, the other a slight, darker skinned Kyrgyz descendent of ancient warriors or Sogdian Silk Road traders. They were all one and the same when it came to the law. Of course, not every detective saw it that way.

"Why this woman. Why now?"

"Kazakov, my old friend." Rostoff left his place by the window to cross to Chelomeyev's side. "You are entirely too suspicious. They asked and so I ask you. Will you help out our brethren in Biysk?"

And get his nose out of trouble in New Moscow. But that was left unsaid.

"And if I refuse?" Kazakov fingered the pages in the book of fairy tales as he looked down at Chelomeyev. Let the young detective wake up. Let his mind be unimpaired.

Rostoff's gaze hardened. "There are those who say you should have retired after you were shot. So far I have denied them."

Kazakov sighed. Once he might have considered retirement, but at the moment there were undercurrents to his country that filled him with concern. He could not simply sit back in his dacha and allow ill things to happen. "Given the problems I cause you, I cannot see where sending me off to another department will enhance your reputation. At least not with that department." And Rostoff was all about enhancing people's views of himself.

Rostoff shook his head. "But you always tell me that you get results and that someone must take the side of victims even if they are tribal."

Kazakov rolled his gaze heavenward. It was unfortunately true. "All right. I'll leave first thing tomorrow, but on one condition. You must check on Chelomeyev regularly and keep me updated when I call."

Rostoff made grumbling noises but finally nodded. "Better if it was tonight. There are concerns that the entire tribal population could rise up and come down from the mountains. With the spring, the passes are opening."

"Tonight then." Kazakov glanced at Chelomeyev and nodded, though the chances of such an uprising were between slim and none in his estimation.

He touched Chelomeyev's hand. "It seems our reading sessions are to be interrupted, old friend, but I will come back and finish the story of Pig Skin."

As if to prove he would uphold his end of the bargain, Rostoff snagged a chair and seated himself as if to assume Kazakov's role, but instead of reading to Chelomeyev, he pulled a magazine from his coat's deep pockets and began scanning the pages. There was only so far the great Rostoff would go.

In silence, Kazakov turned away. There were many miles before him this night.

———

The village of Biysk lay southeast of New Moscow, deep inside the Pamir-Alay Mountains. By the time Kazakov returned home to his dacha to pack and make arrangements with his neighbor Agafya Ryabkov to feed his cat, Koshka, it was full dark when the land lifted the road out of the fields and steppes that were the heartland of Fergana into the tall mountains that shielded that tender heart from the ravages of the Chinese Empire. It was well known that the Chinese had spread their fingers and spies into these mountains and there were rumors that they attempted to recruit the tribal people as their allies. Of course, there were also rumors that the Ottomans tried the same thing.

He had been driving five hours by the time he came over the pass that gave onto the village. To either side were the massive white peaks of the mountains hulking against the star-laden vastness of the sky. Ahead and below the road, a swath of electric lights pooled in the darkness along the edge of a river that he knew was likely still frozen as it bisected the valley floor. Contrary to the spring thaws that had occurred in the valley of Fergana, here heaped snow ran either side of the road and a thin layer of ice covered the pavement so that he had to slow the Perseus in the corners of the switchback turns that took him slowly down between the spruce trees that verged Biysk's valley.

Once the valley had been a pilgrim destination for Islamic true believers, for it was said that a saint had lived in the crags beyond the village. Others had said the epic hero, Manas, had stopped here to rest during his many battles against the Kipchaks and Mongols. With the advent of Russian Fergana, interest in the valley had waned, but the introduction of skiing from the Anglo-Germans had led to the development of the valley.

Kazakov slowed the Perseus to a crawl. He had brought his ex-wife, Annuschka, here for a holiday on their first anniversary and the lights had been a small huddle in the middle of the valley. Now they spread across its floor. Change had come to the valley.

He wondered what daylight would show.

He followed the switchbacks down to the valley floor, but a sudden abundance of roads turning off from the highway slowed him down. Signs advertised hot pools, hotels, and resorts. The ski hill warranted its own broad avenue. Not where he planned to go.

Before leaving home, he had phoned ahead and made reservations at a small guesthouse that he remembered from long ago. It had been there that he had brought Annuschka—much to her displeasure, for the place held none of the modern amenities of home.

Following his own sense of direction, he wound through a maze of streets toward the river. Hotels and grand resorts grew up beside the road where once there had been fields of sheep and horses brought in from the hills. Before, the valley had been a patchwork of trees and fields. Now, in the darkness it seemed all that he could see were new structures and parking lots.

The road he followed dead-ended in a Y intersection by a thin line of naked trees. He stopped the vehicle and climbed out, sniffing the familiar scent of snow and pitchy woodsmoke. So not everything had changed. And over the purr of the Perseus's engine came the clear music of running water and ice. There might still be deep snow on the ground, but the Biysk River's ice was breaking up. His breath steamed in the cold, but overhead the veil of stars was bound by a familiar crown of peaks.

That, at least, time had not changed.

Taking a guess as to the direction to turn, he took the eastward fork and found himself driving past behemoth resorts—some with bulbous rooflines reminiscent of New Moscow's false Saint Basil's Cathedral—and all blazing with light as if they did not feel safe in their mountain surroundings. In daylight, hotel rooms would look out over the river and the mountains, but at night the drawn curtains apparently helped keep the frightening darkness at bay. Five minutes later, the resorts faded behind him and he found himself in an area that looked vaguely familiar.

Low, stone buildings stood back from a river that was known to flood in spring thaws. Chimneys uncoiled bluish smoke that rose halfway to heaven and then spread across the valley. A few of the structures bore signs with expensive-sounding restaurant names, when they looked like the homesteads he remembered from before. Others still stood amid low stone walls with livestock loafing in the cold night air.

Kazakov sighed. He knew where he was now. He could spot a tribal ghetto a mile away. The original people of the valley had been locked away in a small enclave while the Russian well-to-do chipped at ghetto edges and bought up the rest of the valley. He kept going and found a cluster of small stone buildings close by the river and pulled over to the side of the road.

When he climbed out, all was silence except for the mutter of water and ice. Beyond the western peaks, a glow said where the moon had disappeared. He inhaled the cold night air and eased his shoulders. At least he felt whole and healed and ready to do what needed to be done.

His small valise in hand, he crunched down the side of the road until he spotted the long-remembered sign: *Guesthouse.* That was all it said. No reason to provide a fancy name to stand out when you were the only guesthouse in a small town.

He let himself through the cunningly-wrought stone wall by way of a wooden gate that squeaked in the night. A neatly shoveled flagstone walkway cut between four-foot snowbanks around the side of the house to a bright blue painted door under a single bare lightbulb.

Kazakov knocked once and listened to the stillness, soon broken from within the house by a hollow thump and then the quick thump-thump-thump of footfall.

The blue door pulled open revealing a crone of a woman with thick gray hair pulled into two loose braids; a nightdress and tattered felt robe were pulled around her wasted waist and sagging breasts.

"Yes?" She blinked owl eyes up at him from a rosy-cheeked face still very much as he remembered.

"Ayim Beshimov? Is it you?" He looked her up and down and it had to be, though there were ten years and countless lost pounds masking the diminutive woman he remembered. "It is Alexander Kazakov. I phoned about a room and we talked about the old days when I brought my wife to stay."

The owl expression wavered into something more akin to discomfort. "Yes. Yes, the detective. I remember now. Come in. Come in. Wood burns too quickly these days." She stepped aside to allow him to step past into the same immaculately scrubbed hallway he remembered.

Behind him, Ayim Beshimov clicked off the outside light and turned to face him. The hallway's stone and wood walls were scrubbed to shining. A single bulb swayed from a wire overhead, so light played across her face like a sea of expressions. Happy to see him? Sad?

Something about her suggested afraid.

He smiled at her. "When business brought me to Biysk again, I could not stay anywhere else but here."

Her wide gaze seemed to study him and then she nodded. "It is late. You must wish your room." As he removed his boots, she stepped past him and led him down the hall. "You asked for the room overlooking the river, but it is no longer available. My daughter lives there now with her family."

She led him to a door, swung it open, and flicked on a light. Again, a single bulb hung from the ceiling of a ten-by-ten room. The comforting scent of burning wood came from a glowing fireplace against one wall. On top of the fireplace sat a kettle and warmth enveloped him. A single four-poster bed sat under the window set in the stone wall and a dresser sat against the unpainted wood wall beside the door. A clothing trunk was sandwiched between the foot of the bed and the door. Ayim Beshimov collected the kettle and poured hot water into a plain metal basin on top of the dresser.

"You wash here. There is tea, here. The washroom is down the hall as you likely recall." She motioned at a small wooden box above the dresser. "In the morning there is breakfast at seven thirty. I will see you then."

With that, she backed from the room, pulling the door shut behind her. He stood there, listening to the shuffle of her feet down the hall, the opening and closing of another door, and then silence enveloped him save for the sound of heat rushing up the metal chimney flue.

Sighing about the old saying that you could never go home again, he set his valise on the bed and began to unpack. He had to remind himself that it had been many years since he had been here and many things had obviously changed for both the valley and Ayim Beshimov.

He wasn't sure why he felt sad at the lack of welcome.

2

At seven thirty the next morning, Kazakov was seated on a hard bench in the stone guesthouse kitchen with his back to the wall. A well-worn wooden table sat before him, one of three well-scrubbed tables in the room. A flattened pillow under his ass gave no comfort and the uneven stone wall gave no chance to easing the ache in his side.

The room was warm and getting warmer as heat poured off the ancient clay oven in the corner and the metal tray on the top that held a kettle for water. Ayim Beshimov bustled about the room, her owl-eyed gaze avoiding him as she slapped down a bowl of noodles and broth and a large mug of weak tea. A plate with a generous eight-inch wedge of flatbread was the closest approximation of anything he usually ate for breakfast. Clearly, things had changed at the guesthouse.

His meal settled before him, Ayim Beshimov stood before him with her hands on her hips, clearly waiting.

Obediently he picked up a large spoon and sampled the broth. Surprisingly good with the warmth of chicken and ginger. He slurped up a noodle and nodded. "Good."

She nodded "of course" and went back to her bustle when the guesthouse door pushed open to admit a thin young woman with the same wide eyes as Ayim Beshimov. She had thick, dark hair that must flow down her back, but which was modestly braided and coiled at the back of her neck. She wore a plain gray, woolen work shirt buttoned up the front to her chin and a set of stout canvas trousers. Surprisingly, her feet were bare, and peeking out from her trouser legs were long, refined feet with demurely-painted, pink toenails.

She went to the older woman and spoke quietly in a dialect Kazakov didn't know. Ayim Beshimov responded and the younger woman nodded and turned to face Kazakov.

"So you're the detective they send when an old woman is killed." It was a statement, not a question, and clearly left her with the worst of impressions.

Kazakov couldn't help it: he shrugged, though a shrug was the response of liars and cowards and he preferred to think that he was neither. "I'm the one here, yes."

The woman poured herself a cup of tea and settled behind a separate table, but her gaze clearly assessed him. What did she see?

Old man? Gone to fat? Tired with age the way he slumped at the table?

Kazakov sat a little straighter and sucked in his gut, not sure why he bothered. "I've known your mother a long time. I came here years ago with my ex-wife. I was pleased to be able to return."

The woman simply sipped her tea. "Not mother. Aunt as you Russians would define it. My mother would never come down out of the mountains to—this."

Her lips curled and a disdainful glance trailed around the kitchen. He wondered why Ayim Beshimov had described their relationship differently and why she put up with the insults.

"Well, Ayim Beshimov has always been the best of hostesses. I enjoyed my time here very much." He spooned up more of the broth and finished the noodles, then tore off a piece of the flatbread and dipped it in the remaining liquid. It was chewy ambrosia in his mouth.

"What do you plan to do to catch the killer?" the young woman asked.

"I have no idea. Ask questions of those who knew her. Learn who her friends and enemies were."

Harrumphing, the young woman slumped back against the wooden wall and crossed her arms over her chest. She said something indecipherable to her aunt.

Ayim Beshimov turned to face them. "I think. I think we must be polite. See if he tries, at least."

Kazakov raised a brow at them. "Why wouldn't I try? My job is to find justice for the dead."

Again, the young woman shook her head and would not meet his gaze.

"My niece has lost the skill of smiling at those she does not understand," Ayim Beshimov said as she cleared Kazakov's plates from the table.

"No. I've lost patience with these *mu'dak* Russians who do not give a damn about helping us." The young woman's jaw was set in a hard line. So was her mouth, which was a shame, for it detracted from the beauty she was—the same beauty he could see in his hostess if he looked beyond the wrinkles and the careworn expression.

It was a complaint that often remained unsaid but vibrated in the room when he interviewed one of the Kyrgyz or Uzbek Ferganese citizens. It was like acrid smoke in the room that caught in his chest and those who he spoke to. As a result, often it was as if they spoke different languages and, though they might hear the same words, they understood very different things.

"If you knew me, I hope that you would say something different," Kazakov said quietly. "Perhaps you will reassess me after I have done my job here."

The woman harrumphed again and said something to Ayim Beshimov. The old woman filled a bowl with noodles and broth and brought it to her. The younger woman's black glare held him as if it was all she could do to eat in the same room as him. When she was done, she stood and slammed out of the room.

Ayim Beshimov shook her head. "I am sorry. It has been—difficult here. Aisha works at the White Hill Resort. She has not felt well-treated."

"And why is that?" He nodded at her to join him at the table.

Ayim Beshimov shook her head but poured herself a cup of tea and settled heavily at the table Aisha had vacated. "They give her poor shifts. They steal her tips and then the Russian men make passes at her and the management become angry when she resists. Truly, she is a good woman. She works hard to support her son—my nephew."

"Her son?"

"Young Taalay. He is ten years old and was named after his father." She sighed.

"What is it?" he asked, keeping his voice down. It was as if the two of them existed in a quiet place with only the music of the fire in the chimney around them.

"Taalay, her husband, though he was not as lucky as his name. He disappeared a year ago out herding in the mountains. His goats were found wandering, the herd much depleted by wolves."

"I'm sorry. It was a strong marriage?"

"As strong as these times make any marriage." She shook her head and looked troubled.

He considered how to use this moment of accord to his advantage. "Still, I am sorry. No son should be without a father." It was an unlucky happenstance.

"Tell me," he said softly. "You have lived here a long time. The woman who was killed. You knew her?"

Owl eyes above the rim of her cup, Ayim Beshimov nodded. Her gnarled, white knuckles shook as she set the cup down.

"It was Bermet Aytmatov. She was a healer. She was from a village farther up the valley but had moved down here as a young woman. She still traveled in the mountains, though. In the summer she had a garden and grew medicinal herbs and the best tomatoes, sweet and rich. She said it was a special fertilizer that she used that kept her plants happy. We used to laugh and say it was young Russian tourists she lured to her house like your Baba Yaga legend. Their blood and bones made good soil to walk on." She met his gaze and color flooded up her face. "I apologize. I suppose it was ill-said."

She looked as if she awaited his ire. Instead, he sighed.

"I suppose it was earned. How did Bermet Aytmatov die?"

Ayim Beshimov shook her head. "We do not know. She was found dead on a trail not far from her home village." She closed her eyes. "I did not see, but I hear things. Her neighbor found her. It was not—good. Then a Russian tourist came by and accused her neighbor. He was arrested. There is much anger, for Bermet was held in high regard amongst our people."

"And the neighbor?"

"Where do you think? Still in jail."

Her head was bowed and the sudden opening of the door broke the spell of the silence. A ten-year-old boy pushed inside, black-haired like his mother but without her wide eyes. Instead the youngster had a serious gaze under a head of floppy hair. His considered gaze appeared to take in the world and understand what he saw. He glanced in Kazakov's direction and immediately went to Ayim Beshimov.

The lad spoke to Ayim Beshimov softly in his own language as if he did not wish Kazakov to hear.

"I'm fine, Taalay. We were just talking and the talk brought up memories. Now come sit down and I will bring you breakfast. This is

Detektiv Kazakov from New Moscow." She pushed herself up and went to the pot on the oven, ladled a bowl of noodles and broth, and brought it to the boy. All the while Taalay eyed Kazakov as if assessing what he saw.

"You are very like your mother," Kazakov said.

Taalay shook his head. "Mama says I am like my father." He thought a moment. "You catch criminals."

Ayim Beshimov took dough from a bowl and patted it flat in her hands before reaching into the top of the oven to affix the bread to the clay oven wall.

Kazakov inclined his head. The odor of baking bread filled the room. "I try."

"There are bad men in Biysk. You must catch them." Taalay used a spoon to begin sucking up his breakfast. Kazakov finished his tea and stood as Ayim Beshimov brought the flatbread out of the oven and gave it to the boy.

"I will see you both this evening, I hope. Thank you for your information." He bowed his head and stepped out the kitchen door to the hall. He went back to his room to recover his greatcoat, hat, and gloves and, from in his valise, his weapon. He strapped on his holster and replaced his suit jacket and then hauled on his coat and gloves.

When he left the room, he found Taalay waiting for him. "You are a detective. Do you catch killers?"

"When I can," he said and stepped past the boy toward the door.

"There is a killer in the valley. There have been many deaths."

Kazakov turned back to him. "What are you talking about?"

"Old Bermet Aytmatov, she's not the first. A bunch of the elders have died."

"Elders die, Taalay. They are old."

The lad shook his head. "You sound just like Grandmother. She doesn't want to believe. But Mama knows. She does."

The boy's finality wasn't a surprise. Children lived in a world of black and white—like make-believe. "And what does your mama know, Taalay?"

He looked solemnly up at Kazakov as if trying to decide. Then he shook his head again. "Many things. Not to believe in Russian men—even detectives."

He turned and scuttled down the hall and into the room that Kazakov had been expecting to stay in.

Stranger and stranger, but the sentiment of distrust was not unknown to Kazakov. In New Moscow he was one of the few detectives who could have a conversation in the old city and have a hope of gaining the truth. He'd used his friendship with the Medical Examiner, Khalil Khan, one of the few Kyrgyz who had found a place in Russian establishment, albeit a tenuous one, and he had also helped bring the killers of a favored Kyrgyz son to justice. That brought credibility with a people for whom credibility of the police department was in short supply.

In New Moscow.

Here in the mountains was clearly another story.

He followed the hall to the front doorway, but his boots were nowhere to be found. Finally, he followed his gut and checked outside the door. Bright sunlight flared in his eyes, instantly blinding him. Cold withered away any warmth in his exposed skin. He scanned the snowbanks and there they were—half-buried in the blue-black shadow of the house and half frozen to the ground.

Sighing, he pulled them loose, brought them back into the house. The leather was hard, the fur lining almost brittle. Lesson learned: if it was important, leave nothing of his outside his room. He pulled the boots on and his toes were instantly frozen, but it could not be helped. His toes would warm soon enough in the Perseus. Gloves pulled on and coat buttoned, he stepped outside.

Cold sucked the breath out of him and he pulled his hat on, flaps down over his ears. Then he traversed the yard between snowbanks and reached the road.

Thankfully, the Perseus was where he had left it and apparently unharmed.

———

Unknowingly, he had driven right past the new Biysk police station last night. It sat sandwiched between a small wood-and-glass resort hotel that must have been one of the oldest in the valley and a grand behemoth of a new resort full of glass and steel beams. In the clear morning sunlight over the icy mountain peaks, the first showed signs of hard wear in the weathering of the siding and the collapsing structure of the tall fences that divided the hotel property from that of the police station. The new hotel gleamed in the morning sunlight.

He pulled into the police station parking lot that was marked with a small, hard to spot sign that read Biysk Public Safety Building. He could imagine the town fathers demanding that signage and those words because surely a Russian Resort could not have crime. At least that was the image they were determined to present. Which perhaps explained the need to bring in a detective from elsewhere in the face of a murder.

The building was a concrete block structure with wood window sills and wooden pillars flanking the main door as if that could soften the bleak exterior. Dark windows stared blankly out at the parking lot. Not exactly a place to welcome visitors.

Sighing, he locked the Perseus, then trudged up the four stairs and inside. The dry heat in the interior hit him like a wave after the mountain chill. He stood in a small reception area that smelled pleasantly of new wood, though there was no sign of the source of the smell in the plastic and metal waiting room chairs. Two walls to either side and a tall faux-wood counter ahead blocked access to the building beyond. An officer in a uniform ironed to a shine sat behind the counter reviewing documents and blocking access via the small gate that waited at one end of the counter.

He looked up when Kazakov entered. The officer was middle-aged, with a thick head of dark hair and graying temples. He had gray eyes, too, with squint lines at the corners, probably from too many hours in the snow.

"Can I help you?" he asked in a surprising baritone.

"Detektiv Alexander Kazakov, New Moscow Police. I was sent at your Chief Inspektor's request."

The officer raked him with his gaze and stood. Then he limped back a pace so Kazakov could see the cast on his leg.

"Egorova! He's here!" he called down the corridor behind him. Then he returned to his chair. "Take a seat." He lifted his chin at the chairs along the wall.

As if that was going to happen. He wasn't some civilian. He was a detective and he was here to do a favor to these people.

Arms behind his back, he paced the waiting area.

And waited. And waited some more, trying to breathe away his anger at being left there. The uniformed officer seemed perfectly satisfied ignoring him. The officer continued to shuffle papers—until the sound of footfall came from the corridor.

Kazakov paused his pacing. The uniformed desk officer looked up from his papers as the crisp footfall approached. It was lighter and faster cadenced than the pace of most detectives.

A woman in a dark gray suit stepped up to the counter and opened the gate in the corner. She stepped through and held out her hand. "Detektiv Kazakov. Welcome to Biysk. I am Detektiv Elena Egorova."

She had a cool, firm handshake that she kept short and pulled her hand back to her side. In her lace-up brogues, she was considerably shorter than Kazakov—perhaps five-foot-six he estimated. A thick head of honey-blonde hair was tied back in a loose ponytail. She had plain, fresh-scrubbed features that made her look younger than the thirty years he estimated her to be.

Though she wore a crisp white blouse buttoned to her collarbone, a severe, boxy suit jacket, and loose-fitting trousers in a gray flannel, he could better imagine her clad in ski apparel, her pale cheeks pinked in the cold and her gaze sparked with laughter. Instead she assessed him with a serious gaze. Two small gold hoops caught the light in each earlobe.

"You are here about the murder?"

He nodded.

"Come with me." As if she was ordering him. She stepped through the gate and waited for him, then settled it back in place before leading him crisply down the hall. There were three offices to either side of the hall before the space opened up to a large central area of desks and uniformed officers.

He stopped and checked the clock on the wall. Almost eight thirty.

"What is it?" Detektiv Egorova asked when she stopped at one of the desks. It was neater than most in the space and held an unmarked blotter and a small crystal shoe that held paper clips. Clearly, this was her workspace.

"At this hour, uniformed officers are usually on patrol in New Moscow. And detectives do not share an office with them."

She settled into the desk chair and nodded to the empty chair beside the desk. He seated himself.

"This is not New Moscow, Detektiv. Biysk's guests do not like to see police cruising by. They prefer to think that they have left crime behind. That is why it is so important that we solve this murder. It may not have been a tourist who was killed, but she was found by tourists and their horror has seeped into the other resort guests. People are leaving and we cannot have that."

Her clear, earnest gaze would have been charming if not for her words.

"So the only value in solving a murder is preventing the economy from suffering?" He shook his head. "I find that exposing the truth is enough justification."

Her open gaze dimmed a little and she sat back in her chair. "I see. The great New Moscow detective has come to rescue us in the mountains. He deigns to share his immense experience with us. How lucky are we?"

"I did not ask to be here. Apparently, someone from Biysk requested my presence." He remained where he was, wondering what she would do next.

Finally, she sighed. "I'm sorry. I do not take well to being told I must accept a new partner—especially one brought in from outside. Unfortunately, we do need assistance in keeping a lid on this whole thing."

He nodded. "I understand. I, too, prefer to work alone. At times it is not a good idea."

"A partner is good to use as a sounding board, or so it is said." But her gaze remained skeptical.

"So it is said." He found her lips curved into a slight smile at him.

"It seems perhaps we have more in common than I had thought. And now we have a problem in common." She inhaled and stood. "Perhaps we could have tea while I run through what we have?"

He hunched up out of his chair and bumped her desk, rattling the glass shoe and its contents, and feeling Egorova's sharp glance. The shoe was more than a simple office decoration.

Detektiv Egorova turned on her heel and led him out of the squad room toward the rear of the building and to a set of concrete stairs. She started down. Cold radiated off of the cinder block walls and he was glad he still wore his great coat, though he'd been tempted to take it off in the squad room. The stairs were poorly lit by single bulbs on the walls at each landing. They went down one floor to the basement and stepped through a door and out into another reception area guarded by an older woman with short gray hair who typed at her desk.

Detektiv Egorova nodded once in the receptionist's direction and led Kazakov through another closed door. The scent of death, formaldehyde, and pine cleaning fluid greeted him and he knew where he was. The room was concrete and chrome with water running in a sink against the wall, and a drain recessed in the middle of the floor. Fluorescent lights glared overhead and surgical lights had been positioned to illuminate the table in the center of the room.

Two paper-gowned men in protective glasses stood above a body on an autopsy table, their faces masked against the splatter and smell. In the corner by the door hung a selection of white doctor's coats and a long black greatcoat similar to what Kazakov wore.

Detektiv Egorova paused. "Dr. Alexeev, I thought you would not have started."

The doctor's blue eyes looked up at her from behind his mask. He was the taller man of the two and blond, compared to his darker-skinned companion who was wielding scalpel and probe.

"My associate, here, thought it better to begin. He may be able to make it back to New Moscow today. May I present Dr. Khalil Khan." The good doctor's voice through the mask was chill as the room.

A familiar gaze turned in Kazakov's direction. Khan nodded in greeting.

"Detektiv Alexander Kazakov," Kazakov said to Dr. Alexeev. "Dr. Khan I know very well."

Dr. Khalil Khan was virtually unique in Fergana, a man of the tribal people who had inhabited Fergana long before the arrival of the desperate Russian refugees fleeing from the Ottoman sacking of the original Moscow. Those tribal people had taken the Russians in. In thanks, the Russian culture bloomed and overtook and excluded the very people who had helped them. Khan was unique because his brilliance in medical school had led to a position in Fergana's government bureaucracy as a medical examiner. In addition, he ran a clinic for his people in New Moscow's old city. He was also a long-time friend of Kazakov's though lately that friendship had been strained.

"I drove up early this morning after getting the call late last night," Khan said through his mask. "Why waste time, when there is a body waiting." He changed the scalpel for forceps and tugged something from the body to deposit in a waiting tray. He leaned over the tray. "Interesting. It appears to be a bullet fragment, but it was a knife that ruptured the aorta. That's what killed her." He stepped back from the body and pulled his mask down, revealing his handsome, slightly oriental features, which matched his dark gaze. "Lots of bruise marks on the face and upper torso as well. Someone clearly wanted to stop her and finished the job."

At a nod from Khan, Dr. Alexeev quickly sutured the open chest cavity closed. Khan retreated to the sink to pull his gloves off and wash his hands.

It was good to see the little M.E., and yet Khan had an aura of distance around him. Perhaps it was just the cool attitude of Alexeev, but there had been brief moments of chill between Kazakov and Khan, too. Those had arisen whenever a question came up about the loyalty of the Kyrgyz and other tribal peoples. Unfortunately, it had happened frequently in Kazakov's last case and strained their relationship.

"I'm told our victim was found outside," Kazakov said.

Detektiv Egorova's gaze widened slightly at his knowledge given she had told him nothing so far. He looked at her. "What do we know?"

He caught a slight smile from Khan. Usually it was the little M.E. who received such a question at the crime scene.

Detektiv Egorova shoved a stray bit of hair over her delicate ears and her expression firmed. "She was found early morning by a Russian tourist out alone for a morning ski. He spotted a man kneeling over something and went to see what it was. It turned out it was the old woman, our victim."

"Bermet Aytmatov," Kazakov said. "Never just a victim. Never just an old woman. We must think of her with a name."

Detektiv Elena Egorova's lips hardened, so clearly she did not like to be corrected. Then she inhaled and nodded. "Bermet Aytmatov, yes. The Russian called for help on his phone and when he described what he'd seen to the police, the man found with the old woman was arrested."

"He is still in custody?" Kazakov asked and glanced at Khan, but the M.E.'s face was a well-trained mask.

"Of course. He had blood all over his clothes and the old woman—Bermet Aytmatov was dead. He was brought in for questioning."

"Three days ago."

Again, that tell-tale firming of lips as if Detektiv Elena Egorova swallowed what she would like to say. "If he would speak to us and provide a statement, it might be possible to release him."

And having someone in custody would no doubts keep tourists calm and local businesses happy.

"And what does forensic evidence say?"

A low cough from Alexeev reminded Kazakov that he was not in the privacy of a detective office.

"Perhaps it would be better if we go out to the crime scene and you will show me."

"I would like to go," Khan murmured.

Kazakov nodded and turned back to Egorova. "Which detective examined the body at the scene?"

Color rose up her neck and cheeks. In another situation it might be becoming. In this one it was more indicative of anger or shame.

"Her body was collected by a team of officers sent to the scene. I was given the case the morning after." She would not meet his gaze.

"But surely another detective attended," Kazakov said.

"There *is* no other detective."

The situation and process she described was so foreign to everything police were taught at the academy and so wrong from a detective's perspective he was momentarily lost for words. He blew out a breath and nodded. "Then I suppose it is even more important that we visit the scene. When did it snow last?"

"Hard? The night before Bermet Aytmatov died, but there have been fine skiffs of snow off and on ever since."

That was something. Not everything might be destroyed, though he knew there was likely not much left of the scene given the hiker and the police presence. Unless someone had actually had the sense to protect it. Given what he'd seen so far, it didn't seem likely.

"What did you think of the scene?" he asked.

Egorova shook her head. "You will see when we visit."

Thanking Dr. Alexeev, Kazakov led the way out of the examination room, Khan just behind him.

The M.E. stopped them. "Kazakov. I need to complete my report while the information is still fresh in my mind. I should also be able to provide a slightly better time of death. Just give me an hour."

They agreed to meet in an hour in the parking lot and Kazakov and Egorova retreated to the squad room. Where, in New Moscow, the detective squad room would be virtually empty as officers conducted their investigations, here even the uniformed officers cooled their heels at desks or taking phone calls. It was one of the rare times that he had ever thought of Rostoff and his fellow detectives in a positive light.

At Egorova's desk, he faced her.

"I'm sorry," she began. "They moved her before I could do anything. The town council did not want to chance more tourists seeing anything and they wanted the trail open. I was furious when I found out."

Kazakov waved away her explanations. "It is done. I am sorry that I put you on the spot down there. I know this is difficult for you, but we need to work together on this case—regardless of what the town council wants. You are young enough you will remember procedures from training. That is what I want to follow. First, we need to find a quiet office to work from. Then we need the file and an evidence board so that we can begin to assess what we have as evidence comes to us. Can you arrange that?"

She nodded.

"Good. The second thing I want is to interview the man who was found with her and the Russian tourist who found him with Bermet. Then I will want to speak to the attending officers and those who moved her."

"That… that may be more difficult. The tourist has returned to New Moscow. The first officer on scene left yesterday on vacation."

Kazakov stilled. There was something wrong here. It was too much as if someone was trying to make this investigation impossible, but then, he was known for his paranoia.

"We will start where we can and work from there. We will look at the scene. Then the man in custody. He is not going anywhere. While we wait for Khan, get us that office."

He commandeered her desk to make his own notes as she hurried away to do whatever was needed to arrange a private space. The desktop was impossibly neat: no loose pens, no pieces of paper or files. No yellow message slips. Was that what she was like in her personal life, as well? How did her husband deal with such order? But then, he did not recall seeing a ring on her hand. On the other hand, he had never worn a ring, either. Rings were impractical in his line of business.

And then there was the glass slipper on her desk. For all the utilitarian purpose she'd found for it, it was still a surprising piece of femininity. It reminded him of Chelomeyev and the fairy tale that Kazakov had been reading. Pig Skin. A princess hiding behind a pigskin only to be discovered by the glass slipper she wore and lost one night.

He looked up as Detektiv Egorova approached with a dour expression. He couldn't imagine her as a princess.

3

———————

"There is a problem," Detektiv Egorova said when she arrived at the desk from the corridor beyond.

Kazakov sat back, waiting. Around them, the sea of desks held uniformed officers murmuring on the phone or amongst themselves, filling the stuffy air of the cavernous room with a grumble and hum that was more akin to his ex-wife's communication offices than any place to conduct a murder investigation.

"And what might that be?"

"The shift officer questions the need for a private office. We are all police officers. Such an investigation should be conducted in the open, not in secret."

Kazakov nodded and stood. "Where can I find this shift officer? I would like to meet him."

Egorova studied his face and perhaps he wasn't as good as he thought he was at disguising his anger.

"His name is Anatoly Nikitin." She checked around them, but no one was paying any attention. "He is not a good man to cross," she said, low-voiced.

He nodded. "Introduce me, please."

With a quick nod, she led him back the way she had come, through the sea of desks and too many eyes watching their comings and goings. This was what he did not like. He did not like the fact that they could not hold a candid conversation or post their evidence in a way that would help to make connections.

In the hallway beyond the squad room, she knocked on a closed office door.

"What is it now?" came a male voice from beyond the door.

Egorova gave Kazakov an I-told-you-so glance and opened the door. "Sir." She stepped inside. "May I present Detektiv Alexander Kazakov."

She stepped aside to allow Kazakov to enter.

It was a closet of an office, barely wide enough for Nikitin's oversized desk and a narrow path that he could edge past to his chair. The air was dry and stale with failed deodorant and Nikitin's body odor. There were no guest chairs.

The top of Nikitin's desk was awash in files. The one in front of the man was open and covered with red marks from the pen he held. Kazakov had met men like Nikitin and knew what he faced—a bureaucrat consumed with dotting i's and crossing t's. Not the kind of police officer Kazakov respected and not the kind of officer who ensured good police work.

Nikitin was sharp-featured with slightly bulging eyes and thin blond hair that allowed the scalp to show through. He had broad shoulders, but his arms were spindly in his well-pressed, long-sleeved shirt. His pallor said that he was clearly not a man who enjoyed the outdoors.

"It is a pleasure to meet you," Kazakov said and slightly inclined his head. He left out the "sir," for he had been brought in as a special favor to the Biysk commander and technically Nikitin's rank as sergeant was no greater than Kazakov's detective status.

Nikitin eyed him. "I repeat. What is it now? I already told Detektiv Egorova that it is impossible for me to find you a private office. We have no free offices in this building and certainly nothing private. This is not New Moscow, Detektiv." His lips curled down with disdain.

Kazakov managed a smile as he looked down on Nikitin. The man clearly had no idea who he was dealing with.

"The scenery alone tells me that I am not in New Moscow, but the need for a private space to conduct the investigation is nonnegotiable. Either I have space here or I find a space in the village and send the bill to the Biysk Police. Your choice."

Shoving back from his desk, Nikitin pushed upright, but couldn't quite meet Kazakov's six-foot-two in height. "Are you defying my orders?"

Kazakov simply met his gaze. "I am telling you what I need to conduct this investigation. Obviously, the case is sensitive because you asked for assistance from New Moscow. I need the space or I return to New Moscow."

"It was the Chief who asked for help—not me. Egorova could have conducted the investigation herself. Hell, we have already caught the killer!"

"And have not helped calm the already troubled relationship between the police and the tribal peoples."

Nikitin's face went rigid. "It was an old woman. She lived alone with no family. You think the tribals will cause an uprising on her behalf?"

"She is a victim of murder. Her death deserves a complete, objective investigation." Kazakov checked his watch. "I will make other arrangements for an office. Thank you for your time."

He turned and left the office, trailing Egorova behind him. Behind he heard the scrape of cloth against wood as Nikitin came around his desk. Then the door slammed shut behind them.

"It's my turn to apologize. You will likely pay the price for my insistence."

Egorova shook her head. "It will blow over. It always does."

But there was something akin to admiration in her gaze. She was young. She had yet to learn that standing up for yourself also required payment.

At her desk, they gathered the file into a briefcase. A call came in that someone named Khan was waiting for them at the front desk.

"Send him through," Kazakov said.

There was silence on the phone and then "But, sir…"

"We will be right out." Kazakov hung up and sighed. "Is it truly so bad here that a respected medical examiner is not trusted in this building simply because of his ethnic background?"

He didn't wait for an answer but threaded his way back through the desks to the reception area. He waved Khalil Khan over and turned to the desk officer. "Meet Dr. Khan. He is a guest from New Moscow just as I am and he is critical to this investigation. If he is to share his expertise, he must be allowed into the building. Do you understand?"

The officer on the desk looked to Egorova for confirmation. She nodded.

"Sorry, sir. It won't happen again." He nodded at Khan. "Sorry, sir."

Khan remained unperturbed and nodded before preceding Kazakov out the door.

"Derr'mo!" Kazakov swore. "Is it always like this for you?"

Khan looked toward the horizon, but the blue-white mountains blocked his view. "It is nothing new and the mountains are beautiful, are they not? I learned long ago to let the affronts go. Otherwise I would go mad at them."

It was a revelation Kazakov had not expected. An insight into a world he could never experience. His respect for Khan only grew.

He turned to Egorova, who looked pale and serious in the brilliant sunlight. Already slight frown lines had etched themselves on her young features.

"I should ask you the same question: Is it always like this?"

"Unfortunately so," she said with a nod. "There—there is a clear division in this town."

Kazakov shook his head. "And we need to cross it."

He offered the Perseus, but in the end Egorova produced the keys to a large four-wheel-drive vehicle with higher clearance from the road. They climbed in with her at the wheel and Kazakov had to stop himself from bracing. It was not so much that she was a female, it was more that he did not like to be driven at all. When he glanced back at Khan, the M.E. was grinning.

"This must terrify you."

Egorova frowned at them. "My driving is not that bad."

"It is not," Khan agreed. "But our friend, here, prefers to always be in control."

She cocked a brow at Kazakov.

He crossed his arms and settled back in his seat. "Just drive."

At this hour of the morning, the valley was waking up and the trails beside the roads were full of tourists clad in bright red, blue, and yellow jackets gliding along the ski paths toward the ski hills. The mountains surrounded Biysk on all sides, their peaks glowing white against the blue. High altitude winds stripped snow off the tops that turned to rainbows in the rarified air. A dust of silver filtered through the air and hazed the windscreen.

Egorova drove through the village, past the modern resorts with their red-stained timbers and glass, and past the turnoff that Kazakov had taken the night before that led down to the cluster of low, stone houses that were all that remained of the original Biysk village. Smoke rose in long threads from the chimneys as if the village itself dangled from above. The low stone walls that Kazakov remembered partitioning the small farms and land holdings had virtually disappeared. Instead a phalanx of high-end clothing stores sat next to a New Moscow chain grocery store, a music store, and a laundromat. A bank of Chinese, Ottoman, and Anglo-German restaurant chains completed the erosion of what Biysk had been. Gone were the small stone tea shops he remembered. The Russian Fergana and beyond had clearly invaded this part of the tribal country.

And once again the native people were being pushed out, or at least marginalized in a country that had been their own.

The vehicle turned down a lesser traveled road that led to the far end of the valley. The land rose up under them, and beside them a string of stunted aspen and poplar trees followed the frozen riverbed and the expensive dacha that rose up beyond new concrete walls. In spring he could imagine this road being chancy with floods and washouts, but for now the snow, ice, and frozen soil made for bumpy but safe travel.

Gradually the sleek dacha fell behind, and huddled villages of old, low-slung, stone houses regained their place on the steep terrain. There were still ski trails beside the road and occasional flashes of brightly clad skiers seeking places less traveled, but the mass of tourists had been left behind as the road wound uphill.

They left the frozen river behind as it cut through a chasm of stone. The road switchbacked up the mountainside and Egorova dropped the vehicle into a lower gear. From where Kazakov sat, the mountainside fell away, straight down to snow-covered rocky fields.

Then the vehicle lurched up and over an edge and they were on a small frozen plateau that sloped up between the base of two mountains. At the narrowest point sat another cluster of stone houses. Egorova slowed as they followed the road through the village. At their passing, people exited their houses or stopped what they were doing. They were all small, dark-skinned people with the same epicanthic eye-folds as Khan, but while the men wore typical trousers and jackets, the women still wore tribal dress of felted skirts and leggings. Thick shawls wrapped their shoulders.

He glanced over his shoulder at Khan, but the M.E. was engrossed in the view out the window. When he turned back to Kazakov, his face held no expression, but Kazakov was certain it was a mask. Over anger? Defeat? Longing? Determination? Probably a combination of all of them, for Khalil Khan was a man determined to help his people both as an example and as a goad to a better life amongst the Russians.

Kazakov just wasn't certain how far Khan would go to achieve those ends. Certainly the M.E. had been closemouthed when Kazakov had come to him about explosions in New Moscow that authorities claimed were perpetrated by young tribals.

They left the town behind and Egorova slowed further. The ruts and holes in the road made traversing it difficult and set the old bullet wound in Kazakov's side aching from bracing himself. Finally, Detektiv Egorova nodded upslope to what looked like a tumble of rocks near a cliff face. "That was Bermet Aytmatov's home. I came up and took a look yesterday morning while they were calling New Moscow for help."

Kazakov's perspective of the tumble of rock shifted and it became an uneven, sloped, slate roof and stout stone walls. "I'd like to hear what you found," Kazakov said.

"Of course." Egorova kept going up the slope and finally pulled the vehicle over into an area of snow clearly flattened by a number of vehicles. "And we are here."

She parked and turned the engine off, then pointed out the window. "There is a little-used ski trail that runs over there, about thirty feet from the road. Bermet was found beside it with a man from old Biysk bent over her."

Kazakov opened his door, climbed out, and stood. The air was cold in his face like a bracing slap as he steadied himself against the vehicle. His side ached, but it *was* healing.

Khalil Khan climbed out of the back and stood there as if breathing in the scenery. He seemed to glow with new energy as if this valley, this air, fed a different part of him than could ever be sated in New Moscow.

"This way." Egorova, having collected a bag from the vehicle, set off through the snow, surprising Kazakov with her speed and balance over the slippery ruts. The trip up had taken an hour and the shadows had shrunk, making it difficult to distinguish the curves and dips of the snow. But Egorova, in her caramel-colored coat and blue hat pulled down over her ears, simply seemed to float across the snow. Then she stopped and waited for Kazakov and Khan to join her.

She stood at the edge of an area that had clearly been flattened by too many feet. In the center of the flattened area, a large brown stain suggested where Bermet Aytmatov had lain. Kazakov swallowed back an oath.

"I take it that it was not like this when she was found?"

"I don't know," Egorova said. "But this is what I found when I arrived."

"Did no one think to take photos?"

"Yes. Yes, there was one bright light among the six officers who came to collect her and the suspect. They are in the file."

Kazakov grunted his approval and then nodded at Khan, who produced three paper coveralls. "We should not contaminate the scene any further."

Khan doffed his coat and pulled on the coveralls, and then waited for Kazakov and Egorova to do the same. Egorova opened the bag she carried and produced a camera.

"Dammit! It's cold," Egorova said as she huddled in her useless coveralls. Her suit jacket would give her little warmth, unlike Kazakov's turtlenecked sweater, but even that was next to useless in the biting cold and the wind off the mountains. But she gamely began taking photos of the scene and surroundings that would be helpful to others who might need to understand just where the murder had occurred.

"We'll make this as quick as we can," Kazakov said and let Khan take the lead as he followed the edge of the scene to the closest point to where the body had been. Then he knelt in the snow next to the bloodstain.

Kazakov stayed where he was, knowing Khan was as good as it got in assessing a crime scene. Always, in the past, he and Khan had compared notes to build up a picture of what had happened—not just from a police perspective, but also from the scientific side of Khan's knowledge.

Khan studied the blood.

"By the amount of blood, I'd say she was killed here." He shook his head. "The scene is so degraded it is almost impossible to say anything else—except perhaps that the amount of blood suggests that she had been here for some time before she was found. It is highly unlikely that your suspect killed her. Why would he stab her and then remain at the scene?"

Standing, he began to search the scene. Kazakov and Egorova joined him, spiralling out and out from the epicenter of the blood stain.

The day was quiet around them, the noise of the valley left behind so that there was only the crunch of the snow under their feet, the wind amid the large boulders that littered the slopes, and the creak of river ice heating under the sun. The chill air froze the tip of Kazakov's nose and he pulled his hat lower over his ears as he carefully examined the earth around him.

The angle of the sun made the tracks clear. Too many similar tread boots mashing the snow around the body, almost as if they intended to destroy evidence. A fleck of red mashed down in a tread stopped him.

"Egorova. A photo please?"

She came and photographed what he had found and he gently fished it out of the snow and placed it into a plastic evidence bag. He held it up for examination.

"Looks like a strand of wool, like from a scarf or hat or mittens," Egorova said.

Kazakov scanned the area. "We're near the trail. There could be a lot of traffic like our witness."

Egorova nodded. "The trail leads down into the valley, as you saw. Very few cross-country skiers take it though. Up there are only remote villages. These days a lot of them are empty. Families are moving away."

"To where?" Khan asked, coming up beside them.

Egorova shrugged, the sunlight catching in loose strands of her pale hair around her face. "Who knows? Farther back in the mountains? They don't exactly love the valley people—or the tourists."

Kazakov stepped over the ruin of the crime scene to the edge of the trail. "Which way was Bermet going when she was killed? For that matter, why wasn't she killed on the trail instead of fifteen feet off of it?"

"Chased? Egorova suggested.

"Perhaps," Kazakov said and followed the trail farther up the valley. He left Khan and Egorova to complete the examination of the remains of the crime scene and kept climbing. A hundred feet up, he spotted a brown patch on the snow beyond a drift that partially blocked the side of the trail.

He took a cautious route toward it, noting a line of tracks that paralleled the trail but did not near it. He stopped slightly uphill from the brown spot to examine the tracks. Small. Flat bottomed like the traditional felted boots some older women wore. He needed to know what Bermet had been wearing, but he bet he could describe them. His ancient neighbor, Agafya Ryabkov, wore similar boots when she was out in the snow.

He turned toward the brown spot and the sun caught two bowl-shaped indentations in the snow.

"Egorova! Khan! I found something here." A second crime scene? He didn't think so, but he wanted Khan's opinion.

The detective and the M.E. trudged up to his position.

"Small steps of what looks like felted boots. What she was wearing, correct?"

Egorova nodded.

Kazakov pointed out what appeared to be a second blood stain and Khan carefully crossed to the scene and bent low.

"There are only her tracks and the blood. She could have been shot here, I suppose, but I would expect to see her footprints stagger or her body print in the snow because the bullet impact would a considerable blow." He crept closer, Egorova at his shoulder, documenting as he closed in on the bloodstain.

"She went to her knees there."

It confirmed what Kazakov had thought. "To rest?"

"Could be," Khan said.

Kazakov crouched down in the snow where he was. The drift of snow blocked his view of the trail and could potentially block anyone's view of him. "It was early morning when she was found, which means it's highly likely that she was killed at night. If that was the case, she could have ducked down to hide from someone she expected to come on the trail."

Khan studied the scene in front of him. "That fits with what is here."

Kazakov turned and looked up the slope that was gradually being squeezed into a narrow pass between two massive mountains. His gaze followed the faint gray line of the trail used by villagers and the occasional skier and he set out along it, questions parading through his mind.

What was Bermet Aytmatov doing here in the middle of the night? What or who was she running from? Where had she come from?

Ignoring his cold toes and using the palm of his hand to warm his nose, he started up the hill.

In the best of investigations, a team would be called in to follow the trail back to the origins, however he dared not trust the clod-footed Biysk constables to protect and preserve what they found on the way. He looked back at Egorova and Khan. Khan had said he was going back to Moscow, but Kazakov was going to ask him to stay. In Biysk, it seemed, they were the team.

4

The wind blew sheets of snow off the peaks and then released them into silver ice that filtered down around them as they trudged up the slope seeking the place where Bermet Aytmatov had first been injured. The cliffs of the mountains closed in around them, leaving only a narrow path and the hope that the terrain would widen ahead. The sun sent their shadows into long spectral shapes across the smooth snow and showed the dark path that had been Bermet's last scramble for her life.

Considering the injuries she had sustained, the old woman had done miraculously well. He supposed the cold had helped by slowing the loss of blood, but still, where had she come from? How far had she traveled and why had she been injured in the first place?

The sun fell behind the western peak and suddenly the slope was bathed in shadow. Bermet's trail was lost in the blue-tinged light. Kazakov paused and turned back to his companions. Khan was fine, though he stomped his feet where he stopped behind Kazakov.

Egorova struggled up behind them, still carrying the camera equipment, still only clothed in her suit and coverall.

She reached them and shuddered, then hugged herself. "We go on, yes?"

The detective was clearly freezing. Bright pink cheeks had white patches. To use the camera, she had worn only gloves. Derr'mo, he was going to put his partner in the hospital if he wasn't careful.

He looked up the trail. If it was him alone, he would go on, but there was no way Egorova could do it clothed as she was.

"We go back. Night is coming and it will only get colder. We close the trail and the road to stop any further contamination and come back again tomorrow."

"But there's t-t-too much chance of m-m-more evidence being lost," Egorova said.

Kazakov chuckled. "There'll be more than evidence lost if we don't get you warmed up." He turned around and looked down at the detective. "Now let's head home."

It was a struggle down the trail as the daylight faded swiftly once the sun had fallen. The cold increased and Kazakov was concerned for the detective, but Egorova seemed made of sterner stuff than he'd estimated. They made it back to the vehicle and climbed inside, Egorova still insisting on driving after five minutes inside with the heater roaring.

The ride down the valley was a difficult one with the deep ruts and holes barely visible in the swiftly fading light. Egorova's knuckles were white on the wheel as she fought the bucking vehicle to keep it to the trail. Eventually they reached the area by the river.

"We need to put up signs and fencing to discourage people from going farther," Kazakov said. Khan had already agreed to remain in the village. He would call his department head when they got into town.

"I doubt that signs or police lines will stop the locals," Khan said softly from the back seat. "This is their country. They won't be told where they can and cannot go."

Kazakov glanced back at him and read the truth in the M.E.'s gaze. He nodded and sighed. "Still, we put up the signs and the line to stop tourists. I'll talk to my hostess and see if she can get word to the Kyrgyz to have a care with the crime scene." He glanced back at Khan. "Maybe there's something you can do, too."

Khan nodded. "I will speak to my contacts."

Egorova and Kazakov climbed out of the vehicle and Detektiv Egorova dug tape and signs from the rear of the vehicle. It surprised him a little that they were so well equipped given how the department had botched things so far. Together they used two trees to string red plastic emergency fencing across the trail and hung signs from the trees saying the road/trail was closed.

When they were done it would be easy enough to pull down the rickety structure, but they had to hope that the tourists would obey.

It was four o'clock when they reached the Biysk police station and piled out. After the long ride down, Egorova, thankfully, no longer looked like an ice cube.

"It was a good day's work," Kazakov said. "Thank you for your help."

She looked up at him. Even after the arduous day, her gaze was bright. "What do we do about the office space?"

He nodded. "Leave that to me. Tomorrow, come to my guesthouse and bring the case file and evidence."

He told her where he was staying and her eyes widened slightly. Apparently not many Russians stayed in the old village. Then she left him for her office and presumably to report their findings to the redoubtable Nikitin.

Kazakov turned to Khan. "So. What do you think?"

Khan blinked up at him. "I think you have a dead tribal elder, and her people will not take well to this case being mishandled."

"I got that." Kazakov nodded. "Apparently someone in this department did, too, or we would not be here."

"The trouble is, those below that wise pundit do not ascribe to the same views."

Kazakov nodded again and clapped Khan on the shoulder. "I'm glad you're here. At least I have someone to depend on and can have confidence in the information you provide me. Where will you stay?"

Khan's gaze eased away. "With friends. There are long-time friends of my parents living here."

Meaning, from what Kazakov understood of Kyrgyz ways, these friends might not be direct family, but there were blood connections. The entire Kyrgyz people were woven together into such clans and the connections were powerful. It was the same blood ties that had Ayim Beshimov describe Aisha, her niece, as her daughter.

"And you stay with Ayim Beshimov," Khan said. "She is a good woman and much respected. I am surprised you know her."

Kazakov heard the unspoken question. "In another life I brought my wife here for an anniversary. She did not care for the experience—too rustic for her taste, I suppose. But then the writing was already on the wall for our marriage. The trip was a last effort to save it."

How many times during that visit had he stood outside Ayim Beshimov's watching the stars come out and smoking to overcome yet another confrontation on a trip that was supposed to renew their vows? The sky above him now had the red columns of sunset painting the mountain peaks. When the red faded would come the slow parade of stars. He used to feel that he could hold up his hand and touch the glow of the Milky Way. Given the many hotel resort lights now, that would no longer be possible.

Something else stripped away, hidden behind the pigskin of too much Russian light. The Kyrgyz, at least, did not live that way.

"It saddens you to remember."

"Not at all," Kazakov said and turned to the M.E. "It is simply the masking of so many beautiful things and the loss of others."

Khan's lips curved. "Be careful, Detektiv. I will think you have become a philosopher."

The evening air chilled Kazakov and he stomped his feet. "A philosopher detective. I might as well shoot myself. This job is hard enough without reflection."

Khan simply cocked a brow at him and then checked the sky. "I must be going. I will see you tomorrow at Ayim Beshimov's." And then he set off, not in a vehicle but down the road with a stride that Kazakov found surprising. He had never seen the M.E. truly move before, but with this easy stride he could cover many miles.

Kazakov reclaimed his Perseus and returned to the guesthouse. He would change from his suit, tie and sweater into something more casual and then go out for a meal.

When he pulled up at Ayim Beshimov's, all looked the same as last evening. The evening's fading light lay on the old part of town as darkness. There were no streetlights here and virtually none of the houses had lights over their doors. After the lights and traffic of the resort area around the police station, it was as if the old part of the valley lay muffled under a dark blanket. Climbing out of the Perseus it was just that quiet, though a dog barked in the distance farther up the valley.

At the thick wood door, he stomped his boots clear of snow before stepping inside. Then, carrying them, he followed the hallway to his room. The door was locked, but when he let himself in, the scent of cleaning fluid met him. So someone had been in—likely either Ayim Beshimov herself, or... Aisha?

"Your boots should be left at the door," Ayim Beshimov said from behind him in her crackling voice.

He jerked upright and turned to greet her. This evening she wore a black felted skirt and stockings under a pink floral blouse. Both garments hung on her diminished frame.

"Aah, but this morning I found them outside. I thought it better to keep them out of—the way." Not out of harm's way, for that would offend her.

Still, slight pink patches formed on her cheeks. "Outside?"

"In the snow." He nodded.

She held out her hand. "Boots. You give to me and it will not happen again."

By the glint in her eyes, there was no denying her. Kazakov gave up the boots.

"Thank you." He turned to go into his room, but then stopped. "Ayim Beshimov, I have a need that will help in my investigation. Have you a room that we might work from? The police station—it does not seem like a…suitable…place."

Her gaze was black onyx, pitted with time. Then the darkness seemed to brighten and she smiled, revealing a line of yellowed teeth. She nodded.

"I have just the right room! You come." Still holding his boots, she stumped off down the hall. With her diminutive frame, it was as if he followed a living felted doll.

At the end of the hall, a low door of mismatched boards blocked her way. She nodded back at him. "This should do, I think."

Kazakov had his doubts. The door looked more like the entry to an old barn. Many of the old houses were actually built above the barn so that the animals' heat helped warm the house in winter. In the face of her certainty, he held back shaking his head.

From a chain around her neck, she selected a key, unlocked the door, and swung it wide open. A gust of chill air found Kazakov's face. It brought with it the scent of dust and age.

"You look." Ayim Beshimov gestured him forward and he ducked his head and stepped inside.

Not a barn.

Instead it was an ancient makeshift office. A door had been placed across two sawhorses to form a desk. Boards placed strategically on the stone walls formed shelves that were laden with books. More books were stacked in corners. Kazakov picked one up. It was covered with Ottoman script. The next one was, too. He glanced back at Ayim. She stood, smiling, as she waited at the door.

Stout stone floors radiated cold, but he could imagine a fire in the silent iron stove in the corner would soon dispel the worst of it. The ceilings were low for someone of his height, but the room was large enough that it could hold another makeshift desk and, if he could get a piece of plywood, they could lean it against the wall for an evidence board. Or perhaps they could find such a thing in the Biysk police station.

"What is this place?" he asked as he continued his inspection. A simple wooden stool sat behind the desk. Utilitarian, but not helpful when you did your best thinking leaned back with your feet up.

"It was my husband's office. No one has used it since he died."

And that was farther back than his last visit.

"You would let us use it, when you have protected it all this time?"

When there was no immediate answer, he looked up from a stack of Chinese magazines and found himself the subject of Ayim Beshimov's appraisal.

"I hear you work with a Kyrgyz doctor. I hear you act fairly with a Kyrgyz family over the death of their son. Bermet Aytmatov needs fairness, too. You spent time on the mountain today—not like those other *osurak* police. That is truth. That is fairness. In those clothes, you freeze your ass off." She snorted laughter. "I think you are a fair man who will find Bermet's killer and so you must use this place to find truth—just as my husband tried to do."

"We will need lights and there will be more people than just Khan and myself. We will need to remove your husband's books and magazines. And I will need the price for the rental."

She waved a hand at him. "No price. Just find Bermet's killer. I have a light." She stepped inside and pulled a string that hung by the door. A single lightbulb flickered and flared to life. "And I am used to many feet."

He looked back at the room. He'd thought to use his own guesthouse room, but this was far better. He left the room for the hall. "Thank you. The room is perfect. You will be compensated."

She removed the key from a clutter she wore around her neck. "Take it. You will want to keep your things secure. My husband always did."

He accepted the heavy old iron key and locked the room behind them. Then he checked his watch. "I need to get changed and go for dinner."

"You will have dinner with us," Ayim Beshimov said with a certainty that brooked no disagreement.

Such an invitation was unusual to say the least. Not even Khan had invited him to a meal with his family.

"I would be honored," he said with a slight bow.

Ayim Beshimov patted his arm, her ancient bird eyes glittering like a hawk's. "I think you are a good boy. Don't let me down."

And then she shuffled back toward the kitchen, leaving him to use the common washroom and return to his room.

The room's small stove had been kept lit but banked through the day so the room was pleasantly warm. The replenished kettle on the stove produced warm water that allowed Kazakov to wash his hands and face. He changed clothes and peered at himself in a mirror tarnished with age. His misty image might once have held promise, but now he just looked old and tired. He had seen a lot in his years in policing and most of it was bad. The years had also not been kind to Fergana. He wondered what it would look like in the mirror. Mostly faded.

And sad. He wondered what had consumed Ayim Beshimov's husband so much, so many years ago. Apparently, he had never found the truth. That was sad, too.

The hall was cool after the warmth of his room. Through the low ceiling came the sound of the wind. At the kitchen door he knocked once and entered. Ayim Beshimov bustled around the room, just as she had done this morning, but this time Aisha and Taalay were helping.

"What can I do?" he offered.

Ayim Beshimov verbally shushed him to the table. When he still didn't move, Aisha glanced crossly in his direction.

"Do as she says."

He went, settling at a larger table in the corner where, presumably, the family ate together. Taalay rushed over with a tea pot and four cups and poured a cup of tea while he shared a shy smile with Kazakov. The steam rose in the air as the youngster ran and returned with a bowl of sugar and a pitcher of milk and then stood smiling beside the table.

"Spoons," Kazakov whispered and Taalay brightened and ran to get them.

"Would you stop running like you owe him or something," Aisha snapped. "These Russians, they think that is true already. You set the table and that is all."

Chastened, Taalay's smile faded and he backed away. Then he winked and flashed a smile and rushed away to Ayim Beshimov's side as she ladled what looked like *samsa* into a bowl. The boy brought the bowl of meat and vegetable dumplings to the table and then rushed back to help his great aunt with a steaming bowl of *plov*, the rice steaming and rich with mutton, carrot, and onion. Ayim Beshimov tilted the metal cooking surface off the oven, reached in, and hauled out a large round of flatbread.

This she tossed on a wooden platter and swiftly sliced. She brought it to the table, herding a slightly less willing Aisha with her.

At the table she nodded Taalay in beside Kazakov and seated Aisha by her side. The old woman sat down facing Kazakov.

"There are those who would say it is not proper for a strange man to be housed in a house of women and children and less proper for enemies to take food together, but you are not a stranger to our people and I feel you are not our enemy either. Please." She nodded at the table. "Eat."

Aisha did not try to hide her disgust. Instead she sat scowl-faced as Ayim Beshimov served them all and gave Kazakov the larger portion.

"He is just another Russian policeman."

Ayim Beshimov held Kazakov with her gaze as he sampled the plov and nodded. "Good. Very good."

"He seeks the truth. I read it in his eyes and in his sadness."

"Phht," Aisha said. "You're half blind, old woman."

Kazakov chewed the tender mutton and rice. He broke open a dumpling with his fork and rich gravy escaped. He ate with relish as the family murmured around him, talking about Taalay's schooling and the problems of Aisha's job.

"What about you, Detektiv? What will you do for your investigation?"

Taalay's question brought him back from his thoughts about the murder scenes and how to interpret them. It really seemed the old woman had been running from something deeper in the mountains. How far she had come was the question.

Taalay's dark gaze was intent. So were the two women's.

He nodded. "To take this investigation forward will take time. I have seen where they found Bermet and where she was injured, but there are things to learn farther into the mountains, I think. I wish to interview the suspect, and review the documentation collected to date. And the police who were first on the scene. I have their reports but…well, I will trust my own interview more than something written."

Aisha's frown faded a little. "You see? He agrees that the police do not do what they should."

"Hold on." He held up his hand to stop her thoughts. "I am saying that those police were out in the cold and that sometimes at the end of a shift, all that matters is getting home and to warmth. Things may be left out inadvertently."

Again Aisha snorted. She pushed back from the table and turned to Ayim Beshimov. "Thank you once more for a delicious meal, but I cannot stay here and listen to the lies of a Russian. Taalay, finish your meal and come to the room."

She turned and left.

Taalay hurriedly scraped his bowl clean and scrambled after her. At the door he sent Kazakov an apologetic smile.

"I'm sorry," Kazakov sighed. "I should not have ruined your family dinner. In future I can take my meals in the tourist village, though I fear the food will not be so tasty."

Shaking her head, Ayim Beshimov stood to remove the empty plates. Kazakov stood to help her but was waved back. "A man's place is at the table."

A tradition that his wife had never held with. He doubted Aisha did either, but he sat as his hostess commanded.

"I am sorry for Aisha's behavior. As I said this morning, she still mourns her husband."

"How did he die?"

"Disappeared, like so many in the mountains. His body was never recovered. That is also how my dear husband died, so long ago. Aisha's husband, a fine man, went up with two Russians who wished to climb old Kara Kuldja mountain. None of them were ever heard from again. Searchers said there had been an avalanche. In the spring, when more searchers went to recover bodies, there was nothing to find. The wolves and snow leopards must have had their fill."

Kazakov nodded and filed the knowledge away. He had learned at a young age about the treachery of mountains when his only uncle was killed in a skiing accident. And then there had been the reports of entire regiments of Ottoman and Chinese soldiers lost as they attempted to circumvent Fergana to foment their war. The mountains were a place of ice, tribal people, and ghosts.

"The mountains are a hard place to live, I think. Many say just move to the lowlands, but the mountains get in the blood," Kazakov said. Certainly, he'd had enough of such conversations with his ex-wife about his dacha, which was only set in the gentle foothills by comparison with what he had experienced today.

"Death is a constant companion," Ayim Beshimov said.

"But Bermet's death is not the same. We have a body. We know she was killed, and not by the mountains. We will find her killer."

He thanked her and returned to his room for the evening. After banking the fire and adding a log, he went to bed early but lay there with the feeling that he had missed something. As with all cases, this was one with many layers. There was the killing, but there were layers masking the motives and the motives were what he needed to find. He finally opened the curtain above the bed and peered out at the cold stars over the valley. There was much to do in the morning to peel back what had happened to Bermet Aytmatov.

5

———————

The next morning Kazakov woke with blazing sunlight in his eyes through the open curtain. He groaned and rolled over, but then checked his watch on the bedside table. Seven thirty. He'd overslept. He left the fire unstirred, went out to the shared toilet, and then came back and bathed and dressed in a warm shirt and heavy trousers. Then he headed for the kitchen.

Ayim Beshimov was there with eggs scrambled and served with flatbread, its crust still crunchy and warm from the oven. He wolfed it down and thanked her just as a knock came at the guesthouse door.

Trailing Ayim Beshimov down the hallway, they found Khan and Egorova waiting. Khan was dressed in stout trousers and boots, and a heavy parka that looked as if it had seen years of wear, with the hood pushed back so his dark hair gleamed in the sun. Egorova wore a trim, navy-blue, wool coat that came down to her knees and what appeared to be a suit underneath. She held a police evidence box in her arms.

"Let me introduce Dr. Khalil Khan," Kazakov said. "This is our fine hostess, Ayim Beshimov."

"Salam-aleikum!" Khan said and half bowed a greeting. He clasped Ayim Beshimov's hand and kissed it, then placed a kiss upon each of her cheeks.

The old woman caught his face in her palms. "You! It has been years since you have graced my home!"

Egorova stood behind Khan, the sunlight on her face. Ayim Beshimov's attention turned to her. She nodded, but her smile was more forced.

"This is Detektiv Egorova of Biysk Police. She is working on this investigation."

Egorova stuck out her hand, but Khan caught it and pressed it back down, under the glittering regard of the old woman.

"Come in," Ayim Beshimov said and stepped back from the door to allow entry.

"Thank you for the use of your home," Egorova tried again.

Kazakov shook his head at her and then led them inside. When their boots were off and Ayim Beshimov led down the hall, he pulled Egorova aside. "She is not partial to Russians or police, but she will give you a chance to prove yourself. Her niece, Aisha, is less trusting, so be prepared."

She nodded at him, but her lips firmed in a line.

Kazakov unlocked the door to the old office and ducked inside. The others followed him in. He told them what the space had been. "So we must clear the old books and magazines out, but they must be treated with respect. I have space in my room, so we will put them there until our investigation is done. Egorova, I'd like you to get this office set up. A board for the wall to work on—at worse, a piece of plywood will do, I think. A second desk for against the wall. Can you do that? Perhaps Ayim Beshimov can help you."

Egorova nodded, but the two women eyed each other with distrust.

"In the meantime, Khan and I are going back up the mountain to follow Bermet's trail."

Egorova opened her mouth as if to protest, but then nodded. In her good wool coat and crisply ironed suit, she was a city girl sent to the country and she knew it. A long hike into the mountains was not what she was suited for—at least not until she was dressed for the task.

"I expect you will have things arranged when we get back so that we can get to work."

"I will have things ready for you."

"And see what you can do about finding our witness and first attending officer. We will want to speak to them as soon as possible."

She nodded.

"What can I do to help?" Ayim Beshimov asked.

Kazakov turned to her. "Please. Help Detektiv Egorova. And if you could pack Khan and myself a lunch, that would be much appreciated."

She bustled back to her kitchen with purpose and Kazakov turned back to the room. "We need to make this work. If we conduct the investigation from here, there is far more chance of getting information from the Kyrgyz people."

"It was an inspired choice," Khan said.

"Not inspired. Ayim Beshimov offered."

Khan smiled his inscrutable smile. "Like I said, inspired."

Kazakov glanced down the hall where Ayim Beshimov had disappeared. "How do you know my hostess?"

Khan shrugged. "I have been coming to Biysk for years. She is a friend of the family."

Kazakov should have expected it. The links between the Kyrgyz people were strong.

He left Egorova with the keys to his room, traded for her camera, then claimed a heavy parka that he had packed against just such an exigency. Then he and Khan headed out with a backpack of provisions courtesy of Ayim Beshimov.

They took the Perseus up past the barrier they had put up the day before. The rutted track was just as rough and far more difficult in the lower-slung vehicle, but they made steady progress and were up in the alpine area above the blue spruce and aspen of the valley by ten in the morning.

The morning sun was glaringly bright on the snow as they drove the vehicle up the road to the place Kazakov had last spotted Bermet's trail. There, they parked and set off on foot, following the boulder-strewn trail up the narrow pass between the mountains.

"Fresh ski tracks." Kazakov pointed out a single set of narrow tracks that led up the mountain. Someone had ignored their barrier across the trail.

"Tourists get lost out of bounds all the time," Khan said.

"In mountains where even the locals disappear, they should be cautioned."

Khan chuckled. "You clearly don't have children. Teenagers don't listen to anything."

Kazakov looked at the tracks. "Teenagers ski downhill. They look for speed, not an arduous uphill climb."

Two hours of hard walking with their pack of food and their breath was like bellows, but the ski tracks still flowed up the edge of the trail.

"I can tell I am no longer a fit young man," Kazakov said as he stopped for a breather and peered back down their path. At this time of day, with the sun at this angle, Bermet's trail was easy to spot like an uneven thread of ink on the snow to one side of the wider stain that was their trail. Far below, the sun reflected a bright eye off the windscreen of the Perseus and beyond the vehicle, farther downhill, lay the smudges of smoke from the village below and the glints and glances of sunlight off of moving vehicles. Across the valley the white slopes of the ski hill were busy.

"The years weigh the limbs," Khan said philosophically. "Look there."

Kazakov turned to look forward to where the path they followed turned slightly down into the next valley, but this one never reached a level low enough for trees. Instead, boulders stood along the narrow road and at the far end was a cluster of low stone houses.

Frowning, Kazakov studied the place. "What is wrong with this picture?"

"No smoke," Khan said.

With the wind barely a breeze this morning, there should be smoke, either pooling above the houses or lifting straight up to the mountain tops before higher winds dispersed it. Instead, there was nothing.

"And no other sign of life, either."

Together, Kazakov and Khan left their vantage. Bermet's trail followed the main trail down toward the village. So did the ski tracks.

Thirty minutes later they reached the edge of the village. The snow between the houses showed the patterns of many feet, so someone had been here. The ski trail cut right through them and between the houses, appearing to pause at a house or two where the tracks showed that the skier had clearly sidestepped to a door. To peer inside? Or was the skier looking for something or someone?

Bermet's trail ended in a mess of tracks at one end of the houses where her footprints disappeared in amongst a kaleidoscope of others.

"So she came from here," Khan said, inspecting the snow-covered ground.

"Perhaps," Kazakov said and retrieved a cigarette butt from the ground. "Look."

Khan bent over his hand. "A filtered cigarette when in the mountains most the smokers roll their own tobacco—when they can trade for the leaf at all."

"Worse," Kazakov said. "I know this brand. See the light tan lines on the filter? There are American cigarettes that have just such a design."

Khan frowned. "Surely there are others."

Perhaps there were, but the importer of such American cigarettes was the murder victim in Kazakov's last case. What on earth did a murdered cigarette importer and a murdered tribal woman have in common? He had to be imagining a connection. But such a cigarette was an exclusive luxury.

On the other hand, it might have been smoked by a rich skier on holiday…

He bagged the cigarette butt and pocketed the bag before continuing to inspect the village.

The snow was churned as if many people had been here at once. Hoofprints showed that horses had been here, too, but that was nothing unusual as the tribal people depended upon their horses for meat and milk as well as transportation. In the high country, beyond the people's sheep and goats, there was little else.

The first house that they entered was of stout stone and low-roofed so Kazakov had to duck to enter. Snow had been scuffed inside. A hearth stood dark and empty. Shelves stood empty. There was nothing else except the sound of their breathing and the wind in the eaves. They left that house and checked the others. All were the same—stripped of belongings. Not a shoe, a rag, a pot left behind.

When they were finished, Kazakov stopped in the center of the houses. "Stranger and stranger. Could they have all packed up and left?"

Khan looked thoughtful, then worried, but then shook his head. "It is too early to head for the summer pasture higher up the mountains."

"Then why would they go?"

Khan hesitated but then shook his head. "I don't know."

Together, they passed through the village to where the trail continued on into the mountains. The snow was torn with the passage of the villagers, but two slim tracks glided over the top. The skier had come this way, too. Seeking the villagers?

The trail narrowed around them until they traversed a narrow path with the mountain uphill and a cliff below them, disappearing into blue-shadowed depth. Ahead, the narrow passage between the mountains carried on for a long way before opening up into sunlight.

When the sun was directly above them, they shared the food that Ayim Beshimov had given them: fresh flatbread wrapped around the plov from the night before. They munched in silence as they kept going, the boulders at the bottom of the cliff revealed in stark light. They would have to turn back soon if they were going to get the Perseus and themselves down off the mountain by nightfall.

"Have you noticed about the trail?" Khan asked.

Kazakov glanced a question at him as he picked his way through the ruts and holes.

"The hoofprints cut through the footprints. The horsemen came behind the villagers, and the skier last of all," Khan said.

"Following to help any stragglers?"

Khan simply cocked a brow at him.

Something more nefarious? "You're suggesting that the villagers were driven out? But why?"

It made no sense at all, and yet the evidence was there to be interpreted however the interpreter saw fit.

They kept going, and finally the trail widened out a little. Still, the footprints churned the trail ahead of them, but a shadow on the snow at the edge of the steep mountainside caught Kazakov's attention.

He stopped and bent low. The churning of feet had sent a spray of snow across whatever he'd spotted. The pattern of footprints was different here, too. At the barest edge of the mountainside, heavy footprints from the village half-obliterated another set, smooth-soled and clearly headed down the mountain.

"Khan."

The little M.E. joined him and Kazakov indicated the shadow in the snow. Carefully, Khan brushed the intervening snow away. A crimson splatter had been absorbed by the snow.

Kazakov straightened and retrieved the camera from the pack where he'd stowed it with the food. He took numerous photos and then looked down the trail toward the distant sunlit valley and then back the way they had come. Already the sun had slipped behind the western peak and the view of the depth of the boulder-strewn canyon was slipping into shadow.

"We go another thirty minutes and then we turn back. It won't help us any to be caught here at night," he said.

They carried on as the mountain's breadth shadowed the trail and the wind came up, sifting icy crystals down to sting their cheeks and noses.

Their breath came in plumes as they finally reached the end of their allotted time. Kazakov stopped and stood there.

Ahead the churned trail led farther into the mountains. To where, he had no idea.

He glanced down at Khan and then nodded at the tracks. The skier's tracks continued on into the distance.

A normal tourist would be headed back, afraid of nightfall in the mountains.

Clearly, it was no ordinary skier.

———

Reluctantly, they turned and followed the waning afternoon sunlight back toward the village and the trail back down to the Perseus. There was no other person on the trail, so clearly their barrier and warning had deterred other tourists and even the locals. Except the skier.

They arrived back in town after dark and stopped for a meal at a tourist cafe. It was poor fare after Ayim Beshimov's cooking the night before, but mutton stew filled his belly with warmth. Then he drove back to the guesthouse with Khan after the M.E. refused a ride to where he was staying. Bone weariness filled Kazakov's body when he turned the vehicle engine off, both from the long walk and fighting the Perseus on the long drive down the mountain. After dark, headlights had distorted the trail so that in a few places he'd almost high-centered the vehicle. He sat back in his seat. Khan looked out the passenger window.

"I came up here for an old woman my father had known and respected," Khan said. "Now I wonder what is going on."

Kazakov glanced at him. "You *knew* Bermet Aytmatov?"

Khan gave a slight nod. "She was like a great aunt to me when I was very young. She was kind and wise and a truly gifted healer. It was her early teachings that made me want to become a healer. She is why I became a doctor, though I think she was hurt that I did not apprentice with her."

"This cannot have been easy for you." He could feel his friend's sorrow. In New Moscow Khan would have been kept far from such an autopsy. Official channels must have been wholly unaware of Khan's familial connections, and yet he had done his duty. It must have cost the little M.E. plenty.

"When death comes like dawn, you wake up laughing at what you thought was your grief," Khan said softly. Then he smiled softly at Kazakov. "It is a Rumi quote about the illusion of this life. He said that everything about us is a dream and only we sleeping beings consider it real. Bermet is in a better place and so I cannot feel grief, only sadness that I had not come back to see her."

"If you knew her, you must have some idea what she was doing up there in the mountains."

Khan shook his head. "Knowing her, she was probably visiting a patient. Even in her seventies she was filled with endless energy."

"So this could have been a regular trip she took?"

"It is possible."

Kazakov patted his hands on the steering wheel. "Then we need to find someone who knows what her regular patterns were. That may tell us where she had come from, but we still need to get back into the mountains to follow her trail."

Khan's gaze was inscrutable. "Knowing where she came from does not tell us what happened to that village. There were women and children there, along with elders."

Kazakov took in this information. It was logical that such a mix of demographics would be present in any village, but something about the way Khan said it suggested that he had closer knowledge.

"What do you know, Khan. What else haven't you told me?"

The little M.E. just shook his head. "It is late—eight o'clock. I should get back to my friend's house."

He opened the door and slid out to stand in the cold. Kazakov clambered out his side and looked across the hood of the vehicle at his friend. His breath steamed in the cold air. He had his collar pulled up and his fur hat pulled low. In the dim light, his eyes were fathomless hollows.

"I will see you tomorrow?" Kazakov asked.

"What do you plan?"

"There are interviews that must be conducted. I would like you to examine Bermet's clothing and effects."

Khan's gaze felt heavy on Kazakov's skin, even though he couldn't see Khan's eyes.

"I think—not tomorrow. I have other things to see to. The next day, perhaps. Look for me in the morning."

And if he wasn't there, well, wait until the next day. But Khan wasn't Kazakov's subordinate.

"In two days, then." Kazakov nodded and watched as the small

Kyrgyz man walked away into the night. Where he was staying, Kazakov still didn't know; and apparently Khan liked it that way.

When even Khan's footfall on the crunchy snow at the side of the road had died away, Kazakov once more looked up at the heavens. There were stars there, but they were lost in the mask of tourist lights. Wondering what was hidden behind the darkness of Khan's gaze, he went inside.

6

The next morning Kazakov rose to find there had been a skiff of snow overnight. There was a thick tracery of frost on his bedroom window and the wood stove hadn't completely held back the cold. There was a thin trace of ice on the wash water he'd used the night before.

After a visit to the shared toilet, he waited for fresh water to heat in the kettle and did stretching exercises to relieve some of the tightness in his muscles from the day before. In the process he nearly knocked over the piles of books and newspapers from the old office, which were stacked precariously in a corner.

The new snow would doubtless have fallen heavier on the mountain slopes, making it even more difficult to follow Bermet's trail. He regretted his decision to rest his tired muscles and conduct interviews today, but they had to be done and time had already degraded the trail. Besides, who knew how far the old woman had come? For all he knew, she could have been visiting family in China and been injured on the trip home.

No, he had made the right decision. He could make enquiries here about Bermet's habits and where she might have been. Hopefully the news of his investigation had spread through the old village and had been taken positively. That might mean doors would open to him that would have remained closed to Egorova.

Dressed, he headed to the kitchen to find Aisha and Ayim Beshimov deep in conversation in the Kyrgyz tongue. At the sight of him, Aisha slumped in her seat, her arms crossed over her chest. Ayim Beshimov stood and busied herself making him breakfast. She thumped a mug of black tea on the table before him and he added his sugar and milk and sighed appreciatively.

"Thank you. I missed your good cooking last night and a last cup of tea, but we arrived back so late it was unfair to disturb you."

"You were gone for a long time," Ayim Beshimov said as she quickly flattened and stretched a ball of dough on a wooden counter.

"It takes a long time to get into the mountains," he said and sipped again. "We followed Bermet's trail far back past the first small village where the pass widens out."

Aisha shook her head slightly. "I suppose you caused trouble there, too."

Ayim Beshimov's warning glare flashed in her niece's direction.

"Actually, there was no one there." Kazakov made a show of staring into his tea while he surreptitiously studied their reactions.

Utter silence filled the room except for the crackling fire in the oven. Kazakov looked up and found both women looking at him.

"What do you mean?" Aisha demanded.

Ayim Beshimov left her bread for the table. "There are eight families there. They can't be gone. It is too early to leave for the high meadows."

Kazakov shook his head. "I have no explanation."

He told them of the tracks they had found but left out Bermet's bloody prints.

Ayim Beshimov said something in Kyrgyz to Aisha and the younger woman left the room. Then the older woman looked back at him. "I'm sorry. There are people to be told." She went back to her bread and punched it down a final few times, then slapped the round to the inside wall of the oven. When she faced him again, her face was red—whether from the oven's heat or emotion, he couldn't say.

"Where could they be going? What is farther up the trail?"

"There are other villages. Smaller. With less. White Stone Village was rich by mountain standards. They kept to the old ways even though they were able to trade with us. Good people all of them."

"And Bermet worked for them? They knew her?"

Ayim Beshimov nodded as she stirred more plov in a pan to reheat it.

He thought of the bloody tracks he had found farther up the trail. "Would she go to them for help?"

"Of course. It is the mountains. We help each other when needed. Who is to know when you might need help yourself, and Bermet never said no when help was requested."

"But if she was in need, she would go to them?" he persisted.

"Of course."

The bread came out of the oven in a golden round that Ayim Beshimov quickly sliced and brought to the table. A plate of plov soon sat before him and he wolfed it down as if he hadn't eaten the night before, the richly spiced mutton gravy absorbed by the rice and vegetables, the flatbread used to scoop up huge mouthfuls.

When he was done he sat back, feeling satiated.

"Tell me. How far into the mountains did Bermet travel?"

Ayim Beshimov shook her head. "That I can't tell you. You might talk to her nephew, Osman. He sometimes traveled with her when the distances were too far."

"And where can I find this Osman?"

"He lives in the old village: a small house with his mother and father. I can have Aisha show you."

He nodded his thanks, wondering why the nephew hadn't been with her this time when it looked like Bermet had traveled some distance.

A thud, thud, thud came from the front of the house. Ayim Beshimov stood, but Kazakov checked his watch and beat her to the hall. "It will be for me. Detektiv Egorova, most likely."

It was, indeed, Egorova, who stood hunched in her blue coat, her collar up around her neck, her arms laden with an evidence box.

"Good morning, Detektiv," she looked up at him. "I hoped you would be home so that we might examine this evidence together. Have you checked the office?"

He shook his head as he stepped aside to allow her to entry, then took the box from her so that she could remove her boots. Together, they went down the hall.

"How was your trip to the mountain?" she asked.

Kazakov held off answering her until Egorova let them into their investigation room and pulled the string to turn the light on.

It was much changed from the last time Kazakov had seen it. All the old papers were removed. The table, floors, and walls had been scrubbed and another board had been set up across two sawhorses against one wall, leaving the room with two sizable work spaces. The stool had been pushed into a corner and three real chairs of chrome and plastic, which looked like they came from a lunch room, sat at the desks. A blackboard had been nailed up along one wall with the name of the victim written at the top like a reminder that this was a person that the world had lost—not something pitiable lost under the anonymity of a victim label. The room was even warm; the little iron stove had obviously been left banked yesterday evening.

"Did you do all this?"

"Yes. Though Ayim Beshimov and Taalay helped with the cleaning."

"Well done. Well done indeed." He set the evidence box down on the side table and then stirred the last of the fireplace ashes into life before adding wood. At the evidence table, he pulled the file box toward him and flipped it open. "Walk me through what we have."

He pulled the investigation file out first and scanned the contents. The file was neat. Small, precise writing provided a good summary of the investigative process to date. The entry wasn't long, given Egorova had just received the file before it was roughly taken over by Kazakov. He needed to update it with what he now knew.

On the other side of the file were the various notes and statements of the attending police officers and on top was a copy of the autopsy report Khan had dictated yesterday.

They read it together, Egorova reading over his shoulder. Bermet Aytmatov was in her early seventies, though that information was likely based on Khan's knowledge of the woman, not the autopsy. She had been killed by a knife wound, though a bullet wound was also present. The woman was in excellent physical condition but showed signs of hypothermia one would expect with long exposure to the cold and loss of blood. Debris had been removed from under her fingernails and combed out of her hair, but not yet analyzed.

"The evidence supports Bermet having traveled a great distance in the mountains before finally being killed. Given the prior wound, it suggests she was running from someone or something."

Egorova nodded as Kazakov flipped the autopsy report up to read the documents beneath. The suspect's brief statement was next. Kazakov scanned it as Egorova talked.

The suspect, a man named Meder uulu Jolon, denied any responsibility. His story was that he had headed into the mountains to visit friends and had found the body. He had turned the body over to see who it was, and was found like that by the tourist. That was all he would say.

Beneath that was the report of the attending officer, first outlining what he'd found when he first attended the scene and then outlining what had happened when other officers were called in. It took only a few minutes to finish reading the report.

"Sketchy," he sighed.

Egorova nodded agreement.

"So what else do we have?"

Egorova had laid out the bagged evidence box contents on the table. She tapped her finger on a large bag containing bloody, felted clothing. "Bermet's clothing when she was found. There isn't much. One of those felted skirts and stockings. A jacket. A shawl. A blouse, the latter three all bloody."

Her touch traveled to a pair of felted boots. "Boots. Smooth soled and felted and furred inside. They must be toasty given how far she walked."

Her hand bounced away to another bag, this one containing what looked like a courier bag stitched of patched fur and hung on a long, braided band that could be slung over a shoulder. "The bag was found near her body and contains what look like herbs and potions, from what we can determine."

He glanced from the bag to her face. A small frown showed Egorova wasn't as certain of her assessment.

"Tell me," he said.

"Well… it could be nothing. Nikitin thought it was nothing. But there are differences in the plant materials contained in the bag. Most are dried herbs, but there were a few fresh things, too, or at least fresher. They hadn't been dried, but had been wrapped in a bit of paper in the bottom of the bag as if they were hidden."

"Show me."

Egorova pulled on sterile gloves before opening the plastic bag. She spread a white cloth that she produced from somewhere over part of the table and set Bermet's bag in the center before carefully removing the contents. "When I heard another investigator was coming, I tried to leave things more or less as I found them." She leaned over the bag and carefully pulled out what looked like a carefully folded paper packet.

It was made of lined white paper similar to what was found in the squad room but had a glossy finish unlike anything the squad room possessed. This was more like what he'd seen in Rostoff's office or that of the executives.

It was folded crisply into three to create an envelope and the ends were then folded over to enclose whatever was inside. Egorova gently folded back the ends, allowing the heavier paper to gradually unfold itself until its contents were revealed.

Three withered leaves lay on the paper, their green color faded to brown at the edges, their luster fading. Kazakov used a pen tip to flick the leaves apart.

"Nothing distinguishing. Nothing that would clearly give a motive for murder." But then these were likely simply leaves carried for treatment purposes and had nothing to do with Bermet's killing. He fingered the paper. Through the gloves it felt thicker than most paper he was used to. "This paper, though—it's far more expensive than the regular police issue. How did it come into the hands of a Kyrgyz healer?" he asked.

"She might have found it discarded by a rich tourist. There're enough around in Biysk these days. Or someone else could have found it and given it to her." Egorova was looking at him, awaiting his verdict.

With the pen he shifted the folded paper farther apart and slid the leaves to one side. In the yellow glow of the lantern light, the bottom of the paper didn't look as smooth as the folded sides. He leaned down to angle his vision of the paper. A faint tracery of lines covered the bottom as if there was a design or writing.

"There," he said and nodded.

Egorova followed his example and leaned down to look. "Writing." She bit her lip. "It doesn't look Russian."

He read her chagrin when she looked up at him.

"Anyone could have missed it. We need to get it analyzed and the paper also. The leaves, as well."

Egorova nodded. "I'll see to it. I'll have it photographed before it leaves."

Kazakov looked back at the other items from Bermet Aytmatov's bag. "We need to have these analyzed, too. There may be more than one thing hidden in this bag. Something was important enough to kill her."

"You think she was killed because of something she had?"

"No…" Kazakov shook his head. "I think she was killed because of something she knew. The question is what. This may give us some answers."

He wished Khan was here. The M.E. might have more insight given he knew Bermet. Still, perhaps it was better that he wasn't here given how close to the case he was.

"On second thought, perhaps we might get a swifter examination of these items if they are taken to New Moscow." There was a good chance they'd get a more accurate report, too, given there was less immediate bias than there might be in Biysk. "Yes. That makes sense. I'll call my superior and have him arrange it. We just need to get the evidence down to them."

Egorova's expression worked through a series of emotions. Then she sighed. "Nikitin said you were brought in because of your reputation with the tribal people. I'll transport the evidence."

"It is critical that we have this examined and get the results as swiftly as possible. I know these forensic scientists. They must be stood over to encourage speed, but they will not work swiftly for me." He sighed at the question in her gaze. "I would go myself, but I may have burned too many bridges amongst my colleagues over the years."

Nodding, she swiftly bagged the bag and contents again, then looked up at him and smiled. "When will you make the call?"

He checked his watch: barely eight thirty. Rostoff would not be in yet.

"Not for another hour. In the meantime, let's go to the police station. I'll brief you on our trip to the mountains and we can interview our suspect together. Then I can make the call while you document the evidence and you can be on your way."

Together they locked up their investigation room and headed outside. The sun was bright and placed silver and gold glitter in Egorova's hair. In another job, with a bit of makeup, she might even be pretty, but what she'd seen and done on the job had hardened her features. She drove in her usual efficient manner as Kazakov briefed her on what they had found.

"But what could have happened to all those people? Surely you're not suggesting something nefarious?"

"Khan says that it is too early for the villagers to head into the mountains for summer pastures."

"But it would take many men to make the villagers leave. Where would they come from and why?"

Why indeed? Kazakov left the question hanging in the air as Egorova pulled into the police parking lot.

"You can see that there are a growing list of questions. Hopefully an analysis of Bermet's bag will provide some answers."

She nodded and took the evidence box with her into the station. They arranged for the interview and then deposited the evidence safely in an evidence locker before they went to the interview room.

Bermet Aytmatov's neighbor, Meder uulu Jolon, appeared about Kazakov's age, though the file said he was ten years younger. His shaggy black hair was streaked with grey and a haggard gray tinged his cheeks.

He was of a similar slight build to Khan, but his shoulders were broader, though at the moment they were hunched around his ears where he sat at the interview table. His fingers were long, like a musician's, but he had the enlarged knuckles of a laborer. Or a fighter.

When Kazakov and Egorova entered, Jolon's dark gaze barely rose to them before sinking back to the grain of the table.

Kazakov set a copy of the prior interview down on the table between them and then settled into the chair across from Jolon. Egorova leaned against the wall behind and to one side of Kazakov, so that she could observe the suspect but not be the center of his attention.

Kazakov simply sat there a moment and let the weight of his presence sink in on its own. Meder uulu Jolon was already dreading the worst that could happen.

Kazakov flipped the statement open and turned it so that Jolon could read it. "This is the statement you gave—at least what was written down. Is this really all you had to say?"

He asked it softly, so that even the man across from him might have to strain to listen. Meder uulu Jolon glanced up at Kazakov but did not meet his gaze.

The silence in the room lengthened and Kazakov heard Egorova stir behind him. Let the young detective learn some patience. This was how a true detective got information. Let the person on the other side of the table talk first.

Finally, Jolon pulled the statement closer; he read it silently and then shook his head.

"That's what I thought," Kazakov said softly and exhaled. "I need to know the whole story if I'm to find Bermet's killer. Will you tell me everything you know?"

Jolon blinked and his expression ran the gamut from disbelief to relief to hope to resignation. He slumped back in his chair and looked at Kazakov full on. "Who wants to know and why? I thought you had already decided I was your killer."

But the man was now engaged, and that was what Kazakov had been going for.

"My name is Detektiv Alexander Kazakov of New Moscow police. I have been loaned to Biysk Police to conduct the investigation into Bermet Aytmatov's death. Why do I wish your answer? Because I prefer to convict the *correct* person for murder."

Jolon's gaze skittered over Kazakov's face, then up to Egorova. "Who is she?"

"Detektiv Egorova of Biysk Police. She shares my concerns about this case. Now can you help us find Bermet's killer?"

Focus the man on that instead of his fear for his own life.

Jolon shook his head and his silver-streaked hair fell over his eyes. He pushed it back. "But I don't know anything about who killed her. That is what I told the other officers."

Leaning his hands on the desk Kazakov nodded. "I believe you, but you may know more than you realize. Tell me. Why were you in the mountains that early morning?"

"It was simple. My younger sister, Tasha, was visiting our aunt in White Stone Village. I was going up to meet her and walk her back home."

Kazakov held himself immobile, but he heard Egorova stir once more. "That would be the small White Stone Village where the pass widens for a while?"

"Of course. My family comes from there. I am only here for my work and Tasha lives with me to work and send money to our parents. She also saves for her marriage in the fall. She will be happy to marry and not have to leave the village again."

"Tell me about White Stone Village?"

"It is a good village. Very old. Older than Biysk. Some say it was built when our people escaped to the mountains to avoid the great Khans and the despots of Kokand. It is a snug place in winter even though the winds can be strong off the mountains. In the summer there is the river nearby and the woodlands lower down, but we have few of the problems all the lowland people bring. And of course, in the summer most of us travel up to the pastureland. It is good there, rough with stone and the grass is sparse, but our herds are hardy and they do well on the southern slopes of the mountains. It is good to be up in the mountains where you can feel Allah's breath on your face and read his thoughts in the stars."

"You mention herds... what kinds of animals does the village have?"

"Goats. Sheep. A few dogs? Why? What is this about?"

"That is all?" Kazakov asked? "No chickens? No horses?"

Jolon shook his head, clearly confused by the direction of the questions.

"When was the last time you visited the village, Jolon?"

"A week ago."

"And how did you find it?"

"I found it well, thank you. My family was fine and Tasha did not want to come home but she did because she knew she would return this week. She cried a little as we walked the trail back to town and was so happy when she headed back to the village again." His dark gaze narrowed and his hands formed fists on the table. "Why all these questions about the village? You can talk to Tasha. You can talk to the headman or my family. They can tell you. White Stone Village is a good place. They would not hurt Bermet!"

Kazakov nodded. "Tell me about Bermet Aytmatov."

Jolon's knuckles whitened as he gripped the side of the table. "She is a healer. She would visit whenever anyone asked her." He shrugged. "People loved her."

"And yet someone killed her," Kazakov said.

Jolon leapt to his feet. "No one in White Stone Village would do such a thing! I will not let you say such a thing. It was me. I killed her!"

"No you didn't, Jolon. You didn't kill her and neither did anyone from White Stone Village—at least I don't believe so. Now sit down." He nodded Jolon back into his chair.

"How—how do you know I didn't? That no one from the village did?"

Kazakov leaned his elbows on the table and leaned forward. "Because when we went to the village yesterday, no one was there. There were tracks of people heading into the mountains. They appear to have been accompanied by riders on horseback."

Jaw slack with surprise, Jolon sank back in his chair. "I don't understand…"

Kazakov shook his head. "Neither do we. Can you think of who the people on horseback might be?"

Jolon shook his head. His expression worked as if he was still trying to comprehend what Kazakov had said.

"Had White Stone Village any enemies that you knew of?"

"No! It was a village! Of people! Tasha!" Jolon stood up again. "Are you telling me that Tasha is gone? And my family? Everyone?"

Kazakov glanced up at Egorova. She came to the desk.

"We need your help, Jolon," Egorova said. "We need your help to find them. Anything you can think of—please tell us."

Jolon's gaze darted from Kazakov to Egorova and around the room like a bird seeking escape. "I have to go. I have to see."

"There is nothing to see except a trail into the mountains," Kazakov said.

"We have to follow it! It has been too long already."

Kazakov nodded. "I followed it into the mountains on foot as far as I could go in a day and it went on farther."

"Please! Get me out of here! I have to find them."

Kazakov sighed and pushed back from the desk. "For the moment you will remain here, but we will see what we can do about arranging your release."

"You don't think I killed Bermet?"

Kazakov shook his head. "I don't, but there are others who will need convincing."

They left Meder uulu Jolon to be returned to his cell. There was much to consider.

"You don't believe he killed her," Egorova said when they were out in the hall.

Kazakov glanced at her. "Do you?"

She looked thoughtful a moment. "He could have. Even if she was wounded elsewhere, he could have finished the job when he found her."

"And what would be his motive?"

She shook her head. "I don't know, but we might still find one."

"Perhaps." He shook his head. "There's something about this case that I don't like. It's as if there is a cloud that floats around to obscure our eyes so we cannot get a sense of what happened in those mountains." Or as if he was color-blind to what was happening. He couldn't say what gave rise to the feeling, but it *felt* as if there was something happening that was far bigger than Bermet Aytmatov's death. Until he understood what, he could not understand the old woman's murder.

7

The Biysk squad room was busy when Kazakov and Egorova walked in. There were more uniformed officers than normal crowded in one corner of the room. The noise level was higher than the quiet phone interviews and typewriter sounds of Kazakov's first visit and an electric charge seemed to shiver in the air. He and Egorova looked at each other and then he followed her to her desk.

"You call who you need to in New Moscow. I'm going to take the photos and to check on what's happening." Egorova left him to make his call and then threaded her way through the desks to a uniformed officer. She bent to speak to him, and the way her hand grazed his shoulder said that this was not just any officer. He was young by the look of him. He listened to her, nodded, and spoke. Egorova was young. Let her have her romances. It must be difficult being a woman and the only detective in Biysk.

Kazakov turned back to his task and dialed the phone. It purred in his ear and then clicked as the receiver at the other end was picked up.

"Detektiv Chief Inspektor Rostoff's office." The clear voice of Constable Dabria Smirnova came through the phone.

"Dabria. It is a pleasure to hear your voice. How are you?" The lovely constable had been injured in an explosion that had blown out the glass in the executive offices. The result had been a number of small scars across one cheek and her forehead.

"Detektiv Kazakov. So you are still around. I am fine, but I heard rumors that you were dead or retired when I was recovering."

"I think your boss may have started those rumors out of wishful thinking," Kazakov said with a smile.

She chuckled.

"Now he has me on a case in Biysk of all places, but I need help getting the lab to rush analysis of some evidence. I am sending a detective to New Moscow with the evidence. Her name is Egorova. Perhaps you can help guide her through the minefields…"

"A female detective? How interesting. Of course I will help her."

He knew it would give her hope, for Dabria was a bright young police officer held more or less captive from real police work by her work as Rostoff's glorified secretary.

"May I speak to Rostoff? I'm hoping he will smooth the way for her."

"I will, but have a care. He is in a foul mood today."

He felt Egorova's presence and waved her to her chair. The line clicked and rang.

"Rostoff." The Detektiv Chief Inspektor's voice was brusque.

"Kazakov here." He would keep it brief and to the point. "I'm calling from Biysk." He told Rostoff what he had told Dabria. "I need you to call forensics and ensure that they put a rush on this."

There was silence on the phone.

"You are telling me that your little murder in Biysk is more important than what has occurred elsewhere in Fergana? Perhaps she secretly is an important candidate in the election? Or she is the grandmother of a candidate?"

Kazakov closed his eyes. Yes, Rostoff might have set him on the case, but this was always the way with the man.

"There is no political connection that I know of, but the woman is dead and an entire village has disappeared."

"Let me guess—a tribal village. What is it about you and these people, Kazakov? I doubt they give a damn about you! Hell, maybe they killed the old woman and headed into the hills to escape."

Kazakov bit back a retort to the wild theory. It *was* a possibility, however remote. "We are hoping analysis of the evidence will provide clues to their location and where Bermet Aytmatov came from."

More silence on the phone and Kazakov could imagine Rostoff looking out of his office window, his ire once more rising at the empty pedestal in the center of the city square where once a magnificent statue of the Tsarina, Yekaterina, had stood. It rankled Rostoff immeasurably that the statue had been destroyed and more so that it had not already been replaced.

"Fine. Send the evidence. I will do what I can. Dabria can help with this."

"Anything you can do to expedite the analysis will be appreciated. Thank you, sir." He knew the "sir" would help mollify Rostoff.

He hung up and turned to Egorova. "Done."

"It does not sound like it was easy." Around them the noise level had grown as officers left the squad room.

"Like you and Nikitin, with Rostoff it never is. When you arrive in New Moscow, seek out Constable Dabria Smirnova. She will help you and prepare you for an audience with Rostoff."

He nodded at the departing officers. "Didn't you say Nikitin prefers his officers to be invisible? What's going on?"

Egorova nodded. "There's a problem. Apparently, some politician is arriving in Biysk to make a speech. There are rumors that the tribals have planned a protest."

"Why should that be a problem for us? Whether we agree or disagree with their complaints, it has no bearing on the investigation. Neither does a politico."

"That might be the case in most situations," Egorova said, but leaned in close. "But Bermet Aytmatov's name has been mentioned as has Meder uulu Jolon's. Apparently, the rumor says that Bermet was killed by Russians and then Russians falsely accused Jolon to cover their tracks. They plan to confront the politician and demand justice."

"Derr'mo," Kazakov muttered. Such claims would make their investigation more difficult. And a protest about Bermet's death and Jolon's incarceration would ensure emotions ran high. "You'd best be on your way to New Moscow. Here's the name of a place to stay if you haven't a place in mind." He wrote down the name of a guesthouse and handed her the paper. "If things blow up here, there may be no hope of getting evidence out to Forensics. Too many other things will take precedence."

She nodded and stood, retrieved the evidence package from her desk drawer. "I'll take the photos and then leave. I'll call you once I reach New Moscow."

"Drive safely," he said, as she turned to go. "Egorova?"

She glanced back at him.

"Who's the politico?" How the complaints were managed would depend on the politician.

"That Reformation Party fellow; that Boris Bure. Why?"

Feeling almost unable to breathe, Kazakov managed a nod. "No reason," he said and was glad he was still sitting.

Boris Bure, here. The man was the stepfather of a murder victim named Yekaterina Weber, and the associate of an Anglo man who had turned out to be a Chinese spy turned double agent for the Ottomans. In every case Kazakov had been involved in since the Yekaterina murder, there had been hints of Bure somewhere in the background, like a shadow lurking. Bure was also a vocal proponent of Fergana for Russians and his rhetoric had suggested that the original people of Fergana were terrorists who should be removed from Ferganese society or expelled from the country altogether.

He watched Egorova's bright figure cross the room and disappear toward the parking lot. His limbs felt numb. For that matter, so did his brain. The word "bloodbath" kept repeating in his brain. Why the hell was Bure coming here just when things were most sensitive due to the Bermet Aytmatov case, when he knew it would be flame to explosives?

Unless he wanted the explosion…

It would give more credence to his storyline that the tribal Kyrgyz and Uzbek people and their brethren were the source of Fergana's problems, not the obsession with long-lost Russia that was bred in the bone of Fergana's displaced Russians. That same obsession with Russia's past greatness made the country little more than an outpost of quaint tradition and advancements borrowed from other countries around the world. What did Fergana have to celebrate, save the fact that it existed? Even the Americans could stand on the fact that in the face of insurmountable odds they had demanded their independence and had maintained their democracy. They even exported more than they imported, with an economy based on traditional cotton and tobacco as well as new technology. Unlike them, Fergana had an economy like the ancient Silk Road outposts upon which it was built—based on the tariffs charged for shipping between the two enemy empires. That and the sale of Fergana's land and mineral rights to foreign companies.

But sitting here would do nothing to stop things from happening. He needed to warn the villagers that they were playing directly into Bure's hands.

He left the police station and walked back to Ayim Beshimov's guesthouse in the brisk air and sunshine. The roadsides were slush from the traffic until he reached the old village of Biysk, where footpaths pitted with prints ran just inside the snowbanks that grew up from the side of the road. Smoke trailed from the chimneys of the low, stone houses. An eagle called from a tree beyond the frozen river and yet, even though the breeze barely disturbed the chimney smoke, there was a tension in the air. Perhaps it was the fact that he saw no one.

Had they already left to begin their protests?

He shoved in the door of Ayim Beshimov's and found her down on her knees washing the floor of the long hallway with a bristle brush.

"So?" She looked up at him and straightened. "It is sorted out now? Jolon did not kill Bermet?"

Kazakov shook his head. "Not sorted, but I don't believe he did. I just need to be able to prove it to those who won't believe it."

Her black gaze clouded and she climbed laboriously to her feet. "That is not good."

Kazakov nodded. "I heard about the protest. The police have planned a response. Ayim Beshimov, this will not be good if your people protest. This man—this Bure—he will be happy if there is violence. He will use it as proof that your people are Fergana's biggest problem. He uses it to advocate for your expulsion from your own country."

She studied his face and sighed. "That is what I told them—the others. I watch the news. I hear what he says, but the others do not listen."

"We have to get them to. The way Bure inflames things, there could be killings. Certainly, there will be many arrests and likely injuries."

"Even Aisha will not listen. She has taken Taalay out of school to go to the protest today."

"What?" Kazakov scrubbed his face. "A protest is no place for a ten-year-old boy. Where are they? I will speak to them."

Ayim Beshimov stepped past him to the doorway to outside. With the door opened, she pointed.

"See there? The house with the white chimney? That is where Bermet's nephew, Osman, lives. The others gather there."

Kazakov followed her gaze to the house with the white chimney. Pale gray smoke rose to the sky over what otherwise might seem a peaceful scene. Inside, though—inside there were ill deeds fomenting. He knew it. The Kyrgyz people had a long history of warfare and were not afraid to exact revenge to right a perceived wrong.

"This is the nephew who often traveled with Bermet?"

Ayim Beshimov nodded.

"Then that's where I'm going." He stepped past her out the door.

"Wait! I will come with you!" she said.

He waved her offer away. "You are busy and I am a big boy."

He left her and followed the footpath around the corner and down the street until he reached the house with the white chimney. It sat low in its small, snow-filled yard, its stone walls gleaming gray in the sunlight, a lone blue spruce like a dark thought beside the doorway. Across the white yard of snow, a well-worn path had been worn almost smooth by many feet.

Kazakov followed the footpath to the doorway and paused. From inside came muffled voices. He knocked once and waited. The voices continued. He knocked again, harder, and the voices faltered. The door yanked open and he found himself facing Aisha's unfriendly glare.

"What do you want? You should not be here."

Kazakov ignored the barrier she posed and pushed past her, inside. "What I want is to stop people from getting hurt and that means that I should be here."

He scanned the room. Unlike Ayim Beshimov's place where the door gave onto a hallway. In this house the front door gave onto a single large room that had three smaller doors off the back—most likely a bedroom, a kitchen, and perhaps a water closet. The main room held a large hearth and fireplace along one wall and a large, mostly threadbare carpet on the floor. Small cushions provided seating to about thirty people who faced three men at the front of the room. One was a younger man of about Aisha's age who stood nervously facing those seated in the room. The second man stood by the young man's shoulder and took center stage. By his confident stance, he was most likely the leader.

The third man sat on a chair in the corner at the head of the room. Khalil Khan met Kazakov's gaze and looked away, a look of what might be disgust on his face.

For a moment Kazakov didn't know what to say. Surely Khan would have tried to talk these people out of such a foolish move. But Khan stood and went to stand at the other shoulder of the man who commanded the room.

The leader was dark-haired and clad in worn canvas trousers, but his unbleached cotton shirt was pristine and ironed to board stiffness. His dark hair with unusually white temples, was neatly combed back from sharp, tribal features and deep-set black eyes. Clearly this was an important man at an important occasion.

"Who are you and what do you want?" the important man demanded. The eyes of those in the room had all turned in Kazakov's direction.

Khan caught the arm of the speaker, then released him as if the touch burned him.

"May I present Detektiv Alexander Kazakov of New Moscow police."

"I repeat: What are you doing here?" The man didn't even glance in Khan's direction. Was that friction between them?

"I've come to warn you. You're playing into your enemy's hands by doing this. If there are any problems, any violence, Boris Bure will claim that you caused it, that your people are the reason for all of Fergana's problems. The Biysk police are already prepared and deployed for your protest."

"And why would you tell us this? You are Russian."

"He could be in league with Bure—sent to stop us protesting so that Bure doesn't have to face those he harms," said Aisha, standing to face him.

"No." Kazakov shook his head. "I am here strictly to investigate the murder of Bermet Aytmatov. I wished to speak to her nephew."

Gazes shifted to the youngster who stood next to the man in the white shirt. He had thick, dark hair cut over his ears and dark, gleaming eyes, whether from excitement or fear wasn't clear.

"Arrest him, too, more like," Aisha said. "Russians are always happy to blame our people."

"That is not so. I base my arrests on evidence—facts, not race. That is why I've come here. Bure is a man who would divide Fergana on the basis of race. He uses your anger to prove his point." He thought of the stories in New Moscow of how troublemakers caused peaceful protests to turn violent. "Even if you plan a peaceful protest, something will happen to turn it ugly. The police will intervene. More of your people will be arrested. Surely there has to be a better way."

He looked at Khan. Surely the M.E. would back him up, but Khan said nothing.

Aisha stood by her chair, her face defiant.

Thankfully, the spokesman looked thoughtful. He glanced at Khan. "You know this man. Is he trustworthy?"

Khan's black gaze slid back to Kazakov. Then he turned a chill gaze on the spokesman. "Trustworthy? Yes. He believes in truth and almost lost his life protecting my family. But he is known to break into places where he is not wanted and to poke his nose into matters he has been told to leave alone." He shrugged an apology in Kazakov's direction.

The spokesman considered. "Do we do as he suggests?"

Khan met Kazakov's gaze and then away. "As I registered earlier, I do not agree with the decision to protest for all the reasons Detektiv Kazakov mentions. But I understand. Our people have been stepped on many times. Do we allow it to continue unchecked, or do we take a stand? That is my sentiment, though I may not agree with your methods."

No. Khan could not do this!

"Khan! Think about it. Why is Bure coming here now? It's well known that there are sensitivities here. Bermet's death has only made the fracture worse. Bure wants a confrontation. People could be hurt. People could die," Kazakov said.

Khan bowed his head. He sighed. "Our people are already dying. Our culture is undermined, our herds decimated, our children unemployed except as laborers. Our land has been taken to build ski hills. What more can you do to us except kill our bodies?" he said softly.

"I am not like other Russians. I work for justice."

Khan simply looked at him, but there was none of the old camaraderie between them. It was a look of bald resentment. Of Kazakov, too? The betrayal felt like a stone in Kazakov's stomach. After all they had been through, it came to this—to old tribal loyalties trumping Kazakov's efforts to save Khan and his family.

Finally, Khan smiled sadly. "But you still allow the injustice to happen. You are Russian. You have been bred to look away, to see only the past greatness of your people."

It couldn't be true. He'd spent his life fighting for justice regardless of ethnicity or gender. His hands curled into fists. He was Russian, true enough, but he *had* recognized the flaws in his country. "There is only so much one man can do."

"Is there?" the leader said. "We have said the same all these years until finally we have joined together to say the injustice cannot continue. If you truly agree with our position, stand with us. Attend the protest and ensure it does not become violent. Ensure our voice is heard."

Kazakov felt the weight of all those waiting for his answer.

"Khan, surely you can do something." But the room felt breathless and overwarm. Everything he had said was true. Everything they had said made sense. But Rostoff would surely fire him for participating in any protest. On the other hand, when had the threat of being fired ever stopped him from doing what was right? Hadn't he taken unpopular positions on virtually every case he worked on to make certain the truth was heard?

"You see?" Aisha's voice broke into his indecision. "He will not do anything that might hurt his prospects. He is just like every other Russian."

"I will do it," he said softly, his insides curdling. Was he doing this out of support for Khan or because he wanted to prove himself to these people? He wasn't sure, but the people still looked at him as if they had not heard.

"I will do it. It may help your message to finally be heard." He leaned back against the wall feeling sick to his stomach as the room erupted. But a space still existed around him as if an odor of untrustworthiness rose from him. He could understand. To them he was some one-of-a-kind creature, not one of them and not quite Russian. It reminded him of the tale of the princess who had chosen to wear a pigskin to escape her father's advances and how the princess was taken into the Tsarevich's father's house as a unique treasure. Of course, in the tale of Pig Skin, the pigskin was simply a disguise for a princess. But these people didn't know what lay underneath the Russian they saw before them. As a consequence they couldn't trust him.

Considering what he'd just agreed to, he wasn't certain he trusted himself.

8

The front of the Royal Yekaterina Resort had been decorated with Ferganese flags that bore the crest of the long-lost royal family in the top left-hand corner of a white field and golden cross. In school they had taught that the cross was a nod to their Catholic faith, but to Kazakov it had always seemed that it bore more relationship to the virtual sainthood to which the Ferganese had raised the original tsarina, Yekaterina.

The flags flapped from fifteen poles that had been placed above the resort entrance. Three news station vans had set up inside, against the rear wall of the resort's courtyard parking, their cameras and reporters ready. The flags hung down the front of the main, four-story building above a glass-domed atrium. They decorated the podium that had been raised to the left of the resort's main door and fluttered from small toy flags clutched in mittened hands by the growing crowd that was filling the resort parking lot and watching the road expectantly for the arrival of Boris Bure. To one side of the podium was a van emblazoned with Bure's smiling barracuda face and a cluster of men and women with mobile phones to their ears and clipboards in their free hands.

It spoke of the machine behind Bure. The crowd—far more than he would have expected to see midweek—spoke worryingly of the breadth of his popularity, especially if these were truly tourists who had given up their ski time in order to hear Bure speak.

Kazakov turned to Khan, who stood stoically beside him. "Please reconsider this. Bure's not going to listen to anything in front of this crowd. You know it. I know it. Please, help your friends understand what a bad idea this is. Surely there must be a better time."

"If anything, we have waited too long," Khan said, his gaze never leaving the stage.

Whatever had gotten into Khalil Khan, it clearly was something he had harbored a very long time. "I am sorry you think that I have not been a champion of your people. I truly thought I had been."

Khan barely spared him a glance. "So do most Russians."

So he was no more than most Russians—at least when it came to this. It left an emptiness inside that he was no more than a stereotype to Khan and a hopelessness for his country. Would it ever be possible that their two people could coexist as equals?

From down the road came the growl of car engines and the crowd stirred as if a wind had swirled through them. Above, the flags clapped in the wind. The sky was blue; the mountains crowned the valley. The police presence seemed focused on the protection of the stage and podium and the resort entrance. Perhaps Khan's people knew better and this would all go fine.

A low-slung black Ziln sedan reached the white stone pillars of the resort gate. It turned into the parking lot, and the crowd parted around it. It was followed by a Ziln limousine and then another sedan. They came to rest in the middle of the crowd, where the doors of the front Ziln sprang open and two men climbed out. Both were big men, tall and broad-shouldered and incredibly fit looking. They pushed through the people to the second vehicle where they shouldered the crowd back and then one of them turned back to open the limousine's rear door.

The resort manager, in a neat gray suit with the hotel insignia on his pocket, and another man, taller and balding in a navy suit, hurried through the crowd from the resort in greeting. The crowd of Russians seemed to draw in its breath as the sun gleamed on a carapace of pale blond hair. Then Boris Bure raised his face to the crowd and rose out of the darkness of the limousine's interior, his arms raised in victory.

He was clad in a black suit and pristine white shirt; a thin red tie hung from his neck and his pale gray gaze slicked over the crowd as if assessing its worth. His gaze seemed to hesitate at the clot of plain work clothes that surrounded Kazakov at one side of the brightly clothed resort goers. Kazakov couldn't be sure, but it seemed that a satisfied smile curved Bure's lips for a moment before he was swept up in the greetings from the resort manager and the man who accompanied him. He was carefully guided by his security detail toward the stage and podium. The crowd flowed after Bure, leaving the vehicles behind. The driver of the first vehicle trailed after them, carrying a brass-bound wooden box from the vehicle.

A movement at the rear of the swirl of tourists caught Kazakov's eye. From the third Ziln exited four men, shorter, swarthy, but dressed as tourists. They entered the flow of people and Kazakov lost them in the shifting swirl of color. Security? Secret Service ensuring all was safe for Bure?

Khan still stood beside him.

"And so it begins," Khan said, and left Kazakov's side to stand off to the side of the Kyrgyz man in the pristine unbleached cotton shirt. Now the spokesman wore a deep blue jacket over top that shone like a beacon amidst the drab blacks and grays and navy of most of his followers. Kazakov and the others remained where they stood, on the opposite side of the parking lot: within listening distance of the podium, but clearly apart. The police seemed to eye them as Bure and the resort owner climbed to the podium.

The man with the resort owner introduced himself as Biysk's mayor and welcomed Bure with a key to Biysk city and then handed the podium over to him.

Bure held up his hands to the sky, to the crowd. "Hello, Biysk. Thank you for gifting me with this lovely blue sky—but then Biysk has always been good to me, because it was Biysk's search parties who found me thirty years ago when I went missing. Thank you to the good people of Biysk!"

This elicited cheers from the Russian crowd, when truly it had been the parents of the sullen men and women around Kazakov who led the searches. They were the experts in these mountains.

But Bure's gaze never strayed from his favored audience, never once acknowledged the true residents of Biysk.

"It's as if history is being rewritten before my eyes," Aisha said as she sidled up to him.

"Mine, as well," Kazakov murmured.

Bure smiled and extended his hands to the crowd, drawing them into his Fergana, a country with a long illustrious history—a direct descendant from Holy Mother Russia, just as he was, by blood, a relation of Yekaterina. A hush fell over the crowd.

"It is not well known, but my forebears brought with them insignia of our royal connections. My father's father's father's great-grandfather was Yekaterina's grandson, Alexander. He escaped with Yekaterina but his identity was kept secret for his safety." Bure nodded to one of his bodyguards, who brought him the box that had arrived with him. He lifted the lid and lifted something out.

Sunlight flashed on something golden and then Bure held up what he had to the sky. Bright colors and gold leaf flashed on a religious icon Kazakov recognized. The Virgin Mary peered out at the crowd, an expression of long-suffering benediction on her face. The colors of the paint were so rich and vivid, there was to question as to either its age or authenticity. Once he had seen this exact icon hanging in the living room of Boris and Natania Bure. At the time he had been the bearer of the news of the murder of Natania's daughter, Yekaterina.

The fact that Bure would use the antique in such a gaudy show just added to Kazakov's disquiet. Why did Bure need to work so hard to justify himself? Didn't he already have the court of public opinion swayed to his side?

Bure led from showing his icon to a speech that spoke of the need to return Fergana to the likes of Russia of old. Fergana needed to regain her power. She sat as the lynchpin between two empires. It was time to use that to the country's advantage, not cower and vacillate between them.

The crowd roared.

It would be a country of great men and women who could pursue their own paths to supremacy in their chosen fields. Fergana would enter a golden age the like of which had only been seen in the time of Our Lady Yekaterina.

Bure's rhetoric became a singsong chant that could almost raise the specter of a parade of great figures across the sky.

"Why do you only speak to half Fergana's people?" A voice cut through the reverie Bure had created. "There are more than ethnic Russians in this country!"

Bure's crowd went quiet and faces craned toward the speaker.

The cotton-shirted man in the vivid blue coat had stepped away from the Kyrgyz contingent into the bare part of the parking lot near the first Ziln sedan. A police officer walked toward him.

Bure's welcoming expression turned stern. "Fergana is open to all contributors."

"Lies!" Aisha stepped forward to join the blue-coated man. Her drab coat and trousers reinforced her darker skin and hair as she stood to face Bure. "How can we contribute if we cannot work? How can we grow dreams if we are excluded?"

"Young woman, if you choose to live in a place like Biysk, you cannot be expected to have great prospects of advancement. Come to New Moscow and see what happens."

"And you think that will make any difference?" Surprisingly, it was Khalil Khan who stepped up beside Aisha and the blue-coated man. "I am from New Moscow. I am a doctor. The only Kyrgyz doctor, though last year alone, twenty-five Kyrgyz youth applied for medical school. Two at least topped scores in Fergana, but they were not accepted. How do your dreams explain that?"

Bure's pale features colored. Behind him, his bodyguards stirred and the police presence shifted toward Kazakov and the peaceful ranks of the Kyrgyz villagers.

"I would say you are mistaken. Your position as a doctor says that is the case."

"Pah." Khan spat on the earth. "One doctor when our population numbers rival yours? When our birthrate will soon have you outnumbered? When we have more children in Fergana's schools?"

The police were closing in on Khan and the other speakers.

Kazakov stepped forward.

"It is as they have said!" Kazakov was surprised it was his own voice. "I am an officer of New Moscow Police. Too many times, if there is a problem, the Kyrgyz are blamed first, even if the evidence does not support it. This good doctor is the only one of his people and is the best I have met in Fergana and yet he must always walk carefully, lest he anger his Russian employers. Where is the equality of that? Where is the equality when police try to stop them from expressing their concerns as is surely the case..."

"Gun! He has a gun!" The shout rose from a side of the crowd away from Kazakov's vantage.

The crowd screamed and flooded away from the podium, shifting around the cars and surrounding Khan and the others. A gun fired. A woman screamed. The police fought their way through the crowd, uncertain where they should be going.

Kazakov used his height to scan the crowd. People in colorful hats and ski jackets slammed into him and off again. Some made for the gates. Some headed for the resort doors. Another shot from behind him spun him around, seeking its source. The Kyrgyz contingent had disappeared like flotsam in the sea of bright colors. He caught glimpses of terrified faces, both Kyrgyz and tourist. Everyone was running.

Not everyone. Kazakov glimpsed a swarthy figure who, head down, allowed the crowd to push him toward the resort gate. But he wasn't running. He walked rapidly with them, letting them jostle around him. One of the men from the third Ziln.

Kazakov went after him, shoving through the crowd, elbowing people aside. But there were too many people between him and his target. By the time he reached the resort gate, the figure was nowhere to be seen amidst the flood of color spreading down the road.

Kazakov kept watch a moment, but the man never reappeared. He turned back to the parking lot and spotted a clot of struggling figures. Police had a group of Kyrgyz men and women backed into a corner of the parking area. They were hemmed in by the resort wall and towering snowbanks scraped from the pavement. One of the Kyrgyz tried to scale the snowbank but a hand yanked him back. The police shoved Bermet Aytmatov's nephew and the nephew shoved back. A woman—Aisha— joined him and suddenly threw a punch. The standoff disintegrated into a melee.

On the podium, Bure's security detail had helped him up off the floor of the stage. They urged him toward the resort, but Bure shook them off. He returned to the podium.

"They ask why they do not have opportunities and here is the answer!" Bure roared. "These are not our people. They threaten and assault us! They bring guns to a peaceful event like this! It is time for all Russians to stand up and recognize the true threat to our safety!" His finger stabbed the air at the Kyrgyz the police were clubbing down.

Kazakov ran to them and pulled the police off. "Stop! Stop, all of you! You're playing into Bure's hands. You're selling his story of the threat of the tribal peoples."

A police club jabbed Kazakov in the gut.

He doubled over. Couldn't breathe. One of the uniformed officers grabbed his arms and twisted them behind his back.

"I'm police, dammit!" he yelled. "Detektiv Alexander Kazakov, New Moscow Police. I'm investigating Bermet Aytmatov's murder."

"Sure you are," the officer said.

"Let me get my wallet and I'll show you."

"You just assaulted an officer!"

The last of the tribal group had been subdued. Aisha bucked and kicked in the police hold. Bermet's nephew nursed a bloody nose. Their leader stood resolute and proudly while the police cuffed him. Kazakov scanned the prisoners. There was no sight of Khan.

Behind them, Bure was still speaking, invoking the people to rise up and assert themselves over this nation, Fergana. The people who had run out into the street were gradually returning. More flooded out of the resort as Kazakov and the Kyrgyz group were hustled toward waiting police vehicles. As Bure's voice rose and fell, Kazakov turned to him.

The man stood like a statue under the crown of mountains, one hand clutching the edge of the podium, the other raised to the sky. But his gaze met and locked on Kazakov's.

Bure's lips curved in a smile.

———

In the rear of a police van crowded to standing room with Kyrgyz prisoners, Kazakov grit his teeth at being wedged into a front corner, the press of humanity not quite as bad as the heavy atmosphere of fear. Thankfully, the Biysk police station wasn't far and the rear doors of the van burst open, tumbling prisoners out onto slushy pavement. Kazakov waited until the other prisoners were clear and then straightened his coat and stepped down to face the uniformed officer in charge of the arrests.

"My name is Detektiv Alexander Kazakov. I am working with Detektiv Egorova on the Aytmatov murder. You have no grounds to arrest me."

The officer—tall, dark-haired, and broad shouldered with a small scar beside his left eye—shook his head. "You'll go with the others. Tell your story at booking."

He grabbed Kazakov's shoulder and shoved him after the others. The van door clanged shut behind him and the engine roared as the van drove away.

———

Three hours spent fuming at his treatment and asking himself what had he expected, Kazakov was released by the Biysk Police with an apology. His fellow prisoners were not so lucky. They were held on suspicion of terrorist activities and locked in crowded cells.

Kazakov reclaimed his belongings from the booking officer and left by the prisoner release door, only to have his mobile phone ring in his pocket. He fished it out and stood in the parking lot in the weak, late afternoon sunshine wishing for a smoke. On the main road, vehicles passed the police station entrance, their tires hissing on the slushy roads.

"Kazakov." The air was cold on his neck.

"Kazakov! Thank God. It's me. I've arrived in New Moscow but the news is full of Biysk. An attempt made on Bure's life! And you were there! I saw some of the footage at a petrol station. They had a television on. Are you all right?" Egorova's voice was breathless.

"I'm standing outside Biysk police station as we speak. What are the reports saying?"

"That there was an uprising attempt. That Kyrgyz Nationalists shot at him, but police intervened before anyone was hurt, though one woman had her leg broken in the stampede to safety. We were lucky more weren't hurt. At least that's what Bure says. That and that all good Russian citizens should vote in this election. Vote for a prosperous Russian Fergana—emphasis on Russian—and for safety in our homes. His speech was magnificent coming on the heels of an attempt on his life."

Kazakov couldn't stop his snort of derision. So Bure's version of events had already gone out. Khan and his damn-fool friends had just fed Bure's machine exactly what they wanted.

"That's not how it happened at all, though the film clips might show it that way. The Kyrgyz did nothing. I know because I was with them when it all went down."

The phone was silent a moment. "You were with them, not just observing?"

Kazakov sighed, suddenly feeling exhausted. "So the news clips didn't show my little outburst..." That was some kind of blessing, at least. "The Kyrgyz were trying to get Bure to hear their grievances." He told her what had happened.

Again Egorova was silent for a moment. "Listen, the reason I called wasn't just to tell you that I'd arrived. I wanted to let you know that when I got here, the whole forensics operations were in a bit of an uproar. Apparently one of their Medical Examiners has gone missing..."

Kazakov stilled and studied the mountains turning blue at their peaks. He knew what was coming. Khan. "The damn fool simply left town because he knew about the murder and he wasn't going to let anyone else touch the body."

From the main road, an expensive, egg-shell white, four-wheel drive vehicle turned into the police parking lot and purred into a parking space on the far side of the lot. The engine turned off and the door opened, releasing a familiar tall man with graying hair swept back from a high forehead and black eyes that gleamed like onyx pebbles above high, Ottoman cheekbones. A luxuriant black moustache supported a hawkish nose with out-swept nostrils that had always made Kazakov think the man scented fear.

Enver Pasha. His gaze slid across the parking lot and found Kazakov.

He was an Ottoman businessman, who Kazakov suspected spied for his government and probably did far more, including arranging murders. Enver Pasha owned a large, multinational shipping company and was diversifying into many more areas. He had also been a person of interest in both of Kazakov's two most difficult recent investigations. Enver Pasha owned a house in Biysk, but that still didn't explain why the man was at the police station.

"What's going on, Kazakov?" Egorova's voice sounded tinny in his ear.

All of Kazakov's internal alarms were going off. Bure and Enver Pasha both here now, on the same day. It couldn't possibly be a coincidence.

"I wish the hell I knew," he said, clicked off, and pocketed the phone.

9

———————

The sunlight glinted on the gray in Enver Pasha's hair, but on this man it meant steel, not age—even if he might be older than the early sixties Kazakov had come to think of him. His dark gaze was just as calculating as Kazakov remembered from their two previous meetings, but this time his lips curved in an unaccustomed smile.

"This is a surprise. Detektiv Alexander Kazakov, if I recall."

The faintly puzzled expression as if he could not quite recall was surely an act, for Kazakov had bested the man before and this was not a man who liked losing.

But then, perhaps it was not a loss in Enver Pasha's mind. That was something to think about and something Kazakov had begun to suspect was the case.

"Enver," Kazakov said. The Pasha was an honorific the man had earned for military service in the Ottoman empire. His first name was actually Ismail. "What brings you here?"

Enver gave a slight shrug and Kazakov prepared himself for a banality or an outright lie.

"My house, of course. And the skiing."

Kazakov picked at a fingernail as if bored. "I'm surprised you're not consumed with your new tobacco businesses." He kept his voice neutral.

Enver's gaze sparked. His lips curved into a hard smile. Clearly, he did not like being reminded that those tobacco concessions had come at a cost.

Another shrug disguised as straightening his rich wool coat around his shoulders. "I have people for that. And what brings you here?"

"Work." Kazakov returned the shrug.

Frowning, Enver looked from Kazakov to the low-slung Biysk police station. "It was my understanding that you were a New Moscow officer. Have things changed? Did New Moscow not appreciate their busiest detective?"

And just why would Enver Pasha care? For that matter, why would a man of such exalted stature and money bother to cross a parking lot to speak to a detective he barely knew and had no reason to like?

Kazakov just smiled. "I have no idea what people higher up and wiser than myself think. But the air is clear here and a man can think."

"Ah! A well-earned vacation, then." Tension seemed to ease across Enver's broad shoulders. Then he cocked his head. "But isn't it a busman's holiday when a policeman spends his holiday at a police station?"

"I'm here to see friends," Kazakov said and kicked at a loose chunk of snow. It skittered across the parking lot and between two police vehicles. "You?" He studied Enver from the tops of his eyes.

Enver Pasha looked uncomfortable but then shrugged again—a serious character flaw. "I suppose I could say the same. A friend asked me to check on another friend."

As if Enver Pasha would ever do anything for anyone if it did not benefit himself. But Kazakov nodded and straightened. "I should let you get on with it, then." He left Enver Pasha and started across the parking lot to the street where his Perseus had been parked before the mess at the Royal Yekaterina Resort.

"Kazakov!"

Enver's call stopped him and he swung around.

The Ottoman stood tall and square-shouldered in the parking lot, his luxurious mustache gleaming under his hawk nose, but still there was something different than the first time Kazakov had seen Enver Pasha at his offices. This time there was something akin to uncertainty, or simply trying something on for size about the man.

"I am throwing a small party tomorrow night. Perhaps you would like to come?"

"Why?" Kazakov asked, for he could see nothing he held in common with this man.

"Perhaps because I think your presence could make things more interesting?" He flashed the same white smile Kazakov had seen in the newspaper photos. "It is at seven o'clock. Ask anyone in town where my house is. They will point you in the right direction."

With a nod, Enver Pasha turned and headed for the Biysk police station door, leaving Kazakov both slightly confused and feeling dismissed.

But then, that was likely Enver Pasha's intention.

———

The interior of the Perseus was surprisingly warm given the chill of the outside air. Slouched low behind the wheel, Kazakov sat without his gloves on, eyeing the police parking lot exit. The falling sun laid the mountain shadows across the valley and while the sky was vivid blue, the light was fading down below. Forty-five minutes later as street lights flickered on, Enver Pasha's cream-colored vehicle turned out onto the road.

Kazakov slid lower in his seat as Enver cruised past. This time he had a passenger that Kazakov recognized. The man in the unbleached cotton shirt and bright blue jacket sat in the front passenger seat listening as Enver Pasha spoke. By the expression on Enver's face, he wasn't happy.

That was interesting. Kazakov watched them down the road in his rearview mirror and then started the Perseus and pulled a U-turn to follow. The traffic was light, so he hung well back as Enver followed the main road away from the old village.

Where on earth was Enver taking the other man? Surely not to his home.

As if on cue, Enver's taillights came on and the vehicle turned away from the river. In this part of the valley, less expensive hotels served the less-well-heeled visitors to Biysk's ski hills. A few older homes still stood amid the prefabricated concrete, glass, and faux weathered wood hotels, but most looked like they were only awaiting the wrecking ball and more of the New-Moscow-type construction.

Enver Pasha's taillights flashed again and the vehicle turned in at one of the hotels. Kazakov drove past the hotel parking lot entrance, did a U-turn, and slid the Perseus into the curb. He hunkered down again, the engine off, watching Enver Pasha's vehicle and occupants.

Enver Pasha's vehicle stayed where it was as the two men spoke. Then the man who had led the disastrous Kyrgyz protest climbed out and headed toward the hotel rooms. Enver Pasha departed and cruised back down the road the way he had come as the Kyrgyz leader climbed the stairs to the second floor.

Kazakov sat up and considered going to speak with the Kyrgyz leader, but that would give away that he knew of the connection with Enver Pasha. Besides, he was not here to investigate Enver Pasha, but to find Bermet Aytmatov's murderer. He could see little chance of a link between the two.

The Perseus rumbled as he started the engine and turned the vehicle around to head back to the police station. He'd wanted to interview Bermet's nephew, and the young man had been one of those arrested with Kazakov. He couldn't think of a better time to interview him.

———

The Biysk police station seemed to hum around Kazakov when he walked in the front door. He strode to the reception desk and barked a request to be allowed through the gate into the squad room. Regardless of his arrest earlier in the day, he had the right to be here—the big-city detective deigning to help his country cousins.

His bravado got him through the gate and into the dimly lit hall that led to the central squad room. The centrally heated air was dry as dust and smelled of old heated ducts and wool. When he came out into the squad room, uniformed officers looked up. They looked askance when he settled at Egorova's desk and picked up the phone and dialed the number for central booking that was listed on the phone. As he waited he heard murmurs of "Kyrgyz lover."

"Cells," came the gruff voice at the end of the phone.

"Detektiv Kazakov here. I need Kurmanbek uulu Osman brought up to an interview room." He used the full name he had seen noted in the booking log when he'd been brought in.

There was silence on the phone. "I'm not sure we've got anyone of that name booked in."

Kazakov rolled his eyes. Surely they weren't going to play this kind of game. "Do I have to come down and get him myself?" he growled.

He heard flipping pages. "N-no. Here he is. Fine. We'll have him brought up to interview room two."

"How long?" Kazakov asked because he'd played these games before and had seen detectives left waiting for half an hour or more.

"Give us ten minutes."

Kazakov thanked them and hung up the phone and took a few minutes to collect his thoughts. Speaking with Enver Pasha had rattled his focus. So had seeing Enver with someone Khalil Khan clearly valued. He thought about the invitation Enver Pasha had extended and wondered whether he should attend.

He'd leave that decision to tomorrow.

———

Interview room two was a tiny cubicle, barely six feet on a side, with two chairs and a narrow interview table that would allow interviewee and interviewer to rub knees under the table. A single bulb glowed yellow within a grilled cage and placed shadow bars threateningly on all the walls. The air was stale as if the air circulation system didn't work in this corner of the building. It was altogether unsatisfactory, but it was what Kazakov was stuck with. He found the break room, made tea, and settled himself to wait.

The subdued Kurmanbek uulu Osman who was brought to Kazakov was a far cry from the fiery-eyed young man who had stood by the Kyrgyz leader in the house in the old village. He was even farther from the scrapper Kazakov had seen in the Royal Yekaterina Resort parking lot resisting the police attempts to put him into a police vehicle. The deep blue bruise across his temple and a crust of red around his swollen nose spoke of how his arrest had been effected. The tender way he moved spoke of other, less visible injuries, too.

Kazakov nodded him to the chair facing the interview room door and to the two mugs on the table. "I thought you'd probably like tea."

Osman eyed the mug and Kazakov suspiciously and glanced toward the door.

Kazakov sat back in his chair. "If you're wondering why you're here, it's like I said at the house: I'm trying to find Bermet Aytmatov's killer. I need your help."

"You're one of them. You set us up." Osman's eyes flashed, but then his eyelids masked his anger.

Kazakov shook his head. "I warned you all—not that it helped. I've been watching Boris Bure for a long time. I've seen how he works. I don't agree with it, and I would like to see it stop—which was the only reason I agreed to stand with you all. That and my relationship with Khalil Khan. I had nothing to do with what happened at the rally other than trying to stop the arrests and getting arrested myself as a result."

Osman simply glared at him and crossed his arms over his chest.

Kazakov leaned forward over the table. "Listen, do you want your aunt's killer found? Because if you do, I'm the best chance you've got."

Uncertainty filled the young man's face and his feet shuffled the floor. Finally, he nodded. "She was a good woman. A treasure."

"I understand you often went with her on her trips to the mountains. You must have cared for her a great deal."

Osman's gaze fell away to the floor and grief and guilt played over his face. "I should have been with her, but we had just come back from the mountains and I—I wanted to spend time with my friends. She said she would be fine. She wasn't going far, she said."

He turned a bleak gaze on Kazakov.

"Tell me about your aunt's trips to the mountains." Kazakov took out his notebook.

Osman thought for a moment. "She went up there a lot. My mom used to say it was because Bermet didn't agree with what was happening to Biysk and so she liked to go to the mountains to clean her lungs. Anyway, she made the trip at least as far as White Stone Village at least once a week. It was sort of a regular thing and some of the villagers from farther back in the mountains would come to her there for her potions."

Kazakov looked for permission from Osman before beginning to take notes and nodded the young man to continue.

"Most of the time she'd maybe treat one or two. A baby with fever or an old one's aches and pains." He shook his head. "Aunty Bermet had her own aches and pains. There were mornings when she could barely get out of bed, her joints were so swollen, but she'd force herself up and get dressed and gather her things and we'd head to the mountains. She always seemed better by the time we got home, but when we'd first start out, she'd have to have lots of help. That's why I always went with her. She couldn't have made it on her own."

"So when you got to White Stone Village, how would it work?"

"Maksat, the headman, would take her into his house and she would wait for the sick and injured to be brought to her. She would set limbs—a doctor she knew showed her how to do it—she would provide medicine and herbs and sometimes she would counsel people."

Kazakov raised a brow at him.

"Things like a couple could not get pregnant. She would provide them suggestions. It often worked. She'd deliver the babies that came as a result. There are a lot of Kyrgyz girl babies named Bermet." He grinned, his eyes gleaming with tears, and suddenly he was simply a nephew grieving for a favored aunt.

"And those she couldn't help?" Kazakov asked softly.

Osman collected his cup of tea and sipped. He sighed with pleasure and looked at Kazakov openly for the first time. "There weren't many. Usually they were people who waited too long to come to her or lived too far away. She was really good at healing."

Kazakov tapped his pen on his notebook. "Let me ask this more directly. Had she made enemies in her years of healing? After a life that long, most people do."

"No." Osman shook his head. "Even the people she couldn't help, she helped feel better about their condition. My aunt always said death was nothing to fear. She used to quote Rumi about dying as a mineral and being born a plant, as dying as a plant and being born an animal, as dying as an animal and being born a woman. She asked when had death brought her something to fear? She saw death as an adventure. The dying that she treated loved her for it and it seemed to give their families relief. I can't remember anyone being angry at her—ever. My aunt wasn't someone you could remain angry with. She was too kind."

It was what Kazakov had suspected. An elderly healer who regularly chanced the mountains would be no ordinary woman. From the way Osman described her, she was nigh on a saint.

"Tell me about the last time you saw her."

Osman sighed unsteadily and took a long sip of tea. "She came knocking on my door early in the morning. She was already bundled up and ready to go, with her bag of medicine and tools on her back. She said that a message had come down the mountain that Sofia, Maksat's daughter, was having difficulty birthing her second child. The messenger was still there and could help her, so I decided to stay in Biysk." He shook his head and sniffed. "I should have gone. I could have saved her. I'm so much stronger than her, I could have stopped whoever did this to her!"

His voice broke and he choked on a sob, then scrubbed his eyes and swallowed back his emotions. "Instead she died alone in the mountains with no one to pray for her soul and now these police desecrate her body." He scrubbed at his eyes and shook his head. "I am sorry."

"So am I," Kazakov said, thinking about the autopsy that must be the desecration Osman spoke of. No wonder Khan had dropped everything to come here. At least it had been loving hands that conducted the procedure. "I think I would have liked your aunt very much. But you couldn't have saved her. At least I don't think so. Tell me, were there times you and your aunt went farther than White Stone Village?"

Osman studied the table.

"There were a few times," he said softly. "But Bermet did not like to talk about it."

His gaze rose to Kazakov. "We went farther into the mountains, high up and into very bad terrain. One time the weather was very bad and I thought we should turn back, but Aunty would not hear of it. It was like she was driven."

"To a village?" Kazakov prompted.

"No." Osman shook his head. "We were met by men on horseback. They blindfolded Aunty and me and put us on the backs of their horses. We were taken far into the mountains. I don't know where. When we arrived, they took Aunty away and put me in a tent. When they brought her back, she was very tired. I asked her what they wanted and she said she did not want to talk about it. She just demanded water and washed and washed her hands as if she could not get them clean. They left us to sleep, but as I fell asleep I heard Aunty repeating her Rumi saying over and over. 'I died a rock and became a tree. I died a tree and became a deer. I died a deer and became myself. Who am I to fear what comes with death?' But it sounded like she was trying to convince herself. She was very quiet the next morning as we were brought back down the mountain and set afoot again to find our way back home. I asked them why they could not loan us a horse, because Aunty was tired and I was afraid we would not make it home, but they didn't even answer me—just turned and rode back into the mountains."

His earnest look said he was telling everything he thought he remembered.

Kazakov nodded in return. "When did these visits begin?"

"About five months ago, just as the snows were settling in the mountains."

"And when did the last visit occur?"

Osman shook his head. "As far as I know perhaps a month ago, but then I think of when I saw Aunty that last time. She had her heaviest winter coat on and her tall furred felt boots. I should have realized that meant something."

"So you think she might have been going back to that place in the mountains?"

Osman nodded, his shoulders slumping. They sat in silence as Kazakov thought about the information.

"Do you think you could take me back to the place these riders met you?"

The younger man nodded.

"Would you recognize the place you were taken?"

A shake of the head. "We were blindfolded and I was kept in the tent. I never saw anything."

"But your Aunty did?"

Osman thought and nodded. "When she came back to the tent, she wasn't blindfolded."

Kazakov sat forward in his chair. "Osman, often people think that they know nothing about a place that they have been if they couldn't see their surroundings, but really, people frequently know more than they think they do. I want you to try something for me that might help us to understand where you were taken."

Osman nodded, but then grew puzzled. "I will do what you ask, but I don't understand why it's so important. Aunty was found between White Stone Village and Biysk."

Kazakov nodded and leaned back in his chair. "She was. Her body was. But we followed her tracks back to White Stone Village and beyond. We found evidence to suggest that she was wounded deeper in the mountains. It suggests that she was trying to escape something or someone. They caught up with her at White Stone Village." He let his story die.

Silence ticked in the room as Osman puzzled it out. Then his eyes widened. "The village…" His worried gaze found Kazakov.

"It isn't there anymore. At least the people aren't. From the tracks it appears that the villagers were taken deeper into the mountains."

"Those bastards!" Osman said. He leapt to his feet. "After all Aunty has done for them, they kill her and hurt our friends!"

It was where Kazakov's thoughts had wandered. He nodded. "So what I need you to do is help me determine where these men might be. I want you to sit back with your hands on your lap and I want you to close your eyes and breathe. Listen to my voice."

Osman did as he was told, but the way his legs vibrated and his hands twitched, he was anything but calm.

"Breathe in. Breathe out." Gradually the rapid rise and fall of his chest slowed and Osman's quivers of energy subsided. When the younger man finally appeared relaxed, Kazakov leaned forward. "I want you to think back to the last time you went deep into the mountains with your aunty. Can you describe the weather?"

Osman took a deep breath. "It was sunny and cold. I was worried about Aunty, because her circulation isn't so good anymore and she gets cold easily. There was a cold wind down the ridge we were traversing. The ice crystals stung my face."

"What way were you facing?"

"The sun is to my left and it is afternoon so we are facing north."

"Is that the direction the wind is blowing from?"

Osman nodded.

"There are horsemen coming for you. From what direction do they come?" Kazakov asked.

They young man inhaled and exhaled. Although his eyes were closed, his head shifted as if he looked around him. "They come from above us, but there is no way that they could live so high. I think—I think they came from behind us, from the west, up over the ridge."

"Breathe in. Breathe out. Now you are on horseback. You are blindfolded."

Osman nodded.

"I want you to think about your sensations. The horse moves under you. The wind against you. You lean to accommodate the horse over the terrain."

Osman nodded again and his breathing steadied. He was still in his chair as if afraid to disturb the memories.

"The horse moves up a slope but it is not so steep. The wind blows down the back of my jacket. I think we traverse the mountain but then the horse turns uphill. The way is steep and I have to hold onto the rider to stop from slipping off the back of the horse. The afternoon is long and the air cools around us." He frowned. "But then there is suddenly sun. I feel it through the blindfold. The cloth is warmed. And then the horse walks a flatter path for a while before suddenly turning down. The wind no longer finds its way under my clothes. It is there, but does not carry such force. The sun is gone again and soon we are in a place where there are many men and horses. I can tell because of the manure smell and the sounds of the men's voices. They help me down and then I am pushed into the tent and my blindfold is taken."

He opened his eyes. "I remember that I barely saw the sun on the sides of the tent except for the briefest time in the middle of the next day, and yet there was none of the lowering feeling of clouds and snow. There must have been tall mountains all around and the valley must have been very small and deep."

He seemed to come out of a reverie and smiled shyly. "Does that help? Will you be able to find Auntie's killers?"

Kazakov looked at the notes he had made and read them back to Osman. "Is there anything else you can think of that you haven't said? Anything else that you might have heard, smelled, or felt?"

Osman's gaze brightened! "The shooting! While I was there I heard gunfire. It didn't sound like one of our rifles."

"And what does that mean to you?" Kazakov asked.

"That there were people there who weren't Kyrgyz or they were Kyrgyz from across the border in China. I've heard that weapons are hard to get there, but it is possible—not like here."

And living in Biysk with the tribes shifting across the slippery backs of the mountains, he would likely have a good sense of such things; but that still gave Kazakov no better sense of what was going on. As if on cue, his head started aching. He thought of the confusing evidence in the mountains, of Boris Bure and Enver Pasha's presence. The two men had been in newspaper photos together and now they were both here; were they somehow in league?

Waiting on the other side of the table was a singular source of information. Kurmanbek uulu Osman was motivated to help him. That was worth a lot in this kind of case.

"May I ask you something?"

Osman nodded.

"What did you think would happen when you interrupted Boris Bure's speech?"

The air had heated up in their time in the room. Sweat beaded Osman's forehead and ran down Kazakov's undershirt.

"I didn't know," Osman said finally. "Zholdosh said it would get our question into the press and into the Russian consciousness."

Although Kazakov had never been introduced, he had to conclude that Zholdosh was the man with the dark hair and gray temples who had led the abortive protest. "Zholdosh is the man in the white cotton shirt?"

Osman nodded.

Interesting.

"Tell me, where does Zholdosh live in the village?"

Osman shook his head. "He does not. He says that if he stays in one place, there is too good a chance that he might be arrested. Instead he moves from place to place every few days and tells very few of us where he goes."

"Who does he tell?"

Frowning, Osman shook his head. "I'm not sure. Aisha probably. Maybe Khan—he is an important man. I don't know."

Sitting back in his chair, Kazakov mulled over what he knew. Then he glanced at Osman.

"Osman, have you ever met a man named Enver Pasha?"

10

———————

It was fully dark outside by the time Kazakov left the station. Though he had spoken to the watch commander, there was no interest in releasing Osman or his fellow protestors. They were leaving it to the higher-ups to determine what to do, given the protest and ensuing arrests had apparently been on the news in New Moscow. The rumor around Biysk police station was that immediate protests had occurred in New Moscow. In the squad room, a television had replayed a news item of Bure standing beside New Moscow's empty pedestal of Yekaterina promising to bring back her greatness and lay her enemies low. There were speculations amongst the pundits as to what this might mean for Fergana's tribals. Some man-on-the-street interviews with Russians showed anger and little interest in Kyrgyz perspectives.

He left with his gut tied up in a knot and stood at the top of the stairs looking out at the diminished stars poking through a thin veil of clouds. The moon had yet to rise and the chill wind cut through his coat right down to the bones. He turned and could just make out the peak of the mountain that stood over White Stone Village, poking up over the roof of the neighboring resort. What lay hidden in that direction that had claimed the life of Bermet Aytmatov and stolen away an entire village? Boris Bure and Enver Pasha—his gut told him they were both somehow involved.

Young Osman had known Enver Pasha.

The Ottoman had found his way into the village and had hired workers from old Biysk to maintain his home. He had also managed to get himself invited to community celebrations and had, apparently, ingratiated himself. Beyond that, Osman didn't know. He also hadn't been aware that Enver Pasha was the man who had gotten Zholdosh released, only that Zholdosh had been taken from cells and not returned. Those still held prisoner were worried that the police tortured their friend.

So just how were Enver Pasha and Boris Bure involved in this whole mess?

The question hung in the cold air around him and Kazakov would have loved a cigarette, but he'd quit years ago and had used his last "emergency" cigarette months ago. He hadn't replaced it. Instead he went down the steps of the police station one more time and out to the Perseus. The engine started with a grumble and he left the station and turned away from the old town. He aimed the Perseus in the direction of the low-rent Russian hotel.

Through the darkness illuminated by the polluting light from the resorts, he retraced his route back to where Zholdosh had settled for the night. He parked on the street and headed for the outside stairs that led up to the room Zholdosh had entered.

The place looked even less appetizing close up. Paint peeled from concrete and faux wood siding. Stairs creaked and groaned under his feet. Garbage littered the long, open-air walkway that led to the rooms. The scent of onions, beets, and strong cigarettes leaked from the rooms in an almost visible fog. Clearly a Russian hotel.

He reached Zholdosh's room. A light gleamed through grimy curtains that covered a window next to the door. He knocked and waited but no one answered. No sound came from the interior.

Had he missed Zholdosh? Was the man refusing to answer?

He knocked again and a door opened one room down. A head poked out. Woman. Russian. Young and sleepy-eyed, her brown hair in a thick braid that hung over her shoulder. "Would you keep it down out there? I've got an early shift tomorrow."

Kazakov eyed her. Probably one of the numerous youngsters who worked the ski hill during the season. "I haven't been here before. What do you mean?"

"Oh!" She straightened. "Sorry!" She went to pull her door closed.

"Hold on a minute!" Kazakov reached her door before it was closed all the way. He caught the side of the door with his fist and it burst open again, almost smacking her face.

She backed up a pace. "I'm calling the police!"

"I am the police," Kazakov said and produced his identification. "I need to speak with the man who's rented that room. Now what can you tell me?"

The girl looked from the I.D. to Kazakov. She twisted her neck unhappily. "He was noisy, okay? At least his company was."

"His company?"

"An hour or so ago. One guy. I heard their voices. They were loud enough they woke me up. There were some thumps and bangs, too. When they didn't quiet down, I pounded the wall. Things got quiet then and it wasn't long before I heard the door close. I chanced a peek outside and the guy left. When I heard the knock, I was afraid he'd come back again."

Kazakov looked back at Zholdosh's closed door. "So he didn't leave with the stranger?"

"I—don't think so..." The girl frowned. "After I saw the one guy, I didn't hear the guy next door go after him or anything. I'd say the guy who rented the room stayed home."

"Can you tell me anything about the man you saw?"

She shrugged. "I only saw him from the back. He wore a black wool coat like most Russians."

"Tall? Short? What color was his hair?"

She shook her head. "How the heck do I know? The sun was down. He was going down the stairs. If I have to guess, I'd say his hair was dark. Now that's all I know and I need my sleep, okay?"

Uneasiness washed over Kazakov. He thanked the girl and let her close her door. Then he returned to Zholdosh's door and knocked again. There was still no answer and he went to the window.

The dirty gray-green curtain hung unevenly over the glass as if some of its runners were broken. The uneven undulation of the fabric allowed him to see narrow slices of the room: an empty bed. A desk with a brightly colored coat thrown over the chair. A wedge of carpet. A foot stuck out from the far side of the bed.

"Derr'mo!" He pounded down the stairs and across the lot to the manager's office. He burst inside. "I need keys to room 232. There's a man down inside."

He flashed his identification as he spoke. The sleepy desk clerk thankfully roused and trailed him out the door to the cold with a key.

At Zholdosh's room the desk clerk paused. "You're sure? I could get in trouble if I let you in and there's nothing there. Our patrons have rights to privacy."

Kazakov grabbed the key from the clerk's hand and unlocked the door. He burst inside, crossing to see behind the bed.

Zholdosh lay staring up at the ceiling, a jagged stab wound in his throat, his white cotton shirt no longer pristine. The hair of his gray temples outspread like wings. The clerk who had entered behind him turned and retched into a garbage can. Kazakov grabbed his arm and dragged him from the room.

"Go back to your office. Call the police and report what has happened. Write down everything you remember from this evening and everything you know—who reserved the room? Who arrived this evening, who was in the parking lot late this afternoon, and so on."

The clerk, still gasping for breath, just stood there until Kazakov grabbed his shoulder, turned him from the room, and shoved him toward the stairs.

The clerk went.

Kazakov turned back to the room. Let the clerk phone. He pulled out his mobile and made the call, too. He explained that he had secured the scene and was awaiting backup and the medical examiner.

"The medical examiner will examine the body at the morgue," said the dispatch officer.

"Not for my case. This is clearly connected to the Aytmatov murder. I want an M.E. out here immediately. If not one of yours, contact Dr. Khalil Khan. He's in Biysk and he did the Aytmatov post mortem."

It was one way to locate Khan and demand to know what was going on. It was also dependent upon Khan having left his contact information with the police station morgue. Kazakov prayed that he had.

He disconnected and stood at the doorway, carefully taking stock of the room. One double bed with the cheap quilted satin coverlet rumpled as if someone had lain there. A chair drawn out at the foot of the bed. The way it was positioned, it could be someone wanting to face the dresser for some reason, or it could be that someone sat backward on the chair and faced the bed.

The bright blue jacket lay on the desk chair as if it had been tossed there. Beyond it, an open door gave onto a closet where another bleached cotton shirt hung and a single small rucksack sat on the floor. So perhaps there was nothing nefarious about Zholdosh staying here. Perhaps it was as Osman had said. What did that mean about Enver Pasha getting Zholdosh released?

Beyond the closet, a narrow door gave onto a bathroom that, even from Kazakov's vantage, reeked of mildew. He stepped inside the room and kept as close to the wall as possible to circle the bed until he stood in the bathroom doorway. There, he turned and scanned the body.

Zholdosh lay with his arms at his sides. His hands were bloody as if he'd tried to stop the wound. A fight? The raggedness of the wound suggested that it had been done in a struggle. Either way, it had been fast and effective. A professional?

The question was why. Once he had the motivation, the most likely suspect became clear. Of course that wasn't exactly becoming clear in the Aytmatov case, except that the old woman had seen something she shouldn't have, deep in the mountains. He had even less information here, based on the little he knew of Zholdosh.

The sound of a siren said the police were finally responding. He turned from the body reluctantly. He would have liked to have searched Zholdosh's person, but that was the M.E.'s purview. He hoped that they had found Khan.

Turning from the body, Kazakov flicked on the bathroom light switch. Pink tiles around an equally pink bathtub bore a slimy gleam from a single lightbulb. A brown-stained pink sink stood in one corner beside a yellow-stained white porcelain toilet. Small, coin-sized tiles lay underfoot, but many had chipped loose from their grout over the years. Over the sink hung a small mirrored medicine cabinet. Without stepping into the room, he used a pen to open the cabinet. A shelf held a bottle of aspirin and pills with a name he didn't recognize in a small blue bottle. Khan would have to have them analyzed.

The sound of heavy footfall on stairs turned him around and he retraced his steps close to the wall.

Two uniformed police officers faced him, a third officer behind them.

"Good. You're here. There's one body inside. Man's name is Zholdosh according to my sources." He glanced beyond them.

No Khan.

"I told dispatch to ensure an M.E. was called in."

The older of the three officers shook his head. He had gray hair at the temples, and flat blue eyes as if they let the world bounce off of them. "Our officer on duty said we did not need the expense for a body found in a place like this. He said you can go and we are to take control of the crime scene."

"Like hell you are. This man has been murdered and there is a link between this killing and that of Bermet Aytmatov. I need this scene analyzed before anything is moved."

The officer shook his head, his expression grim. "We have our orders. You can leave on your own or we are to escort you off the premises and preferably out of Biysk."

Kazakov inhaled and closed his eyes.

"Is the duty officer by chance Nikitin?"

The officer nodded.

Kazakov nodded. There would be no reasoning with a territorial man like Nikitin.

"Let me have five minutes to take notes on the scene and then I will leave." He held his breath.

The uniformed officers glanced at each other. Given there were three of them, clearly they had thought there would be a problem.

The lead officer shrugged. "Five minutes, then."

Kazakov returned to the room. He scanned the floor. The worn tan carpet showed nothing other than years of wear. He went to the bathroom and pulled on gloves before confiscating the two bottles of pills, placing them in an evidence bag and pocketed the bag. Then he went to Zholdosh's body to examine the man.

Nothing in his pockets, not even the wallet he should have carried. When Kazakov shifted him to check his back trouser pockets his arms shifted. A deep slash marred the inside of one wrist as if he'd attempted to ward off the killer, but there were bruises on his knuckles, too. Perhaps he'd given as well as taken. Kazakov checked the other arm but found nothing. Had the man that the girl next door had heard been here waiting in surprise or had he been someone Zholdosh knew?

"Kazakov!" called the cop outside the room. "Time's up."

Kazakov leapt to his feet and grabbed Zholdosh's jacket. Something weighed down one pocket. He quickly pulled out the contents and transferred whatever it was to his own pocket, then tossed the jacket back where it was.

He stepped outside and patted his breast pocket where he kept his notebook. "Done. Thanks."

He eased past the uniformed officers and down the stairs, then casually crossed to the Perseus. The whole time he felt the gazes of the officers on his back and waited for them to demand he stop.

When he backed the Perseus out of its spot, they were still watching.

He drove around Biysk feeling dishonorable. Since when had Alexander Kazakov ever removed evidence from a scene? Yes, it was because he wanted to ensure he had all the information, but what if the Biysk Police decided to fully investigate? Surely Nikitin's attitude wasn't shared by everyone. Egorova was a good example of that.

Unless the reason that they had so few murders on their books was *because* they simply refused to investigate them as such. What had the uniformed officer said? A death in such a place? Didn't death count if it occurred in a cheap hotel? Or didn't it count when it involved one of the residents of the old village or the villages in the mountains surrounding Biysk?

The enormity of what this could mean almost overwhelmed him. He pulled the Perseus over and climbed out at the side of the road. His aimless drive had taken him away from the main resorts and into an area that held newly constructed chalets of local stone and steep roofs. A few, the most expensive, probably, were constructed of timber that glowed golden in exterior compound lights. He stood in the cold wind inhaling the scent of spruce and snow and felt the earth turn less solidly under his feet.

What if Biysk Police were akin to their New Moscow brethren, but worse? In New Moscow they would at least take the report of tribal deaths, though not much effort was put into their investigation. What if there had been a lot of deaths in Biysk, but none had been investigated until Bermet Aytmatov? Her place as an elder and the growing unrest amongst the local Kyrgyz had led to him being sent here as an appeasement. A symbol or a sop?

A sop.

"Derr'mo!" And Rostoff had played along! Unless he hadn't known.

He hauled out his phone and dialed.

The smooth voice of the switchboard operator at the New Moscow police department answered the phone.

"This is Detektiv Alexander Kazakov on special assignment in Biysk. I need to speak to Detektiv Chief Inspektor Rostoff. Please connect me through."

"At this hour it is unlikely he will be in his office, Detektiv."

Kazakov took a steadying breath and kept his tone calm. "I realize that. Forward my call to his home. I know you can do that."

"We are not to put calls through to officers without authorization…"

Kazakov wanted to scream. "This is urgent. Rostoff sent me out here on assignment and now everything is going to crap. I need his direction and his help. Now. Please."

He felt as if he was strangling with politeness.

"It is against policy…" said the dispatcher.

Kazakov gave up on control. "Listen here. Put me through, or when I do get in touch with him I will make sure that holy hell lands right on your shoulders. Do you understand?"

He did not like the bully this case was driving him to become.

There was silence on the end of the phone and for a moment he thought he'd been cut off.

"Yes, sir." The answer was curt and he knew he had made an enemy, but the line beeped and then began to ring again. He checked his watch.

Eleven o'clock. Rostoff was not going to be a happy man.

The line clicked as someone picked up.

"Hello?" A young female voice. A daughter, perhaps?

"Detektiv Chief Inspektor Rostoff, please."

He heard a muffled conversation, so if it was a daughter she was well-schooled in what to do when answering her father's calls.

The muffling ended.

"Rostoff." His voice was gruff.

"Kazakov, here. What the hell is going on?"

"And I'll ask the same thing. What the hell are you doing phoning me at home, Kazakov?" The ambient noise changed behind Rostoff's voice so he was obviously relocating within his home.

Might as well cut to the chase. "You sent me up here to appease the locals, didn't you?"

"I sent you up there because you were the best man for the job. You've got those people's trust here. I thought you could do it there, too. God knows no one else has it and I use the best tools I can for a job."

The best tool for the job or an appeasement. Neither were particularly appealing to Kazakov's sense of self. "Do you know what's going on up here?"

"If I knew, do you think I would have sent you? I'd have told them who to arrest and to get on with it—not loan them one of my detectives."

"Tell me something. You can access the data. Was Bermet Aytmatov the only murder reported up here?"

"Did you phone me at home at this hour to ask me that?"

Kazakov knew he had to tread carefully here. "No. I phoned to tell you that there has been a second murder that appears to be connected to the Aytmatov case, but the local police appear to want to shove this one under a carpet. It makes me wonder whether there have been other unreported murders of local people. That would explain the anger and distrust I've found here. I'm not sure what it means, but I would like you to check the reports tomorrow morning. The man's name was Zholdosh. See if the death is even reported. You can phone me on my mobile."

There was silence again and Kazakov held his breath, expecting an explosion over the phone.

"Zholdosh. I will check. What happened to him?"

"I found him in his hotel room with his throat cut."

Rostoff tsk-tsked. "Why were you even there?"

"I was following a lead, of course." Though a lead to what, he wasn't quite sure. Just what did a connection between Zholdosh and Enver Pasha have to do with Bermet Aytmatov's death? In his heart he knew the town of Biysk was far too small for such things to be a simple coincidence.

He clicked off and stood there, eyeing the stars above him. His mother had told him as a child that if he could draw the right connections between them he would unmask the heavens and understand the face of God. Not that he was religious, but his mother had been. When she'd died, he had tried to draw the lines in hopes of finding her again. Of course, it had never worked.

At moments like this, he understood why he was a police officer. He was still trying to find the connections. Except now it was between facts.

He drew his gaze down from the heavens to the expensive, well-lit chalets. In the summer, they would overlook the river and its line of trees with the crags of the mountains beyond. In the winter, they would have the best views of the snow-encrusted mountains and the white lines of the ski hills. And at night would come the soirees and dinner parties amongst the moneyed people who owned these homes.

One of them was Enver Pasha.

He would attend the party.

11

The next morning was cold and clear. Kazakov had spent the night tossing and turning with too many questions. Thankfully, the weather reports suggested that the clear days would hold a little longer. It gave him hope that he might still go after the White Stone Villagers because their tracks would not have been destroyed. His room was snug within its stout stone walls once he placed another log on the fire. Thankfully his wash water was still warm for him when he poured it from the blackened kettle to wash and shave. When he was done, he dressed in his stout canvas trousers and woolen shirt and sweater. Clear as it was, it would be cold outside.

He pulled the faded quilted covers over the bed and sat on the edge and dialed Egorova's number. The line purred in his ear.

"Egorova," said a sleepy voice. He thought he heard another soft voice in the background.

"It's Kazakov. How is it going?"

She sputtered a moment. "Kazakov. It's early."

He checked his watch. "Six o'clock is not so bad. I thought you'd be up."

"I would be. Normally. But Dabria—Constable Smirnova—showed me around New Moscow. It's been a while since I visited."

It made him wonder where she was raised. He'd just assumed it was New Moscow like most of the police.

"Has there been any word from Forensics?"

"They said they would probably have the analysis of Bermet's bag contents for me today. They were also going to check the exterior of the bag for trace evidence of where she had been." The sleep was fully gone from her voice.

"And the paper?"

"The paper. Yes. They say it is simply high-grade paper, much as you said."

"And the marks?" Derr'mo, why was she making him work so hard to get the information from her?

"A crosshatch doodle. I didn't phone sooner because there was nothing to tell."

Kazakov's shoulders sank in disappointment. It had been such a hopeful lead. "All right. I'd appreciate you getting the results back to me as soon as possible. I have a feeling that things are about to crack open. I need you back here."

He hung up and sat thinking. He'd been so certain that there had been something important on that paper. Had Forensics not done the proper tests to check the paper's provenance closely? Had Egorova not asked them properly?

And just where was Khan? He'd disappeared since the events at the Royal Yekaterina Resort though he hadn't been amongst those arrested like so many of the others.

Kazakov turned his phone over in his hands. Finally, he flipped the top open and tried Khan's mobile number. The M.E. had finally been issued such a phone given he was in the field so often.

The line purred and purred again. And again.

After five rings Kazakov was about to hang up, but he heard a click and then nothing.

Was that breathing? He could imagine Khan standing with his phone in his hands. New Moscow had probably been trying to get in touch with him. Did they know of his role in the Royal Yekaterina protest? If there'd been photos, they likely did, just as Rostoff was eventually going to know Kazakov had been there. Khan probably wouldn't answer his phone for fear of the repercussions. Of course, he could be lying low for fear of what had happened to Zholdosh. If he knew. But why answer the phone at all now? And why stay silent? To maintain plausible deniability with his employers? So he could say that his cell phone wasn't working? Maybe he'd been waiting for Kazakov to get in touch with him.

"We need to meet. Breakfast at my place in fifteen." He hung up and exhaled, praying he'd read things rightly and that Khan wasn't avoiding him.

Pocketing his phone, he left his room and went down the hall to the kitchen. Ayim Beshimov sat at the kitchen table, her hands cradled before her, her scarf pulled tight around her graying hair. This morning there was none of her usual bustling energy and her usually rosy cheeks were pale. Her gaze flashed to him when he entered and there were only bleak years in their darkness.

"Detektiv Kazakov. I have been waiting for you." She sounded tired.

He slid into the table across from her. "Are you all right?"

She met his gaze. "I am worried. Aisha is arrested. Taalay is threatening to get involved in more protests. I waited dinner for you yesterday evening, but you were late."

"About dinner, I am sorry. There were many things happening in the case. I tried to have the protesters released, but there seemed to be nothing I could do. Do you wish me to speak to Taalay?"

The old woman nodded. "If you would. That may help. The boy is worried about his mother, but it was her choices that put her in this predicament. She is an adult. Taalay is not."

He nodded. "Ayim Beshimov, there are so many things about this case that I do not understand. Why would an entire village leave their homes and head into the mountains?"

Her gaze narrowed. "The answer is, they would not. Not until the weather turns toward the spring and the passes are open. They cannot risk their flocks."

Kazakov considered. He had not seen any sign of flocks by White Stone Village, nor had there been animal prints on the trail of the villagers. What had happened to the flocks? He felt a belly flutter of excitement. Could this be a clue?

"I saw no sign of flocks at White Stone Village," he said.

Ayim Beshimov shook her head. "You would not. This close to Biysk, they would send them down to lower pastures. Their sons and daughters would come down to care for them."

"Like Meder uulu Jolon."

She nodded. "He has a job here in Biysk, but he also tends his father's herd."

Could there be a motive here for the disappearance of the villagers?

One was hard to imagine unless the case was much more far-fetched than Kazakov could imagine.

"Where is Taalay now?"

"At school."

"Then I will speak with him later when we are both home," he said with conviction.

Ayim Beshimov's grim countenance appeared to brighten. "I am a poor hostess, making you work for your breakfast."

Kazakov grinned. "And I am a poor guest, because I have invited a friend to join us. Khalil Khan, you remember."

She bowed her head. "He will forever be welcome in my home."

Ayim busied herself making tea that she brought him and reheating thick slabs of flat bread. She reheated a thick mutton stew on her wood oven. Kazakov doctored his tea with sweet milk and three spoons of sugar, his spoon clinking in his mug. When he sipped, the heat brought much-needed warmth to his limbs. He hadn't realized he was so cold. In fact, he wasn't physically cold: the kitchen was warm from Ayim Beshimov's cooking.

But a part of him was chilled from this case. There were too many loose threads waving in the wind, and darkness masked the way those thread ends connected. He felt like a blind man flailing in the wind. And now someone else had died. Just how did Zholdosh's murder connect to Bermet Aytmatov's? Did the man even know her?

For that matter, who *was* Zholdosh? Given what Osman had told him, Kazakov had to think that he wasn't from Biysk.

He looked up at Ayim Beshimov as she stirred her pots and used a fork to flip the bread she was heating on top of the metal sheet she laid over the top opening of the clay oven.

"Does the name Zholdosh mean anything to you?"

Her fork faltered in flipping the bread. She shook her head. "It does not. Why?"

"Because Detektiv Kazakov no doubt considers him a suspect," Khalil Khan said as he pushed open the kitchen door.

Had he been standing there listening? Kazakov hadn't heard the outer door open or the tread of feet down the hall.

Khan was clad in the same thick parka he had worn when Kazakov last saw him at the protest. Unlike the usually immaculately turned out M.E. of New Moscow, his chin held a twenty-four-hour bristle and his gaze held the haggard look of someone who had not slept well. He stepped inside the room and settled himself in the chair Ayim Beshimov had vacated. His usually neat hair was uncombed.

"What do you want, besides information to incriminate Zholdosh?" His brittle gaze bore none of the camaraderie Kazakov had always received.

"How about information that might find his killer?"

"What?" Ayim Beshimov spun around.

Khan's gaze widened.

"I found his body in his hotel room last night."

Ayim Beshimov settled two plates in front of them, heaped with stew and bread, and settled herself in another chair as if she was invited.

Kazakov looked at her. "I thought you didn't know him?"

She raised a shoulder in a shrug. "I thought I should not admit it. I have enough troubles."

"He wasn't from Biysk, was he?"

Ayim opened her mouth, but Khan preempted her.

"Not from here. No."

"Who was he?" He looked from Ayim Beshimov to Khan, but the old woman had learned her lesson and was letting Khan take the lead.

Khan's gaze fell away to his plate of food. He used his spoon to stir the stew as if considering whether to answer.

Kazakov sighed and picked up his fork. He tasted the stew—rich with the gamy mutton flavor. He forked up a piece and chewed the tender meat. "Your hesitation is troubling. You understand investigations and how knowing the victim can point to their killer."

"I can vouch that Zholdosh was not connected to Bermet Aytmatov's murder." Khan had still not tried his food.

Kazakov set his fork down. "And how can you be so certain? There are more events intersecting here than meet the eye." He might not know what they were, but he was as certain of it as he was of his own identity.

Khan's refuting glare returned to the plate before him. He nodded. "All right. I stand corrected. How did he die?"

Kazakov told him and watched horror bloom in Ayim Beshimov's gaze. She got up and busied herself cleaning up her kitchen. Pots and pans clanged and banged.

Khan just blinked and looked away. He tasted the food and set his fork down before sitting back. "The last I knew, he was arrested. I barely got away by slipping back and into the crowd when everyone started running. When I heard the scream of "a gun," I knew you'd been right and that the only thing to do was to get out of there. I've been at my friend's house."

Given the state of Khan's appearance, Kazakov doubted it was the truth. What had happened to his friend? To their friendship? Had it all been a mask that he'd been too stupid to see through?

"So who was Zholdosh?" he asked again, though he doubted he would get the full truth from Khan.

"A helper. What you might call a—a strategist. He was going to help us to get our point across to the government. The protest was part of it." Khan met Kazakov's gaze. "You know. You understand the injustice of the system against my people."

Was that earnestness and appeal to the truth or simply a smokescreen?

"Why would Enver Pasha post bail for Zholdosh? Why would a wealthy Ottoman use his own vehicle to drive a tribal man to his hotel?"

Khan's throat worked. He looked away. "Those are questions I cannot answer."

But his gaze said he knew far more than he was saying.

"Where is he from, Khan?"

The M.E. shook his head. His food remained untouched before him. "Let me help you by examining the body and the scene."

"All right." Kazakov stood up, leaving half his delicious breakfast unfinished. "It was wonderful, Ayim Beshimov. As usual, you have outdone yourself, but duty calls."

He motioned Khan to follow him and went down to his room to reclaim his heavy jacket, hat, and gloves.

Khan scanned the magazines stacked by the door as he waited. "This!" he tapped the cover of the top magazine with disgust. "He celebrates how Biysk saved him, but he forgets it was us!"

Kazakov glanced at the magazine as he pulled on his jacket. The cover of the magazine showed a much younger Boris Bure standing with the mountains peaks like a throne behind him. It was from about twenty-five years before. The headline on the magazine was "Miracle Boy."

Kazakov had seen its like before in newspaper articles that reported on the miraculous survival and recovery of seventeen-year-old Boris Bure after his family was killed in a car crash in the mountains. The young Bure had wandered off from the crash and been lost for two weeks in the mountains, wearing clothing that should have guaranteed he would not survive, but he was found by Biysk search parties two weeks later in remarkably good condition. He owed his life to the searchers that had been led by Biysk villagers, but that part of the story rarely got told.

"That is the past, friend," said Kazakov. "We want to ensure there is a future. Or at least I do."

Khan would not meet his gaze.

Together they left the guesthouse and stepped out into the biting cold. Kazakov's phone rang and he picked up.

"It's Rostoff. I've got those answers for you. A man named Zholdosh was killed in Biysk yesterday. Follow-up yielded no evidence or suspects. Checking the records there have been seven deaths in the last three years —most of them sudden."

Kazakov stirred. "But that makes no sense. The people I've spoken to have mentioned a number of deaths and disappearances…"

"Hold on," Rostoff interrupted. "Given your concerns, I checked the records. There were only five people reported missing and they were tourists. All of them."

Kazakov didn't know what to say except thank you for checking. He hung up and silently climbed in the Perseus.

The Perseus's cab seemed to barely contain his anger or the strained silence between him and Khan as Kazakov guided the vehicle back to the run-down hotel where Zholdosh had stayed. The bright sunlight glared off the snow and made silhouettes of the many skiers headed across the road to the ski lifts. Khan hunkered in the front passenger seat, his gaze locked on the world outside the vehicle.

Kazakov glanced at him. The faint scent of garlic and potato filled the cab from their half-eaten breakfast.

"The call was from Rostoff. Apparently Biysk Police have entered Zholdosh's death as 'no evidence and no suspects' so the case can be closed."

Khan's brows rose.

"I didn't mention that you're here, but you should know that you have a number of people worried in New Moscow. The M.E.'s office and Forensics don't know where you are." The Perseus's tires crunched on the slush frozen through the night.

Sighing, Khan shook his head. "It could not be helped. When I heard Bermet had died, I had to get up here. There was no time to go through channels and ask for leave."

"You still could have phoned and told them where you were."

"Yes." Khan continued looking out the window.

"What have you got yourself involved in, Khan? I know you say it is because your people are held down by Ferganese society, but it has to be more than that."

Khan shook his head as Kazakov turned the Perseus onto the main road. "Sometimes the soul of a people comes under threat. The brave will do something about it—to stop it." He glanced in Kazakov's direction and gave a sad smile. "I always thought that was what we had in common."

Kazakov thought about what Khan had said. "I thought so, too."

The trouble was, they were apparently speaking of different people.

"The last time we spoke in New Moscow," said Kazakov, "I thought you were gathering information for the Americans. We talked about the risk this puts you at. And now you're here and the man I once thought was a friend and comrade has disappeared." He glanced sideways at Khan's profile as they cruised past the Royal Yekaterina Resort. The flags he'd seen yesterday snapped in the breeze. Khan turned away and met Kazakov's gaze.

"How did you get away?" he asked Kazakov.

"I didn't. I tried to stop the police from beating your friends and was arrested along with them. I'm waiting for Rostoff to find out."

He turned the Perseus off the main road into the warren of older hotels that the less well-heeled New Moscow citizen might use. At Zholdosh's hotel he turned into the parking lot and parked next to the stairs that led to the dead man's hotel room. They climbed out into the wind and the snow glare. Three vehicles sat pulled up to the two-story hotel with its outdoor verandah running across the second story. There was no one around.

Kazakov led up the stairs, their footfall hollow-sounding on the wooden risers. At the balcony walkway, he led the way to Zholdosh's room. At the entry he stopped.

There was no tape across the door to signify a crime scene. When he tried the door, it opened and found himself face to face with a cleaning woman and his nose full of disinfectant.

"Derr'mo!" he swore. Though he should have expected it, he hadn't thought the room would be cleaned so soon.

The woman—a young tribal woman with black hair coiled up under a kerchief and worn trousers under a stained blue tunic—leapt to her feet and backed away behind her currently silent vacuum cleaner.

Kazakov flashed his badge. "This is a crime scene."

Her gaze flashed to the place where Zholdosh had lain. Wet brush marks showed where she'd been working hard to get the stain out.

"The manager—he told me to clean the room."

Kazakov swallowed down his anger—whether at the situation or himself for overreacting, he wasn't sure. He should have known this would happen. Hell, he could almost believe this was done purposely to thwart him, but that was his paranoia talking. Sighing, he swung back to Khan. "Stay here. I'll be back."

He left and headed down the stairs and across to the office. Inside, he went to the counter.

"Anyone here?" he yelled.

The manager from yesterday appeared from the rear office, wiping his wide mouth in his narrow face free of crumbs. "Can I help you?"

"You remember who I am?" Kazakov growled.

The young man nodded.

"You remember I asked you to write everything down?"

Another nod.

"Good. You have arranged the cleaning of the room very quickly."

Licking his lips, the young man nodded again. "I try to keep on top of things. My boss doesn't like rooms left vacant too long."

Nothing nefarious there.

"Your notes, please."

The young manager shuffled through his papers and came up with a few sheets of lined paper. "I did the best I could," he said eagerly. "It's just there isn't a lot to remember. And I'm inside most of the time."

"Tell me. The woman in the room beside the dead man's. Is she still here?"

The clerk nervously shook his head. "She checked out last night. Said it wasn't safe."

Kazakov sighed. Nothing was easy in this case. "Then I need her name and forwarding address."

Swallowing, the clerk shook his head. "I have a name: Nadia Tolbanova. That is all. There are a lot of youngsters who come here for the work. But I got the sense that after this she was leaving Biysk altogether."

"For where?"

"I—I don't know."

Kazakov closed his eyes in frustration. Then he sighed and scanned the clerk's notes but nothing leapt out at him. "Thank you."

He folded the notes into his pocket and headed back to the room. He would need to run Nadia Tolbanova's name when he was next in the station.

Khan and the cleaning woman were talking as Khan toured the room. He peppered the young woman with questions in Kyrgyz, but she seemed willing enough to answer, though she faltered when Kazakov walked in the door.

He stayed by the door and let Khan conduct his survey of the room. When he was done, Kazakov turned to the girl. "Was there anything left here when you came?"

The girl shrank back behind her vacuum again and shook her head.

"She said she saw the police take the body in a bag and when she came in here there was only the garbage," Khan said. He lifted his chin at an open garbage bag in the corner. "I've been through it. It's been covered in vomit. There's nothing that jumps out at me, but we should probably take it back to the office."

Kazakov nodded and went to the door. He stepped outside and eyed the door to Nadia Tolbanova's room. From inside Zholdosh's room, Khan and the cleaning woman were conversing. Kazakov should have spent more time with the witness last night. He'd been shoddy in his work. Perhaps he was getting too old for this job.

Khan exited the room and joined him on the walkway. "She says the occupant next door checked out, but she has not yet cleaned the room. Do you want to inspect it?"

Kazakov shook his head. "She said Zholdosh had company. She caught only a glimpse of the man."

Khan's gaze widened. "What did she see?"

Kazakov shook his head. "Not much. Dark-haired. Probably Russian, given his coat." He sighed. "It seems this is not to be easy, friend. Can you answer me one thing? Can you think of any reason Bermet Aytmatov and Zholdosh's murders might be connected?"

Khan's gaze slid past his.

Kazakov continued. "Don't you think that it is odd that a community of people like the Kyrgyz of Biysk have two murders in the matter of a week? Doesn't that seem like more than coincidence?"

Khan finally nodded.

"So what is the commonality, Khan? What connects them? Or better still, what connects them that is so difficult for you to share?"

Khan didn't answer. Instead the damned M.E. led the way back to Kazakov's Perseus. "I should examine the body," he said.

Fighting his frustration, Kazakov climbed in the vehicle. He was tempted to just drive away and leave Khan standing there. How Khan could do this just didn't make sense.

Unless it did.

As he drove, he eyed Khan out of the corner of his eye.

Khan simply sat there, but there was a trace of worry around his eyes. Kazakov had seen a similar look when Khan had found evidence of a spy in their midst and when he'd come to a cemetery to check on Kazakov after the Yekaterina Weber murder case.

Kazakov realized he had been approaching the mystery of Khan all wrong. He needed to think about what he knew of the man. Come up with his motivation and there was every chance that Khan's actions would make sense. It might even shed light on the murder cases—at least why Khan wasn't helping.

He turned the Perseus into the Biysk police station parking lot and parked. "I don't think there'll be any problems examining the body, but I could be wrong. I had to throw my weight around to interview Bermet's nephew."

He turned to look Khan in the eyes. "Did you know that Bermet Aytmatov had been taken to an armed camp high in the mountains? Osman didn't know why, but her services were apparently needed. They were taken in and out, blindfolded, by men on horseback. It makes me wonder whether these same armed men might be responsible for her death and the disappearance of the villagers. What do you think?"

"It is a theory." A flash of concern on Khan's face was swiftly smoothed away. He pushed open the door and climbed out into the wind.

Kazakov climbed out thoughtfully. Khan's reaction didn't exactly mean Kazakov's suspicions were correct, but it might mean that he was looking in the right direction. But armed horsemen didn't explain Zholdosh's death.

The two of them climbed the steps to the station and pushed inside. Kazakov showed his badge and they were admitted. He retraced his steps through the busy central squad room—again the officers were inside on the phone, not on the street as he was used to. The busy hum of conversation faded a little as Kazakov and Khan threaded through the desks and seemed to resume when they reached the far hall. Together they went down to the basement morgue and Kazakov stepped back. Khan stepped up to the reception desk.

"Dr. Khalil Khan. I'm here to examine the body brought in yesterday."

The woman looked him up and down. At the moment, with his scruffy beard and worn winter jacket, Khan didn't exactly look doctorly.

"Let me call Doctor Alexeev."

"Do that. I conducted the post mortem on the Kyrgyz woman the other day. You can tell him to meet me in the autopsy room."

Khan ignored the woman's shock and pushed through the gate into the medical offices. Such was the power of a medical degree that the woman didn't protest. Kazakov shrugged an apology at her and followed Khan through the gate. Behind them he heard the receptionist in a hushed telephone conversation. Hopefully it was with Doctor Alexeev and not the police upstairs.

The sterile autopsy room was empty, just a small room with a cold metal table, a bank of sinks and storage cupboards along two walls, and a large wall of cold storage lockers across from the door. It was a lot of body lockers for a town where there was a rarely a reported murder. Accidental deaths? Old age, perhaps? But those shouldn't require an autopsy…

Khan checked a clipboard next to the door and went to the locker bank to pull open one small door. A slab table automatically rumbled out toward him, the body covered in a simple white sheet. He hesitated a moment as if steeling himself and then flipped the sheet back. Zholdosh stared vacantly up at the ceiling.

Khan closed his eyes and swayed a moment. Then he looked up at Kazakov as if seeking understanding. "It never gets easier when it is someone you know."

With Kazakov's help, they shifted the body to a gurney and then rolled it across the floor to the autopsy table. Khan doffed his jacket and donned surgical gown, mask, and gloves. His gaze was inscrutable above the edge of his mask. "If you are going to observe, I suggest you wear a gown."

Kazakov shook his head. "I have a couple of other things to check while I'm here and I want to check that Osman is okay. And the others."

Khan nodded. "I would appreciate knowing as well. They are my friends."

"And family," Kazakov finished and caught the flash of surprise in Khan's gaze. Of course, Khan had already said that Bermet Aytmatov was more than a name to him. If that was the case, then there would be other family connections in the mountains and Khan had been a family man as long as Kazakov had known him.

With no further comment, Kazakov left the M.E. to his job and headed back up to the squad room. He spotted what he wanted—the metallic block with small screen that was the station's data machine situated in the rear corner. He headed for it and settled in the low chair with his back uncomfortably to the room. The chair squealed as he shifted a little sideways to keep an eye on things. The keyboard tray waited before him. He typed in Nadia Tolbanova and set the search for drivers' licenses. The machine hummed a moment and then dinged with an overlong list of possibilities. Kazakov scanned through them, but none was the woman he's spoken to. Not a citizen with a driver's license. He tried school records next, but nothing came up again. Had the woman not been from Fergana? There were a few hardy souls who came from elsewhere to work the ski hills. If that was the case, finding her would be far more difficult.

Sighing, he changed direction and typed in Zholdosh.

"What are you doing?" A uniformed officer came up behind him.

Kazakov looked up and recognized the gray temples and flat blue eyes of the lead officer who had taken over the Zholdosh crime scene, but the officer's voice was more curious than aggressive. Kazakov hit the analyze button. "Running the name of a murder victim as a good investigator will. Or perhaps you have already done so?"

The officer looked from Kazakov to the data machine. His expression said he hadn't thought of doing so. But he stayed as the machine searched its records and then pinged. A green light flashed and then the screen lit up with a list of names and descriptions.

Kazakov scanned down the list, aware that the police officer was reading over his shoulder. "So what do you see?" Kazakov asked.

The officer glanced at him, surprised. "Number four, I think."

"As do I." He looked up at the officer and hit print to receive a copy of what was on screen. The officer was younger than Kazakov had thought at the hotel, and his blue eyes had grown depth and a sense of eagerness that Kazakov had last seen in Chelomeyev's eyes. "I believe you have me at a disadvantage. Yesterday I introduced myself."

A red stain crept up the uniformed officer's neck to his cheeks. "Constable Igor Nedved. Let me apologize for yesterday. We were told we had another dead tribal and to get rid of the body before it caused problems with the tourists."

Kazakov blinked at how this news didn't agree with the official records Rostoff had accessed. "Another dead tribal? How often does this happen?"

Nedved glanced over his shoulder. "There have been a few deaths."

"A few?"

Nedved sighed and Kazakov's estimation of the young officer went down a notch. "Perhaps more than a few."

"Be precise, officer," Kazakov said through clenched teeth.

"Perhaps twenty bodies recovered from the mountains. I cannot be sure. There were more reported as missing."

The room suddenly lacked air.

"Twenty murders?" he asked softly. And more missing.

A shrug, but of embarrassment. "It was hard to tell with some of them. Wild animals, you know. But the villagers claimed they were unnatural and wanted an investigation. That was why you were called in when the old woman died. She was special, I guess."

Kazakov's thoughts swirled with Ayim Beshimov's husband and Aisha's spouse, both lost in the mountains and never seen again. It was true that the mountains were pitiless, but still... No wonder there were so many doubts he would do anything to find what was happening. No wonder Khan was here. No one else was doing anything.

Except Kazakov, and for some reason still none of the Kyrgyz completely trusted him. Khan's reticence suddenly made a lot more sense.

He turned back to the data machine. "When did these deaths and reports of missing persons start?"

"About three years ago, I think. At least that was when the reports increased. Before that there were always a few reported missing and never found."

Kazakov cringed at the thought that for three years a string of murders had gone uninvestigated. He typed in unnatural deaths and missing persons in Biysk and hit the send button again.

The machine hummed. Nedved still stood with him. When the machine dinged again and the green light flashed, Nedved leaned in close enough that Kazakov could smell the heated wool of his uniform.

There was a list of names, far more than the twenty Nedved had suggested. Kazakov felt sick to his stomach as he hit print and waited for the sheaf of paper to finish printing. He looked through the list of names and got angry. Herders. Messengers. A complete family of four gone to visit family and disappeared only to have the bodies found dead and eaten in the snow. Reports of missing persons brought the total to closer to fifty.

Fifty people murdered or missing from tribes that were already claiming they were excluded by their own country. The reports went farther back than three years, too. The first one had occurred almost twenty years ago.

He stood up and turned to Nedved. "Have any been further investigated?"

The younger man thought a moment. "Not that far back. Three years ago the deaths and disappearances were sent on to old Kalnitski, before he retired, and to Egorova to investigate, but nothing came of it. The mountains are rugged. Aside from the tribals and an occasional crazy skier, no one much ventures into them. There was talk of this being the result of some kind of tribal war…"

"Did anyone talk to the village leaders?" Kazakov asked.

"I—I don't know."

But Egorova must have. He went to her desk and picked up her phone and dialed her mobile. It brrred in his ear twice before Egorova picked up.

"It's Kazakov. I'm looking at some records of past missing and murdered tribals in Biysk."

There was uneasy silence on the phone.

"Ye-es," she said cautiously.

The storm of anger swirling in his gut threatened to vomit out of him. Instead he closed his eyes and squeezed the phone. "Why wasn't there an investigation?"

Another pause. "There was. At first. My partner and I did what we could, but the bodies were found weeks, sometimes months, after they died. There wasn't much left to go on."

As if that was excuse. "So you're saying that there are open files on these cases?"

"No-oo." Another pause. "There wasn't much we could do, was there? So we closed the files."

"And didn't open files for others."

Silence again.

"Didn't you think these deaths and disappearances might be relevant to the Bermet Aytmatov case?"

"I thought—well, if there had been something that connected them, I would have mentioned them."

"When will you be back?" he asked because he could barely stand to speak to her at this moment.

"Kazakov, I'm sorry. I had no intention of keeping things from you. Bermet's death seemed totally unrelated and occurred so close to the village that it didn't seem connected to disappearances in the mountains. Truly, I just never thought…"

"When will you be back?" he repeated.

"Late tonight."

"Then I will see you in the morning." He hung up and slumped back in the chair, thinking, until he became aware of Nedved still there, still looking at him.

"What are you doing tomorrow?" Kazakov asked, looking up at the young man.

"It's my day off. I was planning on reading and studying for the corporal's exam."

"How do you feel about helping with this investigation?"

Nedved's already blue gaze brightened. "Yes!"

"It will mean a long day of hiking."

"I've hiked before."

"Then come to my guesthouse at five in the morning." Kazakov wrote down Ayim Beshimov's address and stood. With a nod and thanks for his assistance, he left Nedved behind and headed back to the morgue.

Khan was still there, his lips moving in silent words as his bloodied, gloved hands sutured up Zholdosh's chest.

"So? What do we know?" Kazakov asked.

"It was a swift death. He wasn't caught by surprise. There was a fight, but a single slash to the neck finished him. He died due to exsanguination from the neck wound. Not surprising, I know. The cut was quick."

"Professional?" Kazakov asked.

Khan's gaze flickered. "Perhaps not."

"Any evidence found in his belongings?" Kazakov asked as he assimilated the information.

"Nothing that shows up on examination. Maybe at the micro-level, but I doubt…" he lifted his chin at the upper floor and the police, "I doubt they will be willing to pay for the tests."

Kazakov dug in his pocket for the evidence bag with the pill bottle he'd confiscated the day before from the crime scene. "What's this? I found it in Zholdosh's room."

Khan read the label and swallowed. He looked Kazakov in the eyes as if he did not want to answer, but he knew Kazakov could get the answer in other ways.

"A medication used for altitude sickness. It is not used commonly because of possible side effects due to the low blood pressure the user experiences. In the worst cases it can cause oxygen deprivation to the brain and thus brain damage."

Working his neck, Kazakov tried to fathom what this might mean.

"Odd that a man born of mountain stock and raised in the mountains has that kind of problem."

Khan didn't answer.

Kazakov pulled the data machine printouts from his other pocket and laid them on the counter before Khan.

"It seems we have a lot to talk about, old friend."

Khan turned a veiled gaze up at him. Then he straightened as if reaching a decision.

"Perhaps it is time."

12

———————

The sun had already passed zenith in the southern sky and was placing long shadows in the snow as the afternoon and evening shoved it aside. The colors had already taken on a rosier hue. Such were the atmospherics in the mountains. An ice-crystal rainbow encircled the sun as Kazakov and Khan slogged through the snow at the edge of the road and turned into the Royal Yekaterina parking lot. There was a good café inside, according to Khan.

The glass lobby doors slid open and then shut behind them as they stepped into warmth. A huge stone hearth filled the rear of the lobby, but the deep armchairs clustered in its heat were empty. The walls were ornately carved and painted in cream and gilt with massive antique-looking paintings of Russian nobility and long-lost landscapes. Overhead, the ceiling bore more of the cream paint and gilt moldings around a round painting of the original Yekaterina after whom the resort was named. Though the artist had placed a curve on her lips, the old tsarina's gaze was cold as she peered sternly down at them. A thick, acre-wide Bokhara carpet covered the massive tiled lobby floor, and tables in the corners held huge, tropical flower arrangements.

The place was altogether more opulent and more disappointing than even the domes of the faux Saint Basil's Cathedral in New Moscow. Here guests were asked to imagine themselves as members of long-lost Russia's royalty. Would his people never set aside the past and live for now and the future? If this place was any indication, it was doubtful.

Inhaling the heady perfume of the flowers, Kazakov followed Khan across the room to a café called the Palace. Blindingly white tablecloths matched the snow outside. Clusters of diners inhabited the tables, the air humming with the clink of cutlery and quiet voices. Khan chose a table in a corner and Kazakov settled uncomfortably across from him.

"You seem to have come here before," Kazakov said.

Khan smiled. "When I visit Biysk. It reminds me why I do what I do."

Kazakov sat back as a waiter arrived at the table.

"Tea, please," Khan said.

"Make that two."

The waiter nodded and left. Kazakov turned back to Khan. "And what is it that you do, Khan?"

The M.E. cocked his head. "You're not stupid, my friend. What do you think?"

"You help your people. You as much as told me that. But what that involves I have no idea." He met Khan's dark, inscrutable gaze.

Khan had the good grace to look away. "You know about my aid to the American, Eric Clinton."

"Your spying."

Khan winced. "I only reported what I saw and heard. There was nothing done to undermine our government."

"You're splitting hairs, Khan."

Khan nodded. "My help was in trade. There was no help for my people from Ferganese authorities even though we asked. So I went elsewhere. The Americans traded medicines and—supplies."

"Weapons?" Kazakov thought of the armed camp reportedly in the mountains.

The waiter brought their teas in fine bone china cups and saucers with a tea pot between them. Khan played mother, pouring the tea and then stirred in his sugar and milk. Kazakov waited, his tea steaming in front of him. Finally, Khan glanced up at him. He shook his head. "The Americans wanted Fergana to remain intact—an ally. They would not provide weapons that could be used against such a purpose."

"And you know this because your people asked. Or you did."

Khan's gaze became shuttered. "You leap to conclusions. But don't my people have a right to defend themselves?"

Kazakov tried his tea. It was strong and bitter on his tongue even with the milk and three sugars he'd added. "I suppose the question is against whom those weapons would be used."

Khan set his cup down. He leaned over the table and lowered his voice. "You know how we are treated. You've said it's not right. Why are you doing this?"

"Because I need to solve a murder—two murders. And I need your help."

Leaning back in his chair, Khan chewed his lip. "I fear we may find ourselves on opposite sides in this thing."

"Try me." Kazakov took another sip of his tea.

"You've said yourself that there are concerns about the outcome of this election."

Kazakov nodded.

"We—my people—have seen the writing on the wall for far longer. Yes, there have always been prejudices against us, but over the past few years it has become something darker. In the cities and towns, crimes are committed against us and go uninvestigated. Our people are tried and convicted of crimes they did not commit. Then our people began disappearing or turning up dead in the mountains that had always been our home and refuge."

He shook his head. "It was as if the entire universe was arrayed against us. And then six months ago this election brought forth rhetoric that blamed us for the ills of the country. Someone planted bombs in the city and we were blamed as if our demands for equality and our racial links to the Ottomans were enough to make us the enemy."

Khan's words were alarming—and painfully sad. Kazakov swallowed back his anger that attitudes in Fergana had brought Khan and his people to this crossroads. Staying silent was difficult, but he held his tongue to allow Khan to tell his story. Let the M.E. decide how far to go—how far to incriminate himself and his people here in Biysk.

"Men trained in the mountains so they could defend us. They patrolled. For a while it seemed the deaths and disappearances stopped. Then Bermet Aytmatov was killed."

Khan's hands lay open on the table as if he had exposed everything to Kazakov. Could he believe Khan? The M.E. had kept things from him before and there were so many details Khan had glossed over—like where the patrols got their weapons. Surely they didn't depend on the archaic rifles Kyrgyz families held.

Kazakov sighed and nodded. He would believe what Khan had said, but would reserve judgement about what the M.E. had left out. Hopefully, Khan would gradually fill Kazakov in.

"And Zholdosh was murdered, as well. But he is not from here. When I saw him, my first thought was that he was taller and broader than other Kyrgyz. That's the truth because he isn't Kyrgyz, is he? Uzbek, perhaps? Lowland Uzbek?"

The inscrutability of Khan's gaze was the answer. Kazakov was on the right track. The man had been a leader and clearly treated with respect, even by Khan. But what was an Uzbek lowlander doing here in the mountains?

In the city, both tribal groups faced the same problems. Was that all it was? Was that enough to make a lowland Uzbek risk his health by taking the medication that allowed him to be here?

No, the stakes had to be higher to get a man to such a thing.

"He was sent here, wasn't he? He was sent…" Kazakov thought of all he knew. "He was sent by the Ottomans. That was why Enver Pasha plucked him from the police station."

The clatter of crockery breaking gave Khan an excuse to look away.

Kazakov waited, inhaling the late luncheon scents of stew and pizza, but Khan said nothing.

"Are you a fool?" Kazakov leaned over the table, his tea forgotten. "You're doing the very thing Bure preaches as the danger of your people! You're proving him right!"

"Do you think I don't know that?" Khan's gaze flashed as he turned back to the table. "I warned them, but these people felt they had no choice. They were armed with antique rifles. You saw what happened when my house was attacked. Five good men lost their lives. They needed something they could depend on!"

Not we. They. Did the distinction mean anything?

Khan's harsh whisper was like a freezing wind. Kazakov scrubbed his face with his hands. This was worse than he'd thought. As bad as it could be, given two murders and the disappearance of a village's people.

And now he, by knowing this, was part of it.

Unless he reported what he'd learned.

The lunchtime scents coiled deliciously around him, but he didn't know whether he'd ever be hungry again. The Ottomans. The Ottoman enemy operating here in the Ferganese mountains.

A visceral part of his Russian soul shuddered for all he'd considered himself enlightened. There was too much ancient animosity bred in his bones and reinforced in everything around him. The Ottoman army had done horrific things to the people of Moscow when the city fell. That it was payback for Russian atrocities in the Crimea didn't make the Russian hate diminish. Nor, apparently, had time healed those wounds.

Khan waited silently across the table, his hands palm down on the table as if he had laid down all his cards. The man Kazakov had thought was his friend had worn a mask just as well at the tsarina in the fairy tale had worn her pigskin. He'd never realized what was underneath.

A traitor, as Bure would name him? A pseudo-Ottoman, or at least someone who desired to become an Ottoman? Or an absolute loyalist, but with loyalty to his people and willing to do what it took to ensure his people's survival?

The latter fit more with the man he knew.

Sighing, Kazakov nodded. "All right. That places a context around the case. Thank you for telling me."

Khan blinked and then shook his head, a slow smile curving his lips. "You continue to amaze me, old friend. I did not think you would take this so well. I should have known better. You are a man—a Russian—but you are first and foremost a detective. I should have known."

Perhaps it was meant as a compliment, but Kazakov realized most men would not have responded as he had. He was a man with few connections —a cat, a neighbor, the M.E. he worked with—afloat in the world. Maria was dead because of him. Pavel Chelomeyev might as well be, given his condition.

But that was the past and he would not live his life possessed by ghosts.

"So who was Zholdosh?" he asked.

"You already know the most important part," Khan said and lowered his voice. His gaze held the same strain Kazakov had seen when Khan's family had been hostages. "Zholdosh was an operative whose task was to activate our people—get them ready to defend themselves."

"So the armed camp in the mountains is a training camp?"

"It *was*."

The emphasis on past tense caught Kazakov's attention. "Was?"

"When your warning about the protest proved to be true, I managed to escape, but most of the others did not. It got me thinking that someone had known what we were about to do and had reported on us. That got me thinking about the tracks in the mountains. Men on horseback." He shook his head.

"The only way the people of White Stone Village would have abandoned their homes would be if they were forced out. That would have to be with armed men. It got me wondering if the camp could have done this for some reason. I spent last night in the mountains hiking to the camp. I needed to find out what was going on."

Khan closed his eyes and weariness settled over him as if he relived his long trek.

"There was no camp anymore." His eyes opened and looked bleakly across the table.

"What are you saying? Had they moved on?"

A small shake of Khan's head, then he leaned over the table. "They were dead. Every last one of them, including the women who cooked for them. Shot. A few shot execution-style, so they must have been taken prisoner first. And there was more…"

A growing horror filled Kazakov's gut. "White Stone Village."

Khan nodded. "They were there, their bodies with the others. They were executed."

The restaurant scents churned Kazakov's stomach, but at the same time things began to make sense.

"Does anyone else know?" Kazakov asked.

Khan shook his head. "There would be an army leaving Biysk if I they knew. Thankfully, most of the men are currently in jail."

"A blessing in disguise, perhaps." Kazakov thought a moment. "So it seems likely that Bermet Aytmatov was at the camp when something happened or someone came. Perhaps whoever killed the lot of them. Perhaps Bermet saw the killing and got away, but was seen. They couldn't afford for word to get out about what had happened, so they tracked her and caught up with her at White Stone Village."

"But why take the entire village away? Why slaughter them?" Khan whispered.

"There must have been something about who they were… But I don't understand why Zholdosh had to die and who killed him. The same people?"

Khan looked thoughtful as his gaze dipped to the table. "Perhaps not the same people, but connected in some way?"

Kazakov nodded. "People wanting the same outcome, perhaps."

"What outcome is that?" Khan asked softly.

"To stop Ottoman interference. That might be part of it." But not all. Definitely not all. He mentally took a step back from the events that had happened to examine the larger picture, but there were still hazy areas like clouds over the sun.

Or a pigskin over a tsarina.

13

─────────

The makeshift office that Kazakov, Khan, and Egorova had established was warm with the pine-scented heat from the little wood stove in the corner. The lone swinging lightbulb placed shifting shadows on the stone walls and the low rafters. The original desk was empty, but Khan and Kazakov stood at the second makeshift table. Kazakov pulled the bagged evidence from Bermet Aytmatov's murder from the file box he'd stored it in and set it before Khan.

"I sent Egorova to New Moscow forensics with Bermet's bag for analysis."

"Anything of particular interest?" Khan asked as he slid the old woman's clothing out of the bag and spread it on the tabletop. If there was evidence to find on the old woman's clothing, Khan would surely find it.

"All her medicines, of course. And there was a packet of leaves wrapped in an unexpectedly high gloss paper for Bermet to have in her possession. I wanted to know where it was from. I thought there were marks on it, too. Maybe something that might mean something, but according to Egorova, Forensics says there was nothing useful."

Khan frowned as he examined the clothing. "Here are the gunpowder traces." He pointed to the back of the old woman's dress. "Here is the knife slash."

He slid his hand into the dress's pockets and then pulled it out again. A small piece of what looked like dried leaf between his fingers. "And what is this, then?"

He placed it on a clean piece of paper and Khan and Kazakov leaned down to inspect it. "It looks similar to the leaves that were in the paper packet." Kazakov said.

"And what were they?" Khan asked thoughtfully.

"I don't know. Egorova simply said the packet told us nothing. Just herbal leaves."

"Let's see." Khan pulled a mobile phone out of his pocket and dialed a number. He tapped his hand on the table as he waited.

The other end picked up.

"It's Khan, here." He held the phone away from his ear for a moment. "I'm in the mountains. There was a family death. Yes. I know I should have sent word to you, but at the time it was very low on my priorities." He listened a bit longer.

"Listen, can we save this until I return? I have fallen into a case and am supporting Detektiv Alexander Kazakov in a murder investigation. A Detektiv Egorova brought some evidence down for analysis. I need you to check the results for me."

He provided the deceased's name and waited until finally whomever he was speaking to came back on the phone. "There was a glossy paper packet. White. There were leaves in the packet and thoughts that there might be marks on the paper."

Kazakov nodded at Khan's description.

Khan frowned. 'You're certain? Is there any chance that the evidence could have been misplaced?"

His frown deepened, but he thanked whomever he talked to and clicked off his phone. Then he turned a troubled gaze to Kazakov. "Egorova was there and brought evidence for analysis, but the file doesn't mention anything about a paper packet and leaves."

"But I talked to her about it. She took photographs before she left. There has to be a mistake."

Cocking a brow at him, Khan shook his head. "You heard me. There's no mistake. The better question is what it means."

Kazakov found one of the room's rickety chairs and sat down. "What, indeed. Either Egorova didn't give them the packet or someone in New Moscow removed that information from the file."

From his initial rocky meeting with Egorova, he'd thought that they had reached an understanding. He'd trusted her to do her job. He didn't want to think that the missing evidence was due to her.

"She should be back some time this evening," said Kazakov. "We will ask her. And have you examine the paper if she still has it."

Another cock of Khan's brow.

Could Egorova be part of the problem? She, like Kazakov, was Russian, and he'd had issues with other detectives before…

Kazakov nodded and sighed. "Highly unlikely if what we suspect is true."

He felt tired and defeated. "What the hell is going on, Khan?"

"Something big. Something that someone does not want us knowing about—enough to kill a band of armed men and an entire village."

Enough to corrupt a young detective. Kazakov scrubbed at his face, hating that he had to suspect everyone. "And the people behind it can reach right into Biysk." And New Moscow, it seemed.

Kazakov checked his watch. It was almost six. "I have a party to go to." He shook his head, feeling entirely disinterested in going. "Don't look so surprised. It's part of the investigation. Enver Pasha has a party at his house. But I suppose you already know that."

Khan's gaze was veiled again.

"Should we go together?" Kazakov asked. "Meet me back here in an hour and we can wait for Egorova and then head over in the Perseus."

Khan helped repack the evidence and then pulled on his jacket. He looked down at himself and rubbed the beard on his chin. "Give me an hour and a half to clean up. If Egorova arrives before me, wait."

And then he left, the stout wood door banging shut behind him. Kazakov packed away the evidence box, still not fathoming what had happened to the paper evidence. Could whoever was responsible for the massacre in the mountains actually reach down into New Moscow forensics? It was reasonably possible that they could reach into Biysk. But how could they reach New Moscow? To what end? He just didn't see the connection. Why kill all those people?

Working backward, it seemed that the villagers were killed because they helped Bermet and had perhaps seen those that killed her. Bermet was killed because she saw the massacre at the armed camp. But why was the armed camp destroyed? And the outlier was Zholdosh. He wasn't connected to what happened in the mountains.

Or was he?

Had he witnessed Bermet Aytmatov's murder? Did he know something about the camp?

Wood popped in the little fireplace, sending a surge of heat roaring up the chimney. In the yellow glow of the single lightbulb, Kazakov suddenly straightened.

Enver Pasha. Zholdosh had been with him just before he was killed. Perhaps the dead Ottoman spy had told his master what he knew. Or perhaps Enver Pasha had had a hand in creating the armed camp in the mountains, through his creature Zholdosh!

Which meant that there was someone beyond the Ottomans doing the killing and Enver Pasha might be next on the killing list. Hell, for all Kazakov knew, the man could already be dead.

Kazakov leapt up and grabbed his coat. He slammed out of the room and locked the door, then ran down the corridor pulling out his phone. He paused to stick his head into the kitchen.

Ayim Beshimov was up to her elbows in flour, kneading dough for her flatbread. She looked up at his intrusion. "You sound like a herd of cattle in my home."

He was taken aback for a moment. "Sorry. I have to go out. Khan or Egorova might arrive. Please make them comfortable for me."

He left and punched in Khan's number.

"Khan."

"Listen. You're on your own getting to Enver Pasha's tonight. I'm headed there now." As he unlocked and climbed into the Perseus he explained what he suspected.

"I'm coming with you."

"No. You're not. You're not a police officer and you aren't armed."

There was silence on the phone and Kazakov looked heavenward.

"Even if you're armed, you're not coming. Get yourself cleaned up and come later. Or come to the guesthouse to meet with Egorova. I'll take care of Enver." He clicked the phone closed and put the Perseus in gear, then spun his wheels heading down the road.

Unsurprisingly, Enver Pasha's home sat amongst the richly appointed homes along the road at the far end of town. The address Enver had given him turned out to be a compound with solid walls made of pale mountain stone that flanked a tall, spiked-iron gate. Beyond the gate, in the shadows of early evening, the land swept down through a field of snow and scattered trees to a well-lit, faintly Byzantine house with many angled roofs that poked above a copse of blue spruce that must grow near the river. The gate was closed, presumably because Kazakov was an hour early for the event.

He eased the Perseus up to a call button and pushed. An intercom beeped.

"Yes?" A hollow-sounding feminine voice asked.

"Detektiv Kazakov for Enver Pasha."

"One moment," the voice said and the intercom crackled and fell silent.

Kazakov tapped his fingers impatiently on the steering wheel. Then the gate buzzed and silently opened like a portal into an ancient stronghold. Perhaps it was.

He drove the Perseus through and noticed the gate slowly close behind him. So the Ottoman had his security, but security that could be overcome. He drove down the long, curved driveway, noting cross-country ski tracks intersecting the snow. The Perseus reached the last stand of trees and passed under their boughs.

He drove into what he could only consider an inner compound within the larger grounds. Strategically placed spotlights lit the area and highlighted a slim, domed tower with a small balcony at the top, presumably for the Islamic call to prayer. The three-story house was built of the same white stone as the outer walls, but here it was smoothed until it shone, except for ornate friezes of swirls and floral patterns over each door and window. A broad expanse of snow spoke of lawns in broad terraces that were stepped up to the house as if it was built on its own small mount.

The whole gave a sense of grandeur and awe that Enver Pasha must have planned.

Kazakov shook his head at the amount of money people would spend to make a statement and urged the Perseus forward along the curved driveways toward the front door.

A broad, arched portico led to a black wood and strapped iron door that might better guard a fortress. To either side crouched stone lions, their fangs revealed in matching snarls. Kazakov pulled up between the lions and climbed out of the Perseus. A cold wind off the mountains blasted into him as if to warn him off the mountain king's home.

For a moment he hesitated. Then he straightened and strode up to the door.

Before he could knock, the door swung open.

He faced a woman.

She was tall and broad-shouldered, with lovely olive skin over high cheekbones that appeared to tilt her almond eyes. Long hair, black as raven wings, was pulled back tightly into a coil at the nape of her neck. She wore a simple black sheath dress and demure pearls and, though her coloring was darker, the suspicious way she eyed him and the alertness of her pose reminded him of another woman standing in another doorway owned by Enver Pasha. Olga Gruenwald had been just as alert and observant and she had been Enver's paid assassin and bodyguard.

At least Kazakov suspected so.

"Detektiv. Welcome. We were expecting you, though perhaps not at this time."

She stepped aside to allow him entry and he stepped inside.

Into a hall of wonders.

The white stone of the mountains had been smoothed to white pavers across a grand foyer. A white forest of carved columns made up the walls, their lengths carved with mosaic designs, and the ceiling was an eggshell dome that soared above the hall as if it tried to capture God's presence in the room. A single black round table sat alone at the epicenter of the room beneath the dome. It held only a spray of huge white, sweet-scented blooms in what looked like a Persian vase. To either side, dark wood doors carved in more abstract designs blocked his view of the closed rooms, but beyond the table, a broad staircase rose two flights to the next floor where a balcony ran above the hall. To either side of the stairs, two broad hallways led deeper into the depths of the house. For all its light color, the heavy stone made it feel like he'd stepped into a tomb or mausoleum.

"Enver Pasha should be down to meet you momentarily." She stayed where she stood by the door, but said nothing more. Instead she swayed lightly on the balls of her feet, like a fighter.

Kazakov's breath seemed to echo in the expansive entry. When he moved, the rustle of his clothing was overloud.

"You are Enver's secretary?" he said.

Her lush lips curved in a slight smile. "Housekeeper."

Just as Olga Gruenwald had been Enver Pasha's previous "housekeeper." Kazakov tracked his gaze across the expansive house. "That must keep you very busy."

She cocked a brow demurely. "I have help."

And it was highly unlikely that those perfectly manicured fingers cleaned anything in this pristine house.

A soft tread came from above and Enver Pasha appeared above them on the balcony like some heroic figure.

"Kazakov! You're early!" The Ottoman smiled as he lightly came down the stairs and greeted Kazakov by shaking Kazakov's hand. Enver was dressed in dark gray trousers pleated at the front and butter-soft black moccasins. His shirt was saffron yellow and set off his darker skin and brought out the amber in his eyes so that there appeared to be coals behind his gaze. A single gold signet ring adorned the little finger of his left hand.

"You haven't taken his coat, Marta. You need to always take his coat." He turned back to Kazakov. "Please excuse her. She is new to her role in this household."

"A replacement for Olga?" Kazakov asked.

Enver cocked his brow. "I suppose we shall see. Olga was with me a long time."

Though what that meant in Enver's world escaped Kazakov. There seemed little loyalty in Enver's world.

The woman, Marta, nodded and slipped Kazakov's jacket off his shoulders.

Enver Pasha's gaze raked over him and widened the barest fraction. "You do understand this is a party, Kazakov. I could possibly loan you some clothes if you have nothing else to wear."

"I'm not here for your party. I'm conducting an investigation and I believe that you may be in danger."

Enver's gaze widened. "Truly? My, my, my. How this visit must have cost you! I'd have thought you'd be happy if I was killed."

"Not when you might have information crucial to my investigation."

Enver Pasha must have seen something in Kazakov's expression, for he suddenly nodded. "Marta. We will have tea in my office."

He nodded Kazakov to follow him and led him down the hall to the right of the stairs to the second door along the hall. He let Kazakov precede him through the door.

Thankfully, the white mausoleum opulence ended here. This was a working man's office with none of the pretentions Kazakov had experienced at Enver Pasha's New Moscow business office. The walls were lined with full bookshelves and the air had the taint of age and dust. The book spines had the worn look of time and frequent reading and Kazakov would not be surprised if Enver Pasha had read them all many times. From the titles he could see, many were history—and not just Ottoman history either. He saw ancient Greek, Germanic, Chinese, and even American tomes. He glanced down at Enver, who had settled himself behind a busy man's desk. Papers were in neat stacks, most of them in a tray Kazakov suspected would be for work completed. Enver Pasha was that kind of man. He would not let work collect for long.

Enver steepled his fingers in front of him. "So? What has you so concerned for my safety."

"I followed you the other day. I saw you get Zholdosh released and followed you to his hotel and then to your home. How do you know Zholdosh?"

Enver pursed his lips and studied his fingers, then met Kazakov's gaze. "How do you think?"

"Let's put it this way: you didn't just happen to pick him out of a police lineup. And he didn't just happen to be here in the mountains. You sent him to help arm the mountain people. So don't play games with me, Enver."

"I see." Enver spoke quietly. "I met Zholdosh in Constantinople. He was in university, but he came with a unique set of skills given his father had led guerilla fighters against the Chinese in the Burmese highlands."

The eastern subcontinent was a simmering cauldron of border disputes between the two behemoth empires.

"I asked him if he was interested in a—liaison role between myself and his cousins, the Kyrgyz of Fergana. He said yes. So when he was in trouble with the police, I, of course, bailed him out."

What had begun as a slow careful choice of words had become a rapid recitation as Enver sorted out his falsehood.

Kazakov nodded. "Do you know how I can contact his family?"

"His family?" Enver Pasha frowned.

"To advise them that their son is deceased. I went back to his hotel after you left him, but someone had been there before me. Zholdosh had his throat slit by someone who knew what he was doing."

Enver's face had paled.

"After considering the evidence, I believe Zholdosh may have come by information pertinent to my investigation into the death of Bermet Aytmatov, and that he may have told you this information. That is why I think he was killed and that is why I think you may also be at risk."

Enver remained silent. In shock? In fear? Or was that calculating mind of his spinning through the lies he might tell. Then he sagged back in his chair.

Kazakov waited for Enver to speak first. He read the struggle in

Enver's face. He was not a man given to the truth. Mostly he considered what this turn of events meant for himself and his country and how he might turn it to his favor.

"I see." Enver finally nodded. "I suppose your conclusion is reasonable, but I do have my security."

"Marta? And how is she to be at your side during an entire party? It is impossible. And given what I know of these killers, I highly suspect a bodyguard will not stop them, nor will a crowd of innocent people. You know, of course, of the missing people in the mountains?"

Enver nodded.

"I believe their disappearances are related." Kazakov repeated his theory, tracing back Bermet's last hours and the resulting destruction of White Stone Village, but he left out the destruction of the armed camp and finding the villagers dead. "These killers will stop at nothing to achieve their goal."

Sighing, Enver nodded. "The Kyrgyz became worried when the disappearances began. They got no assistance from the Biysk authorities, so they came to me. I offered to help by funding an advisor for them."

So this was the way Enver would reshape his story. He wasn't a spy. He was simply funding an advisor.

"The Kyrgyz began to patrol the trails that their people most often used. But still people disappeared. So did some of their patrols. They had to do something. Their ancient arms obviously didn't help them, so they asked for arms and training. Zholdosh helped them. They established a training camp in the mountains."

"A training camp that has been completely destroyed."

"What!" Enver came out of his chair and stood.

Kazakov looked up at him mildly and nodded. "Destroyed, most probably the last time Bermet was there, but she escaped and so they tracked her and killed her and killed the villagers as well. There is something going on in these mountains, Enver. Zholdosh knew what it was. He told you. I need you to tell me what it is."

Enver sank back into his chair, all the superior certainty dissolved from his countenance. "Allah preserve us."

Diminished and clearly shaken, he met Kazakov's gaze. "They are in your mountains. I hoped—no, I prayed that the Kyrgyz might stop them and so find themselves and their strength that they might stand to shoulder-to-shoulder with their Russian and, dare I say, Ottoman brethren."

They? Kazakov wondered, but he would not interrupt, for fear of stopping this unusual flow of information from the Ottoman.

"But from what you tell me, it has not worked," Enver continued, with a shake of his head. "Zholdosh told me that Kyrgyz trackers came upon signs of another outpost higher in the mountains southwest of here. If that is the case, then they have infiltrated much farther than anyone thought and are almost into Ottoman territory. Zholdosh said that they were sending out an armed party to deal with it."

Outpost? Infiltrated? Uneasiness had Kazakov stirring in his chair.

"The armed party must have failed," Kazakov said softly. "And so they brought the ire of their enemies down upon them. That must have been what Bermet escaped from."

"But they had guards, outposts, warning systems," Enver protested.

"That didn't work," Kazakov said to keep the man talking. Surely, eventually, everything would become clear. "Or perhaps they came under false pretenses. In this case, I've learned everyone wears a mask, a pigskin to hide what they really are."

As he said it, he was certain that he had the right of it. They came supposedly offering peace, a truce, and perhaps even bearing gifts. Yes! That was it. And an old woman stole something from this gift as proof of what had happened. They hadn't realized it initially. But someone eventually had.

Kazakov stood up. "What is the location of this other installation? Zholdosh must have told you."

"He—from what I can tell, it's remote and almost impossible to get to unless you find the right path. His men only stumbled onto it themselves."

Zholdosh's men. The implications of that were staggering and Kazakov's stomach clenched. But there was surely only one enemy that could cause such concern in the man before him. Since the death of Yekaterina Weber, he had been confronting the enemy—the despised Ottomans in the person of Enver Pasha. But there were other enemies of Fergana, lesser known, but always out there, threatening.

The Chinese.

14

———————

From beyond Enver Pasha's office doors came household sounds—hurried footsteps from deeper in the house, voices of household staff and caterers—as the last-minute preparations for Enver's party were completed. The office ticked around Kazakov as he considered the man in the buttery leather chair across the well-used desk. Beyond the chair, bookshelves held well-thumbed hardcover tomes including *The Art of War* by Sun Tzu. A Chinese book.

Was this all a ruse? A ploy? Was Enver Pasha still wearing a mask, one Kazakov was too obtuse to see through?

Enver Pasha's smooth countenance told him nothing. He sat behind his desk with one hand over the other on the top of his desk. His black eyes glittered with amber highlights and his black hair was a slick blanket across his skull, only matched by the luxuriant moustache that guarded his mouth. Enver Pasha was a man who would only tell Kazakov what he wanted to—more so, because Kazakov had bested him once before.

"You wish to go there," Enver said. "The fact there is an unknown installation in your country is bad enough. The fact that men from there appear to have killed your old woman and wiped out my camp would seem to make us allies in this, at least."

His words weren't far off from Kazakov's own thinking. But to trust this man—this Ottoman. Every part of him resisted the idea.

He stood up and paced to the window that gave onto the spotlit garden.

Low bushes were dark stains against the snow. Beyond the garden the curved driveway had become a processional of well-lit vehicles heading for the house from the main road. Enver Pasha's idea of a party was a wee bit larger than Kazakov's. And grander.

He turned back to the man and felt like the tables were turned from last time they had negotiated. This time Kazakov was at the disadvantage because he had nothing to point to the location of the outpost in the mountains.

Shadows seemed to fill the hollows of Enver's face, accentuating his high cheekbones and his deep-set eyes. The man was older than Kazakov had originally assessed him to be. At least in his early-sixties, if not older.

"I am not in this alone. I have people I must consult," Kazakov said. Khan's opinion in this would be important. And then there was Egorova. He needed to determine exactly what had happened with the Bermet Aytmatov evidence before he even brought her into the conversation.

"If it means anything, I am mounting a party to the camp and then on to the Chinese installation. We leave tomorrow. You are welcome to come."

Kazakov paused. It was so tempting to agree. He wanted to see this through to the end, but working with Enver Pasha was simply too foreign an idea.

"Thank you for your information. I will get back to you."

Kazakov left Enver in his office and retraced his way to the foyer. Now there was soft Ottoman music coming from a doorway to a room beyond the foyer. It sounded like it came from an orchestra, rather than a recording. Men and women lingered in the foyer, dressed in semi-formal attire and nursing champagne glasses. He eased through the people, feeling out of his depth amongst the money represented in the room.

He needed to get out of here. Needed to phone Khan and update him.

He retrieved his jacket from Marta and stepped outside into cold mountain air that would have been cleansing except for the moneyed Russians climbing the steps to the house. He hurried down the stairs and reclaimed the Perseus from within a school of expensive vehicles. Waiters served fur-wrapped couples steaming drinks as they mingled beside a large bonfire lit at the edge of the yard. Wood crackled and popped and sent sparks surging upward into the clear, cold night sky. He guided the Perseus against the flow of guest vehicles arriving at the house and turned toward Ayim Beshimov's guesthouse when he reached the road.

He pulled out his phone and dialed Khan's number as he drove.

"Khan." The M.E. picked up almost immediately.

"We need to meet. I think the conversation needs the privacy of our office. And we can meet with Egorova there."

"I thought we were going to a party."

Kazakov sighed. "I suppose that comes later. I'll be there in five minutes."

It was Khan's turn to sigh. "I'll be there. You better have a good explanation. You're getting old Kazakov. You keep changing your story."

"The story keeps changing for me. It's like stripping off masks only to find another mask beneath."

Khan was silent a moment and then hung up.

Kazakov rang another number.

"Egorova." Her feminine voice was cool and professional.

"Where are you?"

"Still in the mountains, but I'm getting close. I can see the valley lights below me."

So she was about half an hour out.

"Come to Ayim Beshimov's. I'll meet you there."

"All right." She paused. "Is everything okay? You sound different."

"The case is developing. We need to strategize," he said.

"O-kay. Looking forward to it." She clicked off and Kazakov stuffed his phone back in his pocket, wondering whether his suspicions about her were right.

The issue with the evidence could be explained by misfiling or laziness at the forensic office. Other than that, there was nothing suggesting anything wrong with Egorova. But he'd been down this road before, with fellow officers who *had* turned out to be the enemy.

He passed the Royal Yekaterina Resort and through the gate saw the shadowy forms of Bure's caravan of vehicles still parked in dignitary parking slots. The man was still here. Kazakov had thought he'd be gone, given the election was barely a month away.

With that disquieting information, he drove on and pulled into the snowy slot next to Ayim Beshimov's stone courtyard wall. A battered old First Auto military four-wheel drive was parked on the other side of the gate. Kazakov climbed out and locked his vehicle. The First Auto looked like it had seen hard use far past its time with the military.

He pushed through the gate and went into the house. Ayim Beshimov stuck her head out of her kitchen. "It is you. Good. Your friends are in the office. I bring you tea."

Friends? He had only one in Biysk that he knew of and that was Khan.

Mystified, he thanked her. "Ayim Beshimov, the young Detektiv Egorova will be coming here. When she arrives, can you stop her at the door and let me know?"

She agreed and then he headed to the office.

At the office, he stepped to one side of the door, caution taking precedence. Khan had always been his friend, but something was different now.

Voices came from inside and one quiet voice was definitely Khan. The other sounded familiar, but he couldn't place it. Still, he stood to one side and pushed open the door. Khan faced him at the evidence table. Back to the door, another man stood in a thick fur coat and a fur hat pulled low over his ears. The coat hem ended at neatly pressed trouser cuffs that topped leather pointy-toed boots with two-inch heels. Kazakov stopped. He knew that there was likely only one such set of boots in New Moscow and that they were tooled in loops and flowers.

Eric Clinton turned toward him.

The last time Kazakov had seen the American spy, he'd been shot in the chest and had been driving away for help in a stolen car. Not even Khan had known whether Clinton had lived through the ordeal. To see him now was a shock.

And the man had changed.

Clinton's usually angular face had thinned out so the skin seemed to barely cover the bone. The fur hat was unexpected given Clinton had always shown his flair with a broad-brimmed hat with a slightly curled brim. Kazakov had always thought the hat indicated that Clinton didn't give a damn what anyone thought of him. The Russian-style coat had replaced Clinton's previous shearling jacket and he huddled inside the new garment like a man who couldn't quite get warm.

Kazakov recovered from his shock and stepped into the room. "Clinton! Talk about ghosts! No one would tell me whether you lived or died. My apologies again for dragging you into a firefight."

He caught the man's hand and pulled him into a brief hug.

"That's because they didn't know whether I would—live or die, that is. The embassy has medical facilities. They took care of me. It doesn't look good to have embassy staff turn up at the local hospital with gunshot wounds." Clinton ended with a cough that left him wincing.

Kazakov eyed him. Through the thickness of the coat, Clinton had felt thin.

"Where the hell did you come from? Where did you find him, Khan?" He turned his attention on the M.E.

Khan shook his head. "He found me. He was waiting when I got back to my friend's home."

By Khan's cocked brow, Kazakov knew Khan had questions about just how Clinton had known where to find him.

"So what are you doing here?" Kazakov asked.

Clinton glanced around the room, grabbed one of the two chairs, and sat. Khan stayed where he was. Kazakov hooked a thigh over the edge of the desk. Clinton's gaze flickered between Kazakov and Khan.

Finally he sighed. "I'm not exactly supposed to be here. I'm supposed to be convalescing. I lost part of a lung, you see."

Kazakov winced internally. He'd allowed the injured Clinton to drive himself into New Moscow on his own.

"The plan is to send me home in a week or two, when they think I can make the flight," Clinton continued. "I've been stuck in that damned embassy for over a month. I was going crazy. Then a little bird told me there was trouble in the mountains. I tried to call Khan, but his wife told me he was gone. Believe it or not, I tried to get in touch with you, too, Kazakov. The police station told me you were on assignment out of the city. I thought it was a good chance you were here, too. Then I saw the footage of the riot at Bure's rally and I knew for sure. You looked good on camera." He grinned.

Kazakov cringed. If Clinton had seen it, likely Rostoff had, too. The question was whether it was during the melee, or when he was being trundled into the police van. The fact Rostoff hadn't mentioned it on their call was all Kazakov had to cling to.

Clinton shook his head. "I can't believe Bure, but then I guess I should. It must be easy to blame the incident on the Kyrgyz when you're the man who stands in front of the wreckage of Yekaterina's statue and definitively states that Fergana's tribal people are responsible. Talk about stirring up trouble. The man's a magnet."

All in accord with Kazakov's opinions. Something niggled in his brain but eluded him for the moment. "Why are you here?"

"I thought you'd need a hand, didn't I? Besides, I might have information that's useful to you." Again Clinton looked from Kazakov to Khan and back as if seeking approval.

Or to gage whether they were buying what he was selling.

Kazakov crossed his arms over his chest. Clinton might have helped them somewhat in the past, but he hadn't done it freely. Instead he doled out bits of information when, and if, he thought it was to his and his country's advantage. And no matter that Clinton was here now, supposedly on his own. Once a spy, always a spy.

On Kazakov's investigation or something else?

Clinton had the good grace to color slightly. "Okay. So I haven't always given the straight goods immediately. It's my job, for God's sake. But since I've been laid up, there's been a swirl of information coming through our networks. You'd be surprised to hear how much of it pertains to Fergana. There's a lot of fear out there in the world. We've talked about it before."

They had. If Fergana ended its neutral stance and picked sides in the Ottoman/Chinese standoff, it would give an excuse to the "aggrieved" party to once more fight their enemy. The uneasy world peace would be ended and though there were those who thought it fine to let the two superpowers fight it out, the issue was what would happen when one or the other won. Both the Ottomans and Chinese had shown an inclination toward world domination. There was no question that any winner of an Ottoman/Chinese conflict would then eye the Anglo-Germans and beyond to Anglo-German North America and the string of independent countries that made up the better part of South and Central America as well as the slim string of Eastern seaboard states that made up Eric Clinton's United States. Clinton had previously said that the independent countries knew they didn't stand a chance against such a winner. As a result, the fate of Fergana was important to them.

And to enough others that he wondered who else was meddling in Fergana's affairs.

"So?" Kazakov prompted him. Let Clinton run on and see where that got them. Maybe he would have helpful information.

"Our sources in Constantinople are picking up hints that the Ottomans are arming and training the Kyrgyz."

Khan's gaze flickered away from Kazakov. The M.E. had been an honest man for too long to be good liar.

Kazakov eased his bulk so that more rested on the table. "Go on."

Clinton's gaze flickered over him. "You already knew." He glanced at Khan. "You both did. How?"

"I'm a detective, remember? I have my sources." Kazakov feigned a smile. "Go on."

Eyeing him warily, Clinton thought a moment. "We have people working for us in a variety of locations around the world."

Spies, he meant. Kazakov nodded.

"Lately we have noticed a change. A number of our best sources have suddenly gone silent. We've sent people in to check and the best we can determine is that the people in question have simply disappeared. In some cases, those who have gone in to check have never been heard from again, either." He met Kazakov's gaze. "It leads us to think that something is happening. Something big. Most of those disappearances were in the west of China—Kashi, Turpan, and along the border with Fergana."

Khan hooked the last chair and sat down. Kazakov shook his head.

"I'm not surprised. We've been dealing with disappearances here, ourselves. Police records indicate that over fifty people have been reported as missing in the past few years." He glanced at Khan, not wanting to reveal what Khan had found in the mountains without Khan's permission. The M.E. nodded.

"Khan made a gristly discovery the other day. He went to a camp in the mountains and found everyone dead. A village had been taken as well and he found their bodies there. The murder victim I'm investigating had been at both locations—at least we believe so."

The room was silent except for Clinton's rough breathing. His gaze had widened slightly as Kazakov had told his story. Now Clinton sighed.

"There's something else. A buildup of Chinese forces east of the border. They claim they are running war games in the Taklamakan Desert, but informants say that for a desert war game, the gear is wrong. They say the men go to battle camouflaged for a mountain winter."

15

The stone walls of the old office seemed to radiate cold as Clinton's words hung in the air. The roaring heat from the wood stove couldn't dispel the chill Kazakov felt or the shiver that ran up his spine. The revelation appeared to have taken the last of Clinton's strength. In the space of telling his story, he seemed to have aged. He looked frail. It had been Clinton's robust energy that had fooled Kazakov before. Now that energy was gone.

Painted in light and shadow from the single bulb overhead, Khan sat like a statue by the evidence table as if frozen by Clinton's words. A Chinese buildup at the border as if they prepared to roll right in to Fergana.

"There's no way they'd dare. The Ottomans would respond," Kazakov said. Enver Pasha might not have said it, but it was a certainty nonetheless. The Ottomans wouldn't take any encroachment on their borders lying down.

"The Chinese would advance if they were asked in," Khan said quietly.

Kazakov shook his head. "Leonid Nikolaev's government wouldn't dare. You don't let the Chinese in the back door while the Ottomans are knocking at the front. Not without knowing a war is the consequence and our people would be the first ones in the line of fire."

Khan's gaze bore into him. "You haven't been paying attention to the news, have you?"

Kazakov frowned.

Clinton bowed his head. "There *is* an election coming."

"And Leonid Nikolaev's party is likely to lose, given the Friendship Clothing Company scandal." Khan said softly. "The evidence is mounting that Nikolaev knew that the money they donated to his campaign came from the Ottomans. The fact that the company also apparently funded terrorist actions like the destruction of Yekaterina's statue just makes it more damning, even if Nikolaev had no knowledge of that fact."

Glancing at the American, Kazakov shook his head. "Even if he loses, no Ferganese government would dare."

Clinton simply raised his gaze to Kazakov.

Bure. The man's rhetoric said it was possible.

Kazakov scrubbed his face, feeling tired and like he was seriously treading on areas above his pay grade.

"But I am not politically minded. I have a murder investigation to conduct."

"There is more," Clinton said softly. "Our spies have picked up activity in the mountains. Some kind of installation, they think, judging by the comings and goings. There is a road cutting through mountain passes from the Chinese border…"

Before Kazakov or Khan could respond, a commotion sounded from the hall beyond the office. A hurried knock came at the door.

"Come," Khan said roughly.

Ayim Beshimov pushed open the door. "I am most sorry to interrupt, but the young woman is here. She says she must see you. Taalay is holding her at the door."

Egorova wouldn't like that. Both being told to wait and being detained by a Kyrgyz boy. No, Egorova wouldn't like that at all.

"Thank you. Can you ask her to wait a moment longer? Perhaps take her into the kitchen for tea?"

Ayim Beshimov nodded and withdrew.

Kazakov turned back to Clinton and Khan. "An installation. Where?"

Clinton shook his head. "Difficult to explain, but I have the coordinates."

Voices came from elsewhere in the house. Kazakov needed to deal with one thing at a time and first was Egorova. "So? Do we let her in to meet our American friend? What do you think?"

Khan shook his head. "We have too many reservations at this time."

Better to not reveal Clinton until they were sure what was going on with Egorova and the evidence.

Clinton stood. "I should go."

Kazakov shook his head. "We need the coordinates first."

Clinton's opaque gaze foretold the shake of his head. "Not going to happen, my friend. It's classified. I might, however, take you with me."

The voices were rising down the hall. Kazakov needed to deal with Egorova, but he needed the information.

"We need to discuss this. May I suggest that you wait until I am done? In my room, perhaps?"

Khan gave a slight nod to Kazakov, hopefully indicating Khan would stop Clinton from leaving altogether. Khan stood and he and Clinton took their leave.

Kazakov stood in the office alone, trying to decide how to approach the evidence issue. Egorova was not some suspect to be interrogated. Up until this evidence question, she had proven herself reliable and helpful. But that could simply be a ruse to gain his trust.

He rapped his knuckles on his skull. He was beginning to sound and think like a spy, trusting no one. Why?

This was a murder investigation, nothing more. He could not let himself be swayed by issues larger than finding the killer.

He went to the door. Who was he kidding? Everywhere he turned in this case, there was evidence of something larger, like a shadow moving beyond a curtain, a figure in a mask, an unrecognizable princess in pigskin.

Was that so bad? In the fairy tale, the Tsarina had taken off her pigskin to attend the young tsarevich's ball, but had escaped at the stroke of midnight leaving behind only a fine glass slipper. It was that slipper that had finally unmasked her and she and the young tsarevich had married and all had lived well afterward. Did he dare hope for such a happy ending in this case?

Sighing, he went out into the hall and found Egorova in the kitchen, not only drinking tea, but hungrily devouring a healthy portion of Ayim Beshimov's mutton dumplings. Beside her was the box of evidence she'd taken with her to New Moscow. She looked up when he entered and set down her spoon.

"Sorry. I didn't have a chance to grab a sandwich for the road when I left. I haven't eaten since noon." She spooned another mouthful and scrambled up, nodded thanks at Ayim Beshimov, and grabbed the remains of her flatbread and the evidence box before following Kazakov down the hall to the office.

Inside, he realized the room was actually hot, the chimney vibrating with the roar of heat. He tamped the fire down and settled in the chair Khan had vacated. He nodded Egorova to the other chair but she shook her head.

"So what's so secret that you wouldn't let me in?" She set the box on the evidence table.

"I had—informants—here. They did not wish to be seen."

Egorova's gaze narrowed slightly, but, still with her coat on, she sat and chewed on another bite of bread.

"How was the trip?" Kazakov asked. Get her relaxed and talking.

She shrugged and worked her shoulders, then shrugged her coat off and let it fall over the back of the chair. "Long. Dark. It was snowing in the pass." Another bite of bread and she chewed. Her jaw muscles worked. Her brown gaze was dark, but her face was pale. "The road wasn't great but the four-wheel drive handled it."

"And your time in New Moscow? How was that?"

Another irritating shrug as if she couldn't be bothered to find details to tell him.

"I arrived. I did the work that needed to be done. I came home."

"And how did you find Dabria?"

A slight pink reached her cheeks for the first time. "She is well. She sends her regards."

"You got on well, then?"

A grin. A nod. "We did. It's been a long time since I've been to the city. Too long apparently. She and her friends made me feel welcome."

"Good. Very good." He nodded. "It is good for police women to meet each other. I know Dabria would like more from her career. You are proof it can happen."

Her regard was steady, but she cocked her head. "Sometimes you surprise me, Kazakov. It is hard being a female officer. I thought none of my male colleagues noticed." She looked down at the last bite of bread in her hands. Ate it and chewed. "What was so important that I set speed records getting back?"

Here it was and he still had no better read on whether he could trust her than he had had when he had sent her to New Moscow with the evidence. Less of a read, actually, now that he had suspicions.

"The evidence we sent to New Moscow. Tell me how it was handled, please." He sat back in his chair and waited.

She looked at him and suddenly her face changed, the slight smile she'd gained talking about her city visit and Dabria was pushed aside. She sat up straighter, like a student facing down a disliked teacher.

"I told you over the phone." She sighed. "All right. I had custody of the evidence for the trip into New Moscow. It did not leave my sight. When I took breaks along the way, the evidence was with me. When I got to New Moscow, I went into the police station to call upon Dabria as you suggested. I had the evidence with me. She went with me to Forensics to introduce me and ensure that Detektiv Chief Inspektor Rostoff's instructions for a rush were obeyed."

She finished chewing her last piece of bread as if she was finished her report. Kazakov's silence must have clued her that she wasn't.

"What?" She opened her hands. "Have I missed something? Have I done something wrong?"

Sighing, Kazakov sat back in his chair. "Tell me again how your time with Forensics went."

She went still, her gaze not leaving his face. "After Dabria introduced me, she left. I remained behind to await results. I went with the evidence as far as that goes. They took the bag and took samples of Bermet's various concoctions—none were particularly appetizing, I must say. I waited until they got their results. Most were folktale remedies according to the staff. I have a list for you."

She dug a white sheaf of papers from her inside coat pocket and handed them to him. He scanned the list. None of the names meant anything. Maybe Khan could interpret it.

Egorova stood and folded her coat over the back of her chair before sitting back down. "It was a long way to go for nothing."

He looked up from the papers. "And the leaves and the paper? You have not mentioned them."

She rolled her eyes and looked up and away from him. "I told you over the phone. The leaves are nothing unique: a shrub of some kind found in these mountains and used as a sedative. The paper was chicken scratch—a doodle."

Her gaze was steady. Either she was telling the truth or she was the consummate liar.

"May I see it, please?"

Another roll of eyes and Egorova stood. Her resentful attitude he well remembered from their first meeting, but it had returned full blown—or worse.

She crossed to the box on the table and opened the lid to fish inside. A puzzled expression claimed her face. Then she hurriedly removed the box's contents and spread them on the table. When the box was empty she stopped, her head bowed. "It isn't here."

She turned to Kazakov, apparently dismayed. "Damn it, Kazakov, it isn't here!"

Fatigue flooded through him. "I see. If you had the box in your possession at all times, how could that happen?"

Her face paled. "I don't know. Unless they didn't put the paper and leaves back in the box after I gave them to them for analysis."

"Who, specifically, did you give the leaves and paper to?"

Shaking her head, she paced around the room. "I'm not sure. I'm not sure. There were so many people coming and going to get the analysis completed as swiftly as possible." She stopped by his chair and clenched her eyes closed. She swayed as if she stood in a stiff wind. "I—I think it was an older man—an expert in handwriting, I believe. I can't remember his name, though."

"And what was a handwriting expert to do with the leaves?"

Her glare down at him almost made him stand. Instead he took a steadying breath and kept his regard mildly concerned.

"I don't know, all right? Maybe I thought he'd pass the leaves off to another expert."

"What did this man look like?"

Sitting back in her chair, she perched on the edge. "Kazakov, why all the questions? What's happened?"

"Just answer the question."

"Dammit, Kazakov, you're treating me like a suspect or something!"

He waited—as he would with a suspect.

She slumped back in her chair, dark circles underscoring her tired gaze. "About six foot tall, reddish-blond hair. Blue eyes. He was thin. He wore a white lab coat just like all of them, but I remember his shoes. For some reason they caught my attention. They were brown with a pointy toe, but well-worn, when he was wearing black trousers. A fashion faux pas, you know?"

A fashion faux pas was so far under his radar he must have committed such an error more times than he cared to think. But he nodded. It was a reasonable description that could be used to identify the possible culprit unless the culprit was sitting before him. He wrote the description down.

"How did he provide you with the results of his examination?"

"He came and told me. He told me it would be in the report."

Kazakov nodded. He looked down at the sheaf of papers in his hand. "This report?"

She nodded.

Kazakov began to flip the pages, scanning through the various reports. Reports on the contents of the various bottles and vials. He came to the last page. There was nothing about the leaves or their paper packet. "There's nothing here."

"What? Let me see?" He handed her the package and she snatched it back to begin flipping through the pages just as he had done. She shook her head. "This has to be a mistake. He said it would be here."

"You didn't check when you were in New Moscow?"

"Why should I? He told me what he'd found. Maybe—maybe it's on the original file, but they forgot to include it in the copying. That could happen. We could check..." Then she stopped and looked at him. "You already have. You knew it would be gone."

"Suspected, not knew." Just as he suspected her. "I had reason to call Forensics. I had them read the contents of the reports to Dr. Khan. According to New Moscow, there is no mention of the paper and leaves in their file."

"You think I didn't give it to them. That I destroyed evidence." Her tone was sullen.

"The thought had crossed my mind."

Her head slumped between her shoulders, her hands between her knees. "I would never do that. This job—it is everything to me. A chance to prove that a woman can be a detective and can do the job well. I—I thought I'd proved myself to you." She glanced bleakly up at him. "I will ask to be reassigned from the case first thing in the morning."

He had expected denial and argument. Could he be wrong? Could the problem exist in New Moscow and not here?

She grabbed her coat and stood. "I am sorry this has happened. I had hoped to learn from you and I have, but I understand that you cannot jeopardize your investigation by working with someone you do not trust."

She slid on her coat and turned to the door, then stopped. "Kazakov, I don't know whether it will help or not, but I did something when I was in Forensics." She dug in her pocket and pulled out a small camera. "I was such a tourist. I didn't know whether I'd ever be back there again, so I took pictures—of the building, of the staff in action, of how they laid out the evidence to examine. I also have the photos of the paper and leaves I took here in Biysk."

She handed him the camera. "I hope it helps."

Then she left him and hurried down the hall, leaving Kazakov even less certain of his opinion of Elena Egorova.

He heard the thump of the guesthouse's heavy front door before he sighed and abandoned his chair. Trust her or not, he didn't know, but she had made a good show of it either way. He looked down at the camera. Maybe her photos could tell them something.

He left the office for his room and found Khan seated on the lonely chair. Clinton lounged on his bed, his sun-bleached hair gleaming in the light from the lone lightbulb.

"How'd it go? She confess?" Clinton asked, swinging his long legs off the bed to sit up.

Khan looked up at him expectantly from where he'd been reading one of the old magazines. When he flipped it closed, it held a photo of a young, pale-blond man on the front, the mountains white crags behind him. The article tag line read, *He Beat the Odds.* Khan set the magazine down and stood.

"It was not what you expected," Khan said.

"It wasn't." Kazakov gave a nod. "She appeared to answer the questions forthrightly. She said a redhaired Forensic staffer took the paper and leaves from her to examine. She seemed surprised that they are no longer in the evidence box. It sounds like she took good care of the evidence until she handed control over to Forensics."

"A lie?" Clinton asked as if that was his expectation.

Kazakov shook his head. "I'm not sure. There is this."

He held up the camera and told them what Egorova had told him. "We need to get the film developed."

Both Khan and Clinton nodded.

"I know a local Kyrgyz photographer," said Khan. "He is reliable and could develop them for us."

"Good." Kazakov removed the film from the camera and handed the film to Khan. "Before you leave, though, can you think of who the Forensic staffer might be? He was six foot tall, blue-eyed, and thin, according to Egorova. He wore pointy brown shoes, well-worn, and black trousers." The detail of the description suggested it was most likely real.

Khan pursed his lips and thought, but then shook his head. "It's not anyone I recognize. They've had some real turnover the past few months."

That was a disappointment. He'd been hoping Khan might know who Egorova described. Now it was a matter of whether the description was even of a real person and that would depend upon whether Egorova lied.

"Then perhaps that is something else you can do? Phone Forensics and ask about this person Egorova described. See if there is a newcomer…"

Khan agreed and left, leaving Kazakov facing Clinton. The American grinned and settled on the bed again, a slight grimace crossing his face.

"That wound still takes its toll," Kazakov said.

Clinton shrugged, and on him, it wasn't something Kazakov resented. For some reason he respected Clinton.

"I've had worse wounds."

"And now you lapse into spy bravado. It was a serious wound. Losing part of a lung is worse. And now you are in the mountains where getting enough oxygen can be a challenge for the fully healthy."

"Aah, but I'm a hardier creature than you give me credit for." Clinton smoothed the bedspread and looked squarely at Kazakov. "So where do we go from here?"

Where indeed. Kazakov studied the low ceiling beams. They were sturdy support against the worst snows the mountains could throw at the low building. If only Fergana had such a support. It was more like the entire country was held up by old Baba Yaga's chicken-legged house. Fitting, actually, given how the old witch could be either good or bad and nobody knew which.

"You mentioned an installation in the mountains. I think we should go there."

"You think that's where your killer is?" Clinton asked, his blue eyes burning in the poorly lit room.

Kazakov shook his head. "Probably not. But the man who ordered the killings likely is. Or evidence of who gave the order, at least."

"You're hedging, old friend. You mention killings and when you do, you glance in Khan's direction as if he's directly involved. What's happened that you're not telling me?"

"Nothing." Kazakov shook his head again. "Or at least nothing that concerns you."

What would an American care if a village and an armed camp were wiped off the face of the earth as if they had never been—every grandparent, man, woman, and child of them?

Clinton stood again and shifted around the bed until he was eye-to-eye with Kazakov. "You forget, Detektiv. I know you. I can see when you are bluffing. There is absolutely nothing in what you've told me that should take you to a mountain installation. What is your excuse?"

Kazakov glanced away from the too-knowing gaze. The trouble was, he couldn't quite put his finger on it himself. There was something like an itch deep down in his gut that came from making connections he was not aware of yet. Enver Pasha's presence was part of the quivering mass of connections. So were Zholdosh's presence and the cigarette butt found by Bermet's body. The death of the camp and the village. Even the arrests at the protest and the disappearing evidence. Those were the most recent pieces that both troubled him and sent him on the scent. But there was a difference, here, too, as if this was simply the most recent veil in a series of mask layers that obscured the truth from him.

He needed to think. He needed to plan.

And he didn't need this American watching him while he did.

"Where are you staying?" Kazakov asked.

"The Royal Yekaterina, of course. Why? I thought we were going to a party—or at least that's what Khan hinted at."

"No party tonight. I have work to do. If you don't have your own vehicle, I'll drop you off."

Clinton grinned. "Subtle as always, Kazakov. But then, it is part of your charm."

Kazakov cocked a brow at him. "You've been talking to Khan." He pulled his coat on. "Now why don't you share those coordinates with me?"

But Clinton stood and pulled his coat on over his lanky, overly-thin form. He grinned. "You think I don't know you plan to leave without me?"

"I could have you arrested and held." Kazakov crossed his arms across his chest. He could take as much as this American could give and give more back. This was Kazakov's country, after all. He had the law on his side.

Clinton leaned in close, a flash of anger in his gaze. "Try it and I'll come hunting you, you hear?"

It was more than an idle threat.

"Duly noted." Sighing, Kazakov led the American out of the room and out of the guesthouse.

The night was cold enough to catch your breath. Overhead a skein of stars spun their web between the mountain peaks as if they all were connected. Perhaps they were, but he was too blind to see. Or perhaps the connection was an illusion—one he'd seen as a child because he needed to.

Shaking his head, he stomped through the crunchy snow to the Perseus and opened the door for Clinton. Then Kazakov rounded the car and climbed in behind the wheel. The engine started with a growl and he did a three-point turn out onto the road and headed toward Clinton's hotel.

"How many years have you been doing this?" he asked with a glance at Clinton. The man sat huddled in his fur coat as if losing his shearling coat and wide brimmed hat had somehow diminished him.

Clinton sighed. "In Fergana, a few years. Otherwise… far longer. A lifetime. They recruited me out of school. The University of Charleston."

Kazakov pondered that as he drove. What would it be like?

"How do you manage all those secrets and lies? I'd think they'd spill out of your head after all this time. How do you keep them straight?"

Clinton smiled. "You keep them simple, of course."

"It's like you live behind a layer of masks."

Clinton chuckled. "Maybe. I don't know. But at least I'm mostly me, not like Collin Archer."

Collin Archer. Another spy and a murder victim, but he, unlike anything Kazakov had ever seen before, had been surgically and cosmetically altered to look Anglo-German. Only the medical examination of his body had revealed the truth. Collin Archer had been born Chinese.

"So there are degrees of spies, then."

Clinton nodded. "Levels of cover, you could say. I'm not very deep. Clearly an American. Clearly with a purpose other than spying. But I make contacts and gather information and keep track of the *mood* of wherever I am. Occasionally I might try to influence someone."

"Like me."

"Like you, but you are aware that someone from beyond Fergana is exerting influence. With someone like Collin Archer, they are inserted very deep into local society. They gather information, like me, but probably from sources they would not normally have access to, and they influence from within by the very fact that they are viewed as one of the people—not foreign."

"Except Collin Archer was presented as Anglo-German, not Ferganese, not Russian."

Kazakov thought about Collin Archer, who had lived with his mask as part of him. What must that have been like, to give up who he was in order to spy for his country? He couldn't imagine giving up the Kazakov he had become—no matter the amount of money offered to him. To live his life amongst foreign people as if he was one of them and yet feel forever apart.

He stopped himself. He lived amongst his countrymen and yet often felt apart from them... The entire Kyrgyz populace felt the same way. So had Maria. Even Chelomeyev. Was that human nature to live desperate lives, their loneliness and truth masked behind what the world sees? It made the world a dismal place.

Ahead, the lights of the Royal Yekaterina spilled over the resort walls and filled the night like a golden dome over the building. He turned into the entrance and stopped by the door. The line of Ziln limousines was still parked against the wall.

Clinton climbed out and leaned back in the Perseus. "You'd probably like to leave tomorrow morning. I'll be ready to go." He held up his hand as Kazakov opened his mouth to argue. "I know you think I'm not fit for this. You probably think I'm a liability. I'm not and I'm going. I've worked too long on this file and I'm seeing it through to the end. Do you understand me?"

In the light from the resort, Clinton's eyes were blue flames. Kazakov nodded.

"I'll pick you up in the morning. But before you go, one question. Amid all these mountains, the least you can do is give me a clue. In what direction is this installation?"

Clinton straightened and looked up at the stars half-erased by the resort lights and then at the mountains. He pointed.

Not east along the river valley and mountain passes beyond White Stone Village, but southward, to the snarl of mountains thrown up when the Indian subcontinent met the Eurasian plate in the far distant geological past. Those mountains were now a jumble of territory claimed by Fergana and contested by the Ottomans due to the proximity to their Moghul India. The Chinese sometimes laid claims too, as an extension of their western border.

16

———————

Kazakov's room was cold when he woke the next morning. The room was dark. His nose and ears were half frozen, but under the tangled bedcovers he was sweat-drenched. The room reeked of the gunmetal stink of his fear. Around him the house was silent, but the pat-pat-pat of fresh flakes were like feather-soft fingers trying to break through the window pane. Soft and deadly came to mind. They would stroke you gently as they froze you to death.

He squeezed his eyes shut and inhaled deeply to slow his racing heart. There was nothing wrong here. Everything was fine. It had only been a nightmare.

A nightmare of everyone around him being skinned alive, layer by layer, as he demanded they remove their masks. Masks that didn't just go skin deep. They were in the flesh. They were in the bone. His friends had flayed their flesh until their bloody remains stood before him. Then they expectantly handed the knives and flays to him. Show them who *he* was.

So he turned the tools on his flesh and dug and stripped his skin, his flesh. But when he was done, there was no Kazakov left—an empty man.

He sat and shivered when his feet met the cold floorboards. He went to the woodstove and stirred the embers and added wood. Soon heat ticked up the chimney and he could feel the warmth. He stood close to it, warming his front and hands, then turning to warm his back. The room smelled faintly of smoke. Unfortunately, his chill was deeper than flesh.

It was a nightmare. Only a dream, probably as a result of his discussion with Clinton. Nothing there. He looked at his watch. Almost four a.m. and they should get away by six if they were truly going into the mountains. Before he'd gone to bed last night, he'd heard from Khan. His photographer friend had rushed through the film development and Khan had the images before him. He'd found a fax machine at a local Kyrgyz shop—the owners had been roused from their beds to help—and he had sent images of the paper and leaves and of the man he suspected was Egorova's forensic technician to people he trusted in New Moscow Forensics. He would hear from them by morning.

Kazakov had also advised Ayim Beshimov of their plans for the next morning and had arranged for mountain packs with appropriate supplies and equipment as well as a trustworthy Kyrgyz guide. Unfortunately, some of the most trustworthy were currently still languishing in police custody.

He dressed and packed the few things that would go with him into the mountains. Extra thick socks, sweaters, and long underwear—why had he thought to bring it?—his gun and extra ammunition, of course. With his heavy parka in hand, he headed for the kitchen and found Ayim Beshimov awake and cooking.

"Sit. Sit. I have tea." She bustled about the room, her cheeks red from the heat from her oven. The luscious scent of frying sausage and potato filling the room.

He shook his head. "I have to go pick up one of my friends." He checked his watch. "Khan should be by any time. Tell him I'll be right back."

He went out to the Perseus. The cold air slammed into him and he pulled his collar a little higher, his fur hat a little lower. The vehicle protested when he cranked the ignition but finally started. He headed to the Royal Yekaterina.

The roads were empty and the ski hills were dark. Above, the sky was alive with flickering stars—enough to impress anyone who hadn't seen it before light pollution dampened their brightness. The mountain peaks were a crown of thorns around the valley. He studied the peaks southward in the direction Clinton had indicated. They were huge and white and topped with wisps of glowing cloud that was probably ice crystals picked up by the blowing wind. Cold.

Even colder than here. He exhaled and watched the vapors freeze inside his car even with the heat on.

What was happening in those mountains? A secret installation. A secret armed camp. Who knew how many secrets those craggy mountains contained.

He pulled into the Royal Yekaterina parking lot. In the corner of the lot still hunkered the low shapes of Bure's Ziln entourage. The fact that the man was still here didn't surprise him anymore. It was as if all the pieces of a game were poised to play. Kazakov just didn't know what game they were playing. He pulled up in front of the door and climbed out. His aging Perseus looked seriously out of place amongst the flock of new vehicles that hedged the expensive resort. He left his vehicle, ignored the footman who came running out as he pulled on a jacket. His tousled hair suggested he'd been sleeping.

Inside, the lights in the wall sconces around the foyer had dimmed, leaving brighter light only over the reception area. The scent of bread baking wafted in from hidden kitchens, readying for the day and the morning rush to the ski hill. He supposed it would be like this at any upscale ski resort, but for some reason he resented it and preferred the simple honesty of Ayim Beshimov's kitchen with its homely scents and plain food.

He found the guest room phone and asked for Clinton's room. The phone purred in his ear two times.

"Hello."

"You ready?" Kazakov asked.

"Be right down."

Five minutes later the elevator dinged and Clinton came out bundled in a down jacket and heavy canvas trousers. Serious-looking boots rose halfway up his calves and his fur hat was pulled low over his head. He carried a well-worn rucksack in his hand, but the gear couldn't hide the hesitation in his stride and the pallor in his skin.

Clinton shook Kazakov's hand. "I was beginning to think you were going to try to do this yourself."

Kazakov looked the American up and down. "Judging by how you look, I probably should have, but you've got the coordinates."

"I'll be fine." Clinton clapped him on the back. "A walk in the park."

"A walk in winter mountains. Think about it. You can still back out." And Kazakov should refuse to take him—hell, the American should be arrested for his own good. But Kazakov needed the coordinates. He led back to his Perseus and returned to Ayim Beshimov's guesthouse. Khan's battered ride was there, but so was a second vehicle—this one a recent model truck with a flatbed that held two, two-person, trail-runner vehicles.

The trail-runners were open vehicles. Instead of wheels, they had side-by-side tracks and a front end like a sledge that the tracks drove up and over or through the snow, mud, or other terrain. They were also hyper-fuel efficient, and these ones looked like they had additional fuel tanks. Khan's doing?

He and Clinton climbed out of the Perseus and took a look at the trail vehicles, but then went inside. Five sets of boots sat by the door. One set was Khan's. Another, well-worn pair of fur-lined felt mountain boots probably belonged to their Kyrgyz guide. One large pair was set neatly against the wall, while the last two pairs, smaller than the others, were worn but unknown.

He and Clinton pulled off their boots and Kazakov led the way to the kitchen. Voices came from beyond the door. Khan's careful voice, a low guttural speaker. A female voice that was Ayim Beshimov and—Aisha?

Kazakov pushed inside. The younger Kyrgyz woman looked tired after her time in jail for the protest, but she worked beside her aunt bringing plates of food to the tables, her face a mask that couldn't quite hide her dislike when she saw him.

Khan sat at one of the tables facing the door, an aging Kyrgyz beside him and two other newcomers in chairs with backs to the door. One was Constable Igor Nedved. The second had blonde hair in a pony tail tumbling down her back. Egorova.

What was she doing here? He frowned a question at Khan, but the M.E. simply nodded him over.

Kazakov glanced back at Clinton. Did he dare reveal the man was working with them? But Clinton simply shrugged and passed him, apparently drawn by the luscious scent of the food. He seated himself beside Egorova and held out his hand as Aisha settled a plate before him.

"Name's Clinton. I'm an old associate of Kazakov's."

"Detektiv Elena Egorova." She nodded back at Kazakov. She introduced Nedved.

"Kazakov," Khan said. "I spoke to my associate in Forensics. He provided results of their review. They were also able to identify Egorova's technician. He is new to the job. Apparently, they have asked Rostoff to become involved."

Whether that would get to the bottom of things was something else again, but it was something. At least it suggested Egorova wasn't involved.

"What are you doing here?" he asked her.

She shrugged as she chewed another forkful of food but caught herself and set the fork down. Swallowed. "I knew you would be going into the mountains. Nedved confirmed it when I went by the office. He said you'd invited him along. I knew you've wanted to go into the mountains since this whole thing began, but the investigation stopped you. By your actions last night, I knew you weren't going to share your plans so Nedved and I kept watch on you. I packed up last night, and when I saw you leave this morning, I went home and brought my equipment here."

"The trail-runners…"

"Are mine," she said with a nod. "But looking at this crew, we need at least one more, preferably two or three. I thought they'd speed the trip along, especially if we're going to be out there awhile."

Khan didn't appear worried at Egorova's inclusion, but Kazakov still wasn't sure he should be convinced.

"So how do we get the additional machines?" If they couldn't, then perhaps that could be his excuse for excluding her.

"You wait one hour and I will have your machines for you," Aisha said. "On condition I go with you."

Egorova nodded. So did Khan. Kazakov sighed. This was going too fast and felt out of control. "How is it you are even here? Last I heard you were still in jail."

Aisha shoved a stray dark hair back from her face. In her worn cotton shirt and canvas trousers she looked sturdy and defiant as if she suspected he would prefer that she still be in jail, but there was a smidgeon of relief in her gaze.

She nodded at Egorova. "She got me. She had to sign her name to my release."

Kazakov looked back at Egorova. "A surety? You signed a surety for her?"

Egorova only nodded and forked more food into her mouth. Suddenly Kazakov realized the mound of wonderful-smelling food was seriously depleted. If he didn't eat soon, he would get none.

He settled at the table and began to spoon food onto a plate. Aisha brought another pot of tea.

"I thought it might reduce your worries about me. Of course, it means Aisha must come, too. I'm not leaving her to get into trouble." She had the gall to grin at him.

His mouth full of the ambrosia of mutton and potato, he sighed and turned to Aisha. "You'd better see to those machines. You, Nedved, go help her." The constable had already eaten a heroic share of the food.

But Kazakov felt as if he had control of absolutely nothing.

It was more like an hour and a half before another vehicle arrived with two more trail-runners. The machines arrived with a crew of five, who all seemed determined to get in Kazakov's way as he tried to manage the increased size of the operation. When he growled once too often, Khan pulled the others aside and loading of their equipment and supplies for three to six days went more quickly then, but it was still nine a.m. before their team of seven reached the trailhead into the mountains. Given the state of the trail, it would be quicker and easier to ride the trail-runners from there instead of taking the trucks into the mountains.

The day was bright, with sun glaring off the mountain peaks and the snow around them. The few trees along the river were ragged beggar silhouettes, the sky itself an unsullied blue. A light wind chilled Kazakov's cheeks, but high up the mountains, ice glittered as it was lifted by high winds. Lower down the flanks of the mountains, flags snapped and whipped around. Across the valley, the ski hills were already busy.

The guide who had breakfasted with them, a wizened Kyrgyz named Kamyrza uulu Sarpek, must have been at least seventy. He led on one machine, hauling a small trailer with their gear. He was a thin-faced, wizened man of medium height and with skin as crevassed with age as a mountain cliff face. He wore a faded green jacket that had gone gray with age and stout trousers over his felted boots. Stray strands of gray hair stuck out of his fur hat around his face. Before they left, he strode about like a much younger man, supervising the vehicle loading, while his knowing gaze assessed the mountains.

Khan and Clinton each drove a machine. Egorova sat behind Khan and Aisha behind Clinton. Kazakov was on the fourth machine with Nedved.

"There will be snow within twenty-four hours," Sarpek said before they left. "But that is not the big storm. That brews beyond the mountains."

Snow did not bode well for what they had planned, but it seemed Sarpek spoke of more than the weather.

By ten a.m. they were buzzing their way up the trail toward the site of Bermet Aytmatov's murder. By eleven they had passed White Stone

Village and were nearing the place Kazakov had recovered Bermet's medicine bag. He urged his machine closer to Khan's.

"You haven't told me what Forensics said about Egorova's photo," he yelled.

Khan glanced over his shoulder at Egorova, who held lightly to his waist. She wore a thick down jacket and ski pants along with thick mittens and a fur hat that tied under her chin.

"It was a good photo," Khan yelled over the roar of the engine. "Tea leaves. They were tea leaves. From what Forensics said, they're of a variety sold mostly in China."

China again. But only mostly. A tea aficionado might have brought the tea in and given it as a gift to Bermet.

"The paper?" Snow blew in his face from Clinton's machine in front of them.

Khan tipped his head. "When they blew the photo up, there were shadows. The chicken scratch described to Egorova was more likely Chinese characters, but they couldn't say what. They were too indistinct."

Kazakov nodded his thanks and guided his machine behind the others as he considered what this meant. Chinese characters on a paper wasn't definitive, either. Bermet could have come by the paper at a store or from an acquaintance and only put the tea leaves in the paper to take them into the mountains for her own enjoyment.

But it was strange, then, that the paper and tea were stolen as if they were important.

Had Bermet taken them when she shouldn't? Had she escaped with them as a warning, only to be hunted down?

The tea was of a sort the Chinese preferred. If, as he'd theorized, Bermet had been taken to the camp for her medical expertise and then something had brought the Chinese into the camp, the Chinese could have brought the tea with him or her. There was a certain sense in that. And then things went wrong and the killing began and Bermet tried to escape, taking with her the tea and paper as evidence. She must have been a canny old woman, but then knowing his elderly neighbor Agafya Ryabkov and Ayim Beshimov, that was nothing uncommon amongst Kyrgyz woman. He probably would have liked Bermet very much.

Beyond the spot where Bermet's bag had been found, Kazakov was in new country. Around them the pass between the mountains had narrowed further, which made it doubly surprising when Khan urged his machine up past Clinton and even with the guide. They slowed and Khan pointed up the seemingly untouched side of the mountain. The guide nodded and motioned Khan forward. His machine crept along as he studied the trail and then suddenly gunned the engine and sent the machine up and over the edge of the trail and onto the mountainside. Egorova whooped like a kid. Khan angled his machine up the side of the slope and soon he and Egorova were above where Kazakov sat his idling trail-runner.

"You think we can do that without getting this thing stuck?" he said to Nedved.

"It's worth a try," the young constable said.

The guide waved Clinton and Aisha forward and they turned sharply, following Khan's lead up into the unmarred field of snow. Kazakov urged his machine forward and followed Clinton's lead. The trail-runner reared up the edge of the well-worn side of the main trail and lurched up and up until he was sure it was going to fall over on him and Nedved. Then its treads found purchase in the snow. The machine plunged down and forward and suddenly he was chugging up Khan's track. What had looked as if Khan had turned onto a wilderness of snow turned out to be a level path hidden in plain sight on the mountain slope. A path that showed signs of recent usage.

A roar behind him said the guide brought up the rear as they chugged up the mountain and toward a higher pass that led away from the trail.

Khan was the first to disappear into the shadows that hid the pass. The glare off the snow made the disappearance instantaneous, as he rounded the side of the mountain into the darkness of the north face of the mountain. Clinton followed and Kazakov was left to track up the slope with only the packed snow as a guide. Then he turned and was suddenly in shadow. Ahead, the two trail-runners had paused where the shadows ended and looked out into sunshine beyond. Kazakov sped up to reach them and cut the engine.

After the echoing roar of the engines, the idling was a welcome reprieve. He glanced at Khan and Clinton and followed their gaze.

Here the slope down the mountains wasn't as steep, nor did it fall so far to reach a mountain valley floor. A snow-bound path led from where they sat down between tall rock guardians that blocked some of the snow. It led down to a bowl bounded by more of the huge fallen stones, but the bowl itself appeared to undulate as if something lay beneath the snow. To one side, the stub of four charred, square walls told where a structure had once stood. Amid a spiderweb of tracks across the snow and signs of digging, at the door of the structure lay a stack of bodies, piled like cordwood. Beside them, four men stood, rifles raised to their shoulders as they scanned the heights. As Kazakov looked, the scan steadied on Kazakov's vantage and the rifles locked in his direction.

"Looks like we have friends," Clinton said. "Anyone we know?"

Khan shook his head. Kazakov wasn't so sure.

The men with the rifles wore white jackets and trousers as if meant to blend in with the snow. If they were laid out amidst the rocks, they'd be very hard to spot. Such equipment spoke of preparation and preparation spoke of one of two parties. He was willing to bet he knew which one it was.

He dismounted the trail-runner and waved away Khan's and Egorova's protests. Hands raised, he stepped from the shadows into daylight and felt vulnerable in front of those rifle barrels as they shifted to him.

"Enver! Enver Pasha!" His voice rebounded like a shot in the pocket valley.

There was a flurry amongst the men below and Khan and Clinton jerked beside him.

"What are you talking about?" Khan asked softly.

"It's the obvious answer. He was funding the camp, wasn't he? And he's been staying in Biysk. He paid the surety on Zholdosh and had him released. It would be logical that he'd wonder what happened here."

In the valley, one man stepped forward. "Who's looking?" called the voice in a Kyrgyz accent. Not Enver.

"Detektiv Alexander Kazakov and associates." Kazakov took three steps forward to where the shadow of the mountain ended and sunlight blazed across his back and shoulders. They wouldn't be able to miss him. He pushed back his parka hood and took off his fur hat. Even in the wind, at this altitude the sun was warm on his head.

Another flurry of discussion amongst the party of men in the valley. The spokesman stepped forward.

"Come down slowly."

Kazakov waved agreement and stepped back to his machine. He started it down the trail between the huge stones loosed from the mountain. Behind came the whine and roar of one of the other trail-runners. And another. And the last.

He made his way down to the floor of the high-altitude valley and into the cleared area between the stones. The pattern of footprints placed calligraphy on the snow around him and the gruesome midden of the dead. There were frozen faces contorted in agony. Men, women, and children with limbs and torsos shattered by bullets and skulls cracked open, their bloody remains lost in the snow. He shut the machine off and held his hands clear of the machine as the others joined him. Each took their lead from him until their group of seven sat in the hushed quiet of the wind amongst stone. The sun's glare was bright and the machine ticked under him as it cooled. He imagined he could hear the faint cries of agony of the ghosts of the murdered. The mask of snow could not muffle it all.

"So," he said, keeping his voice steady in the face of all that death. "Enver Pasha?"

Four military grade rifles still trained toward him. Their barrels were dusky gray and their stocks the color of stone. He'd not seen their like before, but he recognized the square structure and extended magazine of automatic weapons. It was a lot of fire power to reconnoiter the destruction of the camp. Unless that wasn't all they planned on doing.

"It's all right. As I said, I know Kazakov." Enver Pasha stepped from inside the ruined stone structure. Clearly the four other men weren't taking chances with their leader.

Enver crossed the snow and held out his hand to Kazakov. "I see our minds run in similar ways, though I hadn't realized quite the extent of the devastation." He shook Kazakov's hand. He glanced to Kazakov's companions. "I see one or two I recognize. Who are the others?"

Kazakov did a round of introductions, ending with the guide. Sarpek's expression was non-committal as he scanned Enver Pasha's party. Then he stopped and looked taken aback.

Kazakov followed his gaze.

He recognized one face amongst Enver's four companions. Not a man —Marta. Enver Pasha's dark-haired personal security detail still stood with her rifle aimed at them. For all he caught her eye, her readiness to fire didn't waver.

Kazakov looked back at Enver. "I see you come prepared for battle. Do you know something we don't?"

But Enver only shook his head, his attention instead on Eric Clinton. "What, pray tell, is an American doing here?"

"Perhaps you'd like to field this one, Clinton?" Kazakov turned to his companion.

Clinton rubbed his stubbled chin. It would be interesting to know just how Clinton read their situation and what half-truths he would share.

Instead he laid it out to everyone just as he had laid it out to Kazakov and Khan. "It is the American belief and the belief of her allies that the world will be a safer place as long as Fergana retains its neutrality." He met Enver's gaze squarely and a test of wills seemed to ensue.

It was Enver who looked away first, his lips curving in a smile. "I see. So my government and I should not get our way, but neither should our enemy. Instead we must continue to play childish spy games in this vestige of a country. Fergana would be ours just based on our common culture and faith if it was not for the Russian infestation of this place—an infestation that we could excise any time, I might add."

"And risk the wrath of the Chinese," Clinton said quietly.

"You're hated by most Russians. How can you expect to become our allies?" Kazakov asked.

"Not allies. Masters. You would be their servants." Clinton said.

"And you would know all about servants and slaves, coming from America," Enver Pasha snapped. The economy of the small nation still depended upon the buying and selling of humans to perform heavy labor, though most were now domestically bred and raised. Enver ripped his glare from Clinton, nodded to Khan, and scanned Egorova, Nedved, and Aisha before turning back to Kazakov.

"You bring a motley crew on this venture, Detektiv. Do you truly believe that's best? You could easily end up like these lost ones." He nodded at the bodies as if they were simply a tally, not husbands and wives, fathers and mothers and children. Not common villagers brought here to be mowed down.

"I bring the people who can help. Egorova knows the investigation. Aisha knows the hills and contributed to our trail-runners. Clinton knows the location of an installation in the mountains that may have something to do with the murders under investigation." He thought a moment. "Would it be an Ottoman installation?"

Enver was quick to shake his head. "Our installation is in the Kyrgyz people's hearts and minds. But as I mentioned before, we are also aware of a foreign outpost in the mountains. I would be lying if I did not admit to being curious about it. We shall go together. Your guide and my weapons."

Kazakov hesitated. Egorova and Clinton stirred.

"Surely you cannot believe such a place will be unguarded," Enver Pasha said with a shake of his head.

It was a good point, one which Egorova and Clinton must have got. They nodded.

"We could use something more than personal weapons," Clinton said.

So the American was armed just as Kazakov was. Likely Egorova and

Nedved were as well. Carrying a weapon seemed foreign to Khan as a doctor, but then, he was Kyrgyz… Whether Aisha and old Sarpek carried, Kazakov couldn't say.

He turned back to Enver. "I take it your people are equipped for a prolonged trek in the mountains." His group of seven had been prepared for three to six days. "If we work together, you and your men follow my lead. Do you understand?"

Enver Pasha nodded.

"So what have you learned from your examination of the bodies?" Perhaps a warrior's examination would tell something beyond Khan's.

Enver scanned the stacked bodies and the humped snow around them, his expression grave. "Some of the camp members were shot where they stood, others as they ran away. A few fought back from amidst the rocks." He nodded uphill. "They were killed, too. Someone got behind them. It looks like someone—a group of someones—rode into camp. Apparently, they were allowed up close—perhaps some kind of ruse. Then the shooting began." Enver shook his head. "As for the villagers, they were simply herded in and gunned down. Their bodies were all over there against the edge of the camp." He nodded to the other side of the camp.

"Your read matches what Khan and I have suspected. They came in, perhaps were offered a meal, and they offered to share tea in the process." He glanced at Khan and the M.E. nodded.

"The wounds were countless. Some were left to bleed to death. But the death seemed to explode out from this place." Khan nodded at the burned-out hut. "There were camp-member bodies there as well, but most fell as they tried to escape, so our read of the remains concur. Before the fresh snow, it was much clearer." He inhaled. "The difference was that the bodies in the hut had been bound. It seems whoever did this took particular pleasure in burning that lot alive."

Enver looked shaken. Kazakov's stomach clenched.

"Whoever did this will not hesitate to destroy us. Perhaps some of us have second thoughts." Kazakov scanned the group who had come with him. Egorova's pale face caught the sun, but her expression was grim. Aisha looked frozen from within. The guide stoic. Khan, Clinton, and Nedved all shook their heads.

"I'm going on," Khan and Clinton said in unison.

"Me too," Egorova said.

"I will as well," Aisha agreed.

Sarpek, the guide, simply nodded.

It was Nedved who stayed silent. Kazakov turned to look at his companion. The constable's gaze appeared unable to shift away from the mound of bodies. His throat worked as if he could not clear it and his breathing was rapid.

"Nedved," Kazakov said.

The young constable jerked at the use of his name. "Sir?"

"I need you to take on a task for me. It will not be easy because I am leaving you here without a trail-runner, but you told me that you hike these mountains. We'll drop you back on the trail. From there I need you to make your way back into town and file a report. I want Forensics out here as soon as possible and a complete examination of the bodies and a report on my desk when I return. Do you understand?"

Nedved's head jerked in the affirmative. He looked at the sky. "There's enough daylight that I should be able to make it most of the way back to town by dark. I'll use my mobile when I get closer and have someone come out to meet me. By tomorrow morning there will be a full crew out here."

"Good. Ensure they document with photos. You have a camera with you?"

Nedved nodded.

"Then take a few documentary photos before we leave. It may help to light a fire under your bosses."

Nedved dismounted and quickly snapped a few photos as Kazakov and the others turned their trail-runners to follow their back trail. Nedved remounted behind Kazakov.

"Our machines are ready," Enver said. "They are hidden amongst the rocks."

"What—what do we do about the bodies?" Aisha asked. Her black gaze seemed held by that grisly pile. "There are animals…"

"Who will reclaim them," Khan said softly. "But we should bury or burn them."

Kazakov shook his head. "When we return we will build a pyre. For now, we leave them to Nedved and Biysk Police."

Lips in an unhappy line, Aisha finally nodded. Khan did as well, but he brought Aisha forward and, with Enver and the guide, led a prayer for the dead. Kazakov and Clinton bowed their heads. Overhead an eagle soared. And then another. And another. Not eagles. Vultures.

The birds awaited Kazakov's and others' leave-taking and then they would have their way with what was left behind. They had likely already fed on the bodies. Their sharp beaks and talons would gradually strip away the last masks of humanity these poor souls had. It was both disturbing and comforting. Everyone should return to the land that bore them.

Perhaps that was the problem with Fergana. The Russians were, by breed, foreign to these spaces. Perhaps they would never belong and that led to their uneasy clinging to a past they could never reclaim. His small bit of humanity was adrift on the ocean of the world. They might have dropped anchor here, but that would never mean that they belonged.

Kazakov mounted his trail-runner. The others followed his lead. The guide led them in a procession up onto the slopes of the mountain. As they passed around the mountain, the shadows swallowed them up. Kazakov looked back. Through the blue sky, the vultures' black forms settled earthward one by one.

———

At the trail, they bid Nedved farewell and turned away from Biysk and higher into the mountains. They made good time along the packed trail, but as the afternoon faded, the trail became not much more than a footpath straggling through the snow. In the winter, there was not as much traveling amongst the Kyrgyz people. They had their snug homes and their livestock, and most of them stayed close to home in lower altitudes.

The blue sky paled and the mountain peaks darkened into angry crags against the blue. Soon, orange streamers shot up into the western sky. Sarpek slowed his machine and finally stopped. Around them the slopes of the mountains had come together so that they traveled through a narrow, rocky defile. What sunlight there was passed this narrow place by and a chill wind channeled down into their faces. Aisha and Egorova sat huddled in their coats. Kazakov urged his trail-runner up beside the guide.

"Why are we stopping?"

Sarpek pointed to the sky. "Night almost here. This is not a good place, but even worse to try to travel the dark." He pointed ahead and up high on the slope. "See snow? That could fall, and in the night we would not see it. Here there is not such snow." He waved up the mountainsides above them.

For all Kazakov wanted to go on, he could see the logic in Sarpek's decision. He dismounted his machine and went back to the others. "We make camp here."

There was grumbling, but the others dismounted and camp was set up, small nylon tents amid the stones. Aisha and Egorova shared a tent. Khan and Clinton bunked together, and Kazakov and Sarpek bedded down together. Enver Pasha shared a tent with Marta, and the other three of his men had one larger tent. They all came together around a small fire where Sarpek made tea and cooked a meal of rice and leftover mutton that Ayim Beshimov had sent with them. Kazakov sighed but dug in. When he returned home, he was leaving mutton off his menu for at least a month. As the darkness settled around them like another guest at their meagre dinner, the sparks from their fire seemed to ride up and paste themselves upon the sky. Kazakov lay back in the snow next to the fire and watched the stars coalesce and clot above him, remembering how it had looked to him long ago.

Ageless and timeless, the stars were always there, no matter who existed here below. Once he had been a very different man. Now, like everyone else, he was something else again, composed of lost dreams and expectations that had swathed him and weighted him down. He had his masks just like everyone. He wondered what he would be if he just pushed all those intervening losses and expectations aside.

"Penny?" Aisha said as she settled beside him. The others were readying their tents for the night.

Surprised, he looked from the stars to her and sat up.

"I was just thinking about how the stars may be the only things that are real. The rest is just layers of masks we create for ourselves and others," he said softly.

She thought a moment, her dark eyes like velvet, the firelight catching on her hair and cheekbones. "You surprise me, Detektiv. I'd not thought you a man of deep thoughts."

He smiled. "You see? My mask blinded you to who I really am."

She thought about that a moment and her lips curved slightly. "It seems you've caught me. So, Detektiv, what expectations have you placed on me?"

The question was a good one. Kazakov considered before answering. No one else was in earshot. "From what I've seen, you're a woman of many deep thoughts. You are a loyalist to your people, and their situation makes you angry."

Mock surprise filled her gaze. "My, my. The Detektiv sees that, too. I will no longer be surprised by you." Aisha smiled, but a hint of wariness filled her gaze as if she was afraid of how deeply inside he might peer.

"Are you having second thoughts about coming?" he asked. The fall of night had brought the cold down off the snows. A chill wind blew down through their defile and brought with it the creak and groan of the great snowfields above them. Even the stars glittered coldly and their small fire, fed meagerly with pine they had hauled with them, seemed futile in the face of the vastness of the night and the mountains.

She shook her head. "This is a venture to discover who killed a Kyrgyz woman. It is right that a Kyrgyz woman should be here. Thank you again for bringing me."

"It's fortuitous that you are here." A surprising stroke of luck, actually, given Egorova had selected Aisha from amidst the detainees as proof of her goodwill. How had Egorova known of Aisha and that she was Ayim Beshimov's niece? "Did you and Detektiv Egorova know each other before today?"

Surprise seemed Aisha's first response, but then she smiled and shook her head. "I've heard of her, of course. First female detective in Biysk, perhaps of all Fergana." She shook her head. "In case you're wondering, it doesn't mean anything to me. She's still a Russian, and I'm Kyrgyz before I am a woman. It is bred in my bones and those of my ancestors."

"Good to know, I suppose." And yet she was sitting here with him almost as if they were friends. He nodded at her and looked back at the glittering stars. Aisha excused herself and he wondered why she had chosen to sit beside him at all. To put him on notice? Clarify her loyalties? Just how had she ended up being chosen to be here? How had Egorova chosen her from amongst the twenty or thirty Kyrgyz in lockup? Had she been telling the truth that she and Egorova didn't know each other? But why lie about such a thing? Because Egorova knew that she was under suspicion?

Beyond the fire, the young detective was deep in conversation with Khan and Clinton outside their tents. Aisha had settled beside Sarpek, who was checking over the bindings of the equipment and supplies on Kazakov's trail-runner. Enver and Marta and his three men, who had the brawn and steady gaze of professional soldiers, had stepped away from the fire and were readying to retire. As should the rest of them. Their precious firewood needed to be conserved.

"I'm going to bed down," said Kazakov to the others, "and I suggest you do, as well. The morning comes early in the mountains and we can't afford more fire."

Khan and the others nodded and ended their conversation. Clinton ducked into his and Khan's tent. Enver and Marta had retired, as had two of his men, the third taking up a position of guard. Aisha headed for her tent and Egorova made to follow, but Kazakov caught her arm.

"The trail-runners—you made a good choice to get around in the mountains," he said. "Thank you."

She nodded as if his appreciation meant nothing and went to move away.

"Aisha as well, I suppose. She has a vested interest."

Egorova shrugged.

"How did you know?" he asked. Aware of Aisha's proximity, he lowered his voice.

"Know?" She glanced over her shoulder at him.

"About her relationship to Ayim Beshimov. That I knew her. How did you happen to choose her?"

Egorova shrugged. "The address in her file. It was a reasonable assumption that you'd know someone else who resided in the house."

A reasonable answer, but he was still dissatisfied.

"So you checked all the addresses, did you?"

She turned to face him, hands on her hips. "A good number. Why?"

Because he still didn't trust her? Because it just seemed too great a coincidence? Because he found himself obsessed with masks and wondering what was the truth that everyone was hiding in this case?

"Just wondering. How are the two of you getting on? She doesn't seem to be an easy person to be around."

Egorova simply looked at him. "Many people aren't. Now you reminded us of the early morning tomorrow. I intend to get my sleep. Good night, Detektiv Kazakov." She nodded primly, once, and ducked inside her tent.

"What was that about?" Khan asked quietly, coming up beside him.

Kazakov shook his head. Behind them, Sarpek had stomped out the fire and gathered the stubs of the wood for use in the morning.

"I'm not sure," Kazakov said. "A feeling? Something does not feel right. How did Egorova know Aisha was known to us? How did Egorova come to choose her? Surely there were others amongst the detainees who would have been better suited to this venture. You, yourself, said that some of the best Kyrgyz guides were amongst them."

Khan blinked and cocked his head. "Good questions, I suppose, but I have no answers." He said goodnight and ducked into his shared tent, leaving Kazakov, the stars, and Enver Pasha's guard alone.

The night air was fresh and smelled of snow and the ash of the tamped-out fire. Their dinner of mutton was still heavily cloying on his tongue. Fatigue and worry weighed on his shoulders.

There was so much that could go wrong. The trip could take longer than the estimated three days. The weather could turn against them. Whoever owned the installation could be ready and waiting for them. They could be walking right into a barrage of bullets and could end up as dead as the White Stone Villagers.

The cold wind found its way down the neck of his jacket and he shivered—both from the cold and from the thought that Maria, a witness in a previous related case, was dead, too. If he died, perhaps he would meet her again, if what the Orthodox church preached was true. He wondered how Chelomeyev's recovery was going and felt remiss in not phoning to find out since arriving in Biysk.

So many lives had been ended or changed in his investigations. All but his, it seemed. He lived in his dacha alone. He conducted his investigations. He had been shot, but he survived. And so he went on. And on. And on.

When would he have enough of the death and dying of Fergana?

Never, said the wind. *Fergana was born out of death and dying and so it will go on.*

Yekaterina Weber was not the first. Bermet Aytmatov was only the latest and not even that given Zholdosh and the death of White Stone Villagers. In some ways they were layers, but instead of peeling them back, they were being layered on top of one another like layers of plaster until what was left of Fergana, of this case, was a malformed…entity? creature?…that he could never see through.

Almost as if it was intended.

It was a terrifying thought and one that sent bile to poison his throat. The cold stars placed a silvery veil across the heavens as he finally ducked inside his tent. The sour scent of Sarpek's clothing hit him.

It was a human scent. A normal scent.

He climbed into his sleeping sack and breathed in deeply to dispel the image of a plastered heap with too many arms and legs crawling across the ground to get him.

17

The third day in the mountains dawned bright and cold so that the inside of Kazakov's tent was coated in frost that glittered in the sunlight through the canvas. Sarpek was already up and out of the tent, so Kazakov stretched luxuriously for a moment. Then the sound of quiet voices outside sent him scrambling to pull on his trousers and jacket. He hauled on his boots and stumbled out of the tent, where a small fire popped and sent a thin straggle of smoke skyward in the still air. Khan, Clinton, Egorova, and Aisha were sipping steaming tea from metal mugs and chewing on segments of flatbread. By unspoken agreement, everyone had cut back on their rations in recognition that their venture could take longer than their planned maximum of six days. A light skiff of snow had softened the trail-runner tracks and their footprints from the night before.

Around them lay the steep crags of the Pamir-Alay Mountains, crowned with snow and the wisps of cloud. Closer, their planned trail led through unmarked drifts up around the side of the nearest mountain. According to Clinton's map coordinates, the installation they sought lay around the mountain's flank and most likely high up its side. It was an area that, according to Sarpek, held good pasture in summer months, but over the past thirty years had become a haunted, no-man's-land. Too many Kyrgyz herders had disappeared with their flocks when they tried to graze their traditional lands. Unfortunately, the authorities hadn't looked into the issue even though the Kyrgyz had reported it.

And according to Egorova, no one had ever investigated those early disappearances.

"So where are our Ottoman friends?" he asked as he joined the others and Sarpek poured him a mug of tea. He took a piece of bread from those on offer and dunked it in his tea and then chewed the crusty mouthful.

"Enver sent his men out earlier to see what is ahead. They are afoot," Sarpek said. "He and the woman are packing up their tent."

As if in evidence, Enver Pasha climbed out and the tent collapsed behind him as Marta backed out, too, handing out bags to him and brushing the canvas floor free of snow.

Kazakov crossed the crunchy snow to Enver. "Where are your men?"

Enver glanced up at him from where he stuffed a spare shirt into his kit bag. He straightened and lit a cigarette, then offered one to Kazakov. It had a pale filter marked with fine tan lines. A very exclusive American make and one that had been tied up in Kazakov's last murder investigation. Against a sudden craving, Kazakov refused it.

"To reconnoiter," Enver said. "We should not walk into a trap. They will spot anyone keeping watch and report back to me. To us."

"Why are you even here, Enver? Sending your men, I could understand, but to come yourself is not like you. It is not how you operate."

Enver's dark brows rose as he inhaled and let loose a long string of smoke. "It isn't? Do you know how I earned my title? And was it not you who told me that I should leave Biysk for fear of an attempt on my life? Have I not taken your suggestion?"

"You know I was talking about you heading back to New Moscow. Some place where maybe we could contain the trouble you cause! Not joining an expedition into these mountains."

Enver scrubbed at the dark beard that had joined his thick moustache after the few days in the mountains. A humorous glint caught in his eyes as he puffed his cigarette again. "So I misinterpreted your suggestion. It brought me and my men to help you."

Kazakov snorted.

But the humor faded from Enver's dark gaze. Another long string of smoke escaped through his nose. "Seriously. You should be thankful. You think you can take on what could be a foreign military camp with that?" He nodded at the people clustered around the fire.

"I don't think we intended to 'take on' anything, other than confirming whether there is something there. For all we know, it could have been built by the Ferganese government."

"Then you are a fool," Enver said and tossed his cigarette to the snow. "Do you really think that you can discover such a place and walk away again? Don't you think that might be what has happened to your Kyrgyz tribesmen?"

The bleakness in his voice was new to Kazakov. Not even when Kazakov had bested him in New Moscow had the man shown such emotion.

"You've lost your own men in the mountains."

Enver looked away. "He was my first contact in the mountains. A good man, Kanybek Beshimov was."

Kazakov stopped. "Ayim Beshimov's husband? He owned the guesthouse in Biysk?"

"The same." Enver nodded. "He had Russified his name from the traditional Nur uulu Kanybek and was one of the first that I spoke with when I began coming to Fergana and Biysk. He had his suspicions—about things happening in this country, in these mountains. He disappeared about fifteen years ago."

Something shivered in Kazakov's skull and sent a tremor down his back. There was something in what Enver had just said and done that fit with the morass of other facts slipping past each other inside his skull.

A shout from up the trail wafted down to them and both Kazakov and Enver turned. One of Enver's white-clad men hurried toward them.

The others tossed their tea dregs over the fire and stood at alert. Enver started out to meet his man, Kazakov beside him.

Enver's man lumbered over the snow to them and then caught his breath. "There is a hidden road just around the next flank of the mountain. It looks as if it has been well-used in the past weeks."

Enver and Kazakov looked at each other. Khan and the others gathered around them.

"That puts it right where I said it would be," Clinton said.

"Did you follow the road?" Enver asked.

The man shook his head. "We did not dare. There may have been watchers we did not spot. We didn't want to warn anyone. The others have gone on to assess the safety. I came back to let you know."

"We should pack up and follow," Kazakov said.

"Perhaps we should wait for their assessment," Enver said.

Kazakov shook his head. "We move forward to the closest position where we can wait for them safely. There is only so much daylight in twenty-four hours and I want to be close enough that we can get farther up that road if possible."

After a moment, Enver nodded.

They hurriedly packed up the remains of their camp and rode their trail-runners as far as they dared, then stopped in the shadows of a natural ring of standing stones to wait. Enver's man left them to meet his comrades so that there was only Enver, Marta, and Kazakov's team.

The morning ticked on, the blue sky like a crystal bowl of ice over them. The wind picked up and gradually hazed the bowl. Sarpek scanned the peaks and shook his head.

"This is not good. There is a storm coming—sooner than expected."

Kazakov followed his gaze. Huge horsetails of snow whipped off the peak above them and appeared to join forces with a haze of cloud streaming north in bands that threatened to constrict the sky.

By noon , Kazakov felt fuming as the weather. The cloud bands had formed into a pillowing blanket of white that masked the landscape with a dead white light. Where the hell were Enver's men? Nothing moved except the wind that froze Kazakov's nose and cheeks—until he pulled his scarf up over them, copying Egorova and Aisha. He paced up and down the slope, ostensibly to stay warm, but really because he felt trapped. It was the interminable wait that was killing him.

Finally, he went to the others. "We've waited long enough. I suggest we move up the road now or we're going to be caught here in the storm." He didn't mention retreat from the storm. Retreat wasn't an option, though Sarpek still watched the sky and shook his head at what was coming. A great storm, he'd said.

"I say we wait for my men," Enver Pasha said. "Let them do their jobs. Otherwise there's no telling what we might meet."

"Just what is it that you're so afraid of, Enver?" Kazakov asked.

"Yes, what?" Egorova echoed his question, a frown on her face.

"You've been holding us here for hours..." Clinton said thoughtfully.

"Are you really afraid of us being hurt, or are you afraid of what we might find out?" Kazakov said.

Even his magnificent moustache couldn't mask the hardening of Enver's mouth. He shook his head. "Fine. Have it your way, then. We'll go on."

He turned to his trail-runner. The others split up so that Enver's machines weren't left behind. Egorova slid her machine in beside Kazakov as they were getting started.

"What was that all about? What do you think he's hiding?" she asked, pulling down her scarf. Her face was flushed from the wind, but pale points of white on cheeks and the tip of her nose showed the effects of the cold.

"I don't know," Kazakov said. "But my gut says that there's a reason we won't necessarily like." He nodded at her. "You need to wrap your face warmer. Frostbite." He touched his face to match the white spots on hers.

Her mitted hand came to her nose. "I didn't realize. Thanks." She pulled an extra layer of scarf up over her face so all he could see was her eyes. "I didn't tamper with the evidence, Kazakov. This job is too important. This case is."

If this was truly Elena Egorova talking, then she was telling the truth; but he didn't know how many layers of life were plastered on the person before him. Detektiv, Russian, friend, woman, and how many entities combined into one being that he could never fully understand.

It was one thing to respect and honor those layers in a friend he trusted. It was quite another to do so in a woman he couldn't quite be sure he could trust.

He nodded once and started his trail-runner, setting off up the track after Sarpek.

Beyond the circled standing stones where they'd waited, their road curved through the narrow defile between the mountains, but then the path Enver's man had taken swung them aside off the trail and upward onto the mountain through a landscape misshapen with huge fallen stones that now stood swathed in snow. It appeared that white-robed figures formed a silent congregation around them. Then Sarpek disappeared over a hump of snow. When Kazakov followed him over the top, he found Sarpek waiting on a new trail—wider than the one they'd left, but with no marks in the new snow. Beneath that, though, were the puncture marks of horse hooves. Enver's men must have paralleled the road rather than follow on it.

Sarpek didn't wait. When he saw Kazakov, he started upward following the trail. Around them, wind had shaped the snow in some cases like great capes swathed around the standing stones. In others the wind sculpted the snow so some shapes appeared to take wing. The roar of the trail-runner engines echoed off the figures, but amidst the roar seemed to be voices.

On alert, he scanned the landscape around them. A tumble of snow. A shaft of light through the leaden cloud. A shift of shadow. All had him reaching for his weapon.

He didn't like this place. It was a nightmare, actually. Too many places for men to hide with weapons. He could understand the concern of Enver's men and why they'd chosen not to use the road.

But where the hell were they? And just where did this road lead? An installation, Clinton had said, but what did that mean? The word itself seemed to obfuscate clarity.

There were too many questions swirling in his head and the weather was getting worse.

He finally called a halt and let the others talk quietly while he climbed the side of the road. There, in the snow, were the deep boot prints that confirmed that this was where Enver's men had gone. He lumbered back down to the road and climbed onto his machine. They continued up the road, but conditions were worsening.

Huge, white flakes had begun to fall, swirling around them and splattering his face. The flakes clung to his mittens and his jacket until he had a coat of white across his chest, shoulders, and thighs. With little movement his feet had grown cold. He urged the trail-runner up closer to Sarpek. Let them go faster. Let them arrive and find answers. Of course, that was madness and could lead to them walking into a trap.

As if to stymie his need to get there, Sarpek slowed his machine and then stopped so Kazakov had to veer off to avoid hitting the guide's vehicle. Kazakov looked back at Sarpek. "What's the problem?"

Sarpek dipped his head in the direction they were going.

Two trails wide enough that they could have held a full-sized vehicle led into the mountains. One trail led higher up the mountain. The other led almost parallel to the trail they followed for a short while, but then aimed southeastward through a narrow pass between adjoining mountains. A movement far down the lower trail stopped Kazakov. Through the dim light it appeared to be a riderless horse, picking its way lower.

"Horse," Sarpek said, confirming his sighting.

Their party sat at a meeting of the ways, with their trail being only a minor side path off the major thoroughfare.

Khan and Clinton came up beside him.

"Where do you think it goes?" Kazakov asked, nodding at the lower road that the snow was quickly masking in an impenetrable haze of falling flakes. The horse's figure was lost.

"China is that way. It is not far," Khan softly.

"Less than two hundred miles," Clinton said. "Of course the road could turn aside. There are other trails that lead southward into Ottoman Territory. It's not far."

"The Irkeshtam Pass is that way, too, though the Chinese guard it fiercely," Khan said. "Many Kyrgyz people are now trapped on the other side. They cannot come home." His head bowed.

"If we are going, we must go now," Sarpek interrupted. "Snow very bad farther up." He nodded at the uphill road.

It had completely disappeared in a haze of white that masked the mountainside.

Kazakov nodded and they set out, slower now as Sarpek strained to see ahead.

The snow swirled around them so it was difficult to see the lead trail-runner. Kazakov closed the distance between them and the others came in behind. It was too easy to lose one another in these conditions. Kazakov felt for Enver's men trying to make their way on foot. They must have gone a long way to not have returned yet. On the other hand, it would be easy to miss them in these conditions. He consoled himself that they were professionals and must have survival gear with them.

Time passed slowly as they followed the road. Sarpek slowed and the others matched his pace until it seemed they barely crawled up the mountain. Gradually, the road narrowed—still wide enough for a motorized vehicle, but on one side, the mountain slope fell away steeply into shadow. On the other side, the white expanse of mountain grew up beside them into the mass of falling flakes. Enver's men would have had to take the road here. There was nowhere else for them to walk.

The higher they went, the harder the wind whipped the flakes into their faces. Kazakov felt blind in a white howling world. The light faded as the day slipped away and he could barely see Sarpek in front of him. Suddenly the guide stopped his trail-runner, his hand aloft to signal not to go any farther.

The huge flakes had changed to stinging pellets that hissed as they hit the hot metal of the trail-runner's housing and bounced off the frozen white shell of Kazakov's jacket. Sarpek turned his machine off and Kazakov did the same. The others followed suit until the only sound was the wind.

And the sharp, rapid report of automatic weapons.

18

The late afternoon light turned the falling snow into a blinding blanket of gray as Kazakov peered ahead up the snow-covered road. The downhill side of the road was a precipitous cliff, but the snow treacherously masked the exact edge. Uphill, the steepness of the slope made any attempt to leave the road impossible on their machines. In many places the road had been cut into the side of the mountain leaving rocks leaning over the road. Even on foot he doubted that someone could climb very far—at least not without climbing equipment. From ahead, the rapid automatic gunfire came in brief, calamitous explosions and then faded as if there was a battle raging. Enver's white-clad soldiers were earning their keep today.

Or they were dying.

Whoever owned the installation was still home and they weren't happy about being found. Kazakov glanced behind at the Ottoman. Enver's black brows and moustache were white crescents framing his eyes and mouth. Thick lines of worry had formed between his brows. Beyond him, Enver's guardian, Marta, had come alongside and scanned the wall of falling snow ahead like a hound eager for the hunt.

"It appears your men have disturbed someone," Kazakov said.

"They're good men. The others must have been well-hidden, or they stumbled upon something unexpectedly."

"And just what did you expect?"

The snow was a veil between them, but it could not hide the secrets that welled in Enver's gaze. He looked back up the road.

"We thought a Chinese outpost," Clinton said. He and Khan had left their trail-runners behind to come up beside Kazakov. Clinton looked tired.

"I wonder if it is something more," Marta said.

"The fighting has gone on for a long time," Clinton said. "If it was an outpost guard, you'd think Enver's men would have finished him by now."

"So this is something more." It was Egorova joining them this time, Aisha at her heels. The two women looked up the snowbound road.

"It would be a good way to lay claim to these mountains," Aisha said. "These mountains have always been permeable to the shifts of my people and neighboring tribes. Fergana is a crossroads that has seen many masters." Her face twisted in distaste.

"All well and good, but what do we do now? Hold our position until the fighting is over?" Kazakov looked at the others. He'd fought beside Khan before, but he knew nothing of the others. He knew he and Clinton had weapons and he suspected Egorova and Marta likely did as well, but Enver probably did not. He thought it unlikely Sarpek or Aisha were armed either.

"I think one or two of us should go ahead," said Kazakov. "Enver's men know we're behind them. Whoever they're fighting has no idea we're here at all. A couple of us moving fast can surprise them and help finish the fight."

"My men knew we were waiting at the base of the mountain. Unless Salonen warned them, they don't know we've changed position," Enver said.

"I'll go with you." Egorova said. She nodded at Kazakov.

"And me," Clinton said, producing his weapon from inside his parka.

Kazakov nodded. "All right. Marta, I presume you're armed. You stand guard with the others until we return."

The dark woman nodded.

"I should go with you," Enver said. "They're my men."

The man had received his title for his military excellence, so perhaps Kazakov was wrong and Enver was armed and concerned for those he led. But Kazakov had experienced firsthand just how thin Enver's veneer of loyalty was for those who worked for him. Thinking about it, the reason

Enver most likely wanted to go was that he did not want someone else entering the installation before him.

"Come or stay. Your choice. But Marta stays with the others. We'll come back for you when the shooting is over."

She started to protest, but Enver stilled her with a glance.

Kazakov dismounted his trail-runner and hiked his scarf higher on his face. His hat he pulled lower, but none of it helped the fact that he was dressed in dark colors that would stand out in the snow. His companions were as well—except for Enver and Marta. Only the crust of snow across Kazakov's shoulders and chest gave some camouflage.

Kazakov struck out with Egorova at his side. Clinton and Enver came behind. The snowfall had thickened, the icy pellets replaced by small flakes that swirled blindingly in the wind and barely melted against his frozen skin. The snow was almost knee deep, a few inches of new snow on top of a crust that broke under his feet. Underneath the crust was a layer of slick ice that almost sent him sprawling over the cliff until he shifted his path to the uphill side of the road. Whatever the installation was, clearly a lot of traffic had passed this way—enough to pack the snow down to almost impassable, and it had not happened that long ago.

The firefight had settled into sporadic gunfire. He could imagine the combatants circling round through the snow, fading in and out of range and vision. To his right the mountain slope steepened, outcroppings at times completely roofing the road and confirming his assessment that it would be almost impossible to climb.

"Look," Egorova said and stopped. Deep tracks in front of her were slowly being filled with snow.

"It looks like someone started down the mountain," Kazakov said.

Enver studied the marks in the snow. "Could be Salonen's from when he came back to us."

Another explosion of rapid gunfire sounded closer.

"What the hell is up there?" Egorova asked.

"Something or someone very determined not to be discovered. They're going to be concerned at anyone appearing on their doorstep, let alone trained soldiers," Kazakov said as he eyed Enver.

The Ottoman nodded, acknowledging Kazakov's assessment.

He'd been foolish to think of Enver simply as a businessman/spy. The man was also a military man. "What's our best chance?" he asked.

Enver studied what he could see of the road ahead. "We stay close to the mountain slope. We stay low as we near the fighting. My men will try to get upslope from their opponents. We need to try to do the same."

Kazakov nodded. "All right. Weapons to ready."

He led up the road, listening to the gunfire. The sharp reports now had echoes that plagued any attempt to clarify their direction. The road seemed to curve around the mountain and suddenly the mountainside they'd been following fell away from them. Wind blasted them where they stood at one end of a narrow ridgeline that carried the road out into a void of swirling snow.

Rough stone walls to either side of the road were the only thing that told where the road ended and the void began.

Couched low, for the gunfire was close now, Kazakov started across the ridge. Thankfully, the vulnerable crossing wasn't long. The stone walls ended and the swirling flakes revealed a flat open area held on three sides by flanks of the mountain. In the center of the open space sat some kind of treaded vehicle. One door hung open. What appeared to be a dark-clad body lay collapsed and covered in snow close by the treads.

More rapid fire came from his left and Kazakov craned around the edge of the stone wall to see. Snow blinded him. He pulled back and peered above the wall. It was difficult to tell what was happening in the gusting wind and swirling flakes. The horseshoe of enclosing mountain slopes distorted sound, but it was possible to separate two distinct sounds. One group had a heavier sound of traditional automatic rifles. The others, though also automatic, were higher pitched. The long guns he'd seen Enver's men carry up the mountain were a lighter-framed Ottoman make. He had to presume that they could be just as deadly and had as good a range.

"Those are ours, there." Enver pointed through the swirling snow, confirming Kazakov's assessment. Through the snow not too far from where they stood, he made out a steep, rocky slope that ran around the open area. "They must be in amongst the rocks."

"That way are the owners of this place. They've got the heavier rifles." Enver pointed beyond the abandoned vehicle in the snow. "They must have better shelter there." He studied the scene.

Kazakov eyed him. Enver had had an illustrious military career.

"What is your best advice?" Kazakov asked.

Enver looked in the other direction, away from his men's gunfire. "We go that way and circle around them, coming up behind our enemy. They will have no idea we are here until it is too late for them. We have to assume that my men will understand our diversion."

"A good plan," Kazakov said. Clinton and Egorova nodded.

Head down and moving fast, for the snow provided only limited cover for his dark clothes, Kazakov cut right, away from the walled section of road, and ran through foot-deep snow until he reached the wall of mountain. The others came up behind him. Enver at his heels, Kazakov cautiously followed the mountain's curve.

This close, it was clear that the bowl of mountain that held them wasn't natural. Someone had cut into the mountainside to widen the flat area that held the vehicle. To make it better for large vehicles? As a staging ground for an army? Just how big was the installation? Where was it, exactly? How long had it been here?

The swirling snow blinded him as he led them closer to the rifle-wielding owners of this place.

"Look there!" Egorova had sidled up beside him. She caught his arm as she whispered.

He followed her point and through the snow made out a darker arch within the dim gray of the mountain slope ahead of them.

"A gate?" she asked as she peered intently through the snow.

"A tunnel, maybe…" Kazakov said.

"A tunnel would make sense," Clinton said from behind him. "Hard to spot on satellite imagery."

"Easy to defend, as well." Enver's voice held admiration.

Kazakov looked back at him. "Sounds like you wish you'd thought of it first."

He shrugged. "Fergana is a sovereign country. It would not be right." But his slight smile suggested he did not expect Kazakov to believe it.

"So my bet is that they're holed up at the tunnel entrance," Kazakov said.

"Makes sense," Clinton said. He sounded short of breath, but he held his pistol ready. "Do we come up behind them and take them out?"

"If it were only that easy," Egorova murmured.

"We get as close as we can and wait for the next exchange of fire. When they step out to shoot, we take them out. Enver, if you're not armed, I suggest you stay well back. I don't want you getting hit by a stray bullet."

Enver's hand slid into his jacket and came out with a smile and an automatic weapon similar to Marta's. "I do not go unarmed."

Kazakov nodded. "Everyone ready?"

More nods.

Staying close to the wall, Kazakov started forward. The wind buffeted his shoulders and tugged at his hat. It froze the metal of his weapon until he could feel the cold through his mitts. As the intervening snow lessened, the tunnel entrance became clearer. But that meant that he and the others would be more visible, too. Fortunately, the light had faded, but that meant their targets would be less visible.

Another flurry of gunshots said Enver's men attacked. A bullet ricocheted off the rocks over Kazakov's head and he threw himself down. That was the flaw in the plan. Their friends didn't know they were here. Yet.

He scrambled up. The entrance was close, and as the light fell in the mountains, a pale blue glow appeared deep in the entrance. Something that couldn't be seen from above, or probably from anywhere but this close to the entrance. But he could see it and in the dim light he could see movement.

He held up his hand to indicate stop to the others and then pointed. He caught their nods.

Gunfire erupted from inside the tunnel entrance and Kazakov stripped off his mittens and stuck them in his coat pockets. He raced forward, the others like hounds at his heels. The muzzle flash of two weapons came from ahead. He raised his gun and fired. Automatic gunfire from behind him cut past him. In the tunnel entrance, one shooter went down. Another turned and sprayed bullets in their direction. Kazakov leapt for cover amongst the rocky mountain slope. Bullets traced heat around him. He slammed into the ground and elbow-crawled for cover. Egorova was on her belly in the snow, shooting into the tunnel. Clinton had taken cover, but Enver stood in his white parka, shooting boldly into the tunnel.

From beyond the tunnel, more gunfire erupted as Enver's men realized the enemy was otherwise engaged. In the tunnel entrance, another shooter went down. The gunfire stopped. Kazakov leapt up and together he and Enver raced into the tunnel entrance. The snow ended in pavement that floored the tunnel.

He ran up to the fallen shooter and went to his knees. The man's chest was a mass of chewed flesh and blood that spilled over the pavement. He was young, ethnic Chinese, with handsome features, but his black-brown eyes stared blindly as his fingers clawed at his open chest. Then he sighed and stilled. No life there. While Khan might have saved him, Kazakov was far out of his depth.

He crossed to the other fallen man, but a bullet had caught him in the throat. Dead as well. And with them went any information about this place. But it was difficult to believe only these two guards and the one by the vehicle had been left to guard this place. He glanced up as Enver's men arrived and surrounded Enver. Clinton and Egorova inspected their surroundings.

Kazakov stood. The arched tunnel entrance was as tall as three men and at least wide enough for large trucks to pass. The walls were of sprayed concrete covering the chewed-out walls of mountain stone, and the earth had been paved. Clearly this was no small installation. The strange blue light emanated from slim panels set into the walls deeper into the tunnel where the road appeared to lead them deep inside the mountain. A series of empty storage racks and tanks stood along one wall, perhaps for vehicle parts and fuel. Along the other wall was a set of pens bedded in straw. Place for horses? This was a serious installation, incredibly large if the road was any indication, and obviously meant for long term operation.

He wondered how long it had been here. And who was still here. Three dead guards who could no longer provide information. So few just didn't make sense for a secret place of this size.

The slight tire grooves in the pavement suggested the installation's existence for far longer than he cared to think about. In Fergana. Right under their noses!

He turned to the others. "So. Assessments?"

Egorova came to his side, a camera he hadn't realized she had in her hand. She took a photo of the tunnel entrance. "They took cover in here, but they were more likely trying to protect what's inside."

He shouldn't be surprised she'd remembered a camera. She was a competent detective and had had to document scenes before. Kazakov nodded. Her thoughts matched his assessment.

"A considerable installation. Larger than the estimates I'd received," Clinton said. "I'll be interested to see what's inside." His gaze locked eagerly on the tunnel.

Enver's gaze narrowed on Clinton—the American had avoided the Ottoman and his men through most of the trip into the mountains. Enver stood with his men, all four unscathed from the battle.

"Why only three guards?" Kazakov asked. "Clearly this is something big, so why so few weapons to guard it?"

Clinton frowned.

Egorova looked up from taking a photo of the bodies. "There's only the one vehicle here, too." She nodded out the tunnel entrance at the falling snow that swallowed up their view of the guard's vehicle. "A rear guard, maybe? Maybe the place has been abandoned?"

"A reconnoiter is called for," Enver said with a nod.

Kazakov hesitated. There were three men dead here. His police training said he should take control of and document the scene, but...

"Kazakov!" Clinton's voice floated out at him from where the American had followed the road farther into the tunnel.

Enver and his men moved off down the tunnel, examining the installation.

"Document the Chinese presence," Kazakov ordered Egorova. She nodded and quickly returned to her photos. Kazakov hesitated about leaving her alone, but she *was* a trained police officer. He went after Clinton, passing Enver as he and his men examined a vehicle parked at a curve in the road at the back of the huge tunnel.

There, a slightly narrower road turned steeply down and to the right, as if it dove into the mountain. By the blue light of a panel, Clinton stood next to a concrete wall that held a single steel door with a small keypad panel in the center. Next to the door stood a rack holding steel barrels.

"I suppose it's locked," Kazakov said as he arrived.

"Looks that way," Clinton said, but he dipped his head toward the barrels.

Kazakov frowned as he looked at the door, but his attention followed Clinton's lead.

A small shift of air like an exhalation. The soft rustle of heavy clothing.

Kazakov glanced back at Clinton. The American nodded.

"Any chance of you figuring out how to open it?" Kazakov asked as he stepped back from the door. From where he stood, he could just see the rear of the barrels. There were only shadows.

"Not much," Clinton said and stepped in closer as if he was going to examine the door.

Kazakov lunged and reached behind the barrels, his hand closing on something soft and small.

Whatever it was shrieked and teeth cut into his hand. Against the pain he dragged their owner out of their shelter.

A child was his first thought. Perhaps five feet tall and with a bowl-cut of thick black hair that swung to hide her—yes her—features. She wore a dark blue coat of a fabric far too light for the mountains, and her loose-fitting trousers were the same shade. She wore no hat, but thick mittens covered her hands. Shiny, black, snow-pack boots rose up to her knees and looked suspiciously like the boots the dead Chinese guards had worn. Through the veil of hair, her gaze snaked angrily between Kazakov and Clinton. Then she collapsed to her knees and began to weep, her face buried in her hands.

An act? Who was she? He looked helplessly at Clinton.

The American spoke rapid Chinese at the woman.

Her head jerked up in surprise. "You speak Mandarin!" she said in heavily accented Russian.

Clinton smiled and crossed his arms. "And you speak Russian. What a small world."

The girl—no, woman—looked away. Regardless of her teacup features and bowed lips, the fullness of her voice said this was a woman. She looked away to the ground as if embarrassed she'd given herself away. Or it was an act. Kazakov was reminded of another China doll girl he had met who he'd mistakenly thought was a pawn.

"What do you want? You come shooting at us!"

Kazakov snorted. "I'll ask you the same thing. Who are you? What are you doing here in Fergana's mountains?"

The woman's small perfect mouth set in a line. "I have nothing to say."

Kazakov dragged her up by her arm. "Clinton, why don't you get Egorova and Enver. Maybe Enver can send one of his men back to update Khan and the others."

Clinton's gaze smoothed across Kazakov and the girl. Then he nodded and headed back up the tunnel.

Kazakov shoved the woman at the door. "Why don't you open it for us?" The fact that she resisted suggested that there was no superior force waiting beyond the door. The fact that she had apparently been trying to get inside suggested that there was shelter there for her.

She shook her head. "I don't know how. That is why I was hiding. I could not get away."

It might be the truth, but it was more likely that in her panic to escape the shooting, she simply couldn't get the door to work for her. It wasn't unusual for such a thing to happen when a person was panicked.

"Try."

She shook her head.

"Try!" It was an order and the woman turned to the keypad lock in the center of the door. She punched what appeared to be a random number. The door beeped, but nothing happened.

"See? I don't know the number." She turned such a pathetic gaze on him he almost laughed at the act. She might act a victim, but the fact that she was here suggested she was something more.

He sized her up. "My name is Detektiv Alexander Kazakov. I work for New Moscow police. Do you understand? Do you know what that is?"

She nodded, but her gaze ran calculations.

"Good." He loomed over her, using his size as a weapon. "You can open the door for me or you can wait until my friends arrive. There are people among them who will not take kindly to having to break this door down. If they do, they'll have no reason to keep you around, will they? If it was only me, I might bring you back to Fergana to face charges of spying, but the others—well, they may think that's more trouble than you're worth. On the other hand, if you help us, I might intercede. Your choice."

In the blue light, her skin had assumed a bilious green tinge. Her gaze bore black hate and her jaw was rigid.

Kazakov smiled.

The calculation in her gaze suddenly cleared. She turned and stabbed her finger at the digital keyboard and the door beeped again. A light flashed green and something groaned inside the wall. Then the door popped open toward him a bare half inch.

Surprised and cautious that she had complied, Kazakov caught the woman's arm again as he hooked the door fully open. There was firm muscle under his hand. Definitely something more to this one than the simpering weakling she played. "That wasn't so hard, was it?"

The scent of metal and motor oil wafted out from a darkness only illuminated as far as the light from the tunnel entrance's blue panels could reach. Beyond the door, a few feet of tiled floor faded into shadows. He couldn't make out the walls.

"What is this place?"

Her mouth remained stubbornly closed.

"All right. Your name, then. I have to call you something."

Her glare could have turned him to ash, but she licked her lips. "Li Ji."

Her mouth snapped shut as Clinton appeared carrying one of the installation guard's weapons, with Egorova similarly armed. Enver and his men—minus one—followed behind. Li Ji glared at them, too. A very personable woman, this Li Ji. Not that Li Ji was her real name.

"My friends, Li Ji was kind enough to open the door," he said.

Clinton and Egorova eyed him and Li Ji as if wondering what Kazakov had done to get the job done. Enver simply nodded his men toward the opening. Automatic weapons ready, the two men stepped past Kazakov and into the darkness. A light on the side of each of their weapons flashed on, creating two small searchlights that scanned more concrete-covered walls and blank, tiled floor until they caught on a bank of vehicles parked against the wall. They were small, with two seats and a steering wheel like the small runabouts Kazakov had seen at the New Moscow air terminal. A small open box behind the seats provided space for cargo.

One of Enver's men climbed into one and pushed a button. A light came on and the vehicle's dashboard glowed. A low hum filled the tunnel. Enver's man did something and the small vehicle rolled away from the wall.

"Electric, I'll bet," Clinton said with considerable admiration. "We've had people propose just such an engine, instead of something dependent on fossil fuels."

"Why?" Egorova asked.

"Because we're using up fossil fuels, and electricity is just about limitless. Hydro, wind, or wave action. Even solar."

Egorova shook her head. "Not that. Why did she open the door?"

"Does it matter?" Clinton said and stepped inside after Enver's men. Enver followed, leaving Kazakov and Egorova with Li Ji.

"I don't trust her," Egorova said. "I don't trust this." She dipped her head at the open door. "It's as if she wants us to go in. As if this is a trap of some kind."

"And now you sound almost as paranoid as me," Kazakov said and grinned. "I share your suspicions, but we'll take her with us. That should give us some protection. We can't just stand here. We need to understand what this place is. Besides, I'm beginning to think you were right earlier— the place looks like it might have been abandoned."

She shook her head. "We found one of those white suits like the guards were wearing. That and one of their weapons. They were shoved behind one of the tanks up near the entrance. It's like we're being sucked in. This is all too easy." Her determination faded to helplessness as if the words escaped her. "Call it intuition."

He nodded down at her. "I know the feeling. We need to be on our guard."

"You're going in there? How does this catch our murderer?" Her gaze was bright, her flesh the color of old meat in the unflattering blue light. A sudden brilliance inside the tunnel illuminated Clinton standing beside a wall panel. He waved a hand and grinned his triumph. A long line of blue panels flickered on, leading down into a tunnel, but these provided more light than those outside where Kazakov stood. Enver and his men had commandeered two vehicles and headed off deeper into the installation.

Clinton strolled up, but he moved stiffly and his breath was harsh in the relative quiet. The arduous journey had taken its toll on the injured man. "Shall we follow them? Make sure they don't get up to any mischief?"

Even if Kazakov distrusted Li Ji and the installation, it was a good idea. Kazakov distrusted Enver Pasha almost as much. The man had been entirely too helpful so far and that wasn't like him. Who knew what he and his men could get into? But Khan and the others weren't here and he didn't like the thought of leaving Li Ji and Egorova behind. Though Clinton had been helpful, Kazakov still wasn't sure of the man's motives, while Khan's insights had always been useful even though their relationship had been strained.

"Egorova, you and Clinton go ahead. I'll wait here for Khan." He met her gaze. "And be careful."

The young detective's gaze met his as she nodded. She might have reservations about the situation, but she also appreciated his trust. Head high, she followed Clinton to one of the electric vehicles and climbed aboard behind the wheel, with Clinton next to her. It took her a moment to figure it out, but then the humming machine sped away down the tunnel, Clinton clutching the doorframe.

Kazakov turned back to Li Ji. "What was your position here?"

The woman turned her head away, but a satisfied curve to her lips confirmed a reason to feel uneasy. Something was wrong and both he and Egorova knew it. And yet he'd sent her into the tunnel.

He grabbed Li Ji's arm and turned to her to him. "I asked you a question."

"Secretary. I was secretary."

"You expect me to believe that?"

"I not care what you believe."

Why would a secretary be one of the last people to leave the installation? A "secretary" and three armed men who were similar to Enver's bodyguards. Were the dead Chinese men also guarding someone?

Like this woman?

Or was she only another guard for the installation?

The rumble and whine of trail-runners echoed down the tunnel from the entrance and then Khan, Aisha, Sarpek, and Marta appeared along with the man Enver had sent back to them. All of them stopped when they saw the open door. Then Khan hurried up and the others came behind, Aisha trailing.

"What have you found?" Khan asked, his gaze trailing over Li Ji and then through the open door and beyond.

"Far more than I expected," Kazakov said.

Khan shook his head.

"What is it?" Kazakov asked.

"I'm just surprised is all. A woman here. Now, when it looks like the place has been abandoned or closed for the time being."

Kazakov nodded. "She claims to be a secretary. I'd say she's more than that. Either those three dead men were up here to escort her out of the mountains or she was one of them…"

"Where is Enver?" Marta demanded.

Kazakov tilted his head toward the tunnel and she stepped past to the door and inside, assessing the layout.

"Where?"

He told her and she went to one of the parked vehicles and headed after him.

"Do we follow?" Khan asked.

"Given no attacks and no explosions so far, I suppose so." Kazakov caught Li Ji's shoulder and shoved her through the door. "Time to earn your keep, Li Ji. You're going to take us on a guided tour."

He placed her in the driver's seat of one of the vehicles and took the passenger seat beside her, his weapon in his hand. Khan and Aisha took the next vehicle in line, but Li Ji simply sat there.

"Drive," Kazakov said.

"You can't make me."

He raised the gun to her head. "There are dozens of people who are already dead and I suspect your installation played a role in the death of each one. Most recently your people killed an old woman and wiped out an entire village. Would one death in return be so bad? I already know that you are more than a secretary, so why not quit the act? Tell me what we are seeing."

She looked sideways at him and the light slid over her gaze like a snake's. "The old woman and the village were necessary. They had heard and seen things that they shouldn't. This is—was—a research facility. It has run out of its usefulness, so a decision was made to close it down."

More likely they knew that the investigation taking place into the death of the old woman was drawing too much interest to the area. Interest that would make going undetected far more difficult.

"And what were they researching?" he asked.

The woman shrugged. "High altitude and winter survival. Genetic impacts. You know these tribal people stand the cold and altitude better than most?" Her grin was almost gleeful.

Perhaps that part of her story was the truth, but he would bet the tribal research subjects would not have survived the research.

"Drive," he said. "Take us to the research section."

She cocked her head at him like a bird before it pecked. Then she stepped on the accelerator and steered them down into the dimly lit tunnel. A single headlight showed them the way.

At first the tunnel was devoid of anything other than blown concrete over stone. Then the stone ended and the tunnel walls squared off into a metal-clad corridor as broad as it was tall. Closed doors appeared to either side. Each was closed with a keypad lock glowing in red.

Deeper they went. So far there'd been no sign of Clinton and Egorova, or Marta, Enver, and his men. The place was no small installation. The enormity slowly crept in as the little vehicle kept descending.

"How much farther?" he finally asked Li Ji.

"To research? That is in the deepest tunnels." She grinned at him as if it was a dare.

Deep in the earth would be the most sensitive section. Deepest to be safest. But deepest was also the place dungeons were placed. Deepest was hardest to escape.

"Then what is all this?" He waved at the walls around him, the closed doors.

Her lips curled. "It is nothing. Administration. Bureaucrats. Military. All empty now. They removed the records."

If it was true, it was likely the same below. Interesting, however, that the doors were still locked. "So it doesn't matter what we see. Nothing is left."

"But I will take you as you asked, so that the huge Russian does not hurt me." Her lips curled in a small secret smile. He wanted to help it off of her face.

She stepped onto the acceleration pedal and the little vehicle scooted forward with only a slight hum. Behind came the hum and hushed voices of Khan and Aisha. They'd probably heard his and Li Ji's exchange.

He couldn't shake the feeling that he was missing something even though he was on his guard. He knew Li Ji had layers of deceit hidden behind her sweet-faced mask and still he couldn't discern the nature of the danger, just as the King and Queen and Tsarevich had missed the true nature of the Tsarina in the pigskin.

No.

He had that wrong.

The tsarina had used a pigskin to hide her beauty. This, like his past dealings with such a woman, was beauty and vulnerability used to hide something else.

The vehicle's tires whined on the smooth pavement. Beside him, Li Ji wore a determined expression. To stay alive? To outsmart them? He didn't know and scrubbed his face.

Ahead, shifting lights lit the darkness. The tunnel had stopped its curve into the mountain. A large open area about thirty feet across gave onto a T of flat corridors spread out to either side of them. Blue panels led as far as he could see. The little vehicle slowed.

At the junction, five vehicles sat in a huddle to one side, their headlights like knife blades in the semi-darkness. Weapons drawn, Enver's men stalked down the tunnels. Clinton, Egorova, and Enver inspected the nearest doorways under Marta's watchful glare.

"This damn place is a maze of tunnels and doorways, not one of which will open," Clinton said when Kazakov and Li Ji's vehicle came to a stop. "I've checked fifteen of the damn things myself."

"And me," Egorova said. "They're all locked with an alphanumeric code." Her gaze went to Li Ji. "What have you found out?"

"Not much." As he climbed out of his seat, he told them about Li Ji's claim that this was a research facility focused on winter survival and genetics.

Li Ji sat unperturbed under their consideration.

"Khan? What do you think?" Clinton asked.

The M.E. joined them and listened as Clinton repeated his question.

"In winter, data would be gathered. In summer, they could experiment with what they had learned. Such research might be used to prepare soldiers for winter operations."

"But why here?" Kazakov asked.

Egorova nodded. "Why would the Chinese build such an expensive research facility on foreign soil when half the Himalayan Mountains are sovereign Chinese lands? There's some reason that they had to build here."

They all looked at the runabout vehicle where Li Ji still sat behind the wheel. She said nothing.

"Sorry, Li Ji. It seems that your story has fallen apart again," Kazakov said.

From down the corridor came a crash and they jerked around. One of Enver's men had smashed his rifle stock against a door mechanism in apparent frustration.

Li Ji winced.

"If you don't want a lot of that happening, I suggest you open these doors," Kazakov said.

"Why?" Li Ji spat. "They have been emptied. What can you possibly learn?"

Another crash from down the hall and Li Ji winced again. Enver's men battered the locking mechanisms. Then Marta held up her hand and aimed her automatic weapon at the door.

Enver nodded. Kazakov stiffened at the expected noise.

"Stop!" Li Ji yelled.

Too late. Marta's weapon spat. The door console exploded, spraying sparks. Li Ji screamed and the stink of cordite and overheated wiring filled the corridor.

The door swung open. Beyond, incandescent light sprang to life. Clinton glanced back at Kazakov and ducked inside.

A high-pitched wail emanated from the ceiling. Marta swung her rifle up at the roof. A voice boomed in Chinese.

Li Ji stomped on the vehicle accelerator and it lurched forward, mowing into Egorova and Marta and catching Kazakov in one leg. He spun aside as she swung the little vehicle around in the open space and careened up the corridor toward the tunnel entrance. Kazakov leapt to Egorova's aid. She stood and brushed herself off, apparently uninjured. Marta clambered to her feet rubbing her hip.

Enver dove for Marta's fallen weapon, aiming after the escaping woman.

Bullets pinged off the tunnel walls, but Li Ji's vehicle kept going.

"Derr'mo," Kazakov shouted. "Something's wrong! Didn't you see her face!"

He had to shout over the wail.

"What is this?" Enver waved his hand at the ceiling. The voice boomed in Chinese. The wail continued.

"Clinton knows the language, but I'd say it was something in the lock mechanism. By destroying it Marta set off an alarm."

"More than an alarm," Aisha said, leaving the vehicle she had ridden in with Khan. "I studied in the Kashgar Academy for a short while. My Chinese isn't good, but this seems to be a countdown."

Kazakov glanced up the corridor leading to the surface. Li Ji had been damned determined to get there. "They've set some kind of destructive mechanism in case this place was breached!"

"Just this one door?" Enver asked.

"This one's been breached. The others haven't!" Kazakov yelled over the wail. "Everyone out! We don't know how much time we have!"

He left the others to get to the vehicles and ran to the door of the room Clinton had entered. A far door was open, but there was no sign of Clinton. "Clinton! Out! This place is going to blow—or something!"

"Kazakov, come on!" Khan yelled from one of the vehicles.

Enver's men were smashing door locks until doors opened, checking inside and then running to repeat the process.

"Enver shouted them back and then allowed Marta to hustle him into a machine and up the corridor. Aisha waited in a vehicle. Egorova hesitated beside her.

"Go! I'll be up in a minute!" yelled Kazakov.

"In here!" Clinton's voice floated out beyond another door. "You gotta see this!"

Egorova still hesitated beside the machine that held Aisha.

"Go!" Kazakov rushed inside. The room was little more than four bare walls with metal industrial-sized sinks along one wall and a door across from him. So much for Li Ji's claim of a research center.

He rushed across the room and through the other door. Another room. Still no Clinton.

"Where the hell are you?" he yelled. This room was as barren as the last except that a doctor's metal examination table was bolted down in the center of the room. He slammed past it heading for yet another door that led beyond.

And came into another room with another table bolted down in the middle. But this room held a huge round light suspended on a jointed stanchion above the table. Marks against the bare walls showed where equipment had stood.

An operating room?

For the research? In case of emergencies. An installation this large would certainly require medical facilities. The shrilling siren and booming voice shuddered through the room.

What the hell had Clinton so interested that he wasn't leaving?

As if on cue, Clinton appeared in yet another open door. He flourished a sheaf of papers as he headed for Kazakov.

"It's a storage room, with old file cabinets," Clinton yelled.

"We have to get out of here!" Kazakov said.

"You think I don't know that? The cabinets had been emptied, but I found these fallen down behind the drawers." He stuck the papers in his jacket.

In the corridor, the countdown voice had gone eerily silent. Egorova and Aisha still waited beside their vehicle. Enver's men and the others were long gone.

"Damn you, go!" Kazakov yelled. The fact that the countdown had ended couldn't be good.

Egorova leapt aboard her vehicle and Aisha accelerated up the corridor. Kazakov climbed behind the wheel of the last machine and Clinton threw himself aboard. A whining klaxon filled the tunnel. The ground began to shake.

Kazakov stomped on the accelerator and the little vehicle hummed calmly up the sloping tunnel as if it had all the time in the world. Ahead, Egorova and Aisha's vehicle sped up, but it seemed too slow. Too slow, but still faster than they could run it. Behind them a rumbling overtook the klaxon in volume. Clinton glanced over his shoulder.

"Nothing to see. Keep going," Clinton said.

Kazakov glanced up at the tunnel ceiling. So far so good. The blue panels flashed past as the two vehicles buzzed for the surface. Then the panels went out and the small vehicles' two headlights were the only lights in the darkness. Thank God there were no turns to navigate.

Gradually the darkness seemed to lighten until he could see the rear of Egorova's vehicle.

Clinton looked back again and his face glowed ruddy. "Shit. Go man. Go. There's bad stuff happening!"

Kazakov chanced a look over his shoulder and a puff of hot air caught him in the face. Fire consumed the depths of the tunnel and the inferno was coming for them.

There was no more acceleration available. The little vehicles hummed on. Surely to goodness they had to reach the exit soon.

Heat filled the tunnel and his back felt sunburned. Heat burned the backs of his ears and the plastic steering wheel seemed to soften under his hands.

He looked back again. The flame was closer, rising like a dragon up the tunnel. Everything below them had to be consumed. Just as they would be if they didn't reach the exit.

A gust of cold air said they were almost there. He willed the little machine faster, stomped the accelerator as hard as he could. Nothing happened.

Ahead, Egorova's vehicle suddenly slewed aside and their headlight found a darker square of darkness ahead. He slammed on the brakes and the little machine lurched to a stop. Aisha and Egorova were already running for the doorway. He and Clinton scrambled out. Flames licked toward them along the ceiling and wall, feeding on oxygen. The klaxon stopped midwhine, and in the sudden silence, there was only the roar of the fire. What it was feeding on, he didn't know.

"Come on!' Kazakov yelled and grabbed Clinton's arm.

The two of them threw themselves through the door. Kazakov turned and slammed the tunnel door, praying it locked automatically behind them. Then they sprinted past the empty fuel tanks and storage bins.

Beyond the tunnel entrance, night had fallen and the snowfall had become a storm. Swirling flakes and high wind slammed into them as they neared the cavernous mouth of the installation. They caught up to Egorova and Aisha and stepped out into the night.

Snow stung their faces. The cold stole their breath.

"We have to keep going," Kazakov panted. "We don't know what else they have planned for destruction. They could bring this whole mountain down if they wanted." He had to pray that wasn't the case. There was no way they'd be off the mountain in time. Not in this.

He pulled on his mittens. Pulled the earflaps down on his hat. Aisha, Egorova, and Clinton followed his example and he and Aisha set out in the lead. Sarpek, Khan, and the others along with the trail-runners and equipment had to be just over the ridge. If they were still there. If Li Ji hadn't done something.

Head ducked against the wind, on foot he plowed out into the swirling snow, Egorova at his heels, Aisha and Clinton behind. The Chinese snow vehicle no longer stood waiting. Li Ji's action, probably. The blue glow of the tunnel disappeared behind and they were lost in near darkness and cold and wind. Snow blew into his eyes, cold froze his nose and ears. Wind plastered his jacket against him and bent him almost double. It caught fingers under the edge of his collar and sent chills down his spine.

The snow reached almost to his knees as he cut a trail for the others. He dared not slow for fear of what came behind, but the swirling flakes made him depend on dead reckoning that he would reach the ridge and not fall into the precipice. Still, after he'd gone what he thought was far enough, he had to pause to test each step. With this much snow, the edge of the rock was likely disguised by overhanging snow. He could step down and right through if he wasn't careful.

An eddy in the flakes caused him to change direction. Stone rose up ahead and, relieved, he picked up speed again, racing over the ridge following the tracks of Li Ji's snow vehicle. Sarpek and the others should be waiting beyond.

"Sarpek!" he called.

"Over here," Khan's voice, barely audible over the roar of the wind. A small light appeared to guide Kazakov and the others past the low humps of the snow-covered trail-runners. He caught a whiff of oil and gasoline.

He found Khan kneeling beside the stone wall of the mountain. Sarpek lay in the meagre shelter of a snow-laden ledge. From one of the trail-runners, Khan had found an emergency blanket and wrapped it around the fallen man.

The M.E. looked up at him, his face skeletal in the flashlight's light. "The Chinese woman ran him down. Enver and his men just left him. They took their trail-runners and ran. When I got here, he was unconscious. It looks like almost everything is broken. All I can do is keep him comfortable."

As if comfortable was possible here, with the mountain possibly coming down around them.

Kazakov shook his head. "We have to move. That installation's self-destructing. The whole mountain could go."

"The whole world can go to hell! Sarpek's not going anywhere and I'm not leaving him here."

Khan's voice cracked and Kazakov was silent a moment. The M.E.

was not usually prone to such outbursts. "Then we'll get him on a trail-runner and take him down with us."

Again Khan shook his head. "He's dying. He's going to die here in the mountains that are a part of *our* blood. Take your blasted machines and go. I will stay with him to encourage the *shahada*—the acknowledgement that there is no God but Allah, and to pray over him when he is gone. Such is done with the dying in our tradition and I will not leave a good man alone."

"Nor will I," Aisha said, in solidarity with Khan. "I will pray that he returns to Allah who truly owns him." She knelt beside Khan.

There was no way that this was a safe distance from the installation. If there was any explosion, it was a certainty that it would bring huge avalanches pouring down all along this narrow canyon that the road followed.

"You're both fools," Kazakov swore. He bent down and picked the dying man up in his arms.

"No!" Khan caught his arm. "You can't move him. It will cause too much pain."

Kazakov shook off Khan. "You said he's unconscious. No one is staying here. We'll get him farther down the mountains and grieve with you. He will still be in these mountains." If the old man didn't die in Kazakov's arms.

Against Aisha and Khan's protests and stepping as lightly as he could, he crossed to one of the trail-runners. Egorova ran ahead of him and swept off the snow. She slung a leg over and started the machine, then climbed off and helped Kazakov on.

"This is the right thing," she whispered.

Kazakov wasn't so sure. Khan had gone silent and stood furiously brooding in the darkness beside Aisha.

Kazakov nodded in their direction and got the trail-runner moving as rapidly as he dared. The others would follow.

With Sarpek in his arms, it was hard to steer. The snow and the darkness made it a challenge to see, but the tracks left by Li Ji's machine left a trail he could follow in the trail-runner headlight.

A rumbling behind him said he needed to pick up speed. He pushed the accelerator forward and the trail-runner bucked through the snow. Something was happening at the installation. He checked over his shoulder. A bright flash of light cut through the darkness.

Blinded, he jerked around and slowed the trail-runner.

The explosion blasted through the wind. Heat seared into his back. Snow lifted over him in a tidal wave and Kazakov couldn't see, couldn't hear, couldn't breathe. He slammed to a stop and managed to cut the engine. Snow all around—he was drowning in it.

With Sarpek still in one arm, he floundered up, kicked off the machine, and shoved away snow until his head burst from the smothering cover. He dug Sarpek's head free but couldn't see in the darkness. With his free arm, he checked Sarpek's pulse. Weak and thready, but there. The others?

"Khan! Egorova! Clinton! Aisha!"

Rumbling swallowed his voice. It came from under him, above him, from everywhere, but his vision still failed him and he was caught under one of the road's rock overhangs. The snow vibrated around him, the stone seemed to hum as if the whole mountain was truly coming down. Then the night filled with the rumble of a train as dark snow avalanched down beyond the overhanging rock.

It went on. And on. And on. It seemed like an hour but was most likely only minutes. How could so much snow collapse and not fill in his small refuge? When it stopped, silence fell until the wind's howl reasserted itself. Flakes swirled around him.

"Khan!" he called again. "Egorova! Clinton! Aisha!"

Still no answer, but the wind had likely masked his words. He might be the only survivor and just what had they accomplished? He was a fool to have come here! Had he led everyone to their deaths? Rage and guilt tightened his chest. He was a detective, not a spy, not a hero from a trashy thriller novel. He had come up here hoping to identify who was behind the killings and all he'd confirmed was that it was the Chinese—people like Li Ji. Though she'd more or less admitted it, just where did that leave him?

Mourning a tribal woman, his partner, a foreign national, and his best friend.

He closed his eyes.

19

Cold dawn came, first with the soft gray of dove wings across the sky and then with a deceiving rosy glow around the mountain peaks that were softened by the ice crystals suspended in the air. The storm had ended in the middle of the night and left the mountains frozen and Kazakov feeling suspended in his life, his investigation, in everything, so that he focused in on Sarpek, digging both of them out of the snow and then tunneling down to the trail-runner for whatever supplies he could find that would comfort the dying man. An extra shirt. Another emergency blanket. There wasn't much more he could do. All their water was frozen, so he put small bits of clean snow in the dying man's mouth. Sarpek swallowed the meltwater.

It was enough. Instead of taking a life or focusing on those who took life, for the moment he took comfort in giving what he could to this man who had helped him, but whom he barely knew. Under Sarpek's thick gray brows, his eyelids jerked and shifted as he dreamed in whatever netherworld he walked.

In the freezing morning air, Kazakov knelt beside Sarpek and watched the sun rise in a silent glory of golden columns marred only by an eagle soaring high up on morning thermals.

When he looked back to Sarpek, the mountain guide's eyes were open and his gaze glued to the sky. His lips moved. His breath came in ragged gasps. Kazakov leaned in close, whispering the only thing he could recall about Aisha and Khan's words—that there was only one God.

A mechanical roar masked their voices. Kazakov jerked up and around.

From up the snow-obliterated road in the direction of the installation came three trail-runners carrying four riders. Kazakov floundered to his feet, waving his arms madly. They were here! They'd made it through the explosion and avalanche.

"They'll be here in a moment, Sarpek. They'll know what to say!"

He looked down at the guide.

Sarpek gazed blindly at the sky.

Kazakov went to his knees, checking for a pulse. For breathing. He felt like crying. There was nothing there. Whatever had been Sarpek was gone, leaving behind the flesh he had hid within. He took the old man's hand and tried to remember what Khan and Aisha had said. There was something the Kyrgyz people did and said after someone died, but it escaped him at the moment. In its place he hearkened far back in his memory to the days when his mother had taken him to church.

"O God and Lord of the Powers and Maker of all creation, Who sent Thine Only-Begotten Son and our Lord Jesus Christ for the salvation of mankind, and with His venerable Cross didst tear asunder the record of our sins, and thereby didst conquer the rulers and powers of darkness; receive from us sinful people, O merciful Master, these prayers of gratitude and supplication, and deliver us from every destructive and gloomy transgression, and from all visible and invisible enemies who seek to injure us."

He looked up as the trail-runners arrived and somehow the prayer of Saint Basil no longer seemed appropriate for its plea to nail down human flesh and piercing of souls. "Take care of this good man, oh, eternal Father. He returns to you. Amen."

Khan dismounted off the rear of Egorova's machine and stumbled through the snow. "Sarpek! Is he…?"

Kazakov nodded from where he knelt beside Sarpek. "He died just now, with the dawn. I'm sorry. I couldn't remember the prayers you said to pray over him."

He looked up at them then. The frustrated fury of Khan's expression. Aisha's bleak tears. Egorova stood stoic, still straddling her trail-runner, while Clinton stood behind them.

Khan and Aisha waded through the snow to Sarpek's side and

Kazakov floundered up to give them space. They knelt beside the dead man.

Khan gently closed Sarpek's eyes against the glare of the sky and closed his slack jaw. Aisha straightened the old man's clothing and crossed his hands on his chest. She pulled the blanket Kazakov had found for him up over his chest.

"*Inna lillahi wa inna ilayhi raji'un,*" Khan intoned. Aisha joined him and together they repeated the words over and over.

"We thought you were dead," Egorova said softly. "That the avalanche caught you. My machine quit and blocked the trail for the others. By the time we got it going, you were out of sight and then the explosion happened. We were lucky—just like you, apparently." She nodded up at the overhang of stone. "As it was, we had to dig the machines out this morning." She studied the snow. "Let me guess, yours is down there."

He nodded and turned back to Sarpek's body. He knelt beside Khan and joined him in the prayer. It didn't matter what it meant. When Khan and Aisha were done, they bowed their heads toward Mecca and prayed again. Kazakov waited for them to finish.

When they were done, Khan turned a disdainful gaze on Kazakov. "This is not your faith."

"If it was the right thing to do for Sarpek, I felt it right to join in. I was with him when he died."

Aisha touched his mitten-covered hand. "Then it was kindly done."

"What did the words mean?" Kazakov asked.

"Verily we belong to Allah, and truly to Him shall we return," Khan said. "And the last was a supplication to Allah to forgive us all our sins." Sighing, he stood up and looked down at the body. "We need to rig something to get him back with us. Maybe wrap him in the blanket and carry him over one of the seats?"

"No!" Aisha held up her hand. "I knew him best of all of us. He was Kyrgyz. He loved the mountains and mourned that his elder days deprived him of them. He would have been happy to have died here, among them, and his family would be happy that his body is here."

"But we cannot wash him and do what is required," Khan said.

"Sarpek and Allah will understand." Aisha's voice was final.

Khan finally nodded. "Kazakov, give me a hand. You were with him when he died. That will have to do."

Together they wrapped Sarpek's body in the blanket. When they were done, Khan stood and caught Sarpek's shoulders. Kazakov caught the dead man's feet.

"If we cannot bury him in a graveyard, then we will let the mountains bury him in their breast," Khan said.

Together they hauled Sarpek's body to the edge of the cliff. They hefted him up and swung him out and over for the long fall into the precipice. It was too deep to hear him land and they did not watch him fall. What had been Sarpek was already gone to Allah.

Khan was silent a moment looking out over the snow. Then he turned, his expression unfathomable. "What now?"

"We go back down and continue to look for evidence," Kazakov said. "We might have confirmed that the Chinese killed Bermet Aytmatov, but I'm not sure whether we'll ever know more than that. And we still do not know who killed Zholdosh."

"You never give up, do you? I thought all the evidence pointed in this direction. And the installation is now destroyed," Khan said.

"There are other channels to be investigated. A woman witnessed Zholdosh's murder—at least she heard it. I need to find her. And there are other channels to pursue as well." He thought of Enver Pasha, who was probably down the mountain and well on his way to Biysk and New Moscow by now. The man had to know something more than he was telling.

A low whistle turned both of them back to the others. Aisha was still on her knees in prayer, but Egorova and Clinton intently examined something they had spread on the seat of Clinton's trail-runner.

"Kazakov, you should take a look at this." Clinton looked up. "It's the papers I grabbed."

"Papers?" Khan asked.

Aisha finished her prayers and stood. The sun breached the mountain peaks overhead and poured light down over where they stood. The glare was blinding, but it also posed a danger. The sun would heat the snow and increase the chances that the already unstable mountainsides could give way again.

"From the installation," Clinton said for the others' benefit. "There was a file room. These had fallen underneath the drawers of one of the cabinets. I learned a long time ago to always check there. You never know what you might find."

Kazakov raised an eyebrow. Apparently Clinton made a habit of breaking into places. He slogged through the snow to Clinton's side, Khan and Aisha at his heels.

"What have you found?"

Clinton held the papers firmly on the seat against the brisk wind, which carried with it a scent of dust and smoke, suggesting that something still burned at the installation entrance.

"From what I can make out, it looks like this was more than a research facility. It looks more like a medical facility."

Kazakov frowned. "An installation that size, there'd have to be a first aid team."

Egorova and Clinton both shook their heads. "That's not what these papers are showing."

"And you saw the operating theatre," Clinton said. "That was more than you'd find at a first aid facility. A facility like that—it would cost less to airlift injured and sick out than to build and staff something like that."

Kazakov scanned the top paper while Clinton held the corner. It was a document covered in indecipherable Chinese figures. At the bottom was a sketch of a man with a small mark on his hip. Beside it was a closeup of the area with the mark. It showed a small, elongated pouch built of skin.

Kazakov's breath caught in his chest. He looked up at Clinton, and the American nodded. They both turned to Khan. All three of them had seen a real-life version of such a thing on the body of a dead man—a Chinese spy turned double agent for the Ottomans, to be exact.

"Khan? Is this what I think it is?"

The little M.E. peered down at the document. His lips tightened. Finally, he nodded. "We found just such a thing on Collin Archer's side, but that doesn't mean anything. He was Chinese. Once the Empire had the technology, it would be expected that such a spy would have one."

"Makes sense," Kazakov said.

"What about this?" Clinton asked and slid the top paper under the others to reveal another document.

This one was also covered in Chinese characters and showed a pair of side-by-side photographs of what appeared to be a leg x-ray. The first photo image appeared to show a shaft of metal down the middle of a broken femur and both broken tibia and fibula. The broken bone ends did not touch.

In the second image, it looked like new bone growth had filled in the spaces in the previous photo. Kazakov shook his head.

"What is this?"

"It looks like a procedure to lengthen a leg," Egorova offered.

"That's what the writing says—from what I can make out of it. I read Chinese, but this is highly technical," Clinton said.

"Spies," Kazakov said. "Collin Archer was altered. This is one way to do it."

Kazakov flipped the page up to see what was underneath. More writing. No pictures. Flipped again and it was more indecipherable writing, the pictographs almost beautiful in their simplicity. Flipped once more to the last piece of paper and again it seemed to be a document illustrating a procedure. At the top of the page was an open mouth displaying small, crooked, discolored teeth unevenly spaced in the gums. He scanned down the Chinese figures to the bottom of the page, where the same mouth, judging by a small mole on the chin, now showed a crowd of large, white teeth.

Kazakov peered down at the teeth. Archer had had a mouthful of them. Something squirmed at the back of Kazakov's mind. This meant something, but he couldn't put his finger on what.

"What is it?" Khan asked and came up beside him.

"Teeth," Kazakov said. "Archer's were like this. But where else have we seen them?"

"I don't know what you mean." Khan shook his head.

"I mean that I've seen other people with teeth just like these. I just can't recall who." He tapped his fingers on the page, then let the others fold back into place, hiding the troubling image.

Khan shook his head. "I've no idea." He glanced over his shoulder at Aisha and she met his gaze. Something seemed to pass between them, but Khan only sighed.

"I think we've spent enough time on the side of a frozen mountain. Sarpek has been sent on with blessings. I think it's time to move on—to home."

Clinton folded the papers and placed them in his inside jacket pocket. Egorova pulled her hat down farther on her head and the others followed her example.

Working together, they dug out Kazakov's trail-runner, and with one of their machines, helped to pull it free of the snow. When he tried it, Kazakov's engine turned over and roared to life. Together, they started down the mountain road as the sun rose past noon.

The road was deep with new snow from the night before, but occasionally, in the shelter of outcroppings, Kazakov spotted the tracks of

Li Ji's snow vehicle and the marks of other trail-runners—Enver's team probably. The woman had made it through and was likely headed toward Chinese territory. Were Enver's men after her? Did it matter?

All the way down the mountain, Collin Archer's disembodied death grimace filled his mind. Where had he seen a similar show of teeth? The image floated in the air like that cat-grin from the Anglo children's story.

Teeth transformed as part of a mask. The pigskin tsarina had hidden her true, lovely form under the squalor of a pigskin. Who was the person who hid their true nature behind perfect white teeth? Faces of people he'd met on this case and his last one sifted through his brain.

One face settled over the others and fit Archer's white grin.

Boris Bure.

He almost drove the trail-runner off the side of the road.

It couldn't be. He was allowing his dislike of the man to color his assessment. He glanced over his shoulder at the four riders following behind him. Would they agree with him? Would they tell him he was insane?

It didn't matter. He was certain. Bure's dead-fish smile was the same.

20

It was midmorning three days later when they reached the gutted remains of White Stone Village and the Biysk Valley spread out before them. The sky was painfully blue as if the storm in the mountains had never been. The mountains' white snow incredibly pure as if he lived in a dream. Across the valley the white slopes of Biysk's ski hill were dotted with the small black shapes of skiers blithely making their runs. They had no idea where Kazakov's small group had been, nor what they had seen.

Nor what Kazakov might know.

The naked shapes of the aspens placed a gray haze along the frozen river's channel. The green of the spruce and fir placed shadows over the glistening snow.

And the future.

It had taken too long to come down from the mountain, though the trip seemed to go faster to Kazakov. His mind was busy elsewhere.

On the long journey back, every so often it was as if he shook off a trance and realized his bones rattled with the trail-runner's roar and that his nose was full of the machine's engine smoke. When they stopped to camp, it was all he could do to deal with Egorova and Clinton and the others. Even the scent of food barely roused him, though he stuffed his mouth with the cold mutton and bread they set before him. Every once in a while, a particularly striking mountain scene would rouse him from his reverie and once more he would be caught by the impossibility of his suspicions.

Surely Boris Bure's smile was natural.

For all Kazakov's dislike of the man, he had to recognize that Bure was fast becoming a national hero with his rhetoric of Ferganese greatness in the face of greater foes. His rhetoric was waking up the masses, though Kazakov shuddered at what the man espoused. And then there were the rumors that Kazakov had been hearing in the months since the election was called: that Bure not only was a leader, he had the bloodlines—was able to trace his ancestry back to one of the great Yekaterina's children.

Surely such a man could not be a Chinese spy. It was impossible.

And yet all the denials could not dispel Kazakov's thoughts and the dark dreams that had had him up and pacing the snow at their camp each night.

"What are you thinking?" Egorova had come up beside him as they paused before their last run into the town. Clinton, Khan, and Aisha were sharing their last bits of flatbread as they wandered through the abandoned village. The trail on which they'd traveled had shown the scars of larger vehicles—most likely Biysk Police trying to deal with the carnage found in the Kyrgyz camp. He wondered what the news outlets were saying.

He shook his head. "Just how peaceful it looks."

But for how long? The wind whispered across the snow between the sad-looking stone houses. The air was chill, but the sun was still hot on his face.

"You've been distracted."

He glanced at her.

Her face, usually plain and strained with the stress of police work, had somehow reworked itself in the mountains. Her cheeks and forehead were bright with color and they, in turn, lit the blue of her eyes. Even her lips seemed to have brightened.

Or perhaps it was only his eyes and insides that had changed. Perhaps he saw through the professional mask she had so carefully arranged over her person. The dogged detective was revealed as a woman.

He smiled. "Clinton's pages. They gave me much to think on."

She raised her brows at him in a question, but he shook his head. "Not here. Not now. It's time we were back. I'm sure your boss wonders where we absconded to."

She chuckled. "I'd say Nikitin is probably beside himself. It might almost be worth it to stay away a little longer."

"But we're coming back with nothing to show for our trouble. At least nothing that will help to convict anyone for Bermet's murder."

Her smile disappeared. "They'll close the case. I doubt anyone will want to hear about how she died."

He nodded, feeling the failure. "Her death will count for something. You watch. And there is still Zholdosh's murder to solve."

She looked at him as if seeing him anew. "Is that how you get things done? Never do what they tell you?"

It was his turn to smile. "Haven't you figured that out by now?"

"It's time to get back to town," Khan said, his footsteps crunching on the snow as he came up beside them. "I want to get back to the city. I've been away from home too long."

Kazakov nodded and hailed Clinton and Aisha. They reappeared through the village and climbed on their trail-runners.

The last bit of trail went swiftly. Where the trail met the road, they found an unmarked police vehicle parked, a uniformed officer behind the wheel. At their approach the driver's side door shoved open and the officer climbed out.

Nedved stood looking at them. His disheveled hair and day's growth of dark beard made him look as if he'd been sleeping in the vehicle.

"You made it back. If you weren't here today, I was going to rent a trail-runner and try to find your trail." He grinned.

"Let me guess," Egorova said, looked from him to the vehicle. "Nikitin wasn't happy that you'd helped us and come back to report a massacre in his mountains."

"You might say that. He said if I was so inclined to help you, then I could wait here for you. You're to come into the station and give a statement—all of you."

Kazakov shook his head. "We will. When we're ready." He patted the constable's shoulder. "You might as well follow us. Did Enver and his men come through?"

Nedved nodded. "Some trail-runners came through late yesterday. I think it was them."

"Then you'll need to get their statements, too."

Kazakov revved his trail-runner's engine and headed out. Once they reached the road, they roared up and over the drifts that covered the roadsides to Ayim Beshimov's home, Nedved following more sedately in his vehicle. The trail-runners they left in Ayim Beshimov's yard. Nedved advised that he would head back to the station and advise

Nikitin that they had arrived and would report to the station as soon as possible.

"I will give you a ride to your hotel," Khan offered Clinton.

"You're leaving?" Kazakov asked. "But we have matters to discuss…"

Khan met Kazakov's gaze, but Khan's dark eyes were opaque. "You, perhaps. I am not a police officer. I am only a Kyrgyz medical examiner who does what he must for his family. Now I must get back to New Moscow."

His gaze fell away and Kazakov was struck once more with the feeling he'd missed something. Perhaps in his preoccupation on their trip out of the mountains. But then he could be reading more into it than there was. Khan might simply miss his family.

"You go on without me," Clinton said and Khan turned away to his vehicle.

After Khan and Nedved left for their separate destinations, the American followed Egorova, Aisha, and Kazakov into the guesthouse warmth.

"I thought you'd want to get back to your hotel and report," Kazakov said as he slid out of his boots and coat. Egorova hung their jackets up as Clinton slipped off his jacket. The American shook his head.

"I think there're things to discuss before I do."

Kazakov raised his brows, but Clinton shook his head.

"Let's just say it's pretty clear that you've been doing a lot of thinking. So have I."

Kazakov nodded. He ducked his head into the kitchen to greet their hostess. Aisha went into the kitchen, leaving Kazakov to lead Clinton and Egorova down to the office. Inside, Kazakov took his time lighting the fire in the stove before turning to them.

"Those papers," he said.

"They mean something to you," Clinton said. "I saw it in your eyes when you flipped through them."

"Maybe," Kazakov said slowly. It was as if he was finally waking up and a plan was forming. "The thing is, I'm not sure; and sharing what I'm thinking is certain to bring trouble. I need to be sure."

"What can I do?" Clinton asked.

Kazakov sighed, weary from the long bone-rattling journey and the thought of what was to come. "For starters, let me see those documents again and tell me what they say."

Clinton produced the documents, this time from a silken pouch he carried on a cord around his neck. On the desk he laid them out again, this time side by side.

In the shadows of the single bulb, there were differences between the documents. Figures at top and sides of the pages were different. Even the pages' sizes differed slightly as if the chosen format had changed over time. He hadn't noticed that before.

"These pages aren't connected," Kazakov said after scanning them.

"I would say that every so often a page fell behind the drawer. I have that happen with stockings. One will fall and I never realize until I go looking for that exact pair," Egorova said.

Kazakov met her gaze. Her assessment made sense, but it was hard to imagine Egorova with stockings instead of trouser socks and winter boots, or a fur hat and parka.

But then he could. Even in the harsh shadows of the lightbulb, her female countenance remained.

"So these are the accidental product of years—decades, possibly. An installation like that does not spring up overnight."

Clinton nodded.

"So what do these documents say?" Kazakov asked Clinton. "What do you think the Chinese are doing?"

Clinton scanned the documents, running a finger up and down the lines of characters. "This one," he pointed at the one with the x-ray images, "reads like instructions. It is all about the breaking of the limbs, spacing the ends, and the insertion of plastic rods. Then there is a process for encouraging bone to grow—at least that's what I think it is. It's more technical than my Chinese skills."

"Not exactly material on mountain survival," Egorova said.

Clinton turned back to the papers. "This one appears to be part of a letter rationalizing a need for specific specialists to be sent to the installation." He frowned and bent closer. "Interesting. They must have been picking up a fair number of tribals. They're asking for interrogators. Something about the need to gain clarity on what they know and what they have told others." He shook his head. "Sorry. It just goes on with more rationalizations."

Interrogations and limb lengthening definitely didn't sound like a mountain survival research facility. They might be in a mountain, but so far, the documents pointed to something far different and darker.

Pouring over the third document, Clinton frowned and shook his head. "This seems to be a progress report on the installation from a few years ago. It talks about sixteen 'aliens' captured and 'treated.' No—it's not treated, but that's as close as I can get to the meaning." He shook his head. "We need a Chinese language expert—someone with technical knowledge. I'm not even sure whether the American government has such a person."

Easing his back, Clinton turned to another page—the teeth. "Another 'how-to' page outlining a cosmetic process."

Kazakov nodded. "Collin Archer had such teeth."

"The dead spy. Yes. You mentioned," Clinton said.

"Clearly, we're looking at papers from a spy installation," Egorova said, stirring from where she'd perched on the edge of the makeshift desk. "All of the documents you've read are relevant to spying, whether stopping people who came too close, interrogation, or changing a person's looks."

Kazakov nodded. "The question is what does it mean? Do we look at every tall man and woman with suspicion because of this?" He tapped the document of the bone lengthening. "Everyone with large teeth because of this?" He tapped the relevant document.

Clinton's gaze narrowed. "What is it about those teeth that have you so spooked? You were preoccupied with it all the way out of the mountains."

"So you noticed it, too," Egorova said.

Kazakov faced two sets of enquiring eyes, and these weren't going to accept him just turning away. He turned to the small woodstove to warm his hands. The crackle of flame and the tang of pine smoke filled the room.

When he looked back, Clinton and Egorova were both still waiting. Clinton's gaze had turned watchful. Egorova looked pained.

"You're acting like a guilty man," she said.

"Guilty. Yes. Guilty of suspecting something months ago and doing nothing about it." He sank down into one of the two chairs, sighed, and studied his hands. "Sharing what I suspect is only going to add you to the rolls of the damned."

Clinton raised his brows. "I'm a spy, remember? I'm already damned."

"You could say that about me, too, given I'm stationed in Biysk. The Fergana police might have promoted me as their first female detective, but they sure didn't want me someplace where I might be seen."

Kazakov studied them. Clinton had the lines around his eyes and the quiet demeanor of a man who took in everything around him and found it mostly wanting. Egorova had the hungry look of someone still looking for validation. Clinton would take Kazakov's information as just one more indication of the damning of Fergana. Egorova would learn that all the worst things she might think about her country were true.

Or perhaps worse things. He couldn't look at them as he revealed his wild theory.

"It's the teeth, as you suspected. I looked at those photos and my first thought went to Collin Archer, but when I first saw his body, he reminded me of somebody—at least his mouth did." He looked up at them. "Boris Bure."

He watched the shock flare in both their gazes. Clinton's face shifted to consideration. Egorova unconsciously shook her head in denial.

Kazakov drew in a heavy breath. "I know it doesn't make sense, but that's the direction my mind has gone since I saw that image." He lifted his chin at the documents. "I just can't understand how it could be possible. Collin Archer—he was an unknown person—an Anglo-German. But Boris Bure has a history, a pedigree even. How can he be a spy? Did Collin Archer have the same sort of history? Someone I interviewed said he came from a distinguished family in the Anglo-German empire. If that's true, how could that be? How could two men from such distant places have the same teeth?"

Maybe they could help him make sense of this.

Egorova had sunk back onto her perch on the desk. Clinton settled on the other chair by the work table.

"That is one hell of an idea," Clinton said with a shake of his head.

Egorova stayed silent, but Kazakov could see the information ticking over in her head as she tried to make sense of it.

"Where do I begin to prove such a thing?" Kazakov asked. His words fell softly into the quiet of the room. The fire crackled and spat. Heat rumbled up the chimney. From the front of the house came the voices of Aisha and Ayim Beshimov.

"Bure's been in the public eye for a long time. How could he have ever been replaced by a copy? Surely someone would have known..." Egorova's halfhearted protest faded away.

"On the other hand, it would explain his rhetoric," Clinton said. "Link the Kyrgyz and Uzbek Muslims to the enemy, the Ottomans, and make them the enemy from within. The people get scared and they vote for him. As president he can do a lot of damage by shifting from Fergana's neutral stance." He shuddered at the implications.

Kazakov nodded. During a previous case, Clinton had revealed to Kazakov the reason for the American interest in such things. Clinton and the American Embassy to Fergana were representing an attempt to establish an assembly of united democracies from around the world to stand as a block against the monolith Ottoman, Chinese, and Anglo-German Empires. Their fear was that the winner of any war between the Ottomans and Chinese would lead to the victor turning their eye to the rest of the world. The Anglo-Germans would fall and the small fledgling democracies would be erased. Clinton was under orders to make sure it didn't happen.

"Has Bure even been to China?" Egorova asked. "He's barely been to Biysk as far as I can recall—at least not since he's become a candidate."

Kazakov met her gaze. "It wasn't as a candidate. Think back—or no, you weren't here when Bure had his election rally. He mentioned something there—something I had been aware of, but forgotten. When Bure was a boy, he and his family came to Biysk for a holiday, but on the return home there was an accident. All of Bure's family were killed and he went missing—was lost in the mountains. Local guides tracked him, but it was only two weeks later that he was found—amazingly healthy after the ordeal." Kazakov thought about it a moment. "He mentioned it at the rally, but in a cursory way as if he knew that not saying something might be strange, and he didn't want anyone thinking the matter deserved further examination." A matter of hiding the facts in plain sight.

He met Clinton's and Egorova's gazes. "He was seventeen then, I believe."

"But that's almost thirty years…" Egorova said.

"Wow," Clinton said with a hint of admiration and slumped back in his chair. "If you're right, talk about playing the long game."

Kazakov nodded. "The Chinese Empire has been around a very long time. I suppose one can develop patience."

"My country is young. There's no way they'd wait so long to get what they want."

Kazakov thought about that. "My ex-wife did her advanced degrees in China. She talked about them as an ancient culture that takes pleasure in watching a plan unfold, whether it be a painting, a poem, or a battle. She also talked about the importance of saving face. In other words, the Chinese might be willing to take their time in order to enjoy the fruits of their labor unfolding, but also to ensure that their role in the plan was never visible. They would not want to be known as the ones who started a war—merely as the ones who finished it."

Yes. That made sense. "If Bure is elected, then he can purge the tribals," continued Kazakov, "most likely forcing the Ottoman Empire to react. The Chinese can then intervene as Fergana's saviors."

Clinton nodded slowly. "The world might buy it. What do we do?"

"I'm not sure—yet," Kazakov said. "The trouble is, we only have suspicions and no proof."

"And how does this help find Zholdosh's killer?" Egorova asked. "Isn't this suspicion something else entirely?"

Kazakov wasn't so sure. "Bure might not have killed him directly, but there's a chance Zholdosh knew something. He'd been involved with the armed camp. Perhaps he knew about the installation and how it might be destroyed. If the Kyrgyz camp had become aware of the installation and had plans to attack, the Chinese could have taken action with a preemptive attack. After they had to kill Bermet and the village, too, they probably realized the days of their installation were numbered and that's why they were moving out. Or they knew Bure was almost certain to be elected and the installation wasn't needed anymore. At least not until after the election."

He looked up at the others and shook his head. "I know. Not particularly what our bosses are going to want to hear. How do we explain to Nikitin and Rostoff?"

"They'll say we're crazy." Egorova nodded and looked glumly down at her hands.

With a shake of his head, he stood. "We still need to tell them. I think we should start with Rostoff. There're a few things that have happened that might help to convince him."

Clinton shook his head. "You're being overly optimistic. What do you think you're going to do? Arrest Bure? On what grounds? His followers won't let it happen."

Kazakov looked at the papers on the work table. "We have those. They help to build a case. We'll find more evidence." And there was the skeleton of a plan floating around in his head to do it. But first there were people he needed to talk to.

He hauled out his phone and dialed Rostoff's office number. Constable Dabria Smirnova's melodic voice came at the end of the line. "Inspector Rostoff's office. Constable Smirnova speaking."

"Dabria. It's Kazakov. Is he in?"

"In?" He heard her slight smile in the question and could imagine her seated primly behind her desk hearing the furious fuming that usually accompanied anything Rostoff was involved in.

"What has him upset this morning?" he asked.

"Actually? You. A Sergeant Nikitin just called. Apparently you have disappeared and taken their only detective with you. I won't bore you with any concerns for your safety."

Kazakov chuckled. "Doesn't surprise me. Nikitin would rather I disappeared and he wants Egorova around to bully. Can you put me through? We can't have Rostoff misled, now can we?"

"A moment, please." The line clicked and Dabria's efficient voice disappeared. Then the phone clicked again.

"Kazakov?" Rostoff's voice boomed over the phone as usual.

"Sir." Kazakov said, knowing the unusual show of respect would give Rostoff pause.

"I've just been told you've disappeared."

"We were following a lead that took us into the mountains."

Rostoff stayed silent, waiting as any good investigator would. Kazakov regained some respect for the man.

"We—we found something other than what was expected." He explained about the old woman being tracked back to an armed camp and the relationship of Bermet's death to that of the village and the armed camp.

"But who would do such a thing?" Rostoff said, clearly intrigued.

"That was what we went into the mountains to find out. It took us four days of tracking and three days out. We lost our guide in an avalanche on the way out."

"I'm sorry," the big man had the grace to say. "What did you find?"

Kazakov looked at the phone and then up at Egorova and Clinton. "It is better that we explain in person. I phoned to ask you speak to Sergeant Nikitin on our behalf. Tell him that we have been found and that Detektiv Egorova has come with me into New Moscow. We will be there tomorrow, late."

"You'd best make good time. I want you here before end of shift."

"Yes, sir. Sir… Any word on Chelomeyev?" He'd been remiss on not asking sooner.

"Aah. There is a bit of good news on that front. The doctors tell me there are signs he is regaining consciousness."

"Good news," Kazakov agreed. He thanked Rostoff and hung up, looking from Clinton to Egorova.

"You heard. We'd best pack up and head out. I want to be on the road within the hour."

"But can't we head out tomorrow, early, after a good night's rest?" Egorova asked. "And what of Nedved? We told him to tell Nikitin we'd be in as soon as possible."

Kazakov grinned. "As soon as possible is what it will be, just not what Nikitin assumes. And I will personally apologize to Nedved for the hell that will come his way. As for leaving in the morning, that will get us into the city too late. I have some stops to make before we see Rostoff." He turned to Clinton. "What are you going to do—after you get copies of these documents and give me the originals?"

Clinton stood, stretched, and winced. After the long trek, his features were gray as he gathered the Chinese papers. "Well, it had crossed my mind to sleep, but I suppose I should alert my government of what we've found and suspect. They aren't going to be happy." He shook his head and turned for the door. "I'll drop off the papers inside an hour."

Then he was gone, ducking out the low door, his footfall a metronome down the hallway.

Kazakov swept the room with his gaze. "We pack everything up and take it with us."

He and Egorova got busy, taking photos and reports off the walls and placing them in boxes. Then Egorova left for her home to pack a bag and Kazakov carried the box of evidence down to his room. Inside, he set it on the bed and placed his duffle bag beside it. It didn't take long to pull his few pieces of clothing from the dresser and get them into the bag. On impulse, he tossed in the old magazine with Bure on the cover. The Miracle Man, indeed. Just not for the reasons the magazine had covered. He used tepid water off the top of the unlit stove to wash and changed into clean clothes. It felt good, but a long soak in the metal tub he used at his dacha would be so much better. His entire body ached and his side throbbed from the recent injury that had lost him a kidney. Clinton must be made of sterner stuff to have survived the journey.

Clinton arrived and handed him an envelope with the original documents. Where he'd managed to get copies made, Kazakov didn't ask. Then the American was gone and Kazakov carried his evidence and his bag down to Ayim Beshimov's kitchen. He pushed inside.

"Ayim Beshimov!" He caught her hands. "It has been a most wonderful stay. Your warmth and hospitality have been much appreciated, but I fear the investigation takes me back to New Moscow."

Her wise old eyes blinked at the news. "Aisha has told me of your travels. I thank Allah that you brought Aisha back to Taalay and me and I will pray for your safety. There are dangers treading Fergana, I think."

He could not tell her how much. It was better that he and Egorova and everyone associated with the investigation were gone from her doorway. Hopefully, when things became bad, she and her small family would survive.

Instead, he nodded and thanked her again, settling the bill with a generous tip. "I will tell all my friends that Ayim Beshimov's guesthouse is where they should stay in Biysk for an authentic experience." He didn't mention his dearth of friends.

He refused her offer of a last meal and trundled his belongings and the evidence box out to the fading afternoon and his Perseus. The trusty vehicle started without protest and, under skies heavy with pregnant clouds, he drove to Biysk police station. Egorova was already waiting, looking fresh-scrubbed in clean clothing, high black boots, and a slightly out of style calf-length coat of black, boiled wool more suited to the capital.

He raised his brows at her attire and she colored attractively. "Nice coat," he said.

"I've been saving it for when I eventually get transferred to a larger post," she said.

He wondered how long she'd had the coat and figured probably from when she'd obtained the detective rank. So many hopes dashed in this damned country. But he got the sense that this was the true Egorova climbing into his vehicle. Her gaze was bright and steady. No fatigue here, regardless of all they'd been through, while he felt wasted and aged far beyond his forty-five years. But then there was a time when he would have bounced back more easily, too. A time when he believed in the innate goodness of the world.

He put the Perseus in gear and headed out of the parking lot.

"I saw Nikitin," Egorova offered. She was looking out the passenger window, but he could see her gaze reflected back in the glass in the gray late afternoon. She didn't look happy.

"He said that, as far as he was concerned, the case is closed and my career is over if he has anything to say about it. He didn't like the fact that we went into the mountains without telling him, nor the fact that a New Moscow bigwig called him to tell him what his people are doing. He says I can damn well work for Rostoff, then."

Kazakov smiled. "Not exactly the sort of thing I'd wish on my friends."

She nodded and stared out the window. The Perseus had left the confines of resort hotels and expensive dachas and was climbing the steep road out of Biysk Valley. The asphalt road was pitted with frost heaves. The trees were heavy with snow that had been sculpted by wind into macabre shapes that seemed to reflect how Kazakov felt.

It was hard to believe that it was only ten days since he had driven down this road to Ayim Beshimov's home. Ten days, and it felt like the world had changed. Someone had lifted the masks and veils and something ugly writhed underneath.

"Kazakov! Watch where you're going!"

He came to himself and twisted the steering wheel so he no longer aimed them at a snow bank.

"What's the matter with you?" Egorova demanded.

He scrubbed at his tired eyes and squeezed the bridge of his nose. "Too long surviving on adrenaline, I guess."

"You were off somewhere just like on the journey down the mountain. Do you want me to drive?"

He looked askance at her. "No one drives my Perseus."

"Well, no one will be driving it if you drive us off a cliff!"

He took his gaze off the road to look at her. "Do you happen to know where Bure's family went off the road?"

She looked away. "How did you know I looked up the old file?"

"Because it's what I would have done, and you're way more like me than I care to recognize. And you ran into Nikitin. For that you had to have gone inside. Tell me, how the heck did you get the file out of archives so easily?" He pinned her with his gaze before turning back to the road.

She shook her head slightly. "Not so hard. When you told me what had happened at the protest, I wanted to learn what I could about the man. So I called archives and asked for what they had. Today I phoned in and they told me the juicy parts. The file will be waiting for us in New Moscow."

He was silent a moment. Her action showed initiative that he hadn't necessarily believed was there. Unfortunately, there was a downside to what she'd done.

"What? What is it?" she asked.

"Nothing. Nothing worth mentioning."

"Like hell." She twisted in her seat to face him. "Tell me what I've done wrong this time." Her voice carried resignation.

Finally, Kazakov nodded. "All right. There's probably a very good chance that by asking for that file, you've set off an alarm in someone's ear. Do you understand?"

She shook her head.

"It's highly likely that any time that file is reviewed, word of the review gets back to powerful people—or to Bure himself."

What would it mean to them? If Kazakov's suspicions were true, the Chinese would do just about anything to protect the man that they had positioned to become president of Fergana. Given what he'd experienced in the Weber/Manas murder investigation, there was every likelihood that "anything" would include wiping off the map any detective with the temerity to investigate.

She sighed. "I didn't realize."

Kazakov shook his head as he steered the vehicle around a wooded hairpin turn. The road was still rising into the mountains before it could begin its long descent to New Moscow.

"How could you know? Frankly, I'm surprised the file is there at all. After all these years, I'd think that they'd have managed to make it disappear. Then again, maybe they realized that making a file disappear could make other people suspicious. They couldn't have that."

"You keep talking about 'they.' Who is 'they'?" Egorova had braced her foot against the floorboard and had a good hold on the door handle.

Clearly, the speed with which he took the many turns made her a little nervous, even if she was trying to hide it.

"The powerful people backing Bure. The Chinese. There's got to be people in government who back him, too. Some will do it quietly. Others —won't."

He thought of Annuschka, his ex-wife. She'd done her advanced degrees in communications in Nanjing and had been providing advice to Bure's campaign. At least he suspected so. Did she fully understand who and what she was working for? He doubted it. He doubted anyone had connected Bure directly to China.

"What do you plan to do?"

At the moment he wanted a smoke to relieve the tension that tightened his shoulders. He shook his head. "Unfortunately, I intend to drag a few more people into this danger we're in. People who can help me find information."

"Oh." Egorova said and sat back in her seat. "And Zholdosh's murder? What do we do there? I thought it was important to solve the crime."

Kazakov glanced at her. "I haven't forgotten. Bure and his men were in Biysk when it happened. It could have been them."

Her gaze was appraising. "Some might say you are obsessed and lay everything at Bure's door regardless of the evidence."

Kazakov shook his head. "There was a witness. A Nadia Tolbanova. She saw the killer. Now we need to find her before someone else does."

"You think she's in danger?"

"There were witnesses in other cases involving Bure. They didn't live to tell their story."

Egorova fell silent.

It took the better part of the night to navigate the snowy road from Biysk to New Moscow. Dawn was yawning over the Tian Shan Mountains eastward as they came down out of the Pamir-Alay foothills. The Perseus seemed to want to turn toward Kazakov's dacha, but that was the last place they should go if his investigation was known.

Instead, he turned the vehicle downhill through a localized flurry of snow and into the snow-cleansed streets of New Moscow. Another lie. Another veil lain over the gray stain that was the city.

At five in the morning, the Perseus cruised through nearly empty streets, the multicolored spotlit, fantasy domes of the replica Saint Basil's Cathedral rising over the naked haze of trees along the dark crack of frozen river that sided Potemkin Park. He checked his watch and turned off Suvarov Way into the quieter streets of old New Moscow. Here, older homes sat in small yards with planted trees old enough to throw shade. He pulled up in front of one home that had a plain door and porch. Snow covered the yard, but a narrow path had been dug through to the road.

"Wait here," he said and climbed out.

Egorova frowned.

"It's early, I know. The wife of the man I want to speak with is quite ill, but knowing him, he will be awake. He will see me, but if you're there it may disturb her."

He left her and climbed the four steps to the door. Instead of ringing the bell, he knocked softly and hoped that his assessment of Kasimir Krupin's sleeplessness was correct. He stood in the cold, the slight snow placing a haze between the Perseus and him. The dawn-lit, falling snow masked the growing traffic noise that came from elsewhere in the city and hid the bulk of what Russians called Yekaterina Mountain. In truth, that name was a veneer over what the Kyrgyz and Uzbeks had named Suleiman's Mountain, named after the ancient emperor and holy man who had come here to pray in the same spot that Mohammed was said to have trod.

A slight noise from the house turned him around. A curtain stirred in the small window beside the door. Then the door swung open to reveal Kasimir Krupin looking as rumpled as usual and far more tired. The man had a wild head of graying hair and a set of pince-nez glasses perched on his nose. A white shirt with ink-stained, turned-up cuffs was tucked into a pair of brown woolen trousers held up by suspenders. Once Krupin had been a Chief Financial Officer of a leading New Moscow company. Then he had lost his job and become a leading business reporter in the city. Since Kazakov had last seen him a month ago, the man had lost weight. He just had to hope that Krupin was still as plugged into the city's happenings as he once had been.

"Kazakov. What do you want? Margarete is sleeping, the best she has in days."

Krupin's wife, once the beautiful commanding leader of the city's social scene, was dying of cancer. She had come home to die but had helped Kazakov on his last investigation. At the time, Kazakov had promised to visit again, but time had swept by him and he still had not visited.

"I came to see you, actually. Do you have a few minutes?"

Krupin stepped aside but peered out at the vehicle. "You are with someone."

"My partner," Kazakov said, stepping past the older man into the wood-paneled foyer and felt strange saying it. How long was it since he had willingly worked with anyone? Things were changing—even him. "I told her to wait so we did not disturb Margarete."

Krupin nodded his thanks and led Kazakov into the dining room to the right of the foyer. At least once it had been a dining room. Now books and papers covered the long table that could have served a dozen, and more books filled the chairs and were stacked on the floor. Only one seat remained uncovered and Kasimir lowered himself behind it and picked up a pen. A lined writing tablet sat before him.

"You caught me working. What do you need?"

Kazakov looked around himself for a place to sit. He lifted a stack of books off a chair and perched them on more books on the table. He sat down facing Krupin.

"Boris Bure," he said and watched Krupin's eyes widen.

The newspaperman nodded.

"What can you tell me about him and his backers? Not what's in the news, but what do you know that might not be fit to print?"

Krupin's long, gnarled fingers set down his pen and shoved the tablet away as if afraid of anything that might be written down.

"That—is an odd question from a police detective. I see the police chief and the Minister of Justice at his rallies. Surely you know more than me."

Kazakov shook his head. "My partners and I have already gone far enough that it is likely that alarms are sounding somewhere. I'm not asking you to ask around. I'm asking what you know—about his past, his backers. His connections to foreign governments…"

He let his question hang.

Krupin shifted in his seat. His throat worked, but he did not look away from Kazakov. "You're treading very treacherous ground, my friend. I could be one of his backers. I could be preparing to warn them."

Kazakov shrugged and shook his head, heartened by Krupin's caution. "Maybe. Perhaps. But I don't think so. You've made a second career out of revealing business dealings that others would prefer remain uncovered."

"You think compliments will sway me?" But Krupin half-smiled.

"I think you are long past compliments. Margarete: she is your life."

"She is. I must protect her for as long as she lives. That has kept my mouth closed many times."

A slight noise had Krupin on his feet and rushing to the doorway. "Margarete! What are you doing here!"

Kazakov stood. Just outside the door stood an apparition of the woman he'd seen barely a month before. She was reed-thin bones under a veil of flesh. A silken turban, long flannel robe, and shawl seemed to weight her down. Surely the slightest eddy of air would otherwise pick her up like fluff off of a dandelion. But her skeletal face was still beautiful as she turned fever-lit dark eyes from her husband to Kazakov.

"Detektiv? Tell me that you and this husband of mine were not conspiring to keep your presence from me? It has been too long since you visited and gave me purpose." Her long, pale fingers plucked at Krupin's sleeve as she unsteadily turned to Kazakov and graciously held out a hand like the great lady that she still was. But the hand wavered unsteadily in the air until Kazakov caught it.

Hot and dry as if she was consumed by flames from within.

"Madam Krupin. As always, it is a pleasure to see you. I had some questions for your husband and did not wish to disturb you from your sleep."

She shook her head and looked up at her worried husband. "Kasimir always worries that I do not sleep enough. So I pretend to. For him. But when there is a chance of entertainment beyond those interminable books —well, I cannot stay in bed, then, can I?"

Kazakov nodded but looked at Krupin. Let him decide whether Kazakov should leave.

The old man sighed and shook his head. "Perhaps we should return to Margarete's room. That way she can be comfortable while we have our conversation."

Krupin's arm encircled Margarete's shoulders. "Come, love. Let's get you back to bed."

It was a slow shuffle down the hallway to the room that had once been Krupin's library. Now the walls of shelves had been relieved of most of their books, which had been replaced by glass vases, flowers, and photographs of the Krupins and family and friends. A hospital bed now sat where a desk once had, and a side table held a stack of books and too many medicine bottles. Krupin helped her back to bed and settled her against a thicket of pillows.

She looked diminished and tired compared to the last time Kazakov had seen her, but still she smiled gamely out at him and waved him to a chair beside her bed. Then she rubbed her thin hands together.

"So, Detektiv. I heard you mention that beast, Bure."

Kazakov looked from her to Krupin. "That is a dark opinion of a man who is likely to be our next president."

Margarete shook her head. "I may be dying, but my memory is still good and I remember Boris Bure. I may be twenty years his senior, but I've felt his shove as he pushed his way to where he is today."

"Tell me, please."

"I was friends with Natania Weber. My granddaughter played with Yekaterina when they were both very young—when Natania was still married to Carl Weber. Mother and daughter were both so filled with life and then Boris Bure came into their life. Natania came from an old Russian family so it was a surprise when she married a German banker. Still, it was a happy marriage—at least while Yekaterina was very young. Then they met Boris Bure, who was an up-and-coming functionary of the Ferganese government."

Margarete shook her head as a deep, rough cough tore through her.

Kazakov waited patiently as Krupin helped her take a sip of water from a crystal goblet. Finally she pushed away the cup and swallowed.

"Bure became smitten with her. He was always at their house, supposedly for some other reason, but the rumor mill was churning—again. There had been other stories about Bure—some unpleasantness when he was in school—but everyone always said it was because of what he'd been through in the mountains. He'd come back changed—as if his spirit had been broken. Leastways, his friendships dwindled. Of course, he made new friends. Important friends, it seems."

She leaned her head back against her pillows and closed her eyes. The sound of her watery breathing filled the room, and from under the scent of the floral bouquets came the iron-scent of fever and a hint of something rotting—the cancer inside her, probably.

"Perhaps I should come back another time," Kazakov said softly and stood from the chair beside the bed. "You can sleep after I so rudely got you from your bed."

Krupin shot him a thankful glance but Margarete's eyes flashed open —dark and fighting for life, denying what was happening to her.

"No. I don't know how much time I have, Detektiv. The doctors say it is day-to-day. Let me spill my memories to you while I still can. If it will help, even better."

"It will help."

Margarete swallowed and began again. "I had my run-in with Bure about eight years ago. Bure was barely on the public radar. Carl Weber died suddenly in a car crash that shouldn't have happened. His brakes failed on a return from the mountains. He went off a cliff. Bure was immediately at Natania's side. Her friends warned her of him. He got wind and he came to see me. Told me that if I did not support a marriage it would be a black mark against me. I refused to endorse him. Not too long afterward, Kasimir lost his job." She caught Krupin's hand and shook her head. "I'm still sorry about that."

Kasimir shook his head. "Perhaps my previous employer was Bure's ally."

Kazakov straightened. That was news to him and highly unlikely, for Krupin's previous employer was none other than Enver Pasha.

She looked back at Kazakov. "Needless to say, I was not invited to the wedding and suddenly there were two groups holding charitable events. Natania was not part of that, but still it was as if Bure or his backers were trying to punish me. It was punishment enough to see what he did to Natania. That vibrant woman turned into a fearful frump almost overnight. And then the death of Yekaterina. Tragic. I blame Bure for that, too."

Kazakov held his breath, wondering whether she knew of the nature of Yekaterina's relationship with her stepfather.

She didn't offer anything.

"Why do you blame Bure?" he ventured.

"Because the man was wicked. He doubtless chased her out of the house and so she was ripe to be murdered—a child alone on the city streets."

"I see." He looked at Krupin. "Is there anything more? Anything you know."

Krupin looked affectionately at his wife. "She has summed up our largest dealing with the man."

"But you know more." Kazakov took a leap because Krupin was now a newspaperman. He would do his research.

"Know?" Krupin shook his head, his wild head of hair a halo in the soft light from the two windows that transected the shelves. "What does one ever 'know' about Boris Bure? Yes, there is a profile that is in the public eye, but there are also gray areas that one may never discover."

"Layers," Kazakov said. "Masks."

"Yes!" Margarete and Krupin said in unison.

"Masks that he wears in public and in private," Margarete said. "I often wonder what Natania discovered under those masks."

Kazakov thought back to the last time he saw Natania Bure. "Fear."

Margarete nodded from amidst her throne of pillows. "There have been rumors of Bure for a long time. A temper. Violence, a penchant for young—women."

"A friend once showed me an old newspaper article that he suggested was about Bure," Kazakov said. "It was about a seventeen-year-old boy who sexually assaulted a younger girl. The case disappeared from the newspaper except for the one small article."

"Dedushka." Krupin smiled. "I saw the same article, and those about the death of his family and his miraculous rescue."

Kazakov stilled, but Krupin said nothing more. "Have you, by chance, looked into that more?"

Krupin shook his head and caught Margarete's hand. "Should I have?"

Kazakov nodded. "Tell me, when he came back to New Moscow after that horrible incident, where did he live? His family was dead. Did he have other relatives?"

Krupin frowned and stood. "A moment, please. My memory is not what it was. Let me get my notes."

He left and a few minutes later Kazakov heard voices in the hallway. Krupin returned bearing a worn leather notebook, followed by Egorova.

"I'm sorry," Egorova said.

Krupin waved her protest away. "I insisted. She would freeze to death sitting out there. She is another detective, correct? Your partner?"

Kazakov nodded. "Margarete, Kasimir, this is Detektiv Elena Egorova of the Biysk Police Department. She is my partner on this investigation. Egorova, Kasimir Krupin is an ex-leader of industry and now a business reporter. Margarete—"

"Is a silly old woman who was foolish enough to get cancer," Margarete said. She held out her hand in greeting and Egorova caught it and smiled.

"It is a pleasure to meet you."

But Margarete's gaze was locked on Elena's face. "Do I know you, dear? I feel that I should. Your mother? Another family member? Where did you grow up?"

"In Petersberg, but I left with my mother when I was twelve for New Moscow."

Petersberg was a northern mining town consumed with gold.

"And why did you come here?" Margarete asked, still holding Egorova's hand.

Egorova looked away, glanced at Kazakov helplessly. "A job. My father was killed and my mother needed work. She came here as a housekeeper."

"A house… My God! You're Tasha Velikaya's daughter! I recognize you now, by the cheekbones and the eyes, though you are taller."

Egorova squirmed uncomfortably in the face of the woman's excitement. She tried to free her hand, but Margarete had uncommon strength. "This child is a true descendent of Yekaterina!"

Margarete glanced up at Kazakov. "Surely you can see it. The eyes. The cheekbones. The same as our own dear Yekaterina!" She turned back to Egorova. "Why have you changed your name, dear girl?"

"Because of exactly this kind of reaction. It doesn't matter what my ancestry might be. No one can be sure and there are enough people out there claiming such bloodlines, it really doesn't matter anymore." At last

Egorova freed her hand. She stepped back beside Kazakov. "I'm sorry. I didn't intend this to happen. I planned to stay in the vehicle."

Kazakov looked at the young detective anew. Now that it was spoken, he could see the likeness. But the great-great-great-great-granddaughter of an empress? Could it be? He remembered the small glass slipper ornament Egorova kept on her desk. A princess waiting to be revealed to her public. He shook his head.

"Krupin was gathering his notes about Bure to share with us. I asked him what he knew of Bure's early days after he was rescued from the mountains."

"Here it is," Krupin said from a cushioned armchair against the wall of shelves. The leather-bound notebook lay open on his lap as if he was about to read them a bedtime story.

"It really was a miracle and a sensation," Krupin said. "Here a seventeen-year-old boy in street clothes survives for two weeks in winter mountains. When he was brought back to New Moscow, he was a hero and everyone wanted to know him. With his parents and siblings dead, he had no one except a cousin of his mother whom he didn't know. As a result, a collection was taken in the community and very large donations were received for the miracle boy. It was arranged for Bure to remain in the family home with a couple hired to live with and support him. The municipality of New Moscow offered to pay for their engagement and the University of New Moscow gave him free tuition."

He looked up from reading from his notes. "A very lucky lad, our Bure."

"Who were the couple who cared for him?"

Krupin scanned his notes. "An Ivan and Lada Petrov. A common enough name."

Common enough to be hard to trace. "Do you have anything more on them?"

Krupin shook his head.

"Anything on friends, organizations he belonged to?"

Krupin shook his head again. "As I said, he left his old friends behind and made new ones."

Egorova frowned. "Isn't that strange? Wouldn't it be more normal for a person who'd lost everyone he loved to cling to his friends?"

A reasonable expectation. Kazakov considered. "Who'd he walk away from? Who'd he become friends with?"

Krupin shook his head. "That I don't know."

"I might know something," Margarete said. She seemed to have shrunk into her pillows and fatigue filled her face. Clearly this was too long an interview. "I remember back then. We were planning an event for the young society girls—sixteen-year-olds. They had all arranged their dates and I seem to remember one of the girls was devastated right at the last minute when her beau broke up with her. If I remember rightly, it was Boris Bure."

"Who was the girl?" Kazakov asked.

Margarete went still, her skin translucent as agate stone.

"You already know her. Your ex-wife, Annuschka."

21

———————

On the street outside the Krupin house, the snow was still falling in fine flakes that placed a nacreous pall across the glowing sky. Here and there hints of blue shone through the white veil as if truth was shining through. Of course, that could be a lie, too. Muffled traffic rumble came from the direction of downtown, and even the snow couldn't hide the scent of diesel and coal from the factories just outside the city. The curtains were closed in the rows of houses down the street, so they seemed to slumber in their blanket of snow.

Kazakov turned to Egorova across the top of the Perseus. "So what was all that about your ancestry?"

She shrugged. "Nothing that matters. My mom worked for them, is all. As a housekeeper."

"And she and you are descended from the great Yekaterina?"

Another shrug. "It was a story my mother liked to tell when she could not put enough food on the table. We would snuggle under a blanket and she would tell me grand stories of Yekaterina and say that I was like the pigskin princess—hidden until the right man finds me." She grinned. "Funny, but whenever I'm hungry, I remember my mother's arms warm around me."

Kazakov nodded through the veil of snow. "She was a wise woman, your mother. She gave you a gift that most parents can't or don't. You must love her very much."

"I do. I did. She died a year ago. A hit-and-run when she was walking to her shop. She'd saved enough money housekeeping to open a small store specializing in specialty giftware."

"Let me guess: she gave you the small glass slipper ornament that you keep on your desk." But a hit-and-run…

Egorova went still. "Not exactly. It was part of her estate. Something she had had as a child. She said it had been her grandmother's. I keep it at the office because I'm there more than home."

"Did they identify her killer?"

Egorova shook her head and turned to look toward Yekaterina Mountain. Its bulk was barely visible through the falling snow. Its peak and base invisible.

A hit-and-run. That was one way to be rid of another claimant to the throne—not that there was any throne anymore. Sending another potential rival to work as a detective in a remote mountain village would get rid of another. He thought about the impact of being told from childhood that you were descended from queens. What impact would that have on your psyche? Clearly not much in Egorova's case. But Bure…

Though *this* Bure wasn't the same as a child who had been raised from birth with such tales, clearly as an adult he intended to use the story as both weapon and armor. Had the original Bure family actually been Yekaterina's descendants? As Egorova had said, such claimants were common in Fergana.

He unlocked the Perseus. "We need to find the couple who raised Bure and I need to talk to my ex-wife. I'm going to drop you at the library. There's a man there named Artyom Shepovalov, also known as Dedushka. He works in the periodical department. Tell him I sent you and ask him for help in locating that couple. I'll be back to pick you up in a couple of hours."

Egorova nodded and climbed in. Kazakov slid behind the wheel and started the Perseus. The tire tracks in the street were filling with new snow. He carefully guided the vehicle down the street and across the river to the center of the city. There they had a hurried meal of eggs and sausage —ambrosia after so much mutton the past ten days—at a small diner tucked into a corner between two new construction sites. The worn vinyl chairs around chipped trestle tables were filled with Russian construction workers finishing their tea before their work day started. Kazakov paid the bill and ushered Egorova out to the Perseus.

The library stood in what was now the central shopping and office area. The streets were filled with slush and the sidewalks still were mired in snowdrifts that guarded a narrow walking path cleared along the building faces. In this year's unnaturally heavy snow, shopkeepers had given up trying to undo what the snowplows threw up from the streets. The one exception to the drift-filled sidewalk was in front of their destination—a broad concrete façade with concrete angels at the upper corners of the front door and concrete cornucopia on either side of the foot-high letters that spelled out New Moscow City Library.

He pulled in at the curb in front of the door. "Remember. Artyom Shepovalov aka Dedushka. Don't speak to anyone else about what we're looking for and be careful that no one overhears you. Understand?"

She gave him a look. "I know how to do my job."

She climbed out and slammed the Perseus's door behind her and then stalked into the library. Kazakov sat there a moment, gathering himself. Time to see Annuschka.

His ex-wife's office was in the government communications department, located in the expansive basement of the massive replica of Yekaterina's palace. Actually, it wasn't a replica. More simply a façade of white columns and pastiche cherubs and eagles plastered on a concrete block government bunker. There was nothing of Yekaterina's opulence inside, though perhaps there was her delusion of grandeur. And her ambition.

When he turned on the Perseus's radio, the news programs were filled with the unfolding drama of the current Ferganese president, Leonid Nikolaev. Not only were there claims of political contributions from the Ottomans. Now there was evidence of an illicit deal with the Ottomans for a military installation along the border in exchange for the substantial funding. Boris Bure was front and center in demanding that Nikolaev step down and withdraw from the upcoming election in May. Annuschka would be busy trying to spin the news—presumably in the government's favor, but then, given he'd seen meetings between her and Bure, perhaps that wasn't quite true. He turned the radio off rather than face the bleak future unfolding.

The over three-hundred-meter-long government structure rose like something out of a fairy tale above the snow. The falling snow veiled the white and gilt façade, so he could almost imagine that he was in the original St. Petersburg visiting Yekaterina's palace. The golden statues on the roof glimmered in the diffuse light. The columns rose to seemingly impossible heights, though it was in reality only four floors. A golden eagle-topped wrought iron gate stopped people from using the main entrance at the center of the structure. Instead, Kazakov pulled in at a no-parking area near the end of the north wing of the building.

A gust of wind threw snowflakes into his face when he climbed out of the vehicle. Taking a deep breath to gird himself, he set off up the well-shoveled sidewalk past the low, looped chain fencing to the four stairs to the door at the end of the building. This took him to an interior landing where people could go up to government offices or down to the communications department. He took the stairs down.

The communications department was a cavernous room of cream-colored walls, linoleum, and the scent of too much musty paper and new ink. An old-fashioned wooden counter blocked entrance to the sea of desks that filled the space. The small waiting area was confined to a ten-foot square of worn linoleum and tired plastic chairs. For all the number of desks and the number of people beyond the counter, he was surprised, again, by the room's hush. There were no raised voices, only the quiet murmur of confidence that must be hard to maintain in the face of the media attention on Leonid Nikolaev. Unless, of course, they intended to vote for someone else.

He waited at the counter until he was approached by a young woman in a white blouse and slim gray skirt with sleek black hair pulled back into a ponytail. She must have been all of twenty-two.

"May I help you?" She joined him at the counter.

"Annuschka Yevseyev, please."

The woman eyed him. "Can I tell her who is calling?"

"Tell her it is her ex-husband. One more time."

Her gaze widened and she again looked him up and down. "May I tell her what this is about?"

"No, you may not. Just tell her I'm here and I need to speak with her."

The woman backed away and apparently checked with another woman —this one older. Both of them eyed him, and Kazakov was tempted to simply push through the gate in the counter and cross to Annuschka's office. Finally, the younger woman crossed the room to the hallway that led to Annuschka's office. Kazakov paced the waiting area.

Five minutes later the brisk click-click-click of heels turned him around. There Annuschka was again. Once her blonde hair and curves had been his dream. Now it was a dream remembered but not sought again. She was a tall, lithe woman with full lips and carefully made-up eyes. Slashes of pink highlighted her high cheekbones. She came to the counter and placed her carefully manicured hands on the counter. Bright red fingernails and today her hair was coiled at the back of her head. She wore a simple navy sheath that fell straight from her shoulders, but somehow accentuated her curves.

"Alexander. What do you want?"

"I'm here on business. Again. I suggest that we need to talk somewhere else."

Over her shoulder, desk workers were watching. The young woman in the ponytail hung back a few paces away.

"Now? Must you always choose the most inconvenient times?"

He cocked a brow at her. "I thought you'd remember. Wasn't that always part of my charm?"

With a roll of her eyes, she flipped the counter gate open and invited him into her domain. Then she led him efficiently through the sea of desks, and once more, not to her office but into a small office space furnished with a desk and two chairs.

She turned to face him, arms crossed. "So? What is it this time?"

What indeed. How do you ask an ex-wife about the man who was poised to soon become her and the country's boss.

He sat down in a chair and motioned her to the one behind the desk. "This will likely take a few minutes."

Sighing, she did as bid and crisply settled into the chair, a sculpted brow arched in question.

"I will preface what I am about to ask you with the warning that this is a serious criminal investigation. I will ask for your assurances that my questions will not go any further."

Her gaze grew guarded as she sat back and recrossed her arms. "All right. What's your question?"

"Many years ago you were a young woman planning to go to the social event of the year, but something happened. You broke up with your boyfriend just before the event and ended up not attending."

Annuschka's face was a study in fleeting expressions. Old pain. Grief. Reconciliation. Realization and then peace—that swiftly dissolved into the icy, noncommittal glare of a government communications doyen.

"You dragged me away from important meetings to ask me about my prom?"

"I dragged you in here to ask what happened. Why the sudden change of plans? Why the breakup?"

"For goodness sake, that was twenty-plus years ago. How am I supposed to remember?"

Kazakov shook his head. "Because you used to talk about how hurt you'd been and every time you spoke of prom it was with sadness, pain, and regret. You haven't forgotten. What happened, Annuschka?"

She remained stony-faced a moment and then her shoulders sagged. "God. It was so long ago. Not a memory I go to very often. Funny how something like that remains a fresh wound even after this long." She scrubbed her face with both hands. "The short answer is that he broke up with me."

She looked at him and her lovely eyes held the injury of a young girl—all the intervening years of education and hardening couldn't completely hide her away.

"Can you give me the long answer?" Kazakov asked gently.

"Is it really necessary? How can this relate to a criminal investigation?" Then her gaze widened. "Boris? Are you investigating him?"

"Can you answer my question?" he asked.

Looking as if she didn't know where to turn, she ran her hands back over her hair. Her gaze hooked on the door, but Kazakov had made sure he blocked her way. He waited and finally she nodded.

"If you're investigating him, then you probably know that his family was killed tragically in an automobile accident. He was the only survivor but was lost in the mountains for about two weeks. Those were the longest weeks of my life. You see, Boris and I, we were serious. I really thought that after we finished school we'd be married. I thought he wanted that, too. At least he'd hinted it."

She shook her head and plucked at the cuff of her sleeve. From beyond the door came only the occasional footfall of someone passing by the office.

"When they found him, I felt like I could breathe again after two weeks of holding my breath. When they brought him back to the hospital, I lied my way in to his bedside. I threw my arms around him and cried—until he held me away." Another shake of her head. "He knew me—knew who I was—and he looked the same, but there was something different about him and his feelings toward me. Maybe it was his time wandering in the mountains. Maybe that gave him a different perspective, but once he was released from the hospital and went home, things weren't the same. I —I felt as if I was forever on eggshells around him. At times I'd catch him almost sneering at what I said. After a few months he broke up with me just before prom. It broke my heart, but in some ways, it was a relief. It took a long time to stop crying, though."

She gave him a weak smile. "Is that enough?"

He thought a moment. "I know there are a lot of years under the bridge, but you mentioned that he was different. How?"

"How? He didn't love me anymore. That made him less attentive, less caring. He was harder. I remember once we saw a bird get hit by a truck. Before he was lost in the mountains, he would have helped me try to nurse it back to health. Afterward, he told me that if I wanted to waste my time, go ahead, but he had other things to do. It wasn't too long afterward that we broke up. He said he couldn't be what I wanted him to be."

Or what he'd been before.

"After he came home, where did he stay?" he asked.

She shrugged. "At his home, of course. They moved in a couple to make sure he was okay and they stayed with him until he reached the age of majority, I think. I remember they were at our graduation ceremony. I went over to Boris to congratulate him and he was with them. They never had much to say to me and Boris didn't that day, either. He was likely expecting a scene—I'd had a few meltdowns at school." She gave a rueful smile recalling her younger, more emotional self.

Then she looked sharply at Kazakov. "What are you insinuating, Alexander? Are you working for Nikolaev? Trying to find dirt on Boris?"

Kazakov sighed, feeling the weariness of the long drive. "I wish it was only that. There really is a criminal investigation, Annuschka. A couple of people were murdered and an entire village exterminated and it all may have something to do with your first love." He didn't bother to mention wiping out an armed encampment. That was too close to feeding into Bure's rhetoric—rhetoric that Annuschka may have had some hand in crafting. He no longer knew her sympathies.

"I really don't see how Boris could be involved..." She gave a slight shake of her head.

"Frankly? I'm not sure either, but I have to cover all the bases. I have to look at everything."

"Including the ancient history of a political candidate?" She pushed to standing and came around the desk to peer down at him. "I'm sorry, Alexander. I'll adhere to our agreement, but if I see anything that smacks of a smear campaign on Boris, I'll do everything in my power to fight you."

"We both have to do our jobs, Annuschka. But I thought you worked for Nikolaev…"

She had the grace to color slightly, but it was clear that after all these years she still loved a boy named Boris Bure. The question was whether the man she was loyal to was the same person she'd fallen in love with as a girl. Everything she'd told him suggested otherwise.

He stood to face her.

"I appreciate your help, Annuschka. One last question. Who was Boris close to in school besides you? Did he have a special teacher? A best friend? A group he ran with?"

"If you think I'm going to help you any further, you're wrong. I have better things to do with my time." She pulled open the office door. "I'll thank you to leave."

Kazakov did, preceding her out the door and across the cavernous sea of desks. At the counter she let him out and he turned back to thank her.

She waved away his thanks. "Just don't come back again, Alexander. I will be too busy to talk to you."

Then she was gone, clicking her way across the room as the faces of the workers followed her like sunflowers.

Kazakov turned and climbed the stairs to outside, appreciating the honesty of the wind and the snow that gusted in his face.

Mulling his suspicions, he headed back to the library.

Egorova was waiting for him at the curb, her collar pulled up around her chin in the cold. She climbed in the Perseus and slammed the door.

"Well? What did you learn from this ex-wife of yours?" she asked. Her cheeks were rosy. Her eyes danced. She'd clearly learned something from the old man.

"You first. What did old Shepovalov say?"

She shook her head. "What a character. At first he played the querulous old man with me. Then I mentioned your name and he was more forthcoming. He brought me a stack of newspapers to look through on Bure, but there wasn't much on Ivan and Lada Petrov. I asked him specifically to check and there was nothing. Other than that, there really wasn't anything he could offer me—other than stories of you as a child." She grinned as if she had something on him.

Kazakov pulled away from the curb.

"He suggested that we check the natural statistics registry."

He glanced at her. "I think we check the police data base, too."

They made a stop at the registry, a fourth-floor office not far from police headquarters, and made the request at the counter. Kazakov paced while they waited. Egorova stayed at the counter. She looked pretty and quietly efficient. Professional, he thought and he liked that about her. She'd done her time in Biysk. She deserved better—but then so did Constable Dabria Smirnova. Perhaps policing was not so kind to women. For some reason it held them back.

The clerk, a finely built man with an overly high forehead and balding pate came back from the backroom shaking his head. "Sorry. I checked births, marriages, and deaths. There is no record of them."

Egorova shook her head. "That's impossible. We know these people lived in New Moscow between twenty and twenty-five years ago."

"Well, they weren't born or married here and they haven't died here, either," the clerk said. "At least not under that name."

Not under that name. He stopped Egorova's argument and they went out to the Perseus.

Egorova shook her head at him. "Why'd you stop me? He had to be hiding records from us!"

"Nooo," Kazakov said, another suspicion rising in his head. "I think he was telling the truth."

He headed for the police station and parked the Perseus in underground police parking. He carded them inside past security, where Egorova was given a visitor badge, and then they rode up to the third-floor detective office.

It was a midsized room—large enough to hold the paired desks of nine detectives. The desks were crammed back to back with barely space to walk between them. A single desk sat by itself not far from a small coffee room alcove. There were no detectives present at the moment, but the office smelled of cold tea, cigarette ash, and damp woolens. A double line of fluorescent lights hummed overhead and reflected off the worn linoleum underfoot.

Kazakov led Egorova through the paired desks to the lone one. "Mine," he said. "Make yourself at home. I'm going to run the names."

He left her as she took off her coat. He padded across to the data machine in the corner. It was a behemoth metal box, with a keyboard set in a tray on the front and a large, flat screen set at the perfect height if you were seated in the chair at the keyboard. He settled his coat and himself in the chair and ran each name.

Lada Petrov came up with exactly nothing. No criminal convictions or suspicion. Nothing for Ivan Petrov either. He thought a moment and ran a request for driver's records.

No record of driver's license for either person.

He sat back in his chair. What the hell was going on?

"What's the matter?" Egorova asked coming up beside him.

"No criminal record. No driver's license. What's that suggest to you?"

She frowned. "It's odd, but there are people who don't drive."

He looked up at her. "And have no record of birth, death, or marriage, too?"

Her gaze had gone dark and dubious. "There's the voter's registry. We could check that. And that would include their current address."

Kazakov nodded. "We should check. And I'll get Khan to check health records. People might not drive and they might not vote, but surely they need health care."

He nodded her to another desk—Chelomeyev's—and he wondered how the young man was doing. He'd ask Khan about that, too.

Egorova picked up the phone and asked switchboard to connect her to the Ferganese voter's registry. Kazakov dialed Khan's office. The phone rang in his ear and finally clicked through. A female voice picked up. He recognized the cool voice of the unpleasant receptionist at the M.E.'s office.

"Dr. Khan, please."

"I'm afraid Dr. Khan has not reported to the office today." Her disapproval rang loud in her voice.

"Is he ill? Did he not check in upon his return from Biysk?"

"Who's calling please?" The voice had turned guarded.

"This is Detektiv Kazakov calling. Can you please ask him to contact me as soon as possible when he comes in?"

The woman took the message and hung up and Kazakov missed the old receptionist at the M.E.'s office. But she had been let go to make room for the sour-faced young woman whom Khan suspected was there to keep track of his movements. He tried Khan's mobile.

The line rang and rang, but then it clicked as if someone on the other end picked up.

"Khan, it's..."

The phone went dead and a dial tone filled his ear.

He frowned at the phone in his hand. Accidental cut off? Was something wrong? Or had he imagined the pickup click at the end of the phone? He tried Khan's cell again, but it only rang and rang.

Still frowning, Kazakov hung up. What the hell was going on with Khan? For all they'd had their differences before, Khan had never avoided him. He listened as Egorova uh-huhed into the other phone. Then she thanked who she was talking to and hung up, as well. She looked thoughtful.

"Well?"

She shook her head. "No record of either of them."

Kazakov sighed. "Hard to confirm anything about the young man they cared for when they don't seem to have existed—at least officially. They were seen, though. Annuschka spoke to them a few times."

"And Kasimir Krupin knew their names." She scrubbed her face and looked at him. Fatigue rode in her troubled gaze. "How can that be? Krupin said New Moscow paid them. There was fund-raising to support the young Bure."

"There is that. Unless he was mistaken."

Egorova just looked at him and Kazakov shook his head. "You're right. I'm trying to make allowances. But I don't want it said that I refused to consider other possibilities."

"There's an Anglo-German saying that if it walks and quacks like a duck…"

"Then it has to be a duck," Kazakov finished. But was that the truth? A princess in a pigskin was thought to be like a pig, but was really something else entirely.

"They looked like any Russian couple and that's what people thought them to be," he said quietly. "It's all in the expectations of those around you. If you live up to those expectations, you can be just about anything."

"Spies," Egorova said.

"We still need Khan to check health records, but we should talk to Rostoff." He stood and indicated that she should come with him. He checked his watch. It was barely after lunch. Rostoff would be pleased that they had made such good time. Of course, he might also be angry when he learned what they were pursuing. The Detektiv Chief Inspektor was perennially more concerned about hobnobbing with the elite than with solving crimes. And solving a crime of this nature most of all.

He led Egorova out of the squad room and down the hall from the detective squad room into officer territory. To either side, solid doors gave onto plush private offices that housed officers and their secretaries. He pushed into Rostoff's reception area. Constable Dabria Smirnova glanced up at him and smiled when she saw him. Or maybe it was Egorova she smiled at. Time was clearly healing Dabria's wounds. He barely noticed what had previously been bright red pinprick scars across her cheek and a deeper gash on her forehead.

The blonde receptionist appeared as efficient as always—her desk cleared except for a single document she worked with, her uniform crisply pressed. A message pad and pen easily to hand.

"You're early," she said to Kazakov. "He was expecting you later this afternoon."

"We drove all night."

Her brows rose and she glanced at Egorova. Dabria would know that an all-night drive would bring them into New Moscow in early morning.

"We had some—further investigation—to pursue here. Is he in?" Kazakov asked.

"Just finishing his lunch, I believe. Have you eaten?"

"Not since a brief stop this morning," Egorova said. "I want to thank you again for the lovely time you showed me last time I was here."

"It was nothing. A chance to spend time with another career woman." Dabria turned back to Kazakov. "I will order you lunches."

She motioned to the door to Rostoff's inner sanctum. "Go in. I'm sure he will be pleased to see you."

Seriously doubting Dabria's last statement, Kazakov rapped once on the closed office door.

"Come," came Rostoff's deep baritone from within.

Kazakov pushed inside. Rostoff had worked hard to get this office and position—just not through police work. He was of an age with Kazakov, but instead of focusing on catching criminals, he had become something of a fixer for the officials, diplomats, and wealthy that he aspired to. He'd achieved what he'd sought and now he sat in his office with his wall full of photographs of one Detektiv Chief Inspektor Valerian Rostoff glad-handing with the rich and famous.

The man himself was seated at his glossy wooden desk across from the door. He was a bear of a man, almost the same height as Kazakov but with a growing girth that came from a sedentary lifestyle. His nose and cheeks held the broken veins of the drinker.

Investigation files were stacked on the desk in three neat piles— Dabria's influence, most likely. Rostoff wasn't the neatest of men as indicated by the slight rumple of his shirt collar and pieces of crumpled paper that hadn't quite made it into the garbage bin. The dull, noonday light through the window caught Rostoff from the side and etched age-lines and shadows across his face. He gazed at Kazakov and Egorova blearily and then set his pen down and straightened.

"Kazakov! You're earlier than I expected. Come. Sit. And you bring with you your young Biysk detective, too. Good. Sit. Sit. I have good news for you." He motioned to the two chairs that sat between his desk and the door, but the motion seemed to take effort.

Kazakov exchanged glances with Egorova. This was not what he had expected. But he and Egorova crossed to the two chairs and sat down. Kazakov remained impassive, waiting for whatever it was that Rostoff deemed good news.

"Chelomeyev. It is him. He has woken up." Rostoff said.

Hallelujah! That *was* good news. Kazakov felt a weight lift from his chest. He felt like shouting it from the rooftops, but for the lump that seemed to block his throat. Detektiv Pavel Chelomeyev was the sole witness in a murder case that had links to presumed terrorist bombings that had wracked the city and had exploded in the square just outside this building. And Kazakov might have stopped Chelomeyev's beating if only he hadn't given the youngster just enough information to walk right into trouble.

"When did this happen?" Kazakov asked, his reason for seeing Rostoff fading with the need to visit the young man. Chelomeyev had been beaten unconscious and left for dead and then barely escaped a second attempt on his life only because Kazakov had intervened.

"I just got the call. Apparently, he's fully lucid and asking to speak to you."

Kazakov went to stand. Chelomeyev's evidence could be relevant to the Bure case.

"Where are you going? What do you have to report?" Rostoff demanded.

"Chelomeyev isn't safe on his own. He's the last surviving witness in that bombing case. If word gets out that he's awake…"

"It can wait a few minutes. The hospital has only contacted family and us."

Kazakov sank back into the chair but felt himself vibrating with the need to get to Chelomeyev.

"What of the investigation in Biysk? What have you got?"

Kazakov felt Egorova's glance. Where to begin? "Too much suspicion and too little evidence."

He met Rostoff's weary gaze and recognized his own fatigue. "It was not a simple case. Not at all."

He let Egorova run through the finding of Bermet Aytmatov's body and the subsequent botched early Biysk investigation. Kazakov took over, talking about the anger amongst Biysk's tribal people and how he, Egorova, and Khan returned to the scene of the murder, following the tracks of Bermet Aytmatov back to White Stone Village and how it had apparently been abandoned. He went through the demonstration and the subsequent arrests and the release and death of Zholdosh as well as the description of the killer provided by the female witness.

Then he talked about the rationale for the trip into the mountains and the gristly discovery of the bodies at the armed camp. From there he outlined their venture further into the mountains and the Chinese installation that they found there—and what was found. Through it all he attempted to keep Eric Clinton and Enver Pasha as out of the story other than as shadowy background figures. When he was done, he sighed and sat back in his chair.

"Now we come to the difficult part. As I said, at the installation, papers were discovered indicating some of what the installation was involved in." He pulled the documents from his inside jacket pocket and spread them on Rostoff's desktop. "This," he tapped the document with the x-ray of the limbs. "This speaks of a process for lengthening limbs. This one speaks of creating secret pouches in the hip and this one discusses cosmetic dentistry." He held the dental paper up. "This one caused me problems because I recognized the smile. At first I couldn't place it and then it came to me: Collin Archer, the man found dead outside the Red Veil. He had this kind of teeth, this kind of smile, and he turned out to be a Chinese spy turned double agent."

He stopped for a moment as Rostoff studied the image. There was a flicker of recognition in his gaze. Finally, he nodded.

"The trouble was, there was someone else I recognized with the same kind of teeth."

Rostoff appeared to stiffen. His gaze was flat.

"Boris Bure."

Rostoff threw up his hands and shoved out of his chair. "You must be kidding. You expect me to listen to these suspicions because of a smile? And this?" He grabbed the document from the installation and waved it in the air.

Kazakov didn't rise to Rostoff's state of agitation. That would only lead to confrontation. And Rostoff hadn't actually kicked them out of his office. That said there was still room for more discussion.

"Then think farther back to what we know of Bure. It is a verified fact that when he was seventeen he disappeared in the mountains around Biysk and was unaccounted for until they found him two weeks later. When he was found, he was miraculously unharmed. Not even frostbite even though he disappeared wearing only city clothing."

Rostov's disbelieving glare shifted from Kazakov to Egorova. "You believe this, too?"

"It's true. Sir. I just checked the newspaper records."

"Newspapers and reporters! Pah! They are all just liars." Rostoff paced over to his window and peered out into the main square where the huge statue of Yekaterina had stood on its pedestal until someone had blown it up. The explosion had been blamed on Kyrgyz extremists, but investigation had indicated links to a certain businessman who was a supporter of Bure's. Kazakov's problem was that they had no evidence because the direct witness was dead and Chelomeyev was the only other person who might have more information. Rostoff, thankfully, had believed Kazakov that time, but had urged extreme caution in proceeding.

"There's more," Kazakov said gently.

Rostoff closed his eyes and rubbed his forehead. "Odd. I knew you would say that." He looked back at them, his expression bleak. "So?"

"Bure came back to New Moscow as something of a hero, but all of his family was gone—dead in the same 'accident' that left him alone in the mountains." So it was likely that the string of deaths attached to Bure extended that far back as well.

"In New Moscow there were some problems. There were allegations that he sexually assaulted a much younger student, but that was hushed up. He resided at home, but a couple was arranged to live with him—an Ivan and Lada Petrov—a common enough name. They were paid through donations from citizens for the welfare of the young Bure."

Rostoff nodded, waiting.

"We've tried to trace them, but there is no sign," Egorova said standing up behind her chair. "There is no mention of them in any government records—not births, deaths, or marriage."

"Or driver's license. Or criminal record. Or voting registration," Kazakov added, looking down at his hands. Let Rostoff compute and add up these findings—or lack thereof.

Kazakov looked up as Rostoff returned to his desk.

"That—is odd." Rostoff sank back into his chair and Egorova did the same. Rostoff shook his head. "This is troubling—more so because of the individual's prominence."

Kazakov nodded. "His rhetoric causes a division in the country. A shift away from neutrality could upset the balance of power in the region. If he does have connections to the Chinese, that is what could happen." Derr'mo, he was beginning to sound like Clinton.

Rostoff closed his eyes and nodded, but then he took a deep breath and placed his hands palm down on his desktop. "This is a concern. A very big one, but I do not see how it connects to the old woman's murderer. That is why I sent you to Biysk."

Kazakov felt as if he'd been punched in the gut. Rostoff was going to ignore everything that he and Egorova had worked so hard to get. He swallowed back frustration and nodded.

"The evidence says that Bermet's killer was from the Chinese installation. She witnessed their attack on a Kyrgyz encampment. The Chinese tracked her and killed her, but not before she'd traveled through another Kyrgyz village and possibly told them what had happened. The Chinese abducted and killed everyone in the village, too. This was confirmed by a Chinese national at the installation. Unfortunately, that woman escaped us in the mountains. As for the death of the man named Zholdosh, it could have been Bure himself for all we know. Or one of his henchmen. They were in Biysk at the time. The sole witness described a single man dressed in city clothing."

"But why kill him? He hadn't seen anything to reveal the installation as far as you know. You see? There is where your plots and suspicions fall apart!" Rostoff stabbed the top of his desk with his index finger. "I swear, Kazakov, this all goes back to that dead girl and boy last fall. You've harbored resentment toward Bure since then!"

"No!" Kazakov stood up. "I follow the evidence, but every time that I do it leads me back to Bure! And Zholdosh was working with the armed camp. They had planned an attack on the installation."

Rostoff pushed himself up from his chair. "You will listen to me, Detektiv. You will not speak of this to anyone. Do you understand? If you do, it will mean your job. And yours, too, I suspect." He glanced at Egorova, who had stood with Kazakov. "As I am sure even you can get through your thick skull, this is a very sensitive time with the elections forthcoming. The New Moscow Police Department is not going to be caught up in electioneering. If you want Bure, bring me hard evidence of something."

Rostoff sank back down in his chair. "In the meantime, I will do a little digging. If Bure's caregivers were paid for by the city, surely there must be records of them—a pension, something."

Only Egorova's urging propelled Kazakov through his rigid frustration from his chair to Rostoff's office door. Egorova stepped into the reception area and Kazakov stopped. He half turned back to Rostoff.

"Be very careful, Detektiv Chief Inspektor. These people mean business. Those who are not very careful, die."

Rostoff met his gaze and nodded. "I know my job, Detektiv."

Kazakov closed the door behind him, hoping Rostoff truly did.

22

———————

The hallway from Rostoff's office to the squad room was too long, too hot, and too filled with the scent of old dust and sweat. Kazakov shoved through the door into the warren of desks, Egorova at his heels, and stood there inhaling the stale air. That was the problem with the New Moscow Police—they were old, stale, and dusty as if the entire department had settled into inertia. Worse, the dust had settled over and petrified them so that only the form of a police department remained.

Then he noticed he wasn't alone. Detektiv Artyom Pogolin looked up from his desk, his blunt features noncommittal but his gaze interested.

"Haven't seen you in a while," Pogolin said. He ran gnarled fingers through salt-and-pepper hair.

Kazakov nodded and headed to his desk. "Been on assignment in Biysk. This is Detektiv Elena Egorova, Biysk Police."

Pogolin gave a perfunctory nod, clearly unimpressed, whether by their presence or the fact Egorova was a woman, Kazakov didn't know.

Kazakov picked up his coat. He couldn't stay here or he'd petrify like the rest of them.

"You hear about Chelomeyev?" asked Pogolin.

"I heard he woke up an hour ago."

"Nope. This morning. It was on the noon news," Pogolin said.

"Derr'mo." Kazakov turned on his heel and headed for the door, dragging Egorova in his wake.

"What's the problem? They're calling it a miracle!" Pogolin called after them.

Kazakov waved him away and took the stairs down to the police parking three at a time.

"What is it? What's the problem?" Egorova demanded as she followed.

"Chelomeyev's a witness. They've already tried to kill him once. If he's woken up with his memories, we have to protect him!"

They thundered down to the police parking lot and ran to the Perseus. Their tires squealed in the snowmelt on the parking lot's concrete as they pulled out onto the street. "Call Our Lady Yekaterina Hospital and warn them that there may be another attempt on Chelomeyev's life."

Egorova pulled out her phone and made the call, but finally shook her head. "There's only a recording saying their switchboard is currently overloaded."

"Stay on the line. Let me see what I can do."

He pulled out his phone as he accelerated through traffic. He dialed Khan's office number, praying the M.E. had finally gone in. The officious receptionist picked up.

"Dr. Khan, please," Kazakov said as he narrowly missed a car pulling out from a side street. He nearly lost the phone that he'd balanced between ear and shoulder.

"Who is calling please?"

"It's Kazakov again, as you well know. Is he in?"

"Just a minute, please." The line clicked to hold and Kazakov wanted to roar at her through the phone.

Egorova looked at him, still on hold at the hospital. "Your face is red."

He snarled a thank you at her and sent the Perseus's tail sliding as he turned onto Suvarov Way. He hit the gas pedal and the vehicle leapt forward.

The officious receptionist came back on the line. "I'm sorry. Dr. Khan is not here."

"Why didn't you just tell me that?" he yelled at the phone.

"He *was* here. But now he is gone and no one knows where. Again." Her disgust came through the phone.

He hung up with perfunctory thanks and tossed his phone at Egorova so he could focus on driving. Traffic was far too heavy for him to be driving so fast, but certainty about Chelomeyev's danger filled him.

He turned off Suvarov Way and accelerated up the street and into the parking lot of Our Lady Yekaterina Hospital. The snow had stopped, leaving the hospital seated in a sodden gray parking lot, the park across the lot looming gray and dead-looking in the failing light of midafternoon. He slid the Perseus to a stop at the hospital's main door, leapt out, and ran up the stairs, Egorova at his heels.

He ignored the waiting area of plastic chairs and the reception desk that sat at one side of the tiled lobby and ran past for the bank of three elevators. He stabbed the call button and looked around for hospital security. There was no one at the security desk. He swore, but the elevator dinged open and he dove inside.

Egorova joined him. "Floor?"

He reached past and stabbed the button for the fourth floor. The ride was interminable, but finally the door dinged open and he burst into the corridor, turned, and ran in the direction of Chelomeyev's room. A young nurse with red hair in a ponytail, which made her look even younger, looked up from patient files on desk at the nursing station.

"Sir! You can't run here."

He stopped. "Chelomeyev?"

"Room 422. Don't stay too long. He's having a lot of visitors today."

Kazakov left her and strode down the corridor and around the corner. Room 422 was there, so he'd been moved from his old room.

The room's window curtains were drawn and the room was dark. Through the gloom Kazakov could just make out four beds, three of them empty and bare. The fourth, by the curtained windows, had the privacy curtains half-drawn around it masking the occupant from the hall. The curtain shifted as if someone moved within it.

Chelomeyev?

In three steps Kazakov was across the room. He yanked the privacy curtain aside in a screech of protesting metal track runners. Subdued afternoon light leaked around the window curtains to illuminate a pale Chelomeyev asleep in his bed. The bed covers covered him up to his waist and an open book lay face down on his chest.

But across from Kazakov and leaning over Chelomeyev stood a slim, dark-clad figure with a plastic syringe in his hands.

It fell from his gloved fingers to the floor as shock filled the face of Khalil Khan.

"Khan? What the… what are…?" Kazakov stopped as realization filled him.

Khan's shock smoothed away and he straightened. He wore his dark city street coat and gloves. He glanced down at Chelomeyev. "I heard he was awake."

As if that explained everything. Perhaps it did.

"You've been working for the Chinese," Kazakov guessed, feeling sick. "No wonder helping Clinton was so easy for you. You were already compromised. So what do the Chinese have on you, Khan? You know you could have come to me for help."

"The Chinese?" Khan shook his head, an incredulous look on his face. "You really don't understand anything, do you? Sometimes wrong things simply must be done."

"But you were going to kill a man—a witness to the Yekaterina bombing. His evidence could point the finger at the right people—could clear yours!"

Khan said nothing and a sick feeling crept into Kazakov's stomach. Khan's silence suggested the Kyrgyz were involved in more than he had suspected or wanted to believe…

"Surely, as a doctor, killing a man goes against all your training?" Egorova asked.

"I have never wished to kill, but sometimes a man must examine where his loyalties rest. For me, family is foremost." He met Kazakov's gaze as he spoke as if trying to convey something.

"Family. And by extension, the tribe," Kazakov whispered, wishing with all his heart that he was wrong. "What've you done, Khan? What have your people done?"

Khan shrugged. He looked tired and resigned. "My people? Try the Russians, the Ottomans, the Chinese, the Anglo-Germans. The Americans probably would, too, given half a chance. To all of you, we are nothing but pawns. Enver Pasha wants to use us as an army. The Chinese would use us as mountain guides and spies. The Americans say they want allies, but who knows? You Russians would just like us gone." He lifted his chin, the fatigue pushed away. "But we are here to stay, my friend. Let the Chinese make a farce of the Ferganese election. Let the Ottomans fume and attack. Let the war begin and consume the world, but we Kyrgyz people will persist. The war can bomb this city, these plains, but we will withdraw to our tribal lands. The mountains will hold us and hide us until the rest is consumed. And then the world can start again."

Kazakov felt like he'd been struck. He wanted to sit down. Khan had ripped off his mask. The family man and dedicated M.E. might still exist, but they were shallow disguises for the angry man beneath. The man Kazakov had considered his only friend.

It felt like he was floating loose above the room. And still Chelomeyev slept.

Or…

Kazakov's gaze swept down to the syringe on the floor.

Khan's admission was a stalling tactic.

Kazakov's heart leapt in his chest.

"Egorova. Call the nurses. He's already injected Chelomeyev!"

Egorova looked from Kazakov to Khan to Chelomeyev, then she turned and ran out the door. Her shouts for help echoed down the corridor.

"I thought you cared about Chelomeyev. You brought me news of his beating." A thought crossed his mind. "Was it you?"

Khan gaze hardened. "Not me. There are many forces at work here. A nest of snakes. It is a shame he is so young and one of the good ones, but our young men are dying, too." His gaze saddened as he looked down at the young detective. "There are things he knows that cannot be reported."

From out in the corridor came the sound of Egorova's voice and running feet. Then Egorova and two nurses burst into the room.

Khan shoved Chelomeyev's wheeled bed at Kazakov. It hit him midsection and he staggered back, barely stopping Chelomeyev from tumbling off to the floor. Khan leapt past him and bowled into Egorova and the nurses, then careened out the door.

Kazakov dove after Khan. Egorova's footfall pounded behind. Down the hallway, past the elevator. Khan took a corner and disappeared from sight. Kazakov stopped. There were two possibilities. A surgical elevator door was closed before him. From the lights above it, it was headed down. But a stairwell headed down beside them.

"Which way," Egorova asked, her face eager as a hound's.

"I'll take the stairs. Call me when you see where the elevator stops." Kazakov shoved the stairwell door open and listened. Nothing.

He nodded once at her and started down, his footfall heavy on the concrete treads. The stairwell was plain gray with glaring, grilled lightbulbs attached to the walls of each landing. Was that a rustle? The lightest of treads. He peered down the open space between the railings and caught a glimpse of a shadow on a landing two floors down and moving swiftly.

Kazakov leapt down the stairs after the unseen figure. If Khan got out of the hospital and into the old city, it was unlikely he'd ever be caught. He was too much of a hero to his people, and if he hadn't been before, he certainly would be now.

Kazakov's phone buzzed in his pocket. He ignored it and kept on going. Khan's figure was swift, but Kazakov was gaining. The lobby floor was just below him and he heard the door slam open. Kazakov leapt four treads at a time, sliding down the rails on his hands. He hauled the landing door open. An empty corridor waited on the other side.

Kazakov hesitated. Khan worked in this hospital. He knew its hallways. But where he worked wasn't through these doors, it was one floor down in the Medical Examiner's office. He looked down the last run of stairs. A faint click reached him as if a door was quietly slid shut. He could imagine Khan running through the back corridors past the autopsy rooms to his office and beyond, out through the reception area and up the stairs to the parking lot.

Kazakov plunged out the first-floor door into the corridor. The lobby couldn't be far. He just had to find his way. He passed radiology and ambulatory care. He passed the research wing labeled parapsychology. A larger corridor had a sign pointing toward the lobby. Kazakov set off at a run and came into the open area just as the elevator dinged open. Egorova stepped out and headed toward him.

"You didn't pick up your phone!"

"There wasn't time. I lost him on the stairs but I figure he's gone down to his office to get out of the building. The Medical Examiner's entrance is just outside."

The two of them headed for the door. Beyond, the light had dimmed farther and a light snow was falling once more. The parking lot lights had come on, gilding the falling flakes. Their Perseus still sat at the curb. A man and woman picked their way across the now-freezing parking lot toward the entrance.

Kazakov rushed down the stairs and hurried across the rutted ice toward the stairs halfway down the building that led downward to the M.E.'s domain. The roar of an engine stopped him midstride. A dark blue M.E. van pulled out from the loading bay at the end of the building.

"The Perseus!" Khan said and ran back to the vehicle. He threw himself inside and Egorova barely made it in before he accelerated after the van. He swerved out of the parking lot and down to Suvarov Way, then, glimpsing the Van's taillights, he turned toward Yekaterina

Mountain, the spotlighted statue of the matriarch of the country at the mountain peak hazed in the falling snow.

The road ran around the edge of the old city that had existed long before the sick and dying Russians staggered into Fergana. The Kyrgyz had withstood conquerors and homegrown despots and still they were here, a proud people who had been ground down by the "democratic" Russians.

Kazakov's foot lifted slightly from the accelerator. Maybe Khan did what was right, from his perspective. Kazakov doubted that Khan had killed Bermet—no, that was what had taken him to Biysk. But Zholdosh was Khan's work—Kazakov would bet on it. The female witness had described a city man in a coat just like Khan's, and Zholdosh, intent on drawing the Kyrgyz into taking sides, would have been fair game. Stirring the pot was what Khan was doing. The problem was that now that Khan had been identified, it would further inflame Russian hatreds.

He sped up, expecting the van to turn into the narrow streets that were Khan's home, but instead the van kept going. He followed the red taillights out past the old city, out past the abandoned fair grounds and a construction business to a parking lot at the base of the lone mountain in the city. The van slewed sideways to a stop and a dark-coated figure leapt out. Khan sprinted toward the base of the mountain.

Kazakov slammed on the brakes. The Perseus slid to a stop and Kazakov leapt out.

"Khan! Stop! You're just making it worse!"

The dark coated figure kept going, entering the Russian pilgrimage trail that led up to a viewpoint at the foot of the statue of Yekaterina.

"What do we do?" Egorova asked.

Kazakov went after Khan, thankful that he still wore the heavy boots he'd worn in the mountains. Egorova went with him.

The trail was steep and deep with snow. There were some packed-down patches that were icy from recent warmer weather, but these were mostly hidden under the soft layer of new snow. They followed Khan's trail as the way grew steeper and more treacherous as it followed the side of the mountain. The New Moscow city fathers had not yet seen fit to add railings to guard the steep trail drop-off. Every year a few drunkards fell to their deaths.

"Is he armed?" Egorova asked as she puffed up beside him where the trail widened.

"He's a good shot and he owns at least an old-fashioned Kyrgyz rifle that I know of. He could have something else."

"Should we call for backup?"

He glanced back at her. "Khan's my friend."

Through the fading light, she raised a brow at him.

He kept going, his mind racing through options to deal with the situation. Khan *was* his friend. The fact that he was also a killer was hard to accept. Perhaps the attack on Khan's family had set him on this path. Kazakov squinted through the snow for a glimpse of Khan, but in the darkness there was nothing.

The trail would end eventually. He wasn't sure what Khan would do, but the man was smart. Surely then they could talk. Kazakov could talk sense to him. Convince him to turn himself in. The killing of a foreign agent—the courts might even go easy on him. Perhaps there was a way that the attempt on Chelomeyev's life could be downplayed or kept quiet.

Derr'mo, what was he thinking! Khan had killed a man and tried to kill Chelomeyev.

It was so unlike the man Kazakov knew, it smacked of desperation.

The trail switchbacked up the mountainside. Kazakov and Egorova labored up the trail. Night fell and the lights of New Moscow placed a haunting glow on the snow that would have been lovely except for what it masked below. Khan was like an apparition—occasionally they would catch a glimpse of him silhouetted against the spotlights that lit up Yekaterina's statue.

As they went higher, the wind picked up and the flakes swirled around them, driving into Kazakov's eyes and freezing his ears. He wished for his hat, left behind in his bag in the Perseus. Egorova must be feeling the same, but she came gamely on with him, keeping pace with his longer stride.

An hour later the trail leveled off, and from his visits here as a boy, he knew they were almost at the lookout beneath the skirts of the mountain's Yekaterina. He turned to Egorova.

"You've been here before?"

She shook her head.

"There's a concrete platform at the edge of the mountain below the statue. You can't go any farther—at least not without going off the path entirely. A few hardy souls brave one or another of the other five peaks. Some of the Kyrgyz do it as a pilgrimage, but I doubt he'll try it."

Egorova nodded.

"Just follow my lead," Kazakov said and kept going.

The glare of the spotlights was softened by the snow so it was as if the viewpoint was curtained with light. It blocked Kazakov's view of the platform until he stepped inside the glow. Egorova was hidden by the glare somewhere behind him. Inside the bubble of light, the flakes still fell but the rest of the world disappeared as if he had ascended to heaven. Yekaterina's skirts were hidden by snow, but across the pristine carpet in the platform, a single trail led to Khan.

He stood with his back to Kazakov, peering westward out through the curtain in the direction of the mountain's other peaks. Then he went to his knees and prostrated himself in prayer before standing up to face Kazakov. From somewhere he had produced a gun that looked like the sidearm worn by the installation guards. He pointed it at Kazakov.

"This is Suleiman's Mountain. No matter that you Russians rename it —that you soil it with your statues. It will always be Suleiman's just as my people will always be free." His voice shook as he glanced up at the huge statue of Yekaterina, half seen through the glowing snow. "I should have brought explosives. That's what the Chinese would do. But that would just place more blame on my people."

Blame Khan was already confirming by his actions. Kazakov kept his hands where they could be seen. "Khan. Put the gun down. Let's talk this through. Let's talk about options."

"Options?" Khan's throat worked as he steadied the gun. "I'm afraid we're out of options, old friend. If I die, it provides proof to Bure that the tribal people are the source of all problems. He will be elected and the war will begin. If you die during this investigation, it will be proof that there is some other force in play—some deal with the Ottomans, perhaps. That, too, will play into Bure's hands. He will win the election and my people will withdraw into the mountains as the war begins. You see? No options. It will all come out the same."

It was a chilling assessment made more so by the grief in Khan's voice. He had taken unforgiveable actions and he knew it.

"It doesn't have to be like this. You can give yourself up. Tell people what you know. Tell your story at trial and it will get people talking, maybe even thinking."

Khan shook his head and chuckled. "A tribal on trial? Now who is speaking foolishly? There won't be any news coverage there. I'm just another tribal who broke the law. A terrorist, in Bure's words. No one will listen. No one will hear." He shook his head. "I'm sorry to do this, old friend. If it's any consolation, I have never intended to kill. Zholdosh was an accident. I went to talk to him, to get him to leave. Instead he laughed at me and told me to leave. When I wouldn't, he pulled out a knife and we got into a fight." He shook his head.

"You injected Chelomeyev," Kazakov said. And that was far worse than the killing of Zholdosh. That was betrayal on so many levels.

Khan gave a sad smile and shook his head. The gun barrel rose.

Khan's weapon muzzle flared and roared. Kazakov threw himself aside.

He came up in time to see Khan look surprised. The M.E. staggered back a step. Kazakov scrambled up and leapt for Khan.

Too late. With a sad smile, Khan toppled off the side of the viewing platform.

"No!" Kazakov ran to the edge, but Khan's fall was lost in the glare. He was beyond the light. Kazakov's knees folded under him. He didn't feel the cold.

"Kazakov?" Egorova's voice shook.

He glanced back as Egorova appeared through the glare of snow, gun in one hand, the other gripped her shoulder. She slumped against the skirts of the gigantic statue, a grim smile on her lips. "I'm afraid the bastard got me."

Numbly, Kazakov lurched to his feet. He looked back to where Khan had fallen, but then went to her. Khan was gone, and Egorova needed care. Gently he lifted her hand away to reveal blood seeping thickly through the wool of her coat. "We have to get you to the hospital."

"So we walk down the mountain," she said and turned her face to the trail.

But she staggered when she tried to take a step and Kazakov caught her. He lifted her up and was surprised at how light she was. She struggled in his arms.

"You are *not* going to carry me."

"You don't have much choice. It's either that or we wait here for medics."

She went to protest but he stopped her with a shake of his head.

"If you want to do something useful, call Rostoff and tell him where we are. Tell him we need an ambulance—and a search party. They can meet us on the trail."

She dug in her pocket with her good hand and came out with her phone—now smeared with blood from her hand.

She made the call as Kazakov carried her as gently as he could. He stepped out of the blinding bubble of light and found himself in darkness once again.

23

The wind was cold off the mountains that placed a jagged, white wall against the sky to the north, east, and south. Above, the sky was a fragile blue bowl where two eagles had found a thermal and rose circling, circling. A scattering of poplar, walnut, and gnarled apple trees spread naked limbs and spoke of the microclimate Kazakov stood in. Though the wind was cold, the sun placed more heat on his cheeks than he had felt for months. It felt strange, like a blush at the wrong time given what stood before him.

The gray monuments and mausoleums lay in a tight cluster behind a low fence that apparently had done nothing to keep out intruders. Red paint scrawled threats and graphic phallic figures across the low concrete domes and small tiled minarets closest to where Kazakov stood. The Kyrgyz graveyard seemed to huddle in the midst of an unfriendly world. Not seemed. It did. The low, graceful monuments to the dead stood alone in a sea of white snow that stretched to the mountains.

And to New Moscow.

He glanced over his shoulder, westward, at the blight of the city sprawled lower in the foothills along the river at the base of Yekaterina Mountain. The people of the old city has shifted their graveyard here, out an almost impassable dirt road beyond the reach of the long fingers of urban sprawl, but the graffiti said that someone had found it nonetheless.

That was the trouble. No matter that Khan had promised that his people could fade into the mountains to avoid the conflicts to come, there was no place in this troubled landscape that would take them far enough away. The installation and carnage in the mountains should have told Khan that. The monsters were already out there waiting for him. He just hadn't recognized them through the masks they wore. Or perhaps he hadn't recognized his own weakness and that of his people.

But now wasn't the time for recrimination. Khan was gone and it hurt to have lost his friend. It hurt more to realize that Khan had told the truth when he said he hadn't meant to kill anyone. Not Zholdosh, and Chelomeyev hadn't been poisoned—he'd been injected with a non-lethal dose of an amnesia-inducing drug. Kazakov looked back, past the vehicles parked by the gate through the low fence. He had parked a hundred yards back down the road and walked up to this vantage where he could see, yet not intrude.

Through the monuments, the family and friends of Khalil Khan made a slow, silent procession, except for the soft sound of weeping that was carried on the wind. There was no body, for no body had ever been found though the authorities and the Kyrgyz had searched the mountain. Khan had either fallen into a crevice and been covered by snow, or he'd lived and managed to disappear. By the unusual funeral procession, it seemed his family and the Kyrgyz thought he was dead, for the Kyrgyz did not perform such rites lightly, especially without a body.

The men in the procession had exchanged their embroidered, white-and-black felt *ak kalpak* for plain white *doppa* religious caps, and the women wore scarves over their heads. One woman wore an enormous *kelek* of snow-white cloth in the local traditional turban.

"Is that his family?" Egorova asked from behind him.

Kazakov looked back at her as she indicated the woman in the traditional woman's headpiece. Egorova wore a new red coat that came down to her knees. She looked too festive for the occasion, though her expression was grim and her left arm in a sling from Khan's last bullet. Beside her stood Chelomeyev, who looked too pale and haunted to be out of the hospital, even though he'd been discharged. Khan's drug had been caught quickly enough to be counteracted, but even so, his memory had been affected and he had little memory that would justify Khan's efforts except for the hints Kazakov had given him—something about the New Moscow explosions had, in Khan's mind, implicated the Kyrgyz. Perhaps Khan's efforts had paid off as he wanted.

Chelomeyev wore a mink Russian hat and the collar of his black coat was pulled up, but he seemed to sway in the wind even though he leaned on a cane. Why he was here was beyond Kazakov, but he had insisted on coming when he heard Kazakov and Egorova were heading to the funeral. The way he looked at Egorova, perhaps it was something more.

Kazakov glanced back at the funeral procession. "I don't know. Probably. I helped rescue them from the hostage situation in Khan's home, but I was shot and never met them. Khan never invited me home. He was a private person."

And apparently his family was private, too. Even finding out the location of Khan's funeral had been nigh on impossible until Kazakov literally begged a contact he had at a Kyrgyz print shop.

"Should we go in?" Chelomeyev asked.

"I don't think so." He shook his head and sighed. "I think—I think we stand for everything Khan hated. At least in the end." He had to believe that the friendship and trust he had once had with the man had been genuine.

Through the monuments, the procession stopped beside a larger domed building in the middle of the graveyard. The size and the fact that it was in the middle of the graves spoke of the importance of its occupants. Khan's family must be older and more established than Kazakov had ever known.

There were so many things he hadn't known—hadn't realized—hadn't seen though the veil of masks around him. How the hell he ever thought he was a good detective was beyond him.

Egorova stepped up beside him. Chelomeyev claimed his other side as voices rose in prayer and echoed out across the graves.

"In the mountains, the women aren't allowed at a burial," Egorova said.

Kazakov didn't know anything about the Muslim ceremony and he had no one to tell him. Instead he stood there at attention, watching, as the prayers subsided.

"But here there is no burial," Kazakov murmured, feeling a double loss because how could he even say goodbye to his friend if there was no body? What pain must the family feel?

The procession left the graveyard quietly, heading for the vehicles parked together by the gate.

"In Biysk, the women prepare a funeral dinner. They slaughter a horse and share the meat with the community."

He glanced at her. Clearly Egorova had spent more time studying the people she worked among than he'd given her credit for.

The funeral vehicles started and headed back to New Moscow, though they slowed when they passed Kazakov's Perseus. The three figures by the fence must have been recognized for no one stopped, and soon the sounds of the vehicle engines faded into the distance and there was only the wind lifting the pair of distant eagles and the shush of melted snow falling from the tops of the monuments.

"We should go," Egorova said. "I think Pavel's just about had enough."

Kazakov glanced at Chelomeyev and his face was white, with two peaks of color in his cheeks.

"Head back to the Perseus. I'll be with you in a minute."

The crunch of their footfall through the snow receded and Kazakov inhaled the clear air.

"You came to me so many times and told me to live and not dwell with ghosts," Kazakov told his old friend. "And now, perhaps, you are one." Emotion bowed his head, but he would not give in to it. Nor would he hope that Khan still lived. Khan had given up his life and their friendship when he had killed Zholdosh and become a criminal. But still…

"What is it you taught me? What were the words? We belong to Allah and to him we will return."

Through the monuments and tombs, the wind whistled a haunting tune and Kazakov nodded. "Yes, those were the words, my friend."

"You said there were no options, but I will find one. I'm not giving up. Chelomeyev is awake. His memory will return eventually. Then Bure will be stopped." And the Kyrgyz, too.

But Khan wasn't there to answer him.

From far above, one eagle loosed a battle cry. Kazakov watched the two birds swoop and dive. The chilly air made him shiver. Finally, he shook his head and turned to the long road back to the city. For the moment the air was clear, the masking smog of New Moscow blown away.

By the Perseus, Egorova and Chelomeyev were waiting.

Continue reading the first Chapter of *Ivan's Wolf*, Book 4 in the Detektiv Kazakov Mysteries...

IVAN'S WOLF

The cottonwoods along the Syr Darya River and the hills showing patches of dead grass through the snow were beginning to grow green in the first tremulous April brilliance of sun and warmth. Of course, it was most likely a false promise, because the cold white claws of the mountains still encircled the valley on three sides like a fist threatening to close.

Closer in, the backwater, capital city of New Moscow suffered through the slush and grey streets that were the omnipresent experience of spring in the small country of Fergana. People, and the crag that edged the city and was known to the mostly Russian population as Yekaterina mountain, all seemed to hunker down awaiting the next spring storm. The storms always came. The trees' promising green was only a portent viewed with suspicion, not a hopeful foretelling of milder weather to come.

In the centre of the city, next to the business district with its ten-story tall buildings, sat Yekaterina Square, which celebrated the last tsarina of long-lost Holy Mother Russia. Once, it had sported a tall statue of Yekaterina the Great, but someone had toppled it and quite possibly the Ferganese psyche. At least it felt like that to Detective Alexander Kazakov, who worked out of the grey stone New Moscow *politseyskiyuchastok*—the police station that sat on the edge of the square. The explosion that had toppled the statue had blown out many of the police station windows and injured those inside. Of course, those windows were primarily in offices occupied by *politseyskiy* bigwigs, so perhaps the explosion had been targeted. So far no one had been charged for the crime, though a large part of the city's tribal population—those who called New Moscow's five-peaked Yekaterina Mountain by the far more venerable name of Sulieman's Mountain—still languished in detention.

Many of the city residents, including police, were certain that the Kyrgyz, Uzbek and Tajik tribals were to blame for the recent attacks on the city. Detektiv Kazakov was one of the few who felt otherwise.

"It reminds me a lot of the tale of Ivan Tsarevich, the grey wolf and the firebird," said Detektiv Chelomeyev as he looked up from the documents Kazakov had set before him. The squad room was empty except for the two of them, which was why Kazakov had chosen to produce the documents. The cinder-block walled room was small, with barely room for the dozen other desks, a data machine console in the corner and an alcove for making tea and storing lunches. The other desks were cluttered with papers, typewriters and half-empty, scum-topped, cups of tea, their owners presumably out on enquiries.

The explosions still preoccupied the squad because their failure to capture and convict a subject was looking bad to the public and Detektiv Chief Inspektor Rostoff was feeling the heat of public opinion. The walls of the room were mostly covered with memos except on one side where clear glass panels separated the detective squad room from the elevator and the hallway that led to officer country.

Chelomeyev was young, and was the youngest detective on the New Moscow police force. He also bore the haunted look of his recent hospitalization—too hollow-eyed, pale and thin after three months of unconsciousness after being beaten and left for dead.

"Tell me the story." Kazakov hooked his leg over a corner of Chelomeyev's desk. The young detective might not be Kazakov's partner, for he preferred working alone, but the blond youngster was a good detective. He had also done his degree in Russian folk tales—an interest Kazakov shared. More importantly, Kazakov could trust this youngster along with his partner on his previous case, Detektiv Elena Egorova, to keep their mouths shut and their eyes open. He couldn't say the same of most of the detectives he worked with.

Chelomeyev eyed the papers again. There were eight pages, each in their own separate, plastic evidence, document holder. They had been found in an installation high in the mountains southeast of New Moscow. Each of the documents was evidence of surgical alterations of people to look like something or someone they were not. They documented limb lengthening, removal of epicanthic eye folds and other cosmetic procedures.

"Well, the folk tale tells about the youngest son of a tsar, who goes on an adventure after his two oldest brothers failed to find the firebird who was stealing the golden apples from the Tsar's garden. The youngest son's stallion is killed by a great grey wolf and in repayment the wolf becomes the son's steed and helps him to perform numerous deeds so that he returns to his father's kingdom with a beautiful princess, the firebird and a great horse with a golden mane, all of which he stole from other kingdoms with the wolf's aid. But before he arrives at his father's palace, he is come upon by his two brothers who kill him and claim the princess, the firebird and the horse as their own. The oldest son is to marry the princess, but the grey wolf appears once more and revives Ivan Tsarevich so that he can return home and claim his bride. His brothers are exiled and Ivan and the princess live happy and long lives together. So the wolf is the agent who allows the Tsarevich to return home." He grinned wanly up at Kazakov. "Sorry. I know too many fairytales. My father reminds me of it every time I see him."

Kazakov shook his head, but the story jarred an old memory loose in his head. His mother's face swam before him, telling him a bedtime story about a young tsarevich. It was a long time ago, but perhaps she'd once told him such a tale.

He shook his head. "There's wisdom in the old tales, that's for sure, even if the magic is unreal. Interesting that the evil wolf helps the hero, but if my suspicions are true, I don't think that the real Boris Bure is about to return to the land of the living." He sighed and gathered up the documents and slid them into an envelope that went into his jacket inside breast pocket. The envelope was bulky and barely fit.

"It would be a nice bit of police work if the real Bure could testify for us, but I'm afraid we're going to have to do this the hard way." He patted his pocket. There was nowhere else he trusted the documents to be safe— not in a country that looked to elect as president, a man who was probably a Chinese spy who had replaced the real Boris Bure and killed the rest of his family when Bure was a young man.

Detektiv Chief Inspector Rostoff strode the hallway beyond the squad room and Kazakov tensed. Please let him be heading to the elevator, but the door to the squad room thunked open and Rostoff stepped into the small room. He had always been a large man, but over the years the muscles of youth had softened to more lard and stubbornness. His enduring quality was his ability to supply favors to higher-ups that had led to his early promotions to his current exalted position, though he had never been particularly gifted at police work. Rostoff was all about case closure rates, not about the conviction of the real perpetrator of the crime.

"I knew you'd be here, Kazakov." The big man stepped into the room, his ruddy cheeks the sign that he might often be drinking something other than tea in the china cups he sipped in his office. His thick black hair was worn brushed back from his face as if to advertise a clear conscience.

Still perched on Chelomeyev's desk, Kazakov cocked a brow at him. "And here you tell me I spend too much time out of the office."

Rostoff stepped farther into the squad room—something he rarely did. "I heard that you might be mentoring Chelomeyev. I could split the two youngsters up if you'd prefer a partner?"

Kazakov glanced at Chelomeyev and shook his head. "I work alone."

"I know. I know." Rostoff held up his hands in mock defeat. "With that in mind, then, I am assigning you a case. There is a dead girl, but I understand that there are sensitive parties..."

Kazakov stood. Dead girls were all too familiar to him these past six months. His first meeting with Boris Bure had been over the death of Bure's stepdaughter—a daughter that Bure had apparently gotten pregnant according to DNA tests. His heart thumped a little harder in his chest.

"What girl?" he asked.

Rostoff shrugged and Kazakov winced inside. In his experience a shrug was often a sign of an untidy mind that did not have its thoughts in order. With Rostoff, experience had shown that was definitely the case.

"Some girl—a performer of some kind." Rostoff pulled a folded piece of paper from his pants pocket and coins jingled faintly. "Here's the address. Uniforms are there now and the M.E."

Kazakov nodded and accepted the address, wondering why Rostoff was assigning him a sensitive case, when Kazakov would never overlook evidence in favor of a prominent suspect. Over the years Rostoff had dealt with numerous complaints regarding Kazakov's honesty and clearance rate. It had been a point of ongoing friction between them until the last few months when evidence from Kazakov's cases had led to Rostoff being at least willing to consider Kazakov's wild theories about the terrorist attacks occurring in Fergana. But then Rostoff could simply be trying to sidetrack Kazakov's attention away from the more contentious investigation.

When he met Rostoff's murky brown gaze, surprisingly the Detektiv Chief Inspektor nodded minutely. So, Rostoff thought this new case might be of interest to Kazakov's quiet enquiries.

Kazakov nodded. "I'll get out there." He glanced down at Chelomeyev. "You want to come along?" Chelomeyev had returned to work on light duties since his horrible head injuries, but riding a desk wasn't the young detective's idea of police work anymore than it was Kazakov's.

Chelomeyev was up and slipping into his coat before Kazakov could retrieve his black winter coat from where he'd tossed it over his desk chair.

"Good. Good." Rostoff said as he watched them out the door. Kazakov wondered just what the Detektiv Chief Inspector was sending them into.

———

The address on Rostoff's paper turned out to be a fine old house on Volga Lane, a small, dead-end street that gave onto the curved road that edged Yekaterina Park. The park was a combination of muddy gray snow, barren trees and patches of matted brown grass revealed where the sun shone the warmest. On the opposite side of the street sat stately townhomes modeled after English noble's homes complete with cornices, columns and filigree. Their white paint hid a darker core as some housed brothels and others Ottoman businessmen who sought to undermine the Ferganese government. But turning the corner onto Volga Lane was like leaving Fergana's trying elections and social problems behind. The houses were tidy replicas of Russian dachas as they truly had been a few generations ago. Small, cozy, and built stoutly to withstand Russian cold —unlike the new-dacha style that was more window and less wall.

The street was plowed, the sidewalk shoveled. Old gaslight-style, iron streetlights alternated on either side of the street. The houses stood back in their yards, but covered porches suggested that these people still might take the evening air outside and speak to their neighbors. Dark winter coats pulled around shoulders, but without the usual winter fur hats, those neighbors now milled around the front of Kazakov and Chelomeyev's destination. He found a place at the curb, parked the unmarked police sedan, and climbed out. Chelomeyev unfolded his height to stand on the other side.

The air was almost balmy after the long dark days of winter. Kazakov inhaled. It was almost possible to smell the warming soil, the stirring blood. And there was an election ahead to further stir that blood.

Enough for bloodshed.

Kazakov shook himself from the morbid thought, patted the pack of papers in his pocket and worked his shoulders to settle his heavy coat. More days like this and he'd pack this coat away and go in his suit jacket. Of course, that was when the spring storms would pass through, so he'd keep wearing his coat to keep more snow at bay. Magical thinking, but in a country like Fergana that still lived in a fairy-tale fog of Russia's long-past greatness, a little magical thinking was nothing.

He studied the house with the M.E.'s van out front. Small. Tidy. Painted in the last few years, judging by the richness of the dark brown paint. A wicker rocking chair sat on the front porch, a brightly colored blanket tossed on its back as if someone actually had sat there during the winter months. Along the front edge of the porch, where some people might hang a small string of lights, the owner of this house had strung balls of glass small enough to swing on the wind and glitter in the sunlight. Odd.

The house's small windows had what looked like white lace curtains pulled back so that the place exuded an open, friendly air. As if the place would welcome you in. Except that you might die there.

With a sigh, he led the way through the crowd to the house's hip-high iron gate. A uniformed officer stood there at attention. He was an older officer—the kind often referred to as lifers—with fading brown hair gone gray at the temples and watery blue eyes that were also faded. He met Kazakov's gaze and nodded. They'd seen each other a time or two under similar circumstances.

"You first on the scene?" Kazakov asked.

The officer—Kazakov dug through his memory—Petrov was his name —nodded. "My partner and I were on patrol. We got waved down by the owner of the house. She'd been away and when she got back she found her assistant dead."

Kazakov nodded his thanks and he and Chelomeyev headed across the yard. Unlike many homes in New Moscow whose owners simply compacted the snow and ice on the path to the door, here the owner had made sure that a wide path was clear up to the porch. The three front stairs were even salted, resulting in coarse grains of salt being tracked across the wood porch floor. At the front door he stomped his feet to clean his boots and pushed inside. Chelomeyev followed.

Inside, a broad hallway split just in front of them to lead toward the kitchen in the rear of the house or up a set of stairs. The house was busy with Forensic staff collecting evidence in each of the two rooms that opened to either side of the front door. One was a dining room. The others was—something else.

Bright tapestries covered the walls with unsettling images of broadly spreading trees; of figures that were half men, half women; of snakes devouring their tails. Old fashioned lamps sat on tables with sheer red cloths dangling tassels over their lamp shades. Overhead, the ceiling was a field of stars, while underfoot the hardwood floor was painted in what Kazakov could only assume were occult symbols. A round table sat surrounded by eight high-backed chairs, with one chair back spreading wide, gilt wings as if it was a throne. A forensic technician was taking fingerprints around the room, leaving behind a trail of gray-white powder. The room was atavistic, evoking thoughts of nighttime campfires and ancient seers spinning tales into the starlight.

"I know what this is," Chelomeyev breathed. "I've heard them described."

"Spiritualist," Kazakov said.

"I thought they'd died out years ago," Chelomeyev said.

"Apparently someone didn't get the message." Kazakov turned back to the hallway.

Through an open door at the end of the hall, Kazakov caught a glimpse of the M.E.'s blue paper coveralls. With a last grimace at the spiritualist room and the knowledge that Rostoff was probably laughing at assigning the murder to Kazakov—he headed down the hallway.

It was the sweet, murky scent that confirmed the kitchen was the death scene. He pushed inside into a white modern kitchen far removed from the draperied chicanery of the spiritualist's parlor. White cupboards and counters filled the walls on three sides, the fourth holding a door and a bank of windows over a sink. A white enamel refrigerator and stove and a new stand mixer seemed to confirm that this was the workplace of someone who liked order and everything in its place.

The body on the floor undid that impression. So did the pale, tearful, gray-haired woman seated with a police constable at a small table in an atrium space at the far end of the room. A single glass of water stood on the table between them that the tearful woman turned around and around in her fingers. The table was surrounded by windows, bathing the woman in sunlight that only bleached her further. But then, so did the long, multicolored scarves looped around her neck and the long flowing dress and purple shawl that overwhelmed her thin body.

The body on the floor was not so encumbered. Young, naked, possibly mid-twenties or even younger by her smooth skin. Blonde, just like Yekaterina Weber had been. Kazakov rubbed his side. It still pained him where he'd been shot during the Weber-Manas investigation. This girl's eyes were closed, her face calm and somehow that made her naked body more exposed. She was slim, though slightly pear figured, with long smooth legs and arms and smallish breasts. There were no knife wounds, no pools of blood, simply the deep purple bruising to the lower body caused by the blood pooling and the graying fleshtone that came with the early stages of decomposition. A flash and whir and the M.E.'s photographer had captured another image of the girl.

The M.E. looked up from beside the body. He was a cadaverous Russian fellow with thinning blond hair who rarely smiled and was still more rarely completely accurate in his findings. Not for the first time Kazakov felt the pangs of loss and anger over the disappearance of Khalil Khan, the country's only Kyrgyz doctor who was now wanted for murder and attempted murder.

"Gordiev," Kazakov said and nodded as the M.E. stood up from examining the body. "What have we got?"

Gordiev shrugged. "Female victim, say around twenty years old. No sign of major injury to the torso or limbs. Skull intact. I'd say by the discoloration of the skin that she's been dead a few days."

"Strangled?" Chelomeyev asked from his spot at Kazakov's shoulder.

"No sign of bruising, so I'd say no," Kazakov said.

"It appears her neck is broken." Gordiev stripped off the gloves he'd been wearing. "Very neatly done."

"Where're her clothes?" Kazakov asked, scanning the room.

"Not here as far as I know." Another shrug from Gordiev that set Kazakov's teeth grinding. "Maybe she undressed for our killer elsewhere and came in here where he killed her. Or maybe he killed her elsewhere and brought her in here where she was certainly going to be found."

"Did anyone search the room?" Kazakov asked.

"Not yet. They'll get to it after we remove the body."

"Is there anything to indicate where she was killed or why?" Kazakov asked fighting his frustration. Clearly, he'd become too dependent upon Khan's keen intelligence and dedication to excellence.

Gordiev gave another shrug. "You figure that out and you'll have your killer. That's your job, not mine." The M.E. nodded at his team. "You got your shots?"

His photographer nodded.

"Then we'll be moving the body to the morgue." He nodded to a pair of male coroner's attendants who'd been waiting. They preceded Gordiev down the hallway, presumably to retrieve their gurney.

"Anyone know who she is?" Kazakov asked the room.

"Anna. Anna Konstantinova," the tearful woman choked out. She bowed her head and began to sob in earnest.

"Perhaps you can sit with our witness while I examine the body," Kazakov said to Chelomeyev.

The young detective eased past the body and went to the table to slide in beside the constable. He nodded to the sobbing woman and introduced himself. The woman straightened and nodded and they began to talk.

Good. Chelomeyev even showed the compassion of not immediately bringing out his notebook.

Kazakov turned back to the body, not that there was much to see.

"Who did this to you, little one?" he murmured and walked around her, trying to get a feel for the scene.

The calm, almost serenity on the girl's face suggested that she hadn't been coerced into the room. No, she'd come here willingly and met her death as a result. But what would bring her into the kitchen disrobed? The need for a drink after sex? Or perhaps she'd assumed she was alone and come down naked to the kitchen for a drink. Neither option sat completely right with him, which suggested that there was something here.

There was nothing on the pristine white counters other than the mixing machine. Nothing sullied the sink other than a few drops that suggested someone had run the water today. Probably to get the older woman her glass of water.

The attendants returned with the gurney and the old woman looked away. They quickly lifted the body and strapped and covered it on the stretcher and then left down the hallway. A gurney wheel squealed as they left and closed the house's front door behind them. The sound of voices and a vehicle engine came from the street.

Kazakov pulled open the fridge door and checked inside. Not much there. A bunch of spinach slowly transforming to mush. A jug of milk on the door and a half-drunk bottle of excellent vodka laying on the top shelf. Interesting. He couldn't afford that brand of vodka.

He closed the fridge door and went to the kitchen cupboards until he found the one that held glasses. All the space in the cupboard was full, but he held the cupboard door open.

"Excuse me, Madam. Do you know if this is all the glassware or if anything is missing?"

The woman turned haunted brown eyes to him and rose almost bonelessly from the table. She came to inspect the cupboard contents and sighed. "That is all that I remember."

"Thank you, Madam." He eased her back to her seat again and returned to the cupboard. He leaned in to study the contents and had a sense of déjà vu of his time with Annuschka, his ex-wife. She had been vehement that all glasses must only be put away after receiving a final wipe from a lint-free cloth. Most of these glasses had the same pristine gleam, but two of the glasses on one side had slight streaks on their sides. He made a note to collect them and turned back to the room.

Under the sink was a garbage bin. Inside were moldy tealeaf remains and a half-eaten sandwich, nothing more. He tugged the garbage bin out. Behind it, something was stuffed into the corner. He pulled it out and stood to examine it. A robe hung from his fingers, silken to the touch, but not fine enough for silk. A cheaper copy. He glanced at the woman.

"Do you know this garment?"

She shook her head, her lips pressed into a line. "No one in this house would wear something like that. I would not allow it."

Carefully, he folded the robe and placed it in an evidence bag for collection. Then he went to the table and the constable stood up and left the room. Kazakov slid into the vacated seat.

"I am Detektiv Alexander Kazakov," he said. "You have met my comrade, Detektiv Chelomeyev. May I have your name, please?"

"Magda--Magdalena Sobol—Madam Sobol," she said and laced her ring-laden fingers on the table. Not the usual gawdy rings Kazakov would expect, either. The gold of these rings gleamed ruddy, and the flash of green, blue and red suggested real emerald, sapphire and ruby. The largest ring was a clear-cut square stone that, if a diamond, would be fabulously expensive. It begged the question of how such a woman, living in such a house could afford such riches.

Kazakov nodded at Chelomeyev to take notes and then met Madam Sobol's watery gaze. "How many people live in this house, Madam?"

Her watery gaze met his. "Two. There are two: myself and Anna."

Kazakov nodded. So the robe could be a secret possession of the dead girl—or something brought by the killer. "And who is Anna?"

Her gaze flicked away. "I told you her name."

"Yes. But a name tells me very little. Who was she to you? How did she come to be here?" he urged gently.

Madam Sobol shook her head, her long grey hair shifting around her shoulders. "A silly girl who I was foolish enough to hire. She came to me six months ago with huge claims that she had the gift. She wished to learn from the best, she said. More like pick my bones. I've been doing this for forty years. Did she think I would not see through her?"

"See through her, Madam?" Chelomeyev asked softly looking up from his notetaking.

"Of course, I saw through her! She was an ignorant farm girl, while I come from a long line of women with the sight. She thought that she could come work for me for a time and then go out on her own. Claim that she had learned everything Madam Sobol knows and—look, I am more pleasant to look on than Madam Sobol, too." She shook her head, the sunlight through the windows catching on the lines deepening the displeasure on her face. Deep lines beneath the corners of her mouth seemed to pull her lips into a perpetual frown.

"You did not like her much, then," Kazakov said softly, though she had cried as though she truly mourned. For show? Did she not realize the contradiction?

Those watery eyes turned in his direction and for a moment they seemed to clear and look deep into him with Baba Yaga venom.

"Like? I am a realist, Detektiv. I am getting old. I needed help. The girl's determination to eventually undermine me did not stop her from being a good worker. For that I could appreciate her. So I kept her around and dealt with her prying into my secrets—not that she found any. I am far too good for that. Besides, I knew what her fate would be. It was written in her hands."

"Her hands." Kazakov awaited clarification.

"I read her palm when she first came to me. Fleshy mount of Venus. Truncated lifeline. Clear evidence of what was to come." Her thin shoulders lifted her scarves in a shrug.

"And yet you cry for her." He nodded down at the wadded tissue in her hand.

"Death is always a hard thing. We spend our days running from our own death and yet we begin our death walk from the moment we are born. We avoid thinking about our own mortality, but the death of someone we know reminds us of it. So we cry. Not for the dead—they are already gone

—but for ourselves and the days and weeks that are chipped away from us every moment that we live. It begins slowly enough, but as we age, we see more days behind us than in front and still the days fall around us like leaves that we cannot return to the trees."

Her words seemed to press him into his chair. He knew those days, had seen the piles of golden leaves—treasures lost and blown away just as Ivan Tsarevich had lost everything he worked for until the gray wolf worked his final magic and brought the young prince back to life. Madam Sobol's gaze had grown knowing as she looked at him, as if she knew exactly how her words touched him. A cagey old woman, this one. But then a woman who made her living by telling fortunes surely lived by her wits and her ability to read the people around her.

He glanced at Chelomeyev and nodded. "A reasonable assessment of the human condition. So what were Anna's duties?"

"She cleaned and cooked for me and ran errands. She would make sure that my cards and equipment were where they should be."

Kazakov cocked a brown at her. "Equipment?"

"There were—trappings. Things that customers expected though they did not impact the tellings. I am not a charlatan, Detektiv. I am a consultant. I do not knock on tables or have winds blow through my readings to impress the gullible. In fact, I abhor such things. Anna and I argued over just such matters. She felt that I could gain more fame by using such devices and I told her that she could leave and find another teacher if that was what she was interested in." Madam Sobol cast a sad glance at the now-empty kitchen floor. She swallowed."She chose not to leave."Her eyes closed as if the sight pained her.

"Do you have any idea who she might have invited into your home?" Kazakov asked.

"Invited? Surely she was attacked and killed."

Kazakov shook his head. "You have an open bottle of vodka in your fridge and two newly washed glasses in your cupboard. Then there is the garment that you claim to have never seen before. It is a young woman's garment, Madam. It seems more likely that she had a visitor."

A small twitch found the corner of Madam Sobol's left eye. She looked away, out the window to a small snow-bound yard where neat garden beds were just showing their raised edges.

"She said her family were dead. She had few friends—at least that I saw. A few afternoons a week she'd run errands, but she spent most evenings here with me."

"Think, Madam. Any friends come calling. Any phone calls?"

She shook her head, but her face was troubled.

"And your clients, Madam. Did Anna have contact with them?"

She turned a devastated gaze on him. She shook her head. "No. It could not be. She would answer the door for me to allow me to get ready for a reading. She would take coats and usher the client into my office. Then she would leave us and go to the observation room where she could watch how I conducted my sessions. I hoped she would learn from that that tricks are not what is needed to provide a reputable service. I do not see how such meager contact could suggest that any of my clients could be a suspect."

Kazakov straightened in his chair. "Then it is a good thing that you are not investigating this case if we want to find Anna's killer, Madam. At this moment everyone is suspect, even you. I would say even myself and my partner could be suspects except that we did not know you and Anna Konstantinova existed." He stood up. "I will need to see her rooms and we will need a list of all the places Anna went on her errands and a list of all clients who may have met Anna over the past six months. Please prepare them for us while we inspect Anna's rooms."

"I will do as best I can to recall Anna's errands but I will not provide a list of client names." She scrambled up to face him, a light scent of ashes of roses coming off her heated skin. "My clients are corporate leaders and business people. They are private citizens and appreciate my guarantee of utmost discretion. Providing their names so that you can come clumping up onto their doorsteps—that simply cannot be done!"

He tipped his head down to her to peer at her from the tops of his eyes. "I appreciate your concern for your clients and how it may impact your business, but it must be done. A young woman has been killed. Surely you can appreciate that we must find her killer. If we do not, we leave him or her free to kill again. I promise that we will start with contacts she made on her errands, but you must provide us with a client list. There is no way around it."

Her gaze was stubborn as old locks, but gave way before him. She nodded. "I will try to compose the errand list while you are upstairs. The clients—well, it will take a few days to go through my records to find who visited while Anna was here. Anna's room is upstairs to the right."

Leaving Madam Sobol in the kitchen with pencil and paper and her tissues, Kazakov and Chelomeyev returned to the front hall. The forensic technicians had finished in the two front rooms. Kazakov and Chelomeyev climbed up to the second floor.

From the landing above the stairs a dimly-lit, narrow hall led left and right. To the left, two, facing closed doors left the hall in darkness. To the right one of the doors was open, spilling light into the hall.

Kazakov set off toward the open door, wondering who had left the door open. Judging by the other doors, the preference in this household was for the upstairs doors to be kept closed. The dead girl downstairs? One of the attending police? Or the girl's killer, perhaps.

He reached the door and stopped, motioning Chelomeyev up beside him as he studied the room. "What do you see?"

"Bedroom," Chelomeyev began. His gaze roamed over the room. "Woman's." He frowned. "The bed isn't slept in, but the covers are disheveled as if she had been laying there—or someone had."

"Or, perhaps, both," Kazakov said. It was a bedroom like many others he'd seen in his career. Single bed pressed against the wall with pillows against the wall as if the bed was also to function as a seating area for visitors. According to Madam Sobol, in Anna Konstantinova's case it was for no one at all.

And yet someone had obviously been here. He stepped into the room. In the days since the girl's death any telling scent had dissipated, but there was the possibility that she had had a sexual tryst. He would have to make certain that Gordiev checked for that and collected semen and DNA evidence. He pulled on a set of latex gloves and began a search for evidence.

A tall, battered armoire filled one wall. A small desk-cum-dressing-table also showing years of wear, filled another. The desktop was filled with an orderly array of lotions and unguents that apparently a young woman would make use of. He didn't know what they were. A mirror hazed with age held only a photo of the dead girl smiling in front of a brocade curtain. He went to the armoire first and swung open the doors. Women's clothing hung there, mostly sensible dresses of thin floral cloth. Two cardigan sweaters—one white, one black, both, he supposed, suitable to wear with any of the dresses. A single pair of low-heeled black shoes sat neatly facing the wall beneath the dress hems. Beyond the dresses that were certainly not unexpected, was the interesting way the clothing hung in the cupboard with each item evenly spaced across the length of the rack. That showed a different, methodical and orderly side to the victim.

He glanced at Chelomeyev.

"How many young women do you know who have closets like this?" he asked.

Chelomeyev colored slightly as if he didn't care for a reminder of his exploits with females. "Not many. The girls I know are messier than I am —mostly."

Not that Chelomeyev was particularly messy from what Kazakov had seen of the younger man's apartment.

Kazakov went to the desk-dressing table and began opening drawers. A box of tissue and tubes of lipstick filled the top drawer. A side drawer released a pungent puff of lavender from a froth of silk and lace underwear. For a girl with such sensible dresses and shoes, this was unexpected. He lifted the stack of underwear and ran his hand underneath for often women hid surprising pieces of their lives amongst their unmentionables. Nothing. He slid the drawer in and pulled the lowest drawer open. An old blue metal box filled the drawer, the kind in which people traditionally kept mementos.

He pulled the box out and tried to open it, but the box was locked.

Frowning, he set the box down on the desk top and settled onto the hard-backed, wooden desk chair. The metal was scratched and dented from years of use, but the lock looked sturdy. The top, however, looked frayed around the edges as if someone had tried to pry it open.

Succeeded?

Probably, or else it was unlikely that the box would still be here.

He pulled a pocket knife from his coat and began to pry above the lock. After a moment, the top popped up.

"Glad to see I haven't lost my touch." He grinned up at Chelomeyev.

"You are supposed to use your powers for good," the young detective said.

"This isn't good?" Kazakov motioned around the room.

"And just where did you learn your lock-breaking skills?" Chelomeyev asked.

"A long time ago, when I was in prison." His smile broadened up at Chelomeyev as he saw the young man pause as if he considered whether such an unlikelihood could possibly be true.

Chelomeyev finally shook his head. "No wonder others don't want to partner with you. They don't know when you tell the truth."

"But I always tell the truth," Kazakov deadpanned and for a moment felt an unusual affection for the young detective. It was years since he'd had a partner, except for his recent partnering with Elena Egorova.

Perhaps he had missed the camaraderie more than he knew. But he still preferred to work alone and it was better that he continue that way. He eyed Chelomeyev and hoped the young man wasn't going to expect to do this again.

But then Egorova would be here soon. The first female detective in Fergana was currently moving her household from the small mountain town of Biysk to New Moscow. She had been Kazakov's partner in a murder investigation in the mountains that had blossomed into something much more. Having her in New Moscow meant that she and Chelomeyev as well as Kazakov could continue to quietly look into the larger investigation around Boris Bure.

Kazakov flipped open the metal box and found a stack of old letters tied with a ribbon and a series of children's drawings. He unfolded one of the drawings to reveal a typical childish image of a square-block house with a triangular roof and a series of large stick figures standing off to one side. The image was signed Vasili in childish crayon.

A nephew? A son?

Kazakov went through the other drawings and all were similarly signed. He set them aside and carefully untied the ribbon binding the letters. Even through his latex gloves the paper on top had the thin weight and feel of the cheapest quality note paper. He carefully opened the folded page to reveal the writing.

Dear Anna,

I hope this letter finds you well. Vasili has been asking after you. He sends this picture to his beautiful mother. He wants to know when you might come home for a visit. He is becoming more and more insistent that he does not like it here and wants to be with you. What should I tell him? When might you get over this foolishness and come home for a visit? How long is this to go on? A child needs his mother."

The letter was signed by someone named Lidiya.

So not Anna's mother, because a mother would surely sign as such. A friend? A relative? Someone that Anna paid to care for her son?

He set the letters aside to read more fully and hopefully learn where this Lilya resided. The tone of the letter suggested reproach as if Anna was involved in something that Lilya did not agree with. Something to do with a lover or was it only to do with Anna's apparent choice of profession?

He peered into the metal box. The letters and pictures had not filled the box. There could have been more inside. Something taken, perhaps?

At the bottom of the box was a business card. He flipped it over with his finger.

"Pamir Communications: Taking you to the highest level" read the logo on the card. Beneath was only a phone number.

He had never heard of Pamir Communications.

Finished, he replaced the letters and the pictures into the box and clicked the lock closed before standing up.

"Find anything?" he asked.

Chelomeyev looked up from running his hands between the mattress and the bed frame. He looked about to say something, but then stopped and pulled out a narrow piece of colored paper. He held it up.

"This?" He studied what he held and Kazakov came up to him.

It was a royal purple, three-fold flier, like a brochure for an event. Dates were written on the back.

Chelomeyev flipped the flier over.

On the front, Boris Bure's face peered out at them.

Ivan's Wolf is available at http://www.karenlabrahamson.com/books/ ivans-wolf/ or at your favorite bookseller June 2019.

TO MY READERS

1. Thank you for reading *The Tsarina's Mask*. I hope you enjoyed it. If you did (and even if you didn't), it would be immensely helpful if you would leave a review. Reviews help other readers find this book.
2. Sign up for my Newsletter, and receive a free novel, a novella, and an award-nominated short story. To get your FREE eBOOKS, go to my website at www.karenlabrahamson.com.
3. While you're there, check out my website for information on my books, my adventures, and extra content.
4. For more links and offers, or to chat with me, check out Facebook at www.facebook.com/karenlabrahamson.

THE DETEKTIV KAZAKOV MYSTERY SERIES

Set in an alternate history Russia, the series introduces Detektiv Alexander Kazakov, a loner detective committed to finding the truth for the dead and murdered. The series takes place in a world where Catherine the Great's conquest of the Crimea woke the slumbering Ottoman Empire and brought the great Sultans down upon Moscow. Two hundred years later the remains of the Russian population dream of Russia's past glories, while their new country of Fergana lays like the gristle in a joint between the rumblings of the Ottoman and Chinese Empires. The death of a young Russian girl sets Kazakov on a series of investigations that have implications for the entire world.

BOOKS IN THE SERIES:
After Yekaterina
Mareson's Arrow
The Tsarina's Mask
Ivan's Wolf

ABOUT THE AUTHOR

Karen L. Abrahamson writes fantasy, romance, and mysteries as Karen L. Abrahamson and K.L. Abrahamson. Her best known books are the unique Cartographer series in which secret agents of the American Geological Survey use their powers to take on the purveyors of dark magic. Her romantic suspense and mysteries take readers on adventures to dangerous locations around the world.

Her short fiction has appeared in numerous magazines and anthologies; her short fantasy story "With One Shoe" was nominated for an Arthur Ellis Canadian Crime Fiction Award.

Karen's background includes time as a police officer, corrections officer, and probation/parole officer.

To find out more about her and her writing, visit www. karenlabrahamson.com

ALSO BY K.L. ABRAHAMSON

Aftermath

Afterimage

Terra Incognita

Terra Infirma

Terra Nueva

Other Fantasy

Emberstone

Mutable Things

The Crystal Courtesan

Ice Dragon

ROMANCE, MYSTERY AND FANTASY
FROM TWISTED ROOT PUBLISHING

If you enjoyed this book, you might enjoy other titles available from Karen L. Abrahamson in your local bookstore or wherever e-books are sold or through
www.karenlabrahamson.com

THROUGH DARK WATER: Eagles, Orcas and a killer stalk the kayaking Mecca of Pirate's Cove, British Columbia. On a holiday with her niece, school teacher Phoebe Clay has to solve the case to protect herself and everything she loves. Find it at http://www. karenlabrahamson.com/books/through-dark-water/

AFTERBURN: Vallon Drake, agent of the American Geological Survey, the secret arm of Homeland Security that protects America from illicit changes to its landscapes, discovers her partner smothering in a wall. Now someone is rewriting the Seattle maps and killing AGS agents. Their actions threaten the safety of the entire Northwest and only rogue agent Vallon can stop it.Find it at http://www.karenlabrahamson.com/books/afterburn/

SHADOW PLAY: Star reporter Kaitlin Blackwood arrives in Cambodia and lands right in the case of her missing father. When men try to abduct her, the wrong man rescues her: B.J. McCallum, ex-man of her dreams, who comes with his own heap of trouble. The two must put aside their differences long enough to solve the case—and maybe save themselves in the process. Find it at http://www. karenlabrahamson.com/books/shadow-play/